HIGHEST PRAISE FOR
JOVE HOMESPUN ROMANCES:

We at Jove Books are thrilled by the enthusiastic critical acclaim that the Homespun Romances are receiving. We would like to thank you, the readers and fans of this wonderful series, for making it the success that it is. It is our pleasure to bring you the highest quality of romance writing in these breathtaking tales of love and family in the heartland of America.

And now, sit back and enjoy this delightful new Homespun Romance . . .

TUMBLEWEED HEART
by Tess Farraday

D0816065

Tumbleweed Heart

Tess Farraday

J

JOVE BOOKS, NEW YORK

TUMBLEWEED HEART

A Jove Book / published by arrangement with
the author

PRINTING HISTORY
Jove edition / September 1996

The Putnam Berkley World Wide Web site address is
http://www.berkley.com

ISBN: 0-515-11944-X

A JOVE BOOK®
Jove Books are published by The Berkley Publishing Group,
200 Madison Avenue, New York, New York 10016.
JOVE and the "J" design are trademarks
belonging to Jove Publications, Inc.

PRINTED IN THE UNITED STATES OF AMERICA

10 9 8 7 6 5 4 3 2 1

To Cory,
who always rides to my rescue

ACKNOWLEDGMENTS

No creative work springs full-formed from the writer's mind into the world. Such a "birth" takes many midwives. For their support, knowledge and love, I want to thank mine.

Thanks to Bob Roberts, for hospitality and horses; to Hilary and Betty Winebarger for cattle, cooking and cowboy lore; to Linda Dufurrena whose photographs keep the desert's beauty fresh in my mind; to the buckaroos of the Soldier Meadows, Spanish Springs and Circle Dot spreads for their patience and ability to keep straight faces; to all my buddies and colleagues for helping me keep the faith; to Kathy Sage, eagle-eyed critique partner; to Cici and Grace, inspired librarians, for their tolerance of panic and large dogs; to Gail Fortune, my editor, a woman of rare taste and judgment, for taking intuitive leaps along with me; to Alice Orr for keeping my feet on the ground when my heart was in my throat; to my parents for endless encouragement and to my children, Matt and Kate, for boundless enthusiasm and excitement. You two are my oasis.

One

Raindrops loud as hail lashed the attic windows as Christa closed the door behind her. Her eyes quickly separated substance from shadow: a dressmaker's form, two chairs, a trunk, but no child.

"Patty?" Her voice hung alone. Only when she saw her daughter, asleep, did she breathe again. "Patty, baby."

Christa settled on the floor and laid her palm on Patty's back. Beneath her blue dimity pinafore, Patty's spine lay bumpy as a string of beads. Patty had sassed her aunt Francesca. Again. Discovered in Nathan's study, cuddled in his chair with a doll, Patty had refused to budge.

"Want my daddy!" she'd shouted.

"Then ask your mother why she sent him away! Why is my poor brother with the angels, while she—"

Now Patty was curled up tight on the attic floor, one cheek pressed against the leather-bound travel trunk. Her shoulders jerked in a sleepy sob.

How much could a three-year-old understand? Enough to run and hide. Each day, the accusations grew bolder. Christa had scolded herself for being too sensitive, for imagining a sympathetic neighbor brought suspicion as a side dish for a roast capon. Perhaps her tear-blurred eyes had mistaken stares from passersby. But she hadn't dreamed the continued whispers that provided bitter sauce for a funeral pie of raisins and brown sugar. In time, even Patty would understand.

Rainfall slowed to spatters and the attic walls paled to watery gray. Christa raised the trunk lid. Its lock had broken long ago, a victim of Francesca's cleaning. Still, most trunks hadn't made it this far. They'd been dumped from wagons moving West, after oxen or mule teams died.

Layers of muslin puffed forth camphor, which guarded against moths, and there was a hint of Winesap tobacco. Nathan's smoke clung to everything.

Patty's legs flailed under her skirts, running after dreams. "You're all right. Mama's here."

Cloudy sunlight glinted on a thread of hair at the corner of Patty's mouth and Christa swept it away with one finger. Patty's lips pursed and sucked, not all that long past nursing.

Patty had come here searching for her charm. Christa turned back to the trunk, burrowed under her ivory riding blouse and split kersey skirt until she touched leather soft as velvet and tugged the thong that held the pouch like a necklace. Its stiff quill design pricked her knuckles.

Before she even saw it, she smelled sagebrush, horses, and hot rocks washed with rain. Francesca had dumped its mystic contents in the dustbin before Christa caught her, but the leather pouch still held magic.

The stranger had called it a medicine bag, made by a holy man, out on the Western plains. He'd had it from his father, but when he found her laboring alone in a canvas tent, when he saw infant Patty, still and blue, legs dangling like a dead bird's, he'd lifted the thong from his neck and slipped it over hers.

Fear and joy hardened in a knot above Christa's heart as she remembered how he'd covered Patty's lips and nose, puffing his own life into her tiny lungs, breathing until Patty's legs drew up and kicked. Then he'd crouched back on his boot heels, cradling her, eyes shut, before laying her on Christa's breast.

Now the stranger needed help. Danny's letter, last week, had said so.

Christa felt a thrill, like sparks off a cat's fur. How long had it been since she'd felt excitement? She rubbed her hands up her sleeves and shivered.

Her brother Danny had known, at once, that he couldn't live in bustling Sacramento. It had taken her longer to figure it out. A proper lady didn't miss *sky*, vaulting blue and free of housetops. A corseted wife didn't waltz on ballroom marble, wishing for white sand beneath her slippers. She certainly didn't weep at sunrise, mourning wild desert dawns, aching for a life she'd never lived.

Danny only made her yearning worse, when he returned to the desert and wrote that he was cowboying with the stranger who'd saved Patty. Danny's pencil had ripped the paper when he wrote Hell, no, he hadn't admitted meeting the man before. He liked Patrick Garradine, for helping Christa and for knocking Nathan on his ass.

She swallowed the urge to giggle and glanced toward the stairway door. She heard the horsehair couch lurch across the Turkey carpet. Francesca cleaned with a vengeance; it was the only thing that gave her joy.

Danny had found his own brand of happiness riding the range. Boston had stifled them both, though Christa had dreamed of scholarship as a path to adventure. Her dreams had faded as it became clear that offering a tea tray at Father's study door would be the closest she came to Chaucer. Her brother had scorned books and the father who placed them first, so Dan molded himself after whichever reckless male crossed his path. Nathan had failed them both.

Then Fortune presented Dan with a hero. After he had saved Patty, Garradine had turned from mustanger to rancher. The cowboys called him Trick and said he knew everything worth knowing about horses and the high desert. But he was about to lose every rider he'd hired.

Just weeks before a trail drive that would make or break his ranch, Patrick Garradine's cook had quit. Cowboys were

two-thirds belly and one-third stubborn. They'd ride for a
rancher with a mean cook, a drunk cook, even a crazy cook,
but they wouldn't touch a skillet. They'd surely mutiny, said
Dan, leaving Trick Garradine alone.

She owed Patrick Garradine. Like a wild wolf, he'd
guarded her as she labored. His calm and courage had saved
her baby. Nathan might have fathered Patty, but Patrick had
given her life. And, with no more logic than a she-wolf,
Christa's pain and need forged a primitive bond between
them, marking the stranger her mate.

She shook the absurd thought away. Patrick Garradine
was nothing but a cowboy with plenty of trouble and a need
for a cook. She owed him a debt that hard work and rough
men couldn't stop her from repaying. Even the humiliating
memory of a stranger raising her sodden skirts, seeing her
soiled stockings and blood—even that could not stop her.

In the storm's wake, a raindrop worked its way past the
shingles, along an attic rafter, and dripped onto a tin lantern.
Patty roused and nuzzled closer. Christa lifted her, warm
and floppy, as sunlight streamed through the high pane.
Christa closed her eyes against its brightness and dusted her
lips over Patty's hair. *This* was the debt she owed Patrick
Garradine.

"We're going to do it, baby," Christa whispered, as her
daughter woke. "No more mean voices. No more Francesca."

"Bad!" Patty squirmed upright and pointed at the door.

Christa laughed. Love and hope burst upward like a
fountain. Her chest felt tight with it.

"No more crying for Mama or Patty," she promised. "I'm
going to take you where you can look up into the sky—"

"Inna, 'ky!" Patty echoed.

"—and see the Big Dipper. You'll taste snowflakes on
your tongue, and your pretty blue eyes will see wild horses!
I'm taking you where you'll be happy, Patty babe. I'm
taking you to Nevada."

Two

GOOD THUNDER MEADOWS, NEVADA
MAY, 1870

He dropped the gun-cleaning rags and carried his Winchester with him to the door, unsure he'd heard hooves over the wailing dust storm.

And there she stood. Alive. Three years after he'd allowed her fool husband to take her, still bleeding, across the Black Rock Desert, she stood on his plank porch, wind-flushed cheeks testifying he wasn't staring at a ghost.

"Mr. Garradine, I'm—well, I'm back." She shrugged under her black bombazine dress as if she'd only been to town for a sack of flour.

Patrick Garradine clenched and unclenched his fists. Needing to fill both hands, he took his Stetson from the iron hook beside the door.

Alive, and sure he'd remember her after all this time. It had been one night, a hellish and wonderful night best forgotten. He jammed the butt of the Winchester under his arm, barrel pointed toward the floor, then brushed dust from his hat's brim before he glanced up.

"I see that." He settled the hat and watched her eyebrows arch while she bit her lip.

Still small, nowhere near his collarbone, she leaned forward insistently, peering out from wisps of flaxen hair as she tried to catch his eyes. Before, she'd been fragile as a

5

white silk scarf held up against the merciless sun. Now she looked impatient. And she was hiding something behind her skirts.

"I've come from Sacramento City." She pushed her reticule strings to the crook of her elbow and he noticed the ridge of a wedding ring under her black gloves. "My brother Danny wrote that you'd be requiring a cook. I would like to apply for that position."

"No," he said, slowly. "No, I have a cook, a good cook."

Three years too late, this lady'd come from Sacramento, ten days by train and horseback. Not to say, "Patrick—stop haunting my dreams" or "Darling, I couldn't forget you." No, Christabel Worth, a grown-up lady in high-buttoned boots and silky skirts snagging on his porch boards, wanted to cook beef and biscuits for his hands.

He shook his head. Pretty, smart, and if she'd come all the way out here to him, willing. Her husband should've kept a woman this crazy locked in the attic.

"I'm afraid you crossed the territory for nothing, ma'am."

He met her eyes as the dark centers grew small. Her hands slid off her hips to fall limp at her sides.

"This isn't what I'd planned at all." She said it faintly, but she didn't look puny, just god-awful surprised.

With a wheeze and a scream the wind built again, whirling into the yard as a house-high dust devil.

"Are you alone?" He looked past her shoulder as she raised the black shawl to cover her hair.

"Oh, yes, I am, quite alone. Except for Betsy."

Betsy'd be the gray horse, he figured, stamping and flinging her head at the winds, but well-trained or hungry enough not to bolt from the yard.

"And Patty."

She might have slammed him in the belly, for the effect her remark had. She bent, dipping so her skirts belled out, then gathered in a child, a little blond girl with sunburned cheeks and a thumb in her mouth. Christabel popped the thumb free.

"Mama."

He glimpsed cornflower-colored eyes before they were hidden in Christa's skirts.

"I'm sorry," she said, lifting the child. "She's tired."

"Well, you might as well go inside and sit while I put the mare up. There's coffee." He stopped, shaken by the reality of it. This was no dream. Christa had lived. And the child. The little scrap could suck her thumb and say Mama.

"What does she eat?"

Christa laughed, a gurgling sound like water come to the desert.

Whoa, Garradine. She's no oasis, just a madwoman. The Black Rock damn near killed her and she's crazy enough to give it a second try.

"She'll eat most anything," Christa said. "But I would like to lay her down."

"This is no place for a child, or a lady either, but go ahead. For now." He used the rifle to motion them inside.

In that instant, as the sun lost its battle with both dust and approaching night, the pleading shadows, from before, darkened the woman's eyes. But then she hoisted the child higher, lifted her rustling skirts clear of the porch, and raised her chin.

"Very well, Mr. Garradine," said Christabel Worth. Then she stepped into his house as if she'd built it herself.

He unbuckled the headstall, wiped it, and hung it on the stable's stone wall. He placed the small saddle over a rack and tossed the blanket on top. He'd started brushing the mare's dusty hide before he paused, holding the brush in midair.

He'd smelled strong as this horse the day he'd found her. If he'd never seen the coyotes skulking around her canvas tent, his nights would have been a damn sight more restful. But they would have been nights without Christa. The desert had tried to kill her, and he'd snatched her back. What if, this time, the Black Rock were stronger?

A dream with no right to come true, he'd told each aching vision of her face. And he'd been right. Christa Worth had no business standing in his house. He had no time to tend to a couple of females.

September first, he had to deliver a herd to the railhead. In front of God and a court clerk, he'd made his mark on a contract. Between now and then he had to gather and fatten every bovine wearing his brand.

He turned the mare into the inside corral to feed her. The grain scoop's clang brought Cloud and Imp, his bridle horses, shouldering past her. Bits of corn still clung to their whiskers, but they nickered greedily.

"Get back, you lazy crow baits." Trick rubbed the two muzzles, one black, one white.

Sending her off would be easier if he could forget the pictures that flashed through his mind. Christa, fragile and pale when he found her. Christa's eyes slanted up at him, trying to joke through her shame and misery. Christa's eyelashes, tipped with gold in the lantern light, cradling her baby, touching the small wizened face with light fingers.

This, then, was what it meant to have a mother. The thought had vanished as she looked up, more reverent and thankful than any human should feel, looking at him.

Last of all, memory forced him to see Christa, frail shoulders slumped as she clung to the bundled baby and the wagon bench, while her husband, brassy hair aglitter, danced his mount on ahead.

But she'd brought her baby, a golden, miniature Christabel, back. He stopped the smile by slamming his fist into the stone wall, pulling up in time to keep from breaking it, but too late to keep from stripping the hide off. He needed that hand in working condition.

The gray mare glanced back, hay dripping from her muzzle.

"What're you lookin' at?" he grumbled.

Trick pictured that irresponsible dandy, her husband, and

regretted he hadn't had his Winchester that day. If ever a man deserved killing, that man was Nathan Worth.

Trick knew in his gut he'd be every bit as selfish, reckless, and worthy of killing if he gave in and let Christa stay.

Christabel watched from inside his house, from the window he'd probably timbered, rocked, and cut with his own hands. He entered the stone barn, and vanished. Turning to face this room that was his, Christa still saw his image. Patrick stood just as tall as she remembered. His rider's form was lean and hard, his face darkly tanned with a slash of scar above the left eye. In all, Patrick Garradine was wonderfully different from the paunchy bankers who served as Nathan's friends.

She glanced at Patty, sound asleep on the rough wood-framed couch, then tilted her head back to gaze at the beamed ceiling. The blue shawl fell from her shoulders as she wrapped both arms around her ribs and spun. Could she squeeze hard enough to crush the vaulting excitement shaking her whole body?

This house even smelled right, not like ink, cigars, and the kapok stuffing Nathan's animal trophies. In the entire rock-and-wood cabin, only one oil-wet rag lay out of place. No mildew or old clothes made a lady's nostrils twitch. His bachelor dwelling smelled of wood smoke, coffee, and coal oil.

Christa snatched up the oily cloth and looked for a place to stow it. She pulled aside a calico shelf curtain and found a stack of cloth, neatly folded, corners square. Here sat the coal-oil tin, wiped clean, spout plugged with a chunk of potato. Next to it sat a jar labeled "hartshorn" and another of turpentine. Sacramento housemaids kept fewer cleaning supplies than Patrick Garradine.

Absent, though, were things she'd miss long before turpentine. This cabin held no desk, no pen case or inkwell, not even a wooden pencil, and no bookcase. After dinner, didn't he pull a chair before that fine hearth, shuck his boots and toast his socks while he read? She'd have to show Patrick what his cottage was missing. After all, she'd come to help.

Patty's sleep-soft hands opened and skimmed across the couch, back and forth as if parting water. When she sighed drowsily, there was no catch of tears.

Contentment warmed Christa as she turned back to the window. Outside, Patrick emerged from the barn. He watched the horizon, rubbing one hand. It might take him a bit to become accustomed to her arrival, but she'd help him adjust. Already, she'd acted the proper widow, calling him Mr. Garradine, even though he'd been Patrick, white knight in a Western hat, as he galloped through her dreams.

In truth, the formality was essential. He'd looked stunned when she spoke of his absent cook and blank at her mention of Danny, but, oh, how his eyes had lingered on Patty!

Christa trailed her fingers along the polished mantel above the fireplace. A blue-and-white-speckled cup sat there, and standing on tiptoe, she saw a pocket watch with a face framed in gold scrollwork. A tiny winding key lay beside it, but the watch ticked erratically. How long since Patrick had thought to wind it? If only she had an inkling what time it was.

Too late, perhaps. He'd offered no smile of welcome. His eyes held no smoky glow of memory. In fact, when he'd finally met her eyes, his had been cold. Nevertheless, he could forget about sending her away.

Mama's death had made a return to Boston unthinkable. Christa imagined Father, alone at last in mausoleum stillness, with only a housekeeper to disturb the silence of study.

And Sacramento was little better. She and Patty had traveled for days, and the last two had been so unpleasant, she could not decide which had been most difficult—the dust storms, that stiff-necked little town of Coyote, or trying to politely decipher the accents of her Basque escorts from

Reno. No, Patrick Garradine would have to understand; she would not go back.

She repositioned an ivory hairpin so hard it stung her scalp, then stifled her gasp as boots scraped on the porch and the door opened.

"Mr. Garradine," she said, without waiting, "I do hope you will reconsider hiring me." Christa pressed on before he could interrupt. "In his last letter, Danny told me a fortune-teller's predictions are responsible for your cook's departure. I assure you, Mr. Garradine, I would never fall prey to such silliness as—Musky, is it?"

"Muley." He rubbed the faint shadow of a beard along his jaw.

Mercy! Since the schoolroom, Danny's handwriting had been atrocious. Now it had made her look a ninny, when the good Lord knew she needed no assistance!

Still, Patrick refused to look up. She'd have more luck coaxing a wild buck to eat from her hand.

"Muley. Of course."

He removed his Stetson. "You're talking hogwash, ma'am. And I'm sorry to say it," Patrick said. "The early shift of hands will be back before dark, and I'll have one of them ride with you back to your husband."

Frowning, he searched the hearth before using his shirttail to grab the coffeepot from its hook.

"I don't think it will burn you. The fire appears to have been dead for hours." Christa gestured at the white ash and scolded herself for failing to make fresh coffee.

He nearly knocked the watch from the mantel as he tried to retuck his shirt, grab the blue cup, and pour the coffee, all at once. The disturbance made the watch chatter. Patrick drank the cold, muddy brew, crooked his thumb through his belt, and met her eyes. "It's a bad time. I'll miss even one rider."

To curb her tongue, Christa turned and smoothed her shawl over Patty's sleeping form. All males delighted in calling women hindrances. She should know that by now.

Patrick Garradine sounded no different from her brothers, yelling down from their tree house that it would be a waste of time helping her ascend. She'd scaled that citadel in spite of them, and gloried in their sour looks.

"As for that," she forced out words that sounded ladylike, "I traveled here alone and I *could* find my way back."

Patrick's eyes, surprisingly blue eyes, widened and he retreated a half step.

"But I'm sure that won't be necessary. I'm really quite a good cook, Mr. Garradine." She advanced over the floor he'd deserted. "My soups are smooth as cream and I've been told my desserts would make a French pastry chef weep with envy."

Though she'd hardly set a match to a parlor fire since Francesca usurped her place, Nathan had loved sweets and Christa had slaved to make hers worthy.

"Ma'am, French pastry ain't much called for in a cow camp."

The corner of his mouth, just even with the drooping tip of his black mustache, twitched. He cleared his throat and looked away.

Yes! She wanted to clap in delight. She wanted to wake Patty and prove Mama had been right, after all. Patrick was fighting off a smile.

"But, Mr. Garradine, I can make other desserts. Apple cobblers—I saw dried apples in Coyote—and doughnuts. Cinnamon and sugar doughnuts that will make your mouth rejoice!"

The amusement drained from his face. His tanned fist clenched his coffee cup until his nails turned white.

"That explains the twenty-pound sacks across your saddle. It's a wonder you didn't cripple that mare."

"Really, even with the sugar—"

"The fact is"—he replaced the cup on the mantel—"I don't need a cook."

"The fact is"—she stamped her foot, then lowered her

voice, afraid she'd wake Patty—"you will need a cook, whether you know it or not. Danny told me so."

She'd done it again. He backed away so quickly she snatched his sleeve to anchor him.

"Are you talking about Dan who rides for me?" Patrick watched her hand. "He's in California to visit kin and not due back for weeks, or I'd have him tell you he's wrong."

Feeling as if the floor had tipped beneath her feet, Christa opened her fingers, releasing the blue flannel sleeve. With Danny gone, she had no one to count on but herself. She'd hoped it wouldn't come to this, but she would not be banished.

"I have nowhere else to go, Mr. Garradine. I'm a widow and must work for my living." She turned to face Patty as the pocket watch raced on.

"Damnation, I don't know." His words were half snarl, half groan.

In a display of bad manners nearly as shocking as his language, he turned his back on her. Christa judged it time for a change in tactics.

"Where is your cat, Mr. Garradine? I hear her crying, but I don't see her." Christa watched him frown, considering, and decided her diversion had worked.

"I don't keep a cat, ma'am. One sorry dog, but no cat."

"Perhaps we might call each other by our names, Mr. Garradine. Surely it's proper, since you're to be my employer."

Christa saw his chest expand, stirring the black vest that hung over his shirt. She imagined he held his breath against another outburst. Surely that meant progress.

"I'm not certain I told you my name before," she ventured.

She *was* sure, though. Christa remembered sitting straight up, blurting it through a fog of pain, afraid she'd be buried nameless.

Outside, the wind quit screaming. Inside, the pocket watch hushed. She must know if he remembered.

"Christabel." He drew out her name to three long syllables, then cleared his throat. "You told me."

Joy bounded up and cascaded over her before Christa chided herself. He had recalled her name. For an instant, his dour expression faded. But one hour with the man had taught her sensibility, not sentiment, would win his permission to stay. If he could be swayed by feats of feminine skill, she'd best polish hers. Just now, she'd memorized how he lit the lantern, so she could do it in the future.

Patrick collected a block of matches and broke one off, then squatted next to a low table and turned the lantern's brass key. He lit the wick, adjusted it, and shook the match before looking at her.

"Tell me what kind of sound you heard," he said.

"I—" Christa organized her wayward thoughts. "I heard a cat's cry. It moved—"

Why did he smile when her hand imitated a cat's twining, seeking movements?

"—trying to get in—" She raised her voice as he walked away. Frontiersmen were quite discourteous.

"Where?" His voice came from the other room.

"I couldn't tell, really," she said, tempted to match his rudeness by following. "Perhaps under the house?" She edged closer, but her stomach's rumble ruined her stealth.

Hunger didn't account for the breath that caught in her throat as he emerged, bending at the waist to reach leather strings dangling from a rust-colored gun belt.

Guns. Her head swam as she remembered the stench of gunpowder, the ruined flesh and bone. She shook herself free of the image by focusing on Patrick's fingers, knotting the strings briskly behind each thigh.

"You're not going to shoot the cat?"

"No, ma'am."

Again, the mustache lifted as he swallowed a smile. She didn't believe he was naturally unpleasant.

"I don't shoot cats. I'm just taking a look around. You stay put." He nodded toward Patty.

The door swung on well-oiled hinges as he slipped outside. How silly for him to think of violent trouble, when it was only a cat. Still, his glance at Patty had chilled her.

Was he so worried over Indians? Christa knew trouble had erupted here, but Danny had written that Patrick worked with the tribes. In winter, he'd brought them game and for that they'd named his Winchester rifle "Good Thunder."

She'd noticed daylight spilling into a little pantry off the main room. That meant a window. She could watch his search.

The dark pantry closed around her. Touching the shelves for balance, she felt canned goods and paper-wrapped packages. She stood close to the window. If she squinted, three outlines loomed clear. One was a stone barn and another probably a bunkhouse. A lumpy, chimneyed cook-shack, her future domain, was the one she longed to explore. Once the hands tasted her doughnuts, Patrick wouldn't dare banish her. He needed her, whether he knew it or not.

Bored, she turned her wedding band on her finger, round and round, harder and harder. Patrick still had not crossed the area she watched. Dust, pursued by the wind, spattered under the front door, but she kept her attention fixed on the pantry window. The pane wavered with her reflection as, behind her, lantern light faded and brightened. Then, the door at her elbow moved.

Christa grabbed a can and shrank into the slot behind the door. It felt narrow as a coffin, but she wasn't the one in danger. She'd smash in this invader's skull, call Patrick, and run to her baby.

The dark square of door moved silently, opening the width of thread after thread, shrinking her hiding place. A board creaked, boots paused, then the door slammed back. She fought the confinement, hearing the squeak of her gasp, the crack of her forearms against wood, the can's clatter as it struck the floor.

"Mrs. Worth, could you step back into the other room now for a minute?"

Patrick's voice seemed strangely level after the tumult of sound. Feeling foolish, Christa rushed past him to Patty. To disguise her trembling legs, she sat. To hide her shaky hands, she drew Patty's head into her lap and stroked her hair.

"I might have shot you." His voice remained a monotone.

Christa knew he exaggerated, knew he said it to frighten her. She was grateful Patty was not awake to hear.

Light glimmered on his drawn pistol. It slipped back into his holster with reptilian ease, but in that moment she saw that Patrick Garradine's hands, too, were shaking.

As if she'd been splashed with scalding water, Christa recoiled. What would it take to make this man tremble? What had she done? He must truly believe . . . what he'd said. Christa folded her hands in her lap and sat very still.

"Mrs. Worth, I'm going to put this to you like it was runnin' through my head. Will you listen?"

Christa nodded. He took off his hat, regarding it rather than her.

"You hear something outside, and I'm not sure what it is, since I have no cat." He took a breath. "What I do have is some unpredictable neighbors. The 'utes are friends, mostly, but there are a few wild young bucks among 'em, kids with something to prove. And it's happened that war deserters have wandered this far."

He glanced up, startling her. His black hair and dark skin made *him* look like a young buck. Only his tone—solemn and distressed—made him no renegade.

"You see how a man might get to imagining? Might start thinking he was the only thing standing between—" Patrick stopped short, refusing to finish his grim prediction.

In a smooth stride, he reached the table, snatched up the cup of cold coffee, and sipped.

"I told you to stay put," he said on a sigh. "You couldn't even do that. I came in and you were gone. For that long—" He snapped his fingers. "For one brain-shy second, I set up to shoot someone holdin' you in the pantry."

"I'll never do something that stupid again," she promised, but her mind whirled. He saw danger everywhere! How could she avoid worrying him? "Let me make you some fresh coffee."

"Coffee's not going to do it, ma'am." His glance lingered on Patty. "It's why you and the little one've got to go. You don't know nothin' about this life, and you won't do as you're told long enough to learn. I expect it's your nature, but that kind of ignorance will get you killed."

"But I *will* do as I'm told." The vow soured on her tongue, and he must have noticed.

Patrick shook his head with a half smile.

"It's not worth the risk, ma'am. You were lucky once, but this country don't give second chances." He held up a hand to silence her. "And neither do I."

He turned to the pantry. Christa tried not to soften when she noticed the Indian-black hair, tied with buckskin and soft as a boy's where it curled on his nape.

She understood his fretting, but it was uncalled for. If only she could think of how to prove it.

Patrick returned with two twists of dried meat and a chunk of corn bread. He arranged them on the scrubbed pine table.

"More's in there," he said, "but since Muley's not back and it's coming dark, there'll be no hot meal."

"Let me—"

"Mama . . ."

Patty woke with a tremulous, lost cry. Christa scooped her up, shawl and all, then stood, shifting her weight to a soundless lullaby, rocking Patty, absorbing her warmth.

"No, there'll be no cooking. You can sleep in there." The hands that motioned her toward another doorway were gentle.

"Hungry," Patty whispered.

"It's my room. Clean enough for one night. I'll be in the bunkhouse." He settled his hat and strode toward the door.

"Hungry now, Mama," Patty insisted, one hand turning Christa's face toward her own.

"Just a minute, baby. Mr. Garradine, please."

He stopped.

"Can you please stay? Can we talk this out?"

"Ma'am, I ain't talked this much since the last time we met." He still faced the door, but she saw him shake his head. "I consider myself about talked out."

Patty squirmed and reached toward the table. Christa leaned so she could grab the cornbread.

"Very well, Mr. Garradine," she said. She'd force herself to wake early. She'd create a breakfast that would change his mind before he quit chewing his first bite.

"You've got a long ride ahead tomorrow," he told her. "The stage makes Coyote by about noon, so you best sleep while you can. Evenin'."

He left.

"Sing, Mama." Patty's legs clamped around Christa's waist and she sprayed cornbread crumbs down the neck of Christa's black bombazine.

Christa spun to make her daughter scream with delight, then asked, "Which song, Patty Cakes?"

For the rest of the evening, Christa sang and watched Patty spin in circles to "Oh, Susannah"!—but her thoughts clung to Patrick Garradine and how she'd teach him he needed her, for his own good.

Three

Trick Garradine felt mad enough to chomp a chunk out of his ax. Not one hand had ridden in to explain what disaster had kept them out all night. Stuck outside, he'd shaved using his reflection in the horse trough and laid open a gash long as his little finger. Now, as he hazed all three horses from the yard into the barn half of their corral, he noticed the gray mare moved with a catch in her step. Not quite a limp, but Cloud or Imp had landed a kick to her shoulder.

"Fleabags," he muttered, but both cow horses turned their tails, studying something beyond human ken.

He shut the gate, confining them inside, and watched the gray. She could walk to Coyote, but shouldn't carry a rider. That left Cloud for Christa.

It'd come time to quit thinking of her in a way so forward. It wasn't *Christa* warm in his bed with yellow hair loose and tangled around her arms. It was Mrs. Worth, the same sweet Madonna of his dreams. He should be ashamed for thinking anything different.

Trick blundered into a flurry of sable and white. Its shrill yap would've had a drinking man begging for merciful death.

"Useless cur." Trick sidestepped the dog.

Josh, a young collie jettisoned by wagons moving West, regarded him with worshipful eyes and a fanning tail. Frightened by cattle and most everything else, the dog did nothing to earn his feed.

"Some watchdog." The collie's long muzzle insinuated itself into Trick's hand. "Y'oughta be shot, Josh."

The dog answered with a throaty growl and a lick.

Trick waited for his eyes to adjust to the barn's dimness. The stone structure was short on light, but the cavalry had been more concerned with keeping the stalls arrow-proof. Underground tunnels were said to link the buildings, too. Though he'd never found them, sure as shooting that little girl would. One more good reason to get them going back to where they came from.

He had Imp saddled when he heard his front door shut. Though Imp's black ears pricked at the scuffle of feet, Christa's dust-haloed silhouette in the barn door jarred Trick. How could he want to bang his head against the stone wall at the same time he longed to wind his arms around her?

Christa granted him a nod before inspecting the collie's ears for burrs. He turned back to straighten Imp's headstall, but he couldn't help listening.

"Pretty Joshua," she murmured.

"That's not his name."

"I thought for sure I heard—"

"I don't give animals folks' names. He's called Josh, because he's a joke of a dog," Trick said. "He oughta be—"

"Shot, I know. I heard you tell him."

As Christa peered into the dog's ear, daylight shone through, turning the ear pink beneath her fingers.

"Neither of us believed you," she added.

"Should've," he mumbled, and glanced to see the child emerge from behind Christa. She was a pretty little thing, and determined. She shoved a cup in her mother's direction, so she could give the dog's face a flat-palmed pat.

Christa stepped nearer. He didn't have to turn to know. Summer heat hid in the folds of her skirt, disturbing the dim coolness. The barn smells of straw and horse, stone and mortar, faded under Pears soap and lavender.

"I brought your breakfast in a cup," she said. "Since you wanted an early start."

That was it, then. She'd given in, taken him at his word. He blew out his cheeks and lowered his head. He unhooked the stirrup from the saddle horn and let himself look at her.

Trick judged that if he straightened his arm, his fingers would graze the warm dip of flesh between her ear and jaw.

She looked every inch a lady, with her hair tucked up, pale and neat, and a high-necked white shirt with lace around the collar poking up so her throat showed through the tiny holes. But a lady wouldn't stand so close, or flash those green eyes. Hadn't she learned a lady didn't stare at a man unless she wanted trouble?

"What's this, now?" he asked, taking the cup and peering in.

"Strawberry shrub," she answered proudly.

"Shrub?" He sloshed the cup so the red liquid washed up its sides. "The hell you say."

"No!" The little girl rebuked him with a pointing finger. "Mr. Garradine!"

"Sorry." His apology overlapped Christa's reprimand.

"I don't know how it got its name," she went on. "But I purchased strawberries in Reno, let them steep overnight in a bit of your vinegar, then added sugar this morning."

"I made coffee in the cookshack," he told her. "Why'd you bring this out to the barn?"

For an instant, she looked hurt. God, who could figure a woman?

"I brought it so you didn't have to come up to the house," she said. "What's wrong with a little pampering, Mr. Garradine?"

"Never had it, and never felt the lack," he said. "Here, now!" He jerked Imp's near rein when the gelding tossed his head and sidled away.

Pampering! If she'd grown up in trappers' camps, cavalry camps, and cow camps, she'd know men didn't set store by such foolery. Still, here was this drink, smelling like spring and hand delivered as if he were a king.

Then he understood. She figured on snaring him through his stomach. It wasn't going to work.

"No reason to let stubbornness keep you from tasting something so sweet," she teased, as if she'd read his mind.

Trick lifted the cup and drank, unable to look away from Christa's face. Her brows arched as she awaited his reaction, and he couldn't stifle his pleasure. Sugar and berries were a rare treat, but nowhere near as sweet as watching her tiny bird-bone shoulders rise inside her shirt, shrugging as if she worked such magic every dawn.

He returned the cup and faced the horses still loose in the paddock.

"Your mare's limping. Nothing serious, but there's no sense ruining her. Can you ride that gelding?"

She watched Cloud, then spun around as Patty and Josh wandered from the barn.

"Is she safe out there alone?"

"Safe as in church," he answered. What did she think, there were wolves in his dooryard?

"I just— You said there were dangers I knew nothing of. I must be careful."

Trick rubbed the back of his neck, shamed at being snared by his own loop.

"She'll be all right 'til we're ready to go."

"Fine." She turned back to the horses. "And yes, I can ride that horse."

"You're sure? I have a plow horse I use for the wagon."

"Quite sure." She folded her hands together behind her back and kept her eyes on Cloud. "I can cook and I can ride, Mr. Garradine, but since you're determined to lose me, it's wise you don't know what you're missing."

She made a clucking sound and Cloud came to hang his head over the fence. She gave his white neck a pat, then looked back at Trick like a child issuing a dare.

Christabel Worth was no angel. She taunted him with her

head tipped to one side. It'd serve her right if he called her bluff. Trick took a rope halter and tossed it to her.

"Catch him, saddle up, and ride once around the barn, and he's yours for the day, Miz Worth. Otherwise, I'll be whistling up that plow horse."

She wore a low-crowned, flat-brimmed hat, something like an old-time vaquero might wear. With a smile, she pushed the hat low on her brow and nodded.

The silly hat had no chin strap. It wouldn't last two minutes in a wind, and she might not last much longer on Cloud. The horse wouldn't hurt her, but he was as full of twists as a back road after dark.

Make me a liar, horse. Cloud was so curious his ears pricked forward until the tips almost touched. He dipped his head into the halter. Christa tied him to the fence and tested her knot with a yank. Her skirts swirled past, brushing Trick's boots as she took up the saddle blanket and smoothed it on. Then, with a ladylike grunt, she threw the saddle atop Cloud's broad back.

She fastened the cinch and Trick shook his head. Cloud had fooled her, puffing up his belly so the girth wouldn't pinch. Soon as she put one foot in the stirrup, the gelding would let his breath out. Then, with embarrassing slowness, the saddle would turn and Christa would land on a thick pad of straw, smack on her pretty backside.

Trick considered where he'd place his hands as he helped her up. Under her arms, like he would with a boy? Around her waist? Christa glanced back with eyes so trusting, he knew he should mention the cinch. Her hand rubbed under the ropy white mane and Cloud nuzzled her.

"You're a pet, aren't you, Cloud?" Then she kissed him—Cloud, who smelled like a goat and could buck off a man's whiskers when the mood seized him—she *kissed* him on the muzzle.

Trick crossed his arms over his belt buckle and shook his head. That clinched it, honey. What was it you said? It's wise I don't know what I'm missing? And, oh yeah, no sense letting stubbornness keep me from tasting something sweet? Well, Trick Garradine might be lower than a snake's belly in a wagon rut, but he'd never again get this chance. He knew one sure way he'd get to wind her in his arms, this once. He'd let the little witch fall.

She didn't. Instead, she turned back to the gelding. Then, quick as any seasoned hand, kneed the placid horse in the belly. Cloud gasped in surprise, giving her time to jerk the cinch tight. Christa turned around, hands on hips. She might have ridden some, at that.

"Cloud has some bad habits, Mr. Garradine."

"He's a range pony, Miz Worth, long on tough and short on manners."

She didn't answer, but her told-you-so smile accompanied a whole-body wiggle like that of a delighted pup. He stepped closer to help her mount, but she wedged her boot into a niche in the wall and swung her leg, encased in what looked like a split skirt, over Cloud's back.

She ducked as she rode through the barn door, and he marked her progress by the rollicking hooves and a child's shout.

"Go, Mama!"

Trick chuckled. Lord above, it was tempting to keep her on. Best he didn't let her know how tempting.

"We're burnin' daylight, Miz Worth." He came out into the sun as she rounded the corner at a trot. "It'd be helpful if you'd get your gear, put the child up on your gray, and tell Good Thunder Meadows adios. We're headed out."

"Temptation hath come to Coyote Town, and she rideth a white horse!" The bellow came from a gap-toothed maw surrounded by spirals of gray beard.

"I suppose there's a man in there." Christa blinked at the form raging beneath a sign that announced STARR'S SALOON. For two hours, she'd squinted against stark alkali flats and white sun. She didn't quite trust her sight.

"Close enough. It's just Monk."

She saw Patrick's legs tighten, urging Imp to lengthen his stride. When gunfire cracked, making Christa catch her breath, Patrick turned in the saddle.

"That's just Tommy, shootin' bottles behind the saloon."

"Jezebel rides a pale horse!" roared the bearded prophet. He wore overalls so patched they looked like a clown's motley.

Dazzled by the glare and her inability to figure out a way to convince Patrick to let her stay, Christa had a headache. She also had a child who had asked questions endlessly, and an arm that ached from holding the mare's lead rope. Frankly, her patience for zealots was pretty flimsy.

"Is Monk a man of the cloth?" Christa asked.

Looking back, she saw he'd drawn a crowd from Starr's Saloon. Though Monk's body formed an x across the doorway, men squeezed by him, shading their eyes to stare. Mercifully, the saloon stood at Coyote's north end, a dusty block before the plank walls and shops began.

"Monk's more inclined to proclaim than preach," Patrick said. "Truth be told, he's a prospector, down on his luck, but he came out of the desert spouting scripture." Patrick peered at her from the shade of his black hat. "Folks don't think he's holy, but they're afraid to let him starve."

"I guess you never know," Christa said. Last night, in her search for ways to show Patrick he must let her stay, she'd proposed a number of bargains with God. Though His response had been uncertain, she couldn't believe Monk was His messenger.

Looking over her shoulder, Christa was dismayed to see Monk meandering down the road behind them.

"That's a fact," said Patrick. "Turn here."

Christa reined Cloud into Malloy's Livery and Smithy. The ring of hammer on iron made the gray mare snort. Patty came awake, rubbing her eyes.

"Mama? Mama, I'm hungry."

"We'll leave the horses until the stage comes and go get a meal at Pilgrims'," Patrick said, pointing down the sunbaked street. "Or pickles and crackers at Hacklebord's. I'll talk with Malloy about the horses while you decide."

"*You* decide," Christa sighed. She plucked off her gloves and started to lift Patty down.

"I will, then," he said. He took Patty from the horse and made sure her knees held before releasing her. "Be right back, Mrs. Worth."

What on earth had she done right? Christa stared after Patrick, whose voice had turned hearty. Swinging strides carried him into the dim livery and she could swear he whistled as he went.

"Man, Mama?" Patty asked.

Wheezing from exertion, Monk stormed toward them. He teetered only steps away when Christa swept Patty into her arms.

"Stand back, sir," Christa ordered. Behind Monk stood two more drunkards. Before any of them could speak, Christa raised her chin in warning. "And keep your filthy ravings to yourself."

She assumed the steps behind her were Patrick's, until the blacksmith, his shirt half on, shouldered past.

"You'll not be harassin' women and children on my property!" he shouted. "D'ye hear me, Monk?"

"David, she's the one," whispered Monk, spittle spraying. "The letter? Remember?"

He cupped a hand near his lips and would have staggered closer if the smith hadn't held him at arm's length.

"The 'black widow,'" Monk enunciated. "Folks want a look at 'er, before we hide the goods under tar and feathers. You know."

He lurched forward and Christa ducked behind the smith's broad, muscled back.

"What I know is you'll leave her alone."

This time the voice *was* Patrick's, low and deadly. Christa heard leather squeak before he walked past her, gun drawn, finger curved above the trigger. Her heartbeat surged into her throat. Patrick would shoot that grizzled fanatic if he came at her.

The other two drunkards comprehended and fled. One stumbled as he looked back for Monk. One lifted his knees and ran.

"Monk, you know Trick," said the blacksmith. "What y'might not have heard, since he's so gentlemanly, is Trick Garradine was raised with a milk bottle in one hand and a gun in t'other. He just naturally shoots men like you." The smith gave Monk a shove. "Y'understand? Come lookin' for excitement here, boyo, and you just might find it."

Wordless as a sleepwalker, Monk shuffled away.

Patrick and the blacksmith breathed heavy sighs. Christa judged it a wonder she heard them over her own puffing.

"Wanna play, Mama." Patty stretched her arms toward a leggy child emerging from the livery stable.

"That's me daughter, Rosebud," said the blacksmith. He glared pointedly at the drawn gun and Patrick holstered it.

Christa let Patty slip from her arms as the smith tucked his grimy hand into the waist of his leather apron and nodded.

"I'll introduce myself as well, ma'am. I'm David Malloy, proprietor of this equine establishment."

"A good man to have with you in a fight," Patrick admitted.

Though Malloy slapped Patrick's back with his black-smudged paw, Christa thought Patrick said the words grudgingly.

"I'm pleased to meet you, Mr. Malloy," Christa said, and would have shaken his helpful hand in spite of the soot if Patrick hadn't interceded.

"Yeah, thanks, Malloy." Patrick's voice rasped gruff and his shaving cut faded against his cheeks' crimson flush.

And then he touched her skin. For the first time in three years, Christa felt Patrick's ungloved hand on hers. His thumb grazed the inside of her palm as he folded her hand into the crook of his elbow.

"I'll be back for my geldings soon as the stage leaves," Patrick said. "And Mrs. Worth will be trailing the mare back to Sacramento City. Unless you want to sell her?"

Christa shook her head slowly. Why sell a horse she'd need to carry Patty back to Good Thunder Meadows?

Though her mind had knit and unraveled a dozen plans on the ride here, she'd felt that sweet ache of homecoming this desert offered. She loved its teardrop-small wildflowers growing in the shade of stones, the calico mesas, and cloud banks turning from dull pewter to molten gold in a single minute. She would not return to Sacramento City.

Patrick's flash of jealousy had shone a light on the solution, and Christa was not one to ignore God's invitation, even if He opened the door just a crack.

Patrick cared for her, and certainly he needed her. His baffled appreciation of the strawberry shrub proved that, even if she could forget his pitiful cornbread and jerky supper. Mercy, she could concoct a better meal from the crumbs in her saddlebags!

"Pardon me, Trick." Mr. Malloy's voice, an odd combination of wild West and Ireland, jerked Patrick to a stop. "But if y'think the lady's takin' the stage, I fear I've bad news."

Malloy sounded as if he were teasing, but Christa felt Patrick's arm harden beneath her fingers. Before propriety could halt action, she gave him a comforting squeeze.

"Bad news?" Patrick asked, voice level and smooth as snow.

"Aye. The Yates boys, two of your favorites, rode in not an hour past. Seems they met the stage at Cotton Creek, and Potter—that's the stage driver, ma'am—"

"Malloy—" Patrick threatened, to hurry him.

"Seems like the Paiutes are raiding his entire route. He's bringin' passengers here and dumpin' 'em. He told the Yates brothers he's goin' back to Reno, alone."

Christa took in the sound of a jay scolding. She took in the prattle of raven-curled Rosebud naming off her dolls for

Patty. What she didn't take was offense, as the blacksmith finished.

"So you see, Trick, Potter says the stage is leavin' empty as a banker's heart, and it ain't comin' back to Coyote till long about the time hell freezes over."

A staid Methodist by upbringing, Christa always gave thanks sedately and in private. But just now, behind mild eyes and solemn lips, Christa's heart leapt up and shouted "Hallelujah!"

Four

Beeswax candles pricked the shuttered boardinghouse with light so dim, Christa tightened her grip on Patty's hand. When Patrick released Christa's arm to lead the way, she clamped a lid of good sense over her jubilation and followed Patrick's silhouette toward the aroma of pot roast.

"We like to keep it nice and cool, dear, but it seems dark, doesn't it, coming in from the street? Watch your step on the rug." The motherly woman wore wide-puffed sleeves and a cameo. "Oh, and you've got a little one. I hope Sharlot's rice pudding has set."

After the woman's bustling disappearance, Christa made out a pine-paneled dining room and four tables at which a dozen diners ate. A few broadcloth coats and collars turned her way, but most who stared wore miners' rough overalls. All were men.

"Mrs. Worth?" Patrick beckoned from one end of a table at which only two men sat.

Christa hurried to the chairs across from him. Patrick's arm lay across the table, bracketing them off from the others.

"Mama, I want soup!" Patty reached across a platter of carrots for a white tureen.

All conversation hushed. All silverware lay silent. Chewing stopped. They might have been on stage.

"Patty," Christa whispered, "remember your manners. Ask for the soup to be passed." She glanced up at Patrick, hoping he'd cooperate.

"What's your name?" Loud and querulous, Patty's voice drew chuckles.

"Mr. Garradine." Christa managed the words, though her face burned with embarrassment. It was her own fault. She should have explained, last night. Now she must suffer the humiliation of having a room full of men believe she dined with a stranger.

When Patty's attempt at "Mr. Garradine" came out a frustrated garble, he leaned forward.

" 'Trick' is just fine, sugar."

Patrick's kind words warmed Christa, melting coherent expression.

"No, it's—" Christa began. "She must mind her manners—"

"Whatever you say." He took up the soup ladle.

"Please," Patty recited.

"Please, Mr.—" Christa modeled.

"Please, Mr. Trick!" Patty bobbed her head until her bonnet sagged to one side.

Christa looked at her daughter's tiny hands, folded and fidgety on the tablecloth. A "please" and folded hands would have to be good enough. Manners taught in public made the teacher unmannerly.

"Patty, you are such a good girl," Christa murmured. She untied Patty's bonnet strings and kissed her cheek as Patrick served a soup thick with barley.

"Mercy, such goin's on at table," muttered a woman who paused to offer a plate of biscuits. "I'm Miss Sharlot Pilgrim. The other proprietress. My sister, Adeline, you met. Or would have, had she retained the manners *our* dear mother taught us."

As Sharlot Pilgrim straightened, Christa saw that though Sharlot was angular and Adeline round, the sisters shared rust-brown hair and faded freckles.

Sharlot surveyed the others seated at the table. "Not a gentleman among 'em."

"Ma'am?" A male voice and a platter of beef hurried to prove Sharlot Pilgrim wrong.

Patrick's reach blocked Christa's. He intercepted the platter and a bowl of beans, bacon, and onions before the miner's hand grazed hers. With a bite halfway to his mouth, Patrick seized yet a second offering—this time a basket of green plums—then fell, once more, to eating.

Manners didn't come naturally to Patrick, either. Hunched over his plate, he must have felt her regard. He straightened and dabbed a linen napkin at his mustache.

Living in a cow camp didn't lead to gentle behavior. That was easily repaired, but she did wish for conversation. Not until she'd fed and tidied Patty did Christa realize the men ate in silence.

Such focused chewing stole her appetite. Christa spooned honey over a biscuit. The silver spoon wavered, drizzling her hand as the boardinghouse door opened to harsh sunlight.

"'Scuse me, Miz Pilgrim and Miz Pilgrim, but tell me I ain't too late for supper." The man who bowed to the sisters sported bushy whiskers and a red shirt that Christa feared was his underwear. He smelled strongly of horse.

"Of course not," began Adeline.

"You know you are," Sharlot interrupted.

"I've cheated death once today, so I guess I'll gamble on believing *you*, Miss Pilgrim." He bowed to Adeline, then pulled out a chair and collapsed at the head of their table.

His contented groan lingered as Patrick spoke.

"Potter."

"Hey, Trick, you in for supplies?" Potter drained glass after glass of water with such speed, he might better have drunk from the pitcher.

Patrick ignored Potter's pleasantry. "Blacksmith Malloy says the Yates boys've been telling tales on you."

"Not if they said I was outta business." Potter forked a slab of beef onto his plate, then reached for a dish of gravy. "My *former* passengers are out sittin' in the coach wonderin' where the horses went." He looked up at the Pilgrim sisters, who'd lingered. "I 'spect they'll make their way down here, looking for fodder and a place to bed down."

"Heavens!" Adeline gasped.

"How many?" Sharlot demanded. "And don't you be telling me any more than one or two, Vern Potter."

"Two." Potter split three biscuits with a single knife stroke. "One's a gentleman attorney, headed back to the Barbary Coast after tending business in Boston."

"My, my."

"You don't say!"

"Wonder how he'll like settin' up shop in Coyote!"

A chorus of derision met Potter's news, but Christa didn't laugh. Upon Nathan's death, lawyers had flocked to her parlor. She'd listened as Nathan's lawyers, lawyers from his bank, even Sacramento City government lawyers, squabbled over the disposition of Nathan's investments, debts, and effects. Then they'd turned slowly to her, weighing her profit from the accident. Polite and steady, she'd turned out the lot of them.

She hadn't touched the gun that killed him, but she worried that sharp-tongued provocation—of which she'd given Nathan plenty—might count as incitement to suicide. Even now, she felt as if a bone ridge blocked each swallow.

"You can take one widow-woman and her child as far as Sacramento City." Patrick's voice interrupted her thoughts.

Potter started, as if he'd just seen Christa.

"I'd tip my hat, ma'am, but I lost it in the run. I had them horses' bellies scrapin' the ground. And I'm sorry, but it's against policy to drive passengers through hos-tile territory. I'd venture to say two hunters butchered and a homestead burnt to ash indicates the Paiutes are fair perturbed."

Despite the spate of talk, Potter continued eating. His spoon scraped the dregs of gravy onto his plate and he sopped it with the last biscuit.

"Yessir, Trick, and ma'am." He knuckled his shiny lips. "Soon's I get a slug of John Starr's tarantula juice to wash down these victuals, I'm biddin' Coyote Town fare-thee-well. You'll know I'm coming back when you see my crackerbox stage on the horizon."

Potter stood, took Christa's hand in the same paw he'd used on his lips, and planted a smacking kiss on her wrist. Then Potter lifted his belt, belched, and departed in a swagger that doused two candles.

"Well, hell," said Patrick Garradine.

"No, no," Patty reprimanded wearily. Her eyelids drooped from the long ride and heavy meal.

"Tell you what, sugar," Patrick said, rounding the end of the table. "We'll go to Hacklebord's Mercantile and get a couple sticks of peppermint candy. Might sweeten my cursin' mouth."

Christa glanced at Patty. Nathan hadn't allowed store-bought sweets. She wasn't sure Patty knew what Patrick meant.

As he loomed next to her chair, Patty's eyes traveled up. They passed Patrick's denimed thighs and low gun belt, passed the buckle sagging below his waist, traversed the blue shirt to his sun-dark face and black mustache. He stood quite tall, and Patty's lips trembled.

Don't cry. Christa's tongue poised over words of comfort when the child leaned against her, then peered up at Patrick.

"Candy, Mr. Trick!" Patty giggled. "Candy, candy candy!"

". . . warning to the good people of Coyote . . . a cunning murderess . . . ," read Alvin Hacklebord, mercantile proprietor.

Patrick stared at saw blades and shovel handles. He hated all tools that took him down from the saddle. But shoveling and sawing beat the hell out of Christa yammering about the future. He'd grunted and walked faster when she questioned Potter's declaration that she was stranded until fall. Any Western woman would've known the tribes left off raiding to hunt meat and dry it for the winter.

One row over, sleepy Patty clung like a baby possum

while Christa lifted a black iron muffin tin. Christa stopped like she'd been slapped and turned toward Alvin Hacklebord.

What in tarnation was the man jawin' about?

". . . guilty of her husband's death, but not arrested . . ."

Though heat snakes wavered up off the street outside, Alvin's audience clustered, by habit, at the pot-bellied stove. Hacklebord, of course, could read. He squinted over wire-rimmed glasses, peering at a letter held at arm's length.

Who was the letter from, that Alvin shared it with half of Coyote's shopkeepers? Not that Alvin took responsibility to the U.S. Postal Service too seriously. He saw his store more as a slop bucket than a sacred vessel. If folks didn't show up to claim what was theirs, Alvin appropriated it for his own use.

One member of his audience let her attention wander. Like a she-cat testing the air, dressmaker Polly LaCrosse scanned the store. He couldn't see her face in the shadow of a wide-brimmed tumble of fruit and birds' wings, but Trick guessed she'd sniffed him out.

Polly had a craving for him and it made him skittish. Not that she wasn't a beauty. Tall and built to look good in her fancy frills and furbelows, she was fair, like Christa. No, he corrected, that wasn't so. Polly's blond beauty burned icy dry, like John Starr's champagne; Christa's was like warm honey.

Trick ducked over to the aisle where he'd left her, only to see Christa riding skirts flare as she aimed for the group at the stove. Each step she took left Trick more uneasy.

He'd always hated town talk and town troubles, and his nerves jangled like new spurs. This morning's sass-and-vinegar Christa had disappeared. In her place walked an angel, the sort that carried a sword. Should he warn Alvin how smoothly she'd knocked the wind out of Cloud?"

". . . and so, Sheriff . . ."

Hell, Coyote had no sheriff and no need of one. This letter was surely one of Alvin's interceptions.

". . . beware the black widow, Christabel Worth."

Christa? *Christa* a black widow? A husband-killer? Dizziness lurched around him. Just yesterday he'd thought, if a man ever deserved killing, that man was Nathan Worth.

"Yours in Christian sisterhood . . ."

"Francesca Worth." Christa's words eclipsed Alvin's as she halted near the covey of gossips.

"Her own sister-in-law!" Hannah Hacklebord, Alvin's brow-beaten wife, proved that misery loved company.

"Hannah, hush." Alvin twitched his head toward Christa.

With a gasp echoed by the others, Hannah hushed.

Washing dishes in the cookshack didn't sound so bad, Trick thought. Neither did mucking out the chicken coop, or laying flat on his back, getting mashed under a rank bronc. He'd prefer to be any place but here, with all eyes on him.

Alvin's and Hannah's frog eyes said they thrived on other folks' excitement; Tommy Bluff, wishing he had cold blue gunfighter eyes, instead of blueberry, had left off plinking at bottles to watch the show; the Mexican candlemaker they called Lucy watched Christa with dark eyes and a melancholy smile. Polly's cat eyes glittered and feinted up and down his body. Next, she'd be asking to take a look at his teeth.

How'd folks get so bored they couldn't see what was in front of them? Christa's hands embraced her sleeping daughter. One curved around Patty's back as the other smoothed the child's hair. Christa's were not the hands of a murderess. Nor a meek matron. Suddenly, her fingers spread and she lifted her chin, facing Alvin.

"Excuse me, sir. We haven't met, but I am Christabel Worth."

Like any fear-biter of a dog, Alvin retreated.

Christa shifted Patty and offered Alvin her gloved left hand. Trick knew he should've introduced her the minute they entered the store. Just like he should've presented her to Adeline, Sharlot, and Potter. But he hadn't, because he didn't know beans about manners. Now Christa stood there, hand extended.

Since Alvin didn't choose to shake it, she folded it over Patty's back once more and lowered her head. Next to Polly's stylish bonnet, which appeared on closer inspection to be a Thanksgiving turkey with all the trimmings, Christa's riding hat looked like a black flapjack. Christa looked ready to fight.

He searched for words to stop her, but came up dry. He glared at Alvin.

"Sir—" Christa began.

"Hacklebord, Alvin Hacklebord." The shopkeeper bared his teeth in a nervous grin.

"Mr. Hacklebord," Christa amended, "I would advise you not to trouble the sheriff with that letter. Simply deal with it as you would any trash you come across in a working day. Dispose of it."

Taking Christa's arm, Trick towed her along. "When you folks finish discussin'," Trick said, "I'm willing to pay cash money for a ten-pound sack of rice, a tin of raisins, and a hickory shovel handle."

"Of course, Mr. Garradine." Trying to avoid pots of seedlings arranged in the sunlight, Hannah tripped, steadied herself on the counter, and dodged behind it to consult a ledger.

Trick took Christa's arm and guided her away from the others.

"I'm afraid we're out of those handles." Hannah's jerky movements spilled a can of pencils at her elbow. "I could order one for you."

Trick nodded. He didn't fool himself that this talk fest was over. Someone had gasped as he moved Christa away. Now he felt stares. When he'd mustanged for the cavalry, he'd felt the Paiutes watching, and he'd come to recognize that prickle of dread and excitement. But these stares felt itchy as a mosquito's bite.

"Will that be all, Mr. Garradine?"

"I'm ahorseback. Can't take more, just now."

"I'll return with a more extensive order," Christa cut in.

One of the biddies over by the stove fluttered a fan, moaning as if she'd faint from shock.

"I do hope you'll be able to fill it," Christa prodded as Hannah stood openmouthed.

Boston starch coated each word, reminding Trick she was a city woman, not a Westerner like the rest of them. She'd just admitted to living with him. No one here would take her for a cook, and he didn't have breath to explain. What's more, Christa had best stop talking down to people. Out here, folks had little *except* their dignity. They defended it fiercely.

"And three peppermint sticks, if you please, Hannah."

He hefted the sacks over one shoulder and steered Christa toward the door. Her nose wrinkled as they passed the tobacco and he hurried along a few steps until they reached the empty, sunlit street. Then he turned on her.

"Mrs. Worth." Trick kept his voice low and his arms at his sides as he trapped her between his body and the mercantile's outside wall.

Christa flinched and Trick lost his will to lecture. He cleared his throat and wondered why he'd never noticed the curve of a woman's temple. Just where it joined her cheek, the skin turned from ivory to peach. His rope-rough fingers wanted to test that flesh for softness.

"Yes, Mr. Garradine?"

Softness was the last thing he needed. Between now and August, he had to ride a thousand acres, searching for every head of cattle, gathering the herd, feeding and weaning and driving and selling—*if* he wanted Good Thunder Meadows to be a working ranch.

"Mrs. Worth." He separated one peppermint stick from the others. "I want you to put this in your mouth. Don't take it out to talk to anyone, including me, until we hit the trail for home, understand?"

The red-and-white stick cracked when he slapped it on

Christa's gloved palm. He gave her no chance for back talk, just led the way back to Malloy's. The walk had never seemed so long. At each boot fall, his imagination scourged him with questions. What if he kept this city woman within reach all summer long? What if he'd placed the candy between her lips? What if next time he couldn't resist such sweet temptation?

Trick didn't suffer long. The Yates brothers dealt him a jolt of anger, one feeling he understood just fine.

The twin Rebs had stopped to water their horses at Malloy's. Trick had never seen finer horseflesh than the Yateses' pair of Tennessee Walkers. The men, though, were just hateful.

It was rare to see the two together. They had duties on their home place that Trick wouldn't wish on anyone, even enemies.

As Thaddeus and Arthur Yates told the tale, they'd been barely thirteen when they served with their father under General Beauregard. Shocked by word of Grant's progress down the Mississippi, Randall Yates sent his sons home to protect their mother and sisters. Tragedy outran them. Fire, ignited by patriotic attempts to burn crops before Yankees could eat them, destroyed their farm and family. Behind, in the Battle of Shiloh, a Union cavalryman's dying horse crushed Randall Yates's legs. He survived amputation and recurring fevers, but the surgeon declared him a fading corpse.

When his grieving sons arrived to take him home, Randall asked a favor. Before dying, he wanted to visit a place he'd seen on a schoolroom map: a province called the "Northern Mystery," located somewhere between Canada and California. The twins had saved a mule, a wagon, and three head of hidden bloodstock, so they sold one horse to pay expenses and left Tennessee.

Trick had seen such misery, and lived a piece of it. When a Confederate Minié ball ricocheted off his head, he couldn't speak for weeks. He'd come back to Nevada and served the Union by turning mustangs into warhorses. He counted himself lucky to have survived his battles. When word got around to the Yates family, they counted him too lucky.

Up on their fine red Walkers, the Yates brothers approached. *Just keep riding, boys.* Trick willed them to pass. Since dawn, he'd skirmished with Christa; he didn't feel like refighting the war.

It was Christa, still sucking her candy, who caught their attention.

"Ma'am." They lifted gray Rebel caps which had outlasted the rags of uniforms the two struggled into each April, on the anniversary of Shiloh.

Christa nodded, and stopped. Trick tugged her arm, but Patty had wiggled loose, and stood pointing.

"Pretty horse," she cooed.

Both Yateses smiled, drew rein, and leaned forward in their saddles to talk with Patty.

"This here's Banner," said Thad Yates, his voice earnest as Patty's. "And that onc's Blazc."

"Baze," Patty repeated. "Up on Baze. Up!"

Thad chuckled and Arthur shot Trick a sardonic smile. Arthur Yates drank. He spent his holidays from tending his pa in Starr's Saloon.

Damn. Now Patty stood with both arms raised to the Yateses and Christa didn't say a thing. He thought she was about to, but she only took the peppermint stick from her mouth, swallowed, and recommenced sucking.

"Blaze is a mite touchy." Thad glanced at Christa, then Trick, seeking permission. "But Banner is dog gentle."

"Ma'am?" Arthur drew himself up straight with such ragged courtliness, Trick felt a surge of rivalry.

"Mrs. Nathan Worth is from Sacramento City," Trick said. "During her bereavement, she's visiting her brother at Thunder Meadows." Trick rattled off the lie like a Whig.

"A pleasure to meet you, ma'am," said Thad.

"Our condolences on your loss, ma'am. I'm Arthur Yates and this is my brother, Thad."

Christa looked downright peculiar, standing mute, genteel in bearing, somber in her widow's black, smiling around the red-and-white candy stuck between her lips.

Thad frowned with concern, then turned toward Trick.

"Is she—simple?" Thad mouthed the words with barely a hint of sound.

"Just stubborn."

It was time for them to move on. Past time, but Arthur placed a palm flat on his horse's rump and leaned back against it.

"Well, that's a shame," Arthur drawled. "A simple woman might not feel the indignity of living with a Yank."

Living with . . . Trick told himself not to bristle, told himself to take the words at face value.

With Christa squatting, face to face with Patty, telling her to stay back from the horses, this was no place for rough words or a fight.

"Now, a stubborn woman," Thad continued, "she'd probably notice. No doubt she'd welcome a neighborly visit, now and then."

"I'll know if you step foot on my ranch. You'll pay with your hide." He'd like to knock that jackass grin off Thad's face.

"He'll know!" Arthur mimicked, urging his horse on by.

"Brother, it scares me nigh onto death." Thad followed.

Activity recommenced on Coyote's boardwalks, as if the townsfolk had stayed indoors, safe from gunplay.

Christa took his arm. Thoughts of Rebel treachery faded as he wondered how her touch would feel if he had his shirtsleeves rolled up for work.

"Do you throw down dares like that all the time, Mr. Garradine?"

Trick curbed his tongue long enough to realize she was right. It would be sheer chance if he knew the Yateses had ridden onto his land. Unless they made trouble.

"I try not to," he admitted. "But sometimes I can't help it. For instance, I bet you can't make it all the way home without doin' some cockeyed thing that'll cause my heart to pump and puff like a locomotive, now can you?"

He shortened his stride to match her steps, then looked into her smiling face. He waited. Christabel Worth said nothing. She kept her own counsel and she kept on smiling.

five

Just yesterday, Christa had approached Good Thunder Meadows across the vast alkali flats. This time it felt like a homecoming.

Lulled by the horse's gait, Christa's mind wandered to Boston, her first home, and she thanked her father for his long-ago rage. That night, she'd lingered late at a moonlight croquet party. That night, Nathan had proposed and she'd demurred. But when Father hounded her from room to room, berating—not for the first time—her unladylike conduct, Christa sent word that she'd accept Nathan's proposal if he rekindled his pipe dream of going West.

Now, the sinking Western sun transformed weeds to gold stands of wheat. A horse's hoof in talcum-fine dirt left a print overflowing with lavender shadows. Swarms of swallows formed a garland in the sky, then descended, wrapping the house on the horizon.

Christa saw the ranch house a full hour before they arrived. That, Trick said, had made the creekside site perfect for the fort and remount station. With the materials at hand, he'd turned the officers' quarters into his house and the enlisted men's barracks into a bunkhouse. He'd left the stable and cookshack as they'd been.

"How did you come to own a fort, Mr. Garradine?"

"Dumb luck. When I mustered out, the U.S. Army planned to desert this." He motioned at the expanse before them. "They owed me back salary that never showed up on payroll, so we made a deal. And I stayed on."

A coyote's cry stirred longing she hadn't felt since that long desert dusk, the night before Patty had been born.

"You were stationed here, then, when—"

"That's a fact. Sentimental cuss, huh? For that, I'll be in debt till my dying day." He clucked his tongue in the direction of Patty's mare. "Pick up your hooves, Betsy, and you'll earn grain enough to founder."

With that, the horses broke into a trot toward home.

"I'm eating with the boys. When you see them ride out, come on down to the cookshack." Patrick's voice, raised to carry through the closed bedroom door, woke her.

The sky had brightened from black to ink-blue, she noticed, squinting toward the window. *No please, no thank-you, just—eating, had he said?* Christa burrowed her face into the sheets. *Breakfast before dawn. She'd put an end to that!* Patrick's bedding smelled of sunshine and soap, nothing more. Even sleeping in his bed was no intimacy.

Boots shifted in the other room as he issued another order. "Until then, stay inside."

The door slammed hard enough that she started up onto her knees. Heart pounding, she wondered if Patrick was hiding her.

Christa pushed her hair from her eyes. Had she forgotten to braid it or had it unraveled?

Christa yawned, envying Patty's sprawl in their shared blankets. The child had tossed and muttered all night. Now, Christa let her sleep. Before she coaxed Patty's wispy locks into a plait, Christa decided to tackle her own sleep-mussed hair.

Soon. Christa's knees huddled up under her night rail, making a shelf for her cheek. She hadn't drifted long before serenity hit a snag.

Why was Patrick hiding them? Could he be embarrassed by her sudden appearance at his front door? Did he fear mutiny when her cooking skills fell short of Muley's? Or was he simply at a loss to explain her?

Oh, mercy. What if Daniel had been mistaken? What if Muley wasn't leaving? Christa raised her eyelids and scanned the room. Patrick's house was already tidier than hers, so he needed no housekeeper. She'd come to help, but if he didn't need a cook, how could she?

Not that he'd budged from his first-hour declarations: This was no place for a lady; Trick Garradine didn't give second chances; she didn't "know nothin'" and wouldn't do as she was told long enough to learn.

Of all his protests, only the last troubled her. She'd proved him right, first in the pantry incident, then again yesterday in Hacklebord's mercantile. No lady, no matter how provoked, would have meddled in that closed-circle chatter about her past.

No matter her Western shortcomings, Christa knew how to act like a lady. A lady overlooked such slander. A lady would never scorn Hannah, especially when the *lady* recognized the sickly worry mirrored in the shopkeeper's eyes as they darted after her husband, gauging his displeasure.

Christa heard a bark, a yelp, and men's voices.

"Sakes, Josh, get out of the way."

Boots tramped. There was a cough, then someone spat. Christa shuddered. That was another habit to curb in these womanless males.

"Throw 'im a stick, Jim."

"Humph. Let him throw his own damn stick. I'm saving my ropin' arm."

"C'mon, boys. My tapeworm wants to get fed."

What on earth could he mean? She wished her mother, who'd written that Daniel had "lost his polish" since moving West, could have met the men Dan worked with.

Now she knew why Patrick had kept her apart. And yet she would meet them, eat with them and converse with them, so he'd accomplished nothing. Except that she was forewarned. For Patty's sake, she'd put an end to earthy talk.

Christa's hair was braided and twisted into a high coil when Patty woke. Now, dressed and hungry, Patty kicked her feet impatiently as her mother peered from behind the curtain.

She believed all the men had left. She listened for another door creak, watched for a slip of kerosene light amid dawn's shadows. But how many men comprised the day shift? Or was this the night shift? Though a cluster of them moved toward the barn and corrals, she'd wait a bit.

That should please Patrick, and since he hadn't agreed she could stay, she'd bend. Otherwise, he'd devise some way to send her back, back to a woman who'd branded her a black widow.

The cookhouse door hadn't opened for at least ten minutes. If Patrick waited inside, he'd be growing impatient.

"Would you care for some breakfast, my sweet?" Christa took Patty's hand.

"Candy." Patty jumped up from the couch and ran ahead, towing Christa, who closed the cabin door behind them.

"Not for breakfast," she told Patty, though only Heaven knew what these Westerners deemed suitable breakfast fare.

"The slickest way to clean a rabbit is to start here, cut a hole 'bout this big, grab the hind feet, and then sort of crack the whip with your wrist. See?" Muley, his face gleeful from bald pate to gapped teeth, held up the skinned game for Christa's inspection.

Patrick Garradine had said she could stay, and though he'd said it grudgingly, he'd mentioned nothing about skinning meat.

Firing up the stove had been simple. Pricking nutmegs with her hat pin to check for freshness was no chore at all. Grinding Mexican chili peppers to spice meat that wasn't fresh, adding flour and water to sourdough starter and setting it in the cookhouse window to proof—such culinary tasks were not difficult. But this . . .

Still, Christa wrote down each of Muley's suggestions. He'd finally told Patrick what he'd confided to Dan a month before. He wasn't following a herd of heifers when there were fortunes to be made in Virginia City. Only an extra day's salary had enticed him to stay on a bit longer. So, while Patty pounded pots with a wooden spoon, Christa copied recipes, confident she could do this job nicely.

But the cuts of meat she'd prepared in Sacramento City had come from a butcher's shop, neatly wrapped and tied with string.

"Does Mr. Garradine—" Christa swallowed and covered her lips. She'd come off the cookhouse porch to watch Muley's demonstration, but now she stared past him. Far across the ranch grounds, beyond the range of her quavering voice, Patrick paused in the stable door. "Does he often have a craving for wild game?"

"No, ma'am. Trick and them, they mostly like beef. And ham and bacon, o' course. I have tried 'em on mutton, and chicken. They perk right up when I fry chicken. None's ever left for midday saddlebag fare. But they're not what you'd call picky eaters."

"That's a mercy."

"Excuse me, ma'am?"

"I said," Christa tried to quell her shaky sigh, "my, um, meat preparation skills are somewhat lacking."

"You don't like to butcher, is what you're saying. Neither do I, come to that. And you being a lady, why, it's just natural."

Her hands were actually perspiring. Christa wiped her palms on Muley's gift of an oversized apron.

"Don't worry, Miz Worth. Trick Garradine treats his cooks like gold."

Perhaps. This morning Patrick had spoken exactly seven words to her. Standing as far from her as the cookhouse walls allowed, he'd said, "This is Muley. He'll show you around."

Then, he'd fussed about the cookhouse, oiling door hinges, pounding in a nail from which a calendar hung, frowning at the rafters. Finally, he'd left her alone with the cook.

"The hands do the slaughtering and such. Why, you won't even have to wash dishes."

"No?" Christa managed a weak smile. This happenstance was fortunate. She'd never washed a dish in her life.

*   *   *

Pewter-blue and cloudless, the evening sky stretched behind his house, bare except for a smudged half-moon. Trick felt odd, approaching his own porch as a visitor. He'd keep his hat on, unless she asked him in. Even then, he'd refuse.

Trick eased the kink in his neck, bending it side to side. He couldn't figure why, but he was as stiff as if he'd been thrown.

He'd flat wasted the day. He'd mucked out the stable, tested cinches, cleared out a nest of rats from the feed loft, but mostly he'd spied on the cookshack, making sure Muley acted proper toward Christa.

In late afternoon, when the smell of dinner beckoned, he found Patty asleep under the dinner table. Then he saw Christa. Yellow corkscrews of hair dangled against her high black collar. Red-faced, with arms trembling, she'd drained steaming liquid from a washtub-sized cast-iron pot. He didn't rail that it was too much for her, but he wanted to. He'd eaten the grub she and Muley stewed up, and he didn't rant that she'd be better off in Sacramento, because until the stage ran again, they were stuck with each other.

But it was dusk now. He stood on the dirt apron in front of his own porch, watching gold light seep around the edges of calico he'd tacked up as a curtain for his only glass window. What did women do, after their daily chores ended? Was Christa sewing on a sampler? Cooking up more of that strawberry shrub? No, sir. Practicing her quick-draw, more like. She wanted to stay forever.

He tried to listen to the chorus of crickets, to the bass croaks bobbing up from the creek. Damn. Three years ago, when Christa had sworn she wanted to stay, he'd figured she was delirious. Now she'd dug her heels in, set on making this tough life hers.

He heard a faint sound, like the fall of a card. Christa was awake, then, but he hadn't heard a peep from the girl. Lord knew she was the talkingest child. *Patty*. He wondered if it was a family name.

Over the creek's rushing, he heard chair legs slide on the plank floor inside. It had to be Christa. There wasn't another human on the ranch grounds.

He'd told Muley to get back to the cow camp. For his extra day's wage, he could quit watching a lady do his work and get out to the chuck wagon. He'd cook Friday dinner and tomorrow's breakfast, and tell the riders they were on their own until sundown Saturday. Then they could draw lots for nighthawking, and all but an unlucky two could ride in for Christa's first meal. He hadn't meant for it to sound like a celebration.

He hoped Pete drew the short straw and stayed in camp. He liked the young Texan, but the kid was prickly around Bloody Jim Black. Jim was, no contest, the testiest human Trick had ever met, but he was loyal and tough.

A pale moth bumped the window glass. Trick took the two stairs quickly and rapped on the door.

If she'd taken a moment before opening the door, he wouldn't have caught the glimpse of her chemise. Some kind of scalloped openwork, girlish and white, showed before she tucked her book under her arm and fumbled to close the top buttons. He pretended not to notice, glancing back over his shoulder as if he'd forgotten something, but it was hard not to smile. In her haste, Christa had missed a hole, leaving one button sticking up, an inch above the rest of her collar.

"Oh, Mr. Garradine, do come in." She swung the door wide and he saw a clutter of papers on his table. Of course she could read and write. Hadn't she said she was the daughter of a teacher?

"I was just making lists of what you have on hand in the pantry, in the cookhouse, and a list of supplies we'll need from town. Oh, please do come in. I feel awful for evicting you from your own house."

"Can't have you and the little one sleeping in the bunkhouse with a bunch of smelly ranch hands."

"Still, I'm sure—"

"No, ma'am. This arrangement's for the best."

Her chin came up, and he braced for another battle.

"If you don't mind, since there are so many flying insects, I'll step outside and keep the house free of them."

In the instant before he stepped out of her path, he noticed her lips came level with his chest. And the top of her dress fit tight and curvy. If he had clasped her to him, would his hands have met stiff whalebone or cloth molded to warm flesh?

He stepped back far as he could without tumbling down the front steps. When had it turned dark? Why was he thinking such thoughts of a woman he'd *worried* over, like a dog with one pup, for three years? And how had he come to be standing here with her in the yearning summer night?

"No need to trouble yourself." But Christa already stood outside, swinging the book before her with both hands, looking anything but troubled.

She turned her face up to the stars, like most folks sought the sun. She looked so filled up with longing, he had to speak.

"I thought I'd tell you how I planned things with Muley."

So he did, watching her excitement and anxiety, listening to her scheme for tomorrow's dinner, from the rules she expected to have followed to her girl's blue dimity dress.

"It's all right, isn't it, that I discourage the men from cursing?" She shook her head, and the tassel end of her braid danced on the rise of her bodice. "And . . . and other impolite behavior? They are your men, after all."

To be the ribbon on the end of that braid, he'd trade all rights to being a man! Except, of course, bein' there would do him no good if he weren't a man. Lord, Christa had him spinning like a blind dog in a meat market.

Trick sucked in a breath and fisted one hand hard as it would curl.

"Don't mind your rules a bit. At the cookshack, Muley's king. I own the spread, but the law for every cow outfit I've heard of is 'pamper the cook.' No killin', skinnin', or washin' up. We give you all the time you need to make the best grub you can."

"And you have nine men?" Her fingertips tapped against the cover of the red book, matching like men ranged down each side of a table.

"Yes, ma'am, but you won't have more than six at the table. Probably less. Two men are usually out brush poppin', gathering cattle from ravines and the like. Two stay with the herd. Keep them close together and they start thinking they're one family."

He was stalling, putting off the moment he'd walk back into the dark, alone. But Christa looked spellbound. He couldn't resist her encouragement.

"That helps on the trail, and keeps things safer, once all the range bulls quit staking out their own little territories."

"And then you'll drive them all to Reno." Christa bit off that line of questioning as if scalded.

"First, we'll brand and cut the calves, wean them, and keep 'em penned till their mamas are gone along the trail."

He saw her lower lip come out, probably mourning the mother cows, trudging toward slaughter as their babes bawled, behind. It didn't do to dwell on it.

"So that's how they do it—" She skimmed her thumbnail over the side of the pages, raising a sound like shuffled cards. "—get all that meat on city tables."

"That's how I do it." He shrugged. "In Texas or Mexico, I expect it's different. But I plan on keeping them in close, near water and what grass there is, through summer, then driving as the nights cool off, but before it starts to freeze."

She tucked the book under her arm again, as if she didn't know what to do with it, then chafed the cloth over her upper arms, imagining September's chill breath already.

"Will you tell me the men's names again?"

Trick drew a breath and held it till it hurt. It could be that Christa was stalling, too. He sure couldn't blame her for being lonely in this long desert night.

"Pete—he's a towheaded kid from Texas—and Preach,

he's my *segundo*, like a foreman, sort of. Then there's Slim Jim, Bloody Jim, Silas, Ramon, Dan, of course, Bill Williams, and me."

Christa turned away from him, toward the hills and the traveling barks of coyotes on the hunt.

"Aren't they splendid?" She took a deep breath, just as he had, but damned if she didn't act like she could take in their wildness with one chestful of sage-scented air.

"Some folks think they're frightening, calling out in the dark."

With a huff, she faced him.

"They're not frightening! That sound—" Christa tapped her breastbone, "it pulls something up out of me, something absolutely lonely, but wonderful." She laughed and swished her skirts self-consciously. "I don't know how to say it."

"I know." He couldn't say it either. None of it.

Trick moved down one porch step, bringing himself almost eye level with her. Before he could go, she placed her hand on his sleeve.

"Thank you, Patrick. Thank you for letting us stay."

He wanted to warn her, wanted to tell her he only took this risk because she'd be in greater danger crossing the territory with the Paiutes on the prod. But he was afraid she'd move her hand, afraid he'd miss another breeze with her lavender scent light on it. So he stayed put, until he thought he might have to kiss her.

Trick slapped his hat against his jeans, replaced it and tugged it low.

"Morning comes mighty early around here . . . Christa."

There, he'd said it. Not *Mrs. Worth*. Not *ma'am*. He'd let himself have that much of her, just her name. It rushed through him like a jolt of tequila.

"Best get yourself to bed." He willed his arm to drop from under her hand and forced his boots to walk away.

Six

Christa judged that the black man's sleek, bare head would have topped Patrick's by six inches. From Muley's description, she recognized Bloody Jim Black. He loomed over a scrappy blond boy, trying to teach him some manners.

"Pull your neck back in, boy. I don't feel like tromping your britches before supper."

Muley had described a former slave who blamed his foul temper on being scalped and left for dead. Muley hazarded a guess that Bloody Jim was a mean son of a gun long before he'd crossed the Mason-Dixon line with his copper brown mule, Emperor.

Just now, facing the drawling blond boy, Jim did an admirable job of controlling himself.

"I'm not eating at the same table as a darkie. Not with a lady present."

The young Texan had galloped in five minutes ahead of the others, sliding his bay to a dusty, hind-heels stop at the stable. No more than sixteen and full of himself, he couldn't see his harassment of Bloody Jim looked as mismatched as a sparrow cheeping in the face of a tomcat.

Why wasn't Patrick here to control his men? Two older brothers had taught her the signs of a brewing brawl. With one shove or epithet, this confrontation would flare into a fight.

Right outside her cookhouse. Right before her daughter's

eyes. Right before her first Thunder Meadows supper. She would not allow it!

"Patty, you may ring," she said.

Dressed in high-button shoes and her favorite blue dimity pinafore, hair in two neat plaits, Patty wobbled atop a chair. With a spoon, she set the triangle ringing. But not very well.

The gentle "ding" carried only a few yards, but it was enough to distract the combatants. The cowboys moved toward the cookhouse porch. They paused in front of the first step, looking up at Christa as if she were a queen bestowing largesse on commoners. Pete stood apart, kicking the dirt between glances over his shoulder.

They don't see many women, she reminded herself. Mothers, sisters, shopkeepers in Coyote, perhaps a hurdy girl in Reno.

"Gentlemen, as soon as you've washed up," Christa gestured toward the pump, "I'd be delighted to have you step inside for supper."

Christa pushed Patty inside ahead of her. Relieved to escape their stares, Christa watched steam rise from the thick cuts of beef and the earthen tureen filled with cut corn. Belatedly, she realized two loaves of sourdough bread wouldn't be nearly enough, nor would the two dried-apple pies.

Water splattered from the pump. Hallelujah! They'd heeded her request. Then, boots clattered up the porch. Pete had remained outside, but the other four stood shifting in the doorway.

"Gentlemen, if you'd kindly remove your hats . . ."

If she'd asked them to remove their trousers, they couldn't have appeared more surprised, but they complied and shuffled toward the benches set on each side of a long plank table.

Christa cleared her throat, licked her lips, and wondered how to begin saying grace. Why had Patrick stayed away? With a silly ache in her throat, she decided to press on.

"Pete, don't you feel like eating some grub?" Standing next to the pump, Trick used both hands to slick back his hair, then smoothed the bars of his mustache and straightened his vest.

"I ain't eating at the same table with Jim." Pete squatted to rumple Josh's ears rather than meet Trick's eyes.

"You eat with him." Trick nodded to the range.

"That's different." Pete stood. "There's a lady in there." *You shouldn't allow it,* his eyes told Trick.

Christa had made things damned complicated. He'd come late for supper because his stomach lurched at the idea of watching his men see her for the first time. He'd managed to miss them gazing at her with mooncalf eyes. Now this.

"Suit yourself." He clomped up the stairs and opened the door into heat and silence cooled by her voice.

". . . and for the cloak of safety You provide for each of us in this untamed land, allowing us to make our way to this, Thy bounteous table. Amen."

At the chorus of "amens" that joined hers, Christa's eyes lifted and found him.

"That was mighty pretty, ma'am," said Preach. As *segundo*, only he had the gall to throw Trick a scowl.

"Yes, ma'am." Silas waggled his worm-thin eyebrows. "Preach could take a few lessons."

Blushing, Christa shook her head in denial. Trick saw his men react. They were quiet men and shy of strangers, but Christa's gentle, prim way enchanted them. They'd be lovesick and useless if he didn't stop them. He moved to the head of the table.

"I apologize for being late, Mrs. Worth. It won't happen again." He used his voice like a lash, snapping their daydreams away.

"Now, I didn't have much warning about Muley going, so Mrs. Worth, here, agreed to help out. Mrs. Worth is not a hired girl." The water pitcher shivered as he leaned forward to plant both palms on the table. "She's a lady. She's Dan's sister—"

"Hellfire, who would've guessed," muttered Silas, before

catching sight of Christa's renewed blush. "Sorry." He regarded his folded hands with abashed intensity.

"—and a lady. We'll treat her as such by not eating till she and her little girl sit down, and by using the wreck pan in the back. A man who chooses not to wash his own dish can eat his biscuits and gravy out of his hat, come morning."

All four nodded vigorously. He wished Pete would get his tail in here. Trick hated this speechifying. These men better pass the word to Slim Jim and Ramon, too, because he'd rather be snake-bit then talk each time he came in to eat.

"Anything you want to add, Mrs. Worth?"

"Just—this is fine," she said. "And please, don't wait for me. Eat while your food is hot."

Little chance of it cooling in this overheated cookhouse, but Trick didn't say so. He watched her waver under the weight of male eyes, as the men waited for her to sit. She slipped into a chair at the end opposite him. When Trick picked up his fork, there was a general groan of eagerness.

She'd gone to some trouble to cut this corn off the cob, but he hardly tasted it for looking at her. Gone was the somber riding dress of black. Christa wore a gray calico gown with some sort of dark figuring on it. Before she sat, he'd noticed the sides of the skirt had extra material swooped back like dove's wings. How could a little gray drape focus his eyes on her waist and tidy backside?

Trick stared at his fork tines. Knowing she didn't intend the dress to do such things aroused him all the more.

He cut a bite of beef and found it still pink. He guessed Muley had neglected to tell her they liked meat brown as boot soles. Not that it wasn't tough as leather. Probably she'd cut it with the grain, instead of against it.

So much for her kitchen skills. She'd been out here since daybreak, with time enough to roast seven whole steers rather than these seven steaks. He swallowed the bite, certain she was watching.

Trick let his glance skitter down the center of the table to the end. Next to her own untouched plate, Christa's hands curled into tight fists.

"It's a real fine meal, Mrs. Worth."

Her shoulders drooped with relief. Truth was, he'd never met a human being so dependent on talk.

Her bread didn't have the crunchy crust and tender center of Muley's, but the men couldn't get enough of it. Bill Williams, who always seemed on the verge of saying something important, held his bread and nodded. The others rewarded Christa's anxious silence with lip-smacking and winks exchanged among themselves. Pete stayed outside.

He was a stubborn cub, to stay out in spite of the aroma of cinnamon and apples from Christa's pies.

"I declare," moaned Bloody Jim Black, chewing slowly.

"Yes, ma'am, this is some pie," agreed Preach.

Trick tried to swallow his own grin. She'd been right about pastry. If all her pies and cakes matched this, he'd eat his beef bloody raw just to pass the time till dessert.

As she bent to cut Patty's pie into bites, Trick noticed Christa's buttons. Little round things, no bigger than raisins, they started high on her throat, marched over the swell of her breasts and down to a point below her waist. It was two parts then, not one gown. He remembered the little licks of lace he'd seen on her chemise last night. Then he bit into a piece of crust ruined by a lump of salt.

Good God. The woman had come to him with the idea of repaying a good turn. She had delivered herself and her child into his protection. Her husband hadn't been in the ground a year, judging by her mourning black, and Trick Garradine was wondering if it would take two hands to pop the buttons on her widow's weeds!

"Mr. Trick." Patty's high voice fished for his attention. She displayed fingers shiny with cinnamon syrup. "Candy," she reminded, as if the peppermint had become a code between them.

"Your mama's pie is even better," he said. Then he closed

his trap for the rest of the evening. He hadn't meant for the words to sound so danged cozy.

Josh never barked at a strange rider. He never gave chase when a coyote sniffed at the henhouse, but tonight the useless collie whimpered, stared at the moon, panted, and followed his tail in slow circles. It was nearly midnight when Josh pricked up his ears and stared at the cabin.

"Josh, settle." Things had come to a sorry pass when Trick depended on this dog for company.

Pete Jessup had ridden out before the rest swaggered from the cookshack. They'd patted their bellies, claiming to be half-foundered, but they'd hit their saddles quick instead of lingering for a smoke. Christa's meal had barely blunted their hunger, and Trick figured they'd be poking around the chuck wagon before they crawled into their bedrolls.

Trick squatted outside the stuffy bunkhouse, whittling sticks and watching nighthawks dive for bugs. Three days with Christabel had turned his life on its head.

For her own safety, he couldn't send Christa away. For his own sanity, he couldn't stay with her.

A pale shaving curled up from his knife blade. It quivered, awaiting a final stroke to cut it free.

Should he stay on the range, ride herd every night, and assign one of his hands to keep watch here? That spunky cub, Pete, was a likely choice. Or Ramon. The handsome Californio kept a guitar leaning against the bunkhouse wall. He could sing Patty to sleep while Christa learned the fandango. Not hardly.

The most sensible thing would be to send a rider after Dan. They'd switch places. Trick could search for steers and let Dan nursemaid his sister until fall. Then Christa and Patty could ride with the herd as far as Reno. They'd think it was a great adventure and be safe in the meantime. It was a fine solution, except that he didn't want to leave her.

Trick's blade slid to the bottom of the stick and the shaving fell. His stomach rumbled. Then Josh jumped up and made a deep warble in his throat before bolting toward the house.

Like a roll of silver satin, the creek glowed with moonlight, rippling over the biggest boulders, chuckling as it passed. Christa held each end of her flannel towel. Precise as a tightrope walker, she picked her barefoot way along the water's edge.

She hadn't had a proper bath all week. Last night, exhausted from Muley's cooking lessons, she'd fallen asleep, anyway. Today's confinement with a woodstove banished any pretense of daintiness. She smelled like a drover.

The creek ran high, snatching the hem of her white gown as she hesitated on a creekside rock. Though all the hands had departed, removing her gown would be shameless. And though she hadn't seen him since dinner, Patrick might still be about.

She couldn't think why, but he'd probably be troubled by this. Remembering her resolution not to provoke him, Christa moved downstream. Here, thick stands of willow and cottonwood trees screened her from view. She shook her head, wondering what Nathan would think. He surely wouldn't have allowed her to bathe in a creek.

Christa stepped in up to her knees. The sudden clamp of cold water numbed her feet and she slipped. Before she regained her balance, a bark and splash signaled the arrival of Josh, and she fell to her hands and knees.

"Go on." She pushed his muzzle from her face.

She'd regained her feet when she saw a shadow on the bank. It could only be Patrick.

"Don't shoot," she said.

"That's not a bit funny."

Creating a great rush of water as she stood, Christa wrung out her hem and slogged toward the edge.

"You have no idea, Mr. Garradine."

How bright the flash from his gun would be, here in the darkness. Never mind.

"I-it is s-safe for me to come here, isn't it?" She tried to talk past chattering teeth. "R-rattlesnakes don't swim, do they?"

Patrick bent across the space between them and she braced. He didn't grab her shoulders to shake her, though. He took the flannel towel still hanging around her neck and wrapped it over her shoulders. Damp nearly to her waist, she really needed the flannel lower, but mentioning it would be indelicate.

"No, they don't swim." He pulled his hands back.

"Don't l-laugh at me, Mr. Garradine——"

"I'm not laughing," he said. "Besides——"

"I hear it in your voice, this sort of secret amusement." She reminded herself to remain ladylike and polite. "But I interrupted you."

"No, ma'am, you didn't."

"I *did*. You said you weren't laughing, then 'besides.' 'Besides' what?"

Josh's loud lapping and an owl's query filled the moment.

" 'Besides, what happened to calling me Patrick,' that's all I was going to say."

He spoke quickly, running the words together. It took a minute to sort them out. Then Christa understood.

Patrick stood like a man who'd taken a smack in the jaw and absorbed it, refusing to buckle. Yet he'd only asked that she call him by his given name.

"I think that would be pleasant. For us to——"

"It's a fool idea."

She tried to banish his embarrassment. "You're right. The men might not understand, but surely, when we're alone . . . ? We are partners, after a fashion, aren't we?"

"Partners." He pronounced the word with solid emphasis. Evidently, he could allow a partnership. "Fine."

She almost extended her hand, then remembered how she'd felt, waiting for Alvin Hacklebord to shake it. "Well, Patrick, I'll take myself off, now, so I'll wake early enough to make breakfast."

"There's a timepiece on the mantel, but I'm up at four, rain or shine, summer and winter. I'll wake you, if you like. Hands'll be in about five."

"Thank you."

Christa pulled the towel closer, lifted her soggy hem, and walked toward the cabin. She heard Josh shuffling along behind and quickened her steps before her slugabed mind had her screaming that *four o'clock* did not qualify as morning.

"Mush was good, ma'am." Bloody Jim Black nodded to her as he left the cookhouse. "My mama used to fry it up in a pan where she'd been cookin' ham."

"I'll remember that."

Christa whisked the last crumbs from the tablecloth. Outside, the hens cackled as Jim departed. Dawn had finally shed enough light for the cock to crow and for Patrick to vanish into the stable. In a moment, she'd consult him about Silas's criticism.

Hoofbeats told her she'd almost missed him. Skirts held aside with both hands, Christa bolted down the steps.

"Mr. Garradine!"

Imp shied at her swooping arrival, rolling his eyes as if he took her for a giant chicken. Christa released her skirts and approached horse and rider, slowly. Patrick might believe her a tenderfoot, but he couldn't fault her understanding of the odd imaginations of horses.

He didn't. Instead, he drew rein and leaned one forearm against his saddle horn.

"Yes, Mrs. Worth."

Hidden in the shadow of his hat brim, his face was unreadable, but the angle of his head made her wonder if he was laughing at her again.

"Silas has confided, in the nicest way possible, that my meals aren't large enough."

"He's the confiding sort. Used to be the undertaker. Still keeps his store in town for fixin' folks that pass on."

Christa folded her arms. Patrick's rambling was clearly obfuscation.

"Is he right? Must I cook larger meals?"

Patrick scanned the ranch yard. He frowned at the hens. He brushed dust from Imp's mane. He glanced at the cabin, as if wishing Patty would create a distraction.

"Patrick," she said, almost whispering. "I count on you for advice. It's a small matter to cook more food."

"Well, I've never known a hand who refused more victuals."

"Thank you."

"That's not to say I want them riding out of here lookin' like poisoned pups," he said, backing Imp.

"I understand."

"If you have things you want from town, I'll be going later."

"Oh, I have a list. I'll go with you."

"Not necessary."

Was he being kind or discouraging her because he wanted to avoid an awkward scene like the one she'd triggered before?

"I'd *like* to go."

"It'll take some time to make the evenin' meal, and I'm sure you've got laundry and all."

There was no way to misunderstand that. Patrick wanted to go alone.

"I'll have a list ready."

His fingers grazed his hat brim and his heels touched Imp into a trot. Christa watched him go. The morning sky had gone to light blue and dust rose from Imp's hooves, like wisps of smoke.

What if Francesca's letter were still being passed around? What if he read it for himself? She hoped Coyote's sheriff didn't know the details of Nathan's death.

In a small town like Coyote, the absolute, word-for-word truth might get her hanged.

Seven

When perfume overpowering as whiskey assailed his nose, Patrick knew he'd walked into a trap. Polly LaCrosse rustled toward him, trailing enough bustle to fill a boxcar.

"Patrick, I have been desperately concerned!"

Well, hell. His trials weren't over, after all. After the aggravation of fooling Christa into reciting her list aloud so he'd know if Hacklebord filled it, after leaving the summer glare for the dim, coffee-scented cave of the mercantile, he'd thought he could relax. Blundering into Polly LaCrosse hadn't crossed his mind, but then Fate had a way of surprising a man.

The word triggered an ironic echo of his father's voice.

"Fate? A real man takes Fate by the throat and makes it see things his way." Of course, Dad only faced sudden death and hostile Indians in ten territories. He'd never met Polly.

"Patrick Garradine, let me look at you." Polly pushed him to perform a mortifying turn. "Why, I think all the vital parts are there. My, yes."

"Polly." He held up a hand, signaling that her gift for flirtation was wasted on him.

"Can you blame me, Patrick?"

Polly tilted up her face, and he thought she might lose her bonnet. Oblivious to the armload of irises that had taken root up there, her lower lip quivered and her eyelashes fluttered.

"You are too kind for your own good." She perched one hand on the hip of her purple dress. "You know that, don't you? Taking in that woman, when she's the next thing to a- a- an assassin."

"Whatever that is, Polly, I think you've let your fancies stampede over your good sense."

"I am awfully concerned."

Lace ran in a vee down Polly's bodice. Being a seamstress, she arranged her trimmings as she liked. It was pretty clear which direction she wanted his eyes to follow.

"Mrs. Worth is just a widow with a little girl." Trick examined his gloves rather than Polly's pouter-pigeon chest. "She's nothing like what you're saying."

Hannah Hacklebord bustled in from a storeroom and saw them.

"Why, Mr. Garradine, back already. And Miss LaCrosse." Hannah wagged her head as if sharing a secret.

"Please, help Patrick first. I'm only here for fabric. More Mother Hubbards for the Pilgrim sisters."

Hannah took Christa's list and assembled foodstuffs, even managed to dodge into the back room for a hurried conversation, while she kept up a confab with Polly.

"I know how you hate making those plain dresses," Hannah said, then turned her attention back to Trick. "Mr. Garradine, you just have yourself a rest with a cup of coffee. I asked Alvin to pack your seedlings."

"Of course, the pattern is totally unstylish." Polly examined a bolt of gingham.

"A waste of your talents." Hannah tapped the list on the counter. "Dill, basil, chives, and I suppose you've got your own wild onion?"

He hoped she didn't expect an answer. Commotion at the back door distracted her. It would be Alvin with the plants. If they'd been sitting in the sun like they'd been the other day, he would've just packed up a sack of them. No explaining.

"I've never known you to plant, Garradine." Alvin Hacklebord carried the vegetation-filled box at arm's length, so the shoots didn't tickle his nose.

Hacklebord was right. The only green stuff Trick worried about was grass. He liked his food brown and white, but cattle thrived on stuff like this. If it didn't rain soon, they'd devour every blade on the range.

"Kitchen herbs." Hannah fingered the feathery top of one. "Mrs. Worth has it in her head to bring real cookin' to us savages."

"Mrs. Worth! Imagine letting a murderess prepare your food." Polly shuddered. "You are brave, Patrick."

"I don't know as I'd advise that, Garradine." Alvin shifted a plug of tobacco against his cheek. "Her own sister-in-law—"

"I don't recall askin' for advice."

Wind caught the back door and slammed it twice against the jamb.

"After all, Patrick, you would caution any of us about allowing a stranger into our houses." Polly held a bolt of calico before her, like a shield.

The hell he would. His men had been strangers before he'd flung wide the bunkhouse door and trusted them. Polly jumped to odd conclusions.

"She's no stranger." Damn his mouth. He ought to keep it in the barn where his confidants never repeated a thing. "We met some time back. Before the baby."

That didn't seem to help. Alvin's pencil paused above a scrap of butcher paper. Hannah balanced a big can of peaches. Polly held a length of calico she'd measured from her nose to her fingertips. All three froze in place, conserving energy for gossip that'd start soon as the door closed behind him.

It'd probably make things worse to say her dead husband was a sorry son of a bitch. Instead, he tried a joke.

"I don't have family silver for her to steal and I'm just outside in the bunkhouse. You all will be the first to know if we hang her for horse thievin'."

The wind gave the door another bang.

"I'll carry this out to your rig." Alvin shifted the plants.

Polly set the bolts of gingham and calico on Hannah's counter, then turned back to him.

"Perhaps we have misjudged her, Patrick. You may be right. It might be just the thing for Hannah and me to come calling."

Polly's smug nod worried him. Trick thought of Christa's heat-flushed face as she stoked and stirred the stove. He pictured Patty's dirt-smeared cheeks and the collie fur stuck to her fingers. It took Christa all damn day to cook dinner. Would she welcome narrow-eyed guests and tea parties?

"That's just what we'll do. Patrick Garradine, tell your Mrs. Worth to ready herself for company."

Grease spatters had blistered Christa's hands, forearms, and a spot on her cheek. She'd used a blizzard of flour not only to dredge the chicken but to extinguish flaming fat. Her gray calico was soiled and she had no idea when there'd be time for laundry. Cooking at home, with servants at her heels, had been amusing. This—Christa waved away a fly—was drudgery.

Crossing between the cookhouse and the cabin, she tormented herself with another look toward the barn. Just as galling as insects and toil was the sight of the animal hides flanking Patrick's barn door. She thought she'd escaped such symbols of men's cruelty.

Weathered and worn, the hide hanging to the left had come from a black bear. Bloody Jim said it had hung there since the days Good Thunder Meadows was a fort.

The other skin, a cougar's, lay smooth as tawny velvet, face and tail shading to coffee brown, then black.

Christa looked away from the skins and pumped a bucketful of water.

"Mama," Patty whined.

"Go ahead, baby. I'll be in soon. Play with your sock dolly."

Christa hauled the bucket to the freshly weeded ground near the front steps. She poured, catching her breath as the water soothed her burned hands. While the water soaked into the earth, she recalled Jim's description of the cougar's death.

The cat had been about four years old when Patrick saw her leap on a heifer, snap its neck, and fall to ravenous feeding.

Patrick shot once. Only when the cougar lay dead had he learned why the cat had ventured from her high-country domain. Her maimed paw would have made deer kills difficult and her teats said she was nursing.

"Trick cussed a blue streak over that." Bloody Jim had laughed, oblivious to Christa's despair. "Didn't want to starve no kittens, and wouldn't hush over finding that den."

Patrick didn't enjoy death. Nathan had gloried in the kill. Those facts should have relieved her. Too, Bloody Jim claimed nailing the hide up followed a bizarre Western tradition. Hides were displayed as a warning to others of their kind.

Christa climbed the cabin steps with the bucket bumping against her leg. At least Patrick kept no such trophies inside the cabin. She set down the bucket, bent her head back and stared at the rafters. She heard Patty puttering around in the pantry.

"I can't find my dolly."

"Try to remember where you left her, Patty cakes."

Christa rested her hands on her hips and winced from the pain. Francesca had smeared butter on cooking burns, but Christa couldn't tolerate more grease.

She poured the water into the basin in her room and sluiced her hands through it. She drenched her face and opened her collar to let the water drip down her neck. Heaven.

Two things she'd never thought to appreciate about Good Thunder Meadows were the lack of mirrors and the dearth of friends who might have noticed the flaws she ignored.

She closed her eyes, pressed a wet cloth to her face, and

allowed a quick memory of Patrick at the creek by moonlight.

"Mommy-y-y-y," Patty whined and swung her dolly by
one arm. "Go park tonight?"

"I'm sorry, Patty babe. There's no park here, but we'll go
for a walk after dinner. Would you like to wade in the
creek?"

"No. Tell Mama 'No, no.'" Patty seized her doll's middle
and shook it so hard, Christa feared its head would come
unstitched. Patty knew she wasn't allowed near the swiftly
flowing water.

Christa swooped Patty into her arms and nuzzled her.
Faster than her mother, Patty was learning the new rules this
place demanded. Christa wondered why she'd assumed a
widow, freed from the dictates of parents and husband, was
emancipated.

"You may go to the creek if I hold your hand," she told
Patty. "Shall we bring Josh? I think he likes the water."

"Josh inna house," Patty whispered.

The tickle of her daughter's breath, her secret sharing and
trust made Christa smile.

"We'll see." She placed Patty back on her feet. "I'll ask
Mr. Garradine, after dinner. Now, get the hairbrush and I'll
tidy you for dinner."

"No, Mama, too hot."

"Go on," Christa said, but she agreed.

Patty balked at entering the airless cookhouse. Christa
had promised herself that next summer she'd have Patrick
cut a second window, for improved ventilation.

A metallic sound caught her attention. At first she thought
the men had ridden in early, then Christa recognized the
rumble and clank of the wagon. Patrick was back.

She felt a knot in her chest, a heady mix of elation and
nerves. It reminded her that if she *were* here next summer,
it would mean he'd asked her to stay.

Not that she would. She'd help him through his roundup,
but this ranch and this man were far from perfect. Take the

high-handed way Patrick had snatched her mercantile list and refused to take her along, though she'd all but fallen to her knees, begging. He had given in to her request for a ride, though, and the prospect of a twilight canter had sustained her through the day's heat.

Boots scuffed on the porch outside. Christa twisted her hair into a high knot, stabbed in four hairpins, and twitched her black skirts into place.

His imperious knock reminded her Patrick Garradine was accustomed to getting his own way. So far, she'd been able to accommodate him. She opened the door and managed to smile.

"I brought the little one a present," he said.

Peppermint sticks? Then she saw the other child.

"A playmate. She'll be staying over, if it's all right."

Vexation made it difficult to stifle a retort. Christa's nostrils stung with the smell of singed pin feathers and her hands burned from spitting grease. She'd tolerated the rude intrusion of a sniffing dog and the measuring eyes of half a dozen hungry men. She'd swatted a hundred biting insects and fought the impulse to do the same to her own heat-cranky child.

Christa might have spouted every outraged word if Patrick had presented her with any other youngster.

"This is Rosebud Malloy."

The blacksmith's child was a solemn little owl. Round hazel eyes and freckles were framed by the tightest braids hanging from the straightest part Christa had ever seen. Rosebud gazed up, frowning as if she had trouble seeing.

"Hello, Mrs. Worth. I've come to play with Patricia." Rosebud extended her hand in the most endearing gesture Christa had ever accepted. "I won't be causing you any trouble. And I eat like a bird, me da says."

"I'm sure you'll be no bother at all, and you must eat as much as you like." Christa held the small hand in both of hers and rued her uncharitable thoughts. "How old are you, Rosebud?"

Even the sound of approaching hooves, and Patty's tug at her elbow, didn't distract Christa from this tot with the air of a little old woman.

"Six, but I can read. Da taught me how."

"Ah." That explained her sweet maturity. Patrick couldn't have brought a more welcome guest, but when Christa turned to thank him, he shambled off the porch.

"You know Patty is only three." Christa moved her arm to draw Patty around in front, but her daughter refused to budge.

"I met her at the smithy." Rosebud leaned to one side and bent her fingers in a wave. "I like little children."

All the men had gathered at the stable and the two girls followed at her heels when Christa had the idea. Even though he was busy washing up at the pump in the middle of the yard, Christa rushed to Patrick.

"Mr. Garradine."

His face dripped on his chambray shirt, his hair glistened black and wet, and when he tossed it back, water flew onto her lips. Christa stood speechless at the intimacy.

"Mrs. Worth? Did you need some help, ma'am?"

She heard the crunch of boots on the dirt behind her. She heard Pete's drawl and knew Jim must have stayed with the cattle. She felt the little girls move against her from each side before she could answer.

"No, thank you." Truly, the heat and bugs had scrambled her brain, because even as she answered Pete, she watched Patrick watch her dab the droplet from her mouth.

The other men shouldered for room at the pump and Christa came alert as Patrick stepped her way.

"Mr. Garradine, since it is so warm, and we have a guest," Christa bobbed a half curtsy to Rosebud, "might we bring the table out of doors?"

Resistance darkened the line between his brows, but Patty spoke before he could.

"Picnic, Mr. Trick." She peeked out from behind Christa's skirts.

"What's that?" Patrick raised his voice over the splashing and horseplay behind him.

He jammed both hands on his hips, and Christa covered her laughter with a cough. Her daughter refused to be intimidated by Patrick's threatening stance.

"Picnic," Patty repeated.

"Aw, let's do it, Trick. I smell fried chicken and biscuits and that's reason enough for a picnic if ever there was one." Preach waggled gray eyebrows at the little girls and they giggled.

"Yeah, come on," Silas said.

"Fine, then." Patrick slapped his hat back onto his head. "You two move it outside, but mind the hens and don't blame me if it won't fit through the door. It was built inside that very room."

It took four of them to juggle the table outdoors, and Christa noticed Bloody Jim Black *was* present.

"It's nothing to starve over," Pete shrugged when Trick mentioned the switch.

In private tribute to Pete's change of heart, Christa asked if he would mind offering a blessing. His reply was far from the stammering excuse she expected.

"My pa's a Baptist preacher, ma'am. I never miss a chance to witness."

Though the men shifted on the bench, mumbling of hunger and deprivation, they survived Pete's long-winded benediction.

Christa had peeled potatoes until she lost count, and baked pan after pan of biscuits. Though Silas tapped one biscuit on the table, in sly reproach, he had no trouble choking down five or six. And when she presented a platter of molasses cookies, the men's howls rivaled coyotes baying at the moon.

As she rose from the table, Christa's forearms shook with the day's effort. She could hide weariness from Patrick, but

Cloud might feel her weakness. She hoped not. She'd earned her ride and she meant to have it.

Oh, no. What would she do with the girls? Earlier, she'd assumed Patty would ride along on Betsy. But what of Rosebud? Christa considered the cottonwoods, silver-green and trembling in the evening breeze. Such beauty didn't banish her regret. She supposed the long dusk could serve as time to plant her herb garden, but Heaven help the man who asked why she wore such a long face!

"Mama, can I . . . ?" Patty's words meandered into a blend of question and demand that Christa couldn't decipher.

"Slow down, baby. Tell me again."

Rosebud interpreted, "May we take our dinner, what's left of it," she said, though the girls' plates looked virtually untouched, "down to the creek, for a real picnic?"

"I want to plant some seedlings before dark, Rosebud. And Patty's not allowed to go down to the creek alone."

"She wouldn't be alone, though. Not if I looked after her."

Rosebud's earnest face was persuasive. If Rosebud drew her charm from her father, David Malloy was a man for young widows to avoid.

Christa gathered the girls' plates and ordered Josh to stay, certain the dog would finish their suppers before they could. When they got to the creek, Christa staked out their boundaries.

"If I catch either of you putting one tippy-toe over this line of rocks," she indicated the rectangle of rocks she'd laid around them, "you will be punished. Do you understand?"

Rosebud nodded soberly, but Patty bounced in place.

"Patty? If you don't mind me, if you leave the rocks, I will not ask Mr. Garradine about Josh."

"Yes, Mama. Stay. In. Rocks." Patty shouted to emphasize each word.

Christa took long steps back to the dirt bed she'd

prepared for her seedlings. Worry might allow her to plant just the dill before hurrying back to check on the girls.

Squatting by the porch was undignified, but daylight was too valuable to waste. Christa had just loosened the roots of one plant when a shadow fell over her.

"Let me help with that, ma'am?"

Bloody Jim Black crouched next to her. Before Christa could protest, he scooped perfectly spaced basins in the soil.

"Thank you. I've only planted window boxes before."

"They won't grow, mind you, but you can try."

"This soil is so strange." Christa transferred a seedling from her fingers to Jim's.

Pete Jessup interrupted. "Alkali, ma'am," he said. "Ancient lake, they tell me. And he's no doubt right. They won't grow. Nothing good will come from messin' with Nature, no matter how hard you try."

Christa sighed. Pete must be talking about something other than her garden. His veiled references probably concerned white folks and black. Before she marshaled the energy to issue a lecture she'd been composing for two days, the opportunity vanished.

From under the plank table, Josh delivered a volley of barks that made Christa's fingers open and drop the chive plant. Twisting quick enough to see the collie's lips contract in a snarl, Christa shrank against the porch as he ran by, a growling blur headed for the creek.

"Patty!" Christa screamed once.

Both Bloody Jim and Pete reached for her, but by then Christa was gone.

Eight

Christa found Rosebud and Patty holding hands within their rock boundaries. Josh crossed up and down the bank, stared across the creek, then recommenced prowling and sniffing.

"Mama!"

Patty struggled within Christa's hug, but she didn't loosen the embrace, only grabbed Rosebud, too, as Patrick rode into the clearing. In movements almost too fluid to separate, he marked their safety, lifted one leg forward across his mount's neck, then walked, Winchester angled over his forearm, down the bank after Josh.

Patrick abandoned the whining dog and waded halfway across the creek, surveying up and down, before the other men arrived.

All the while, Patty chattered of fairies and piggitys, of a fried-chicken tea party, and Josh's loud invasion.

"Who we lookin' for, ma'am?" Preach wobbled up in high-heeled boots.

"I'm not quite sure," Christa said. "Rosebud, can you help?"

"We had the party, as Patty said. And I did hear something moving, but, well—I'll be getting spectacles when Coyote's teacher comes. Then I'll be able to see the chalkboard, Da says. I'm rather shortsighted, is all. But I heard something, and Patty called out 'biggity.'"

"Not 'piggity'?" Christa asked. "Like a piglet, perhaps? There are piglets in her fairy-tale book."

"No, Mama. No, no, no!" Patty shook her index finger so vigorously Christa grabbed it. Then she kissed it.

Preach and Silas held guns. Christa felt the veins in her wrists go cold as she pictured them running with pistols drawn and fingers curved above triggers. She felt the uneven footing, saw the darting dog and unpredictable children, and all the food she'd cooked and breathed congealed in her stomach.

"Put them away," she croaked, staring at the guns.

Preach smiled with strained understanding and waved Silas to holster his revolver.

"No doubt you're right about the piglets, Mrs. Worth," Rosebud sighed. "I just thought she said the other."

Preach slogged across the creek. He called out and the Winchester sagged as Patrick loosened his hold and shook his head. In the fading light, Christa couldn't see whether he smiled or frowned. Then Rosebud sniffed back tears.

"I want those spectacles so. I tried to see, truly I did, but I just couldn't."

Patty wiggled a hand free to touch Rosebud's cheek.

"I'm sorry I'm no more help, Mrs. Worth."

"You were wonderful, Rosebud. Here, jump up, like Patty's doing."

"With me legs hooked about your waist? Won't you tip over?"

"I don't think so." Christa braced herself for the little girl's leap.

"Da carries me on his shoulders," Rosebud suggested.

"Then I *would* tip over."

Balancing a child on each hip, Christa turned back toward the cabin. Dusk had shifted to darkness and Christa had made it halfway, safely if not gracefully, when Patty roused herself.

"Mama, horse coming."

Christa's spirits lifted. It would be Patrick, telling her a deer or wandering cow had caused the commotion.

When she turned, she saw only Patrick's black gelding,

Imp, riderless and dragging his reins. She did not have the balance to snag them, so she stepped ahead slowly, hoping Patrick could catch up.

When he did, he surprised her.

"I hear we're looking for piglets and fairies?" As he spoke, Patrick lifted Rosebud from Christa's hip.

When she turned to thank him, Rosebud dangled from his hands as if he didn't know what to do next.

"Da carries me on his shoulders," Rosebud tried again. This time it worked.

"Like a sack of grain?" Patrick asked. "Or a calf?"

He draped the child's arms over one shoulder, her legs over the other, and caught them together in one of his hands. Rosebud's giggles prevented her from speaking, but they stirred Patty, who grumped "No," then closed her eyes.

Patrick stepped ahead to open the cabin door, then set a match to the lantern wick as she carried Patty to the bedroom. Christa heard a chair scrape the floorboards, too, but when Rosebud wandered into the bedroom alone, Christa realized Patrick had gone.

Readying Patty for bed was like dressing a rag doll, but Rosebud, sleepy as she was, undressed and pulled on her nightclothes alone. When the little girl loosened her braids and climbed into Christa's bed, instead of sharing Patty's pallet, Christa didn't have the heart to evict her. Instead, she lay Patty next to Rosebud and pulled the covers to their chins.

Rosebud's lips puckered to speak, then her eyelashes closed against freckled cheeks.

Christa's hands supported the small of her back as she groaned. No ride. No herbs planted. Nothing to show for this day but a burn on her cheek and—

Her baby. Christa sank slowly into the center of her skirts, then knelt, forehead pressed to the blanket covering Patty's chest. Christa condemned herself as an ungrateful wretch, a terrible mother to think such selfish things. Swallowing a sob, Christa stayed on her knees, sending up prayers of thanksgiving.

Trick yawned and lowered his boots from the porch rail. He'd chosen this guard duty and wouldn't be sleeping tonight—especially with Bloody Jim down on his knees, humming and patting Christa's green things into the dirt—so he might as well quit longing for bed.

His cabin door opened. Josh lifted his head and fanned his tail as Christa slipped outside.

"I didn't think that thump was Josh." Her nose sounded stuffy and she cleared her throat before saying, "Patrick, thank you."

The heel of her hand rested on the chair back, but she raised her fingers to rub his shirt, there over his spine.

Yearning came spurting up in him again. He wanted to twist around and grab her wrist in possession, bury his face in her hand, kiss it, move it to his face, and then—Lord knew what.

So he didn't make the first move, didn't ask for such aggravation. He chalked it up to a natural craving, brought on by her female nearness. It had nothing to do with protecting them. It couldn't. Because Christa wasn't his woman and Patty wasn't his child.

Bloody Jim's wordless baritone made Christa start. She hadn't known Jim was down there. Her fingernails grazed Trick's neck as she jumped back.

"Is that you, Jim?"

"Yes, ma'am, giving these poor things a decent burial."

"Thank you. You didn't have to do it in the dark. I would have gotten to them tomorrow."

"I got the bunkhouse lantern. Besides, I'd be awake anyway. Me 'n' Trick are keepin' our eyes peeled for Josh's bogeyman, and these herbs are a sight more entertaining than the boss."

"Chin music don't count when the shootin' starts."

When Christa sucked in her breath, Trick knew he'd done

it again. The gal was gun-shy. Preach had noticed it, too. Trick lowered the Winchester to the porch, but he'd set her off.

"What was it?" she asked. "Do you know?"

Something odd snaked through Christa's voice. It wasn't fear or bluster. Motherly upset? How in hell would he know? Christa was the first mother he'd ever got acquainted with.

"Josh was barking at something. But something serious? Hard to tell." At his name, the collie rose from the porch, shook, and worked his head under Trick's palm. "Can I trust the word of a dog whose brain pan's narrower than my hand?"

"He's useless, but he ain't gutless," said Jim. "He's scared stiff of that brindle cow that keeps slipping away from the herd, but he goes after her every day."

"Yeah?" Trick gave the dog a pat. "Does he bring her back?"

"No, just follows her, dodging around with his tail tucked between his legs, yapping till one of us rides after her."

"Was it just an animal?" Christa asked. "It ate their fried chicken, bones and all!"

"Prob'ly they just pitched dinner into the river," Jim guessed. "Some trout downstream's having himself a feast."

"I don't know." Christa stared at Trick, pressing for an answer he didn't have.

"I think it's too risky to ignore his barking. I think a city child had no business bein' down there alone—"

"Rosebud is no city child and she—"

"—and what's more, Mrs. Worth," Trick raised his voice to teach Christa not to sass him in front of Jim, "I think you had better get to bed—"

"The girls are in my bed!"

"—so we'll have breakfast in the morning!"

He'd ended up yelling. He *never* yelled. Sweet Heavens, so the girls were in Christa's bed. Why had she told him?

Should he call her bluff? Haul her down to the bunkhouse and see what that tied-up hair looked like loose?

Bloody Jim stood and smacked the dust from his pants. "I only stayed to get a head start on breakfast."

"I'll make doughnuts, Jim. Would you like that?"

Quick as a spark, jealousy burned out Trick's desire. What kind of woman was Christa, flashing from worried mama to shrew to sweet-talking vixen, all in a matter of minutes?

"Yes, ma'am," Jim was saying. "Doughnuts would be fine." Then he settled his hat and strode toward the bunkhouse.

Josh pricked his ears toward the creek. He whined, then his toenails clicked on the porch boards as he walked to the cabin door and scratched.

"Patty's been asking if Josh could come in at night."

Christa's voice was too level. He'd hurt her feelings and she wasn't going to ask him pretty please.

"No. I don't allow dogs in my house."

"I'll tell her."

"Don't—" Trick stopped, as disgusted as he was confused. "Tell her whatever you want."

"All right." But Christa didn't move, except to stare up at the stars.

"The Big Dipper!" Her finger stabbed toward the night sky. "Hey, there," she said, as if greeting an old friend. Then she wrapped her arms around her ribs. "I haven't looked at constellations since—" She failed to go on.

Come autumn, he'd watch a different sky. He'd have to walk around back of the house to see the Big Dipper. And Christa would see it from Sacramento City. Would she remember tonight? Or would the streetlights where she lived erase the stars . . . and him?

That would probably be best. But he had her now. What would be the harm of loving her, just a little?

She started for the door.

"Christa. Tell the little one Josh can't spend the night inside, but tell her—"

By damn, the woman made his throat raw from talking!

"Tell her she can have him for a nursemaid for a while tomorrow night, because her mama owes me a horseback ride, right after dinner."

Christa made a little flip of her hand, then touched her lips before going inside, unaware she'd changed the way he'd look at the night sky forever.

Nine

Although the noonday glare hadn't banished memories of last night's stars, the sudden clatter of coach wheels made Christa start as if a schoolmarm's hands clapped her back to attention.

Gliding crow-black and ominous, the hearse trailed a plume of dust across the alkali as it drew closer to the small party headed for town. The girls, riding tandem on Betsy, welcomed the distraction, but it only reminded Christa that her arm ached from holding the lead line.

Somber black with silver trim and oval glass windows for viewing the body, the hearse was twin to the one that had come for Nathan. Sun glinted off the silver harness studs, and Christa squinted against the glare.

"Nice Cleveland Bay horse and a fine coach. Don't suppose I'll go to my rest in one of those." Preach clamped his jaw closed and tugged the gray hat brim that matched his hair. "Sorry, Miz Worth. Don't know why I forgot your bereavement."

"It feels like ages ago." Christa blinked the heaviness from her eyelids. It felt like ages, too, since she'd slept.

Patrick's switch from ogre to friend had left her wakeful. With a book to read, she might have forgotten her desperate run to the creek and Josh's staccato barks. She'd craved a tale of love or intrigue to beat back the darkness and tense listening. But days of searching Patrick's cabin hadn't revealed even a family Bible.

"Does Coyote have a lending library? Or a bookshop?" Christa asked.

"No, but I've heard the Pilgrim sisters have sherry and shortbread on the sideboard and a few books for guests. You might check with them," Preach said.

"Mr. Garradine hides his so well." She fished for a clue. "And Patty's fairy stories are growing rather— I wonder why it's not turning off?" she interrupted herself as the hearse horse loped past the road to Coyote, on across the bone-white desert.

"The departed probably wasn't from around here."

Christa glanced at Preach, weighing the levity in his voice.

"Probably an Easterner," Preach added. "Should've stayed in the city, where it was safe."

"Don't gossip with Mr. Garradine. He frets like a mother hen." Her side glance caught Preach smirking. "At least allow me to make my own mistakes. You'll see they are not life-threatening," she insisted. "And I'll try not to beat you to the services of that fine Cleveland Bay."

"Did you know him before? Trick?" Preach asked.

Know him? Did it count as acquaintance that Patrick had steadied her trembling legs as she labored? Had an alliance knit when Patrick placed an Indian charm over Patty's neck or when he struck her husband for leaving her to live or die, as Nature decreed? Was a relationship forged when he urged her to fight the soul-sapping darkness and vowed he'd give her something to live for?

"Briefly. We met briefly when I traveled west with my husband."

"'Cause I never seen him fuss so, and I thought maybe—"

"I did something foolhardy? No. As I said, Preach, I'm careful." Christa looked back as Patty proclaimed she'd spotted a cloud shaped just like a bunny. "Mothers can't take risks."

"Coming out of nowhere, going nowhere." Preach stared after the coach. "No offense to your widow's sensibilities, but that's what life's about. Some risks find you."

"It's not that your philosophizing is an unwelcome

diversion, but I refuse to see that carriage as an omen. I may be an Easterner, and a greenhorn, but I intend to learn faster than that fellow."

Preach chuckled and Christa hoped he'd stay far from Hacklebord's Mercantile or Starr's Saloon. Francesca had already poisoned a handful of Coyote's citizens, and she didn't want Preach to regret his concern over her widow's sensibilities.

David Malloy had offered tea and fresh-baked soda bread when Christa delivered his weary daughter. Now, as the heady scent of wine-sauced goose beckoned her up the boardinghouse steps, Christa wished she'd accepted.

"I'm afraid you're a bit early for dinner. I—oh!" Adeline Pilgrim swallowed her cheery welcome and Christa knew word of her "wicked past" had spread.

"Miss Pilgrim, I'm Christabel Worth, and this is my daughter, Patricia." *Oh, good girl, Patty, to curtsy like a little lady, and not a witch's whelp!* "We didn't meet properly the other day, although I've despaired of setting a decent table since dining at yours."

"I understood you were going on to Sacramento City." Adeline fidgeted with her dust cloth. "But then, of course, you couldn't."

"I'm cooking for Mr. Garradine now," Christa said. Would employment make her more or less suspect?

"You must find it difficult," Adeline replied. "A lady, in such circumstances."

"No more than you, I'm sure."

Adeline's eyebrows knit together and Christa imagined the woman comparing her parlor's Currier and Ives prints and lemon-oiled deacon's bench to a cavalryman's cabin.

A movement fluttered in the doorway beyond. Did Sharlot Pilgrim stand there, listening?

"Oh! But we're maiden ladies, used to making our living as best we can."

"And I'm a widow who must do the same." Christa held Patty's hand a bit tighter.

Adeline's manners defeated her curiosity over the question of money. She clearly longed to ask if Nathan had left Christa destitute. Should she say so? Or imply what any sensible woman knew: It would be madness to kill her breadwinner.

"I'm afraid Mr. Worth's death was unexpected," Christa began.

"So we've heard." Wiping onion-soaked hands on her apron, Sharlot Pilgrim appeared.

Patty tugged Christa's hand, pointed at Sharlot and whispered.

"Speak up, young lady," Sharlot snapped. "Whispering is impolite."

Patty looked to her mother and Christa nodded, fighting the fear Patty would say something awful.

"Rice pudding lady," Patty said, much as she'd identify a flag, a lily, or a letter of the alphabet.

Sharlot sniffed, battling her pleasure.

"You liked that pudding, did you? Even the raisins? Children are such persnickety eaters."

"Raisins," Patty sighed. There was no mistaking the savor in her voice.

"You must ask your mama to make you some," Sharlot said.

"Mrs. Worth is staying on." Adeline looked pointedly at her sister.

"That's as it may be." Sharlot rolled her sleeves down to a more decorous length and buttoned her cuffs. "Some do and some don't."

"Remember that New Hampshire wig-maker—"

"Departed soon after a coyote ate her cat."

Christa hoped she imagined Sharlot's smug satisfaction.

"And that wheat farmer, the Russian fellow—"

"Adeline, the man was from North Dakota and the crop was flax."

"I beg to differ, Sharlot. He spoke English deep down in his throat." Adeline patted her breastbone. "And sang awful dirges while planting—perhaps it was flax. But his music was Russian and that, more than the soil, kept his seed from flourishing."

"Not that he'll find better soil in San Francisco, which was where he headed." Sharlot untied her apron strings and lifted the bib over her head.

Christa had just untangled the flurry of gossip when the elder sister turned to her.

"Now, Mrs. Worth."

"I have a—well, Mr. Worth considered it a vice." As Christa began, the Pilgrim sisters' concentration intensified. "I am a perpetual reader."

At Sharlot's sudden smile, Christa told the galling truth.

"My husband called me an addict, and I must confess, in Sacramento City, where my energies were less taxed, I read books by the dozens."

"I'm more of a quilter, myself, but Sharlot—" Adeline hushed under her sister's glare.

"Now, I find myself without something to read, and Mr. Garradine's foreman suggested you might have books to lend."

Christa examined the strings on her reticule and waited. She'd finished her appeal lamely, distracted by the contentious looks between the sisters.

"Step into our study, Mrs. Worth." Sharlot moved down a dim hall. "Perhaps we can appease your 'addiction.'"

It could hardly be called a library, this petted collection of seven volumes, but Christa presumed Sharlot's favorites hid upstairs, beyond the reach of guests. Christa understood. The smell of leather bindings and aged paper made her crave the immersion only books offered.

"Ohh." Patty's sigh echoed the one for Sharlot's pudding. "Grimms!"

"No, Miss Pilgrim doesn't have *Grimms' Fairy Tales*." Christa cast Sharlot a quick smile. "These are other stories."

Though the books were an odd collection, Christa longed to empty her dollars into Sharlot's lap and take the lot of them.

Tales, by Edgar Allan Poe, a tattered dime novel whose title had ended *of the Frontier,* a fine copy of *Hans Brinker and the Silver Skates* . . . She touched its spine. Was it too complex for Patty?

"You look pleased."

"Very," Christa said. "My father is a professor of litera-
ture. For all his shortcomings, he did give us this." She
recognized a nibble of homesickness. "Honestly, I cannot
fathom why Mr. Garradine has no books."

"Why would he?" Sharlot asked. "Patrick Garradine is
like most of these Western men—illiterate."

Illiterate. Shame that she hadn't guessed, anger that he
hadn't told her, chased through Christa.

"I don't believe he can write his own name. In fact, I'm
certain he can't. I saw him make his mark at Hacklebord's,
for credit."

Why should it matter? Patrick remained the Lancelot of
her dreams. Except, of course, he'd probably never heard of
Lancelot, Galahad, or any other knight. For Patrick Garradine, the world began in Nevada, twenty-seven years ago.

"It's not a rare thing, Mrs. Worth," Sharlot reproached.
"*We* are the oddities, here."

"But to miss—"

"They don't. People who can't read don't miss it. They
work themselves half to death and fall into bed, glad for
respite."

I can't . . .

He'd love . . .

If only . . .

The room absorbed Christa's silent protests. Patty touched a
plaster cat statue. Sherry shimmered in a glass-stoppered bottle
on the sideboard. Nothing had changed.

"I'm sure you're right." Christa drew her shoulders back
and met Sharlot's indulgent nod. "How silly of me to waste
sympathy where it's not needed!"

"I must return to the kitchen. A dozen hungry mouths will
line up in an hour, and Adeline's hopeless with fowl.
Vegetables are her forte." Sharlot rolled the word, as if
books gave them a shared vocabulary.

"Just select a volume and take it. And leave your purse
strings alone. I daresay you're with us for a while." She

squeezed out a pinched smile or a grimace. "Just bring it back to town when you're finished."

Christa's hand hovered over a book on American fisti-cuffs as Sharlot addressed Patty.

"Next time, perhaps I'll have rice pudding. Today I made anise cakes. Children hate those."

Patty's smile glowed like sunshine. "Nice," she told Sharlot.

The woman's eyes narrowed.

"Humph," said Sharlot. "You have a lot to learn, young lady."

The man who confronted Christa a few moments later had curly muttonchop whiskers of improbable carrot-orange. They did little to compensate for his bald pate and unnervingly low voice.

"If ever a rose bloomed in the desert, I have found her!"

For a madman, he kept his suit and vest well-brushed. In fact, a gold watch chain lapped from his pocket, and only dust-smeared shoes planted wide apart on the boardwalk kept him from appearing a prosperous merchant.

"It's Mrs. Worth, isn't it?"

"It is," Christa replied. Patty hid behind her.

Clearly, the man recognized her. She didn't take him for a citizen of Coyote. One of Nathan's business associates? Perhaps. His immense whiskers and bare head reminded her of someone.

"Perhaps you'd remember me if I were dressed in traveling attire," he said, embarrassed by her confusion. "I'm Jeremiah Smit. We were companions on the journey west."

"Of course, the attorney! You must forgive me." Christa extended her hand. "You were bound for San Francisco."

She wished she hadn't allowed Mr. Smit such liberties in greeting. He wrung her hang so enthusiastically, her black mesh mits abraded her flesh.

"San Francisco, yes. I have a comfortable practice. Only went home for a visit and now I'm stranded here. Thank

God I've the money to set up a little storefront office and cater to the simple needs of—" He tilted his head toward a nearby shop, then recalled his manners. "Whatever are *you* doing here, Mrs. Worth?"

In that pause, Christa saw his surprise turn critical. He took in her dusty riding dress, her apparent ease in this crude hamlet, and, most damning, her lack of a male escort.

"I've been widowed since we last met, Mr. Smit."

"What a shame." Smit still clung to her hand, patting it. "All that way across the country," he mused, "to die in— Hangtown, was it?"

"Sacramento."

"A true shame."

"Mrs. Worth, if you're ready?" Preach stood at a hitching rail just behind her, where he'd tied all three horses.

"Of course."

Preach snatched her mind back to the present. Time to make purchases in the mercantile had fled. At the ranch, there was dinner to get, laundry to wash, and personal preparations before she could ride out beside Patrick. With luck, her first Dutch oven stew was cooking itself. She'd only juggle the lid and coals, and add biscuits for topping.

"Mrs. Worth." Jeremiah Smit moved closer, as if barring Preach's approach. "Are you living in Coyote? I'd consider it a privilege to—"

Christa interrupted before Jeremiah Smit could nudge Preach's eyebrows a notch higher. "I'm employed—"

"Employed?" The attorney blanched until his orange whiskers glowed. "Oh, no, Mrs. Worth, surely not. Whatever your circumstances, that simply will not do. I say!"

"I say you'd best watch how you're talkin' to Mrs. Worth," Preach rumbled. "There ain't nothing improper about a good woman doin' honest cookin' where she's appreciated."

"It's not Mrs. Worth who's at fault, and I'm grievously sorry if you understood me to imply so. But it is the way of the world we live in, sir. Women of breeding do not labor for wages. Am I wrong, Mrs. Worth?"

The little color that had returned to Jeremiah Smit's cheeks would vanish if she told him the truth. She and Patrick had not yet discussed recompense.

"Of course you're not wrong, Mr. Smit, but I'm performing no duties I wouldn't be responsible for at home."

Jeremiah Smit fingered his watch chain, and his lowered gaze opened a window to his mind's meanderings. For pity's sake! Only a man would surmise she meant wifely duties of a conjugal sort!

"Ma'am," Preach said, lifting Patty into Betsy's saddle, "you said you wanted to get back early."

He yanked Cloud's reins free of the rail and offered them. Christa mounted the jigging white gelding. When she turned back to Jeremiah Smit, his jutting chin whiskers and determined eyes offered a rescue.

"Just the same, Mrs. Worth, my situation is such that, should you change your mind, I will eagerly help you for as long as I'm stranded in this godforsaken village, and beyond."

"Thank you." Christa ducked her head so that her hat brim blocked his sincere glower.

"Give ol' Betsy a boot in the ribs," Preach told Patty. "This town air's startin' to smell like hell on housecleanin' day. Let's get on home."

Trick stood in the dim barn doorway, coiling a length of rope while he watched Christa dismount at the cabin. As Preach took the reins and led Cloud his way, Trick strode off toward the henhouse. He was too busy to stare after a closed door.

"Here, chick, chick, chick."

When the child's voice sounded at his elbow, mimicking him, Trick turned and frowned down at her, wondering why Christa had left her running loose.

"You figure on helping me gather eggs before dinner, is

that it?" He hated the chore and shuffled it off on another hand as often as he could, but the little girl's head bobbed in answer.

"C'mon, then."

Christa should have taken over Muley's task, but she'd shown no curiosity over how eggs appeared in her cool box. Did she figure that's where the hens laid them?

"Watch your step, now," he'd said, showing the child into the dim henhouse. "Mainly they lay in their sitting boxes, but one is a sloppy old gal and I find hers in the straw."

With rustling feathers and soft cackles, the biddies remarked on the second human. But the child stepped careful as a dancer and the hens settled.

"What's they names?" she'd whispered.

"They don't have names." Some of the muttering hens were red, some white, none was distinguishable from her sisters. "They're just hens, not pets."

"What are they names?" This time she enunciated each word.

The little scrap thought he hadn't understood her. That sure wasn't the case. He thought she talked fine and he didn't want her believing otherwise.

"No one's named them," he said, surrendering. "I thought that could be your job. Everyone on a ranch has to work. You think on names while we gather eggs."

She'd taken the basket and followed, stepping high in the deep straw.

"These red biddies," he'd told her, "mostly they don't peck. They flutter off their nests, real polite, and let you help yourself. Some are a mite more selfish. They stay put. Then . . ." He'd paused and looked down into blue eyes the size of dollars.

"Then . . ." she coaxed.

"You sweet-talk them. Hens like that. And you ease your fingers along their nest straw, then gentle, along their feathers. Sometimes they do some shifting around, but you won't mind it. Then close your hand over the egg, ease back out, and you got it."

At that, he'd ceased his crooning and held out a perfect white egg between his thumb and forefinger. She'd clapped her hands and dropped it in the basket.

"Careful now, sugar. Eggs break."

The sober transformation of her face had made him smile.

Together, they gathered eggs until Christa's shadow darkened the henhouse doorway. The scent of lavender soap cut through the dust and straw. He noticed how washing darkened her pale hair to the color of honey. She'd twisted and pinned it tight enough to tug the corners of her eyes aslant.

"Patty, let's clean you up for supper."

"Red Gretchens don't bite," the child declared. "White ones peck, peck, peck." Her index finger tapped her mother's skirt.

"Oh." Christa glanced up at him, questioning. "Red Gretchens?"

"It's by me, ma'am. I told her she could name 'em. 'Gretchen' for all the red ones makes as much sense as anything else, I suppose."

"I suppose." Christa lifted her skirts clear of the straw. There was nothing finicky about the movement. It just said she was clean and planned to remain so.

Once she'd gathered a reluctant Patty against her and hustled her through the henhouse door, Christa looked back over her shoulder.

"We're still riding right after dinner, aren't we, Mr. Garradine?"

"Yes, ma'am."

She and the child had almost reached the cabin when Patty refused to tidy up for dinner.

"I have a surprise for you." Christa's wheedling voice floated back to him.

"Candy?"

"No candy."

"Mr. Trick gives me candy," Patty insisted.

"Mr. Trick gives you unrealistic expectations."

He didn't quite have a handle on what she meant, but Christa turned then, shading her eyes to look back across the sunbaked yard at him.

When he recalled the grace of that gesture later, at the dinner table, Trick figured he could forgive her this meal.

Christa had tried Muley's lazy-day stew, but she didn't have the old cook's knack. Chili peppers and salt couldn't cover the taste of scorched flour and burned beef.

Trick chewed and watched Christa hack Patty's portion into bites. Christa glanced back at the men, then bent, despairing, to her task again.

Her fresh-washed hair clung in a damp nest to the exposed nape of her neck. Trick blamed Jeremiah Smit and vanity for the first meal she'd ruined. And there was plenty of it.

"Ah, a senora who is not afraid to add spice to her cooking, *bueno*." Ramon de la Cruz nodded and aimed a reverent smile toward Christa. She blushed and looked away.

Trick stopped chewing. He'd be double-dog damned if he needed Ramon flaunting his Latin charm at Christa's dinner table. Trick gave the vaquero a glare. Ramon pretended not to see.

"I like chicks." The child was hovering at his elbow again.

"Y'do, huh?" He made a quick grab for the pie plate she carried before the pastry could avalanche to the floor. He'd have to be gut-shot to refuse Christa's dried-apple pie. Cinnamon and sugar clouded the scent of charred beef. By the time Christa poured coffee, Trick conceded that when it came to desserts and plain old Arbuckle's coffee, Christa worked magic.

He'd concentrate on that, and not the ride they were about to take together.

Ten

She wore blue. Not sky blue or liberty blue, but not black, either. The men sprawled around the cookhouse, letting supper settle. Pity they hadn't already ridden out. Because he wanted to believe, as he led Imp and Cloud from the barn, that Christabel Worth's blue dress meant she'd come out of mourning.

Just before she noticed his shadow separating from the barn's dim interior, he caught her tugging the hem of the blouse down over the split skirt.

"Kind of baggy, is it?" He couldn't say what he'd really thought.

"You've worked me too hard, Mr. Garradine. I fear I've—what is it they say of horses?—I've 'lost flesh' since reaching Nevada."

She must be joking. But when she glanced around, sort of guilty, he wondered why. He'd bet she didn't like the men watching, any more than he did, and that she fretted over what they thought of their boss riding out with the lady cook.

"Watch him, now." He felt edgy, handing over Cloud's reins. "He's not done testing you. That's for sure."

She smiled like he was a simpleton, but he was right, damn it. No rider knew every horse.

Mounting, he glanced over at the hands again. Yeah, they were getting an eyeful. He couldn't explain what this ride meant. Lucky no one had asked him to.

Neither could he explain why he took her loping away from the herd. He might have taken her out to see his cattle and calves, but he didn't. He rode toward Goldwing Seep, hoping for a pretty sunset.

Evening softened the desert. Stark blue sky now shimmered copper. The white alkali flat turned amber.

Patrick jogged his horse beside hers. From the corner of her eye, Christa watched him. The low sun hit his cheekbones and left his eyes in shadow. Once more, Patrick became the confident, Indian-bronze stranger of memory.

Her side glance failed as Imp shied from a diving blackbird, and she turned to her saddle to look outright. Patrick swayed from the waist, but his legs stayed steady, giving the young horse confidence. Patrick's black hat brim tipped forward as he spoke to Imp.

"Easy, son."

When he caught her watching, Patrick urged Imp forward. They loped on, man and horse merging, advancing into the sepia light until they became a faded daguerreotype, with dust and shadow slanting away from Imp's hooves.

She didn't feel abandoned. As Patrick rode ahead, she reveled in the desert's spare beauty. Even before she'd left Boston, the idea of Nevada had haunted her. Where Nathan and the others saw barrens, she noticed a wildflower waving from the cracked playa. While they complained of sky lowering like an enamelware lid, she watched a ripple of arch-winged birds sailing the sky. Sacramento had tormented her, forcing her to contrast city streets against measureless plains.

Tossing his head so high his mane lashed her cheeks, Cloud sucked in draughts of evening. He wanted to run to Patrick. Christa kept her reins taut, though Patrick's supple strength in the saddle pulled her after him, as well. Cloud tucked his chin and his hooves spanked the desert floor. Why punish them both? Christa loosed her reins and Cloud surged into a gallop.

"Get them, boy." She pressed her hat down and bent her

head to meet the wind head-on and rejoiced as Cloud's reaching, far-flung legs swept her past Patrick and Imp.

In an instant, Imp caught up, and the two horses, black and white, matched strides. Then, Imp's shaking head and stuttering gait told Christa that Patrick reined the black in, refusing to make a race of it.

Christa leaned low on Cloud's neck. The soft heat of horse brushed her cheek, stirring memories of childhood tourneys with her brothers. Always, she'd played Mordred to their Arthur, centaur to their Greek heroes, savage to their soldiers. To her fell roles that called for bashing, maiming, or skewering with sabers. Each plot devised by her brother Daniel had ended with a disastrous fall. Along with self-doctoring, the stunts had taught her horseback agility the boys never learned.

Imp's head jerked aside. His black legs moved like spokes as he veered away from Cloud, toward a tumble of rocks and a stand of reeds. Christa followed, pulling Cloud down to a blowing trot, then a walk. Finally, a quarter mile from the reeds, she halted, dismounting a few yards from where Patrick waited on foot. Her legs' weakness surprised her, since these past weeks had been filled with riding. But nothing this wild. She tried to walk toward Patrick without wobbling.

Christa expected a lecture, but he stayed silent. She breathed the wet-earth smell borne on a breeze, and her arms swung loose. Patrick led the way, shortening his strides to match hers.

"How'd you come to be so spooky around guns?"

She faced him so suddenly, her hat brim grazed his shoulder. When had he noticed? She stepped back. What had she done?

Christa removed her hat. Leading Cloud and carrying the hat left her with both hands filled, or she would have tucked up the tendrils of hair that had fallen loose. Anything to buy time.

She clenched her fists against trembling and took a few more steps before answering him.

"I'm not spooky, just careful."

"C'mon, now. When you came upon me cleaning the Winchester, you looked like I was polishing a rattler. Preach noticed it, too."

"Down by the creek," she said, swallowing past her tight throat. "With Josh weaving around, men on horseback and afoot, all with drawn guns, and those two little girls—you must see that was dangerous."

"Not a one of those men had his gun out."

"I think you're wrong." But was he? Had fear fanned her imagination?

"Think what you like. *I'm* thinking the girls heard the Yates boys sneaking around. The scent of strangers might rile up even Josh."

Her tension eased as Patrick's curiosity turned from her. Christa drew a breath and let her silence urge him on.

"Those boys are bad news." He lengthened his steps, hurrying toward the spring. "They're still fighting the war. Long as they are, I want a gun kept in the cabin. Shoot over their heads if they come sniffin' around."

Fire a warning shot at two high-spirited young men? Christa shuddered. "No, I won't do that."

"Then call me and I'll shoot them."

"You will not. Not on my behalf. The worst things that have befallen me were well-intentioned. Someone doing something for my own good. No, thank you."

When she took steps just as long as Patrick's, Cloud lunged ahead to the end of his reins. Patrick shook his head, then clucked gently. Perhaps Cloud was set on proving himself a horse, not a city pet to be led on a leash, but Christa coaxed him back. The interlude gave her another idea.

"Patrick, I know you've tried avoiding them and it didn't work. What would be wrong if I saw them 'sniffing around' and asked them in for coffee?"

"Don't you do it."

Cloud's misbehavior encouraged Imp to caper sideways, and Christa feared the young horse wasn't completely to blame for the energy Patrick used in jerking him back.

"All right. It just seemed a more civilized way of dealing with the problem. Still," she hedged, "firearms aren't safe near children. I won't have one around Patty."

A bird's cry punctuated their boots grating on the desert floor.

"You will, as long as you're here."

Nothing defiant marked his tone, but he left no room for negotiation. "And it's for her safety. She's not in danger from an uncocked gun or an unchambered bullet. I'm not sure you understand how it works."

For a gaping moment Christa knew he'd offer to teach her, and she went dizzy. She closed her eyes against it.

Would I do this? Nathan had taunted. *Would I, if it were loaded?* The explosion in her memory always made her eyes start wide open, banishing Nathan's face and the dull metal gleam.

"There are some ugly stories," Patrick admitted. "About folks tripping and blowing a foot off—"

A foot. How civilized, how darkly humorous a foot injury seemed, matched against reality.

"—or jerking a rifle out of a wagon bed and having the trigger catch."

She searched for an escape from this conversation.

"That doesn't happen if you're careful. And I wouldn't be anything but careful around you and—your girl."

Why didn't he call Patty by name? She couldn't ask, not when she'd just crossed him over guns. So Christa kept quiet.

"Didn't your husband keep guns?"

"Oh, yes."

His steps stopped, but she kept walking. So what if she'd confused him with the cynical turn of her words?

"Nathan was a big-game hunter. Not for food. There were dead animals all over my house. Stuffed."

"Never saw much point in that."

He wouldn't. Patrick Garradine's every word and action spelled manhood. He wouldn't prove it by killing trophies. No, Patrick's deadly rifle served as a tool.

"Besides, animals don't give me trouble. Maybe an old one with bad teeth goes after a calf, but mainly it's trash like the Yateses. The only manners they've got come from a fear of lead poisoning."

Christa laughed. Patrick Garradine had actually made a joke.

"A man's not good for much if he can't protect those who need his help. Just like you'd protect your daughter."

She stopped and smiled at him. He shook his head and swallowed as if his mouth had gone dry.

"Patrick Garradine, you are a good man. *I'd* protect Patty because she's my child and I love her. We were strangers and *you* protected us because it was the right thing to do."

"Anyone would. Don't be foolish." He squinted past her shoulder, slapping his reins against his palm. Restless.

"Not Nathan."

"Then Nathan was a horse's ass!"

Patrick blushed, and Christa delighted in his sheepish look. She wanted to surround him with a shameless hug, not just for possessing the strength and confidence Nathan had lacked, but because Patrick was humble, totally unaware of his appeal.

He sneaked a look back at her, then turned away again. Boyish embarrassment sat surprisingly well on his dark features. Between Nathan's barbered, manicured good looks and Patrick's rugged disregard for all but cleanliness, there was no contrast. In every way, Patrick proved the better man.

Jittering stomach muscles and confusion made Christa stride ahead of Patrick and Imp. An impetuous mistake now could have him towing her off across the territory, back to

Sacramento, even in the midst of an Indian war. Clucking her tongue at Cloud, who lagged at the end of the reins, she walked on, stopping only when she parted the reeds that fringed the spring.

A wave of warmth shimmered over the pool's surface. The muddy bottom, wavy grass, and tall reeds released the fertile odor of a wet garden. Set down on the bare desert floor, the pool made an oasis.

"This isn't the place—?"

"Naw. That was Rabbit Hole Spring. It's long since dried up."

He remembered.

Disregarding her skirts, Christa sat on a boulder at the edge of the hot spring. She stripped off her gloves, but she wished for the freedom to unbutton her boots, roll off her stockings, and dangle her feet like a child. The warm water would slide between her toes. She felt bold enough to pull her skirt as high as her knees. How would it feel to wet her shins and let the whispering breeze cool them?

Without looking, she knew Patrick remained standing, staring at the Western sky, now molten with the sun's fall. He looked content with evening's silence.

A blackbird wearing chevrons of gold perched atop a reed. He balanced and issued a rusty carol.

Christa's heart swelled as full. Given the powers of an enchantress, she'd conjure the delicate snowstorm globe she'd left behind on her Sacramento dressing table. She'd replace the storm-bound village with this moment of sunfire and Patrick.

"Let go of his reins. He'll stay ground-tied."

She opened her hand and Cloud moved after Imp, nosing wisps of grass. Patrick sat on the rock next to hers. His denimed knees brushed her skirt.

Patrick took one of her hands. He kept his eyes fixed on the sunset, but her pulse beat wild in that hand, pounding crazily, as if she'd tried to grab that blackbird.

"Tell me what happened," he said.

Nothing of consequence, she wanted to say. Instead, she felt the scuff on one of his knuckles. *Only a just end for a man impressed with his own prowess,* she might snicker, except that the pad at the base of his thumb touched her palm in warm intimacy. *Oh, a sort of murder, since I provoked his insane rage.* His hand tightened, urging her to speak, and she knew Patrick wouldn't settle for sarcasm. She delivered the truth, quick as she could.

"I confronted him about his guns. It wasn't the first time we fought over them, but it was the loudest. And he'd been drinking."

She saw it: burgundy wine taken in a room with red velvet drapes falling unfettered to the maroon carpet. Nathan's gun room, so lavish it might have housed a mistress instead of a gun collection, so plush it appeared a haven for clandestine rendezvous, was sure to entice a curious child. He'd glared when she invaded his smoky sanctuary.

Patrick's thumb skimmed across her knuckles and she tried to reward his patience. Her words came out stiff, and too few, sketching only a skeleton of that night.

"I caught Patty pushing a chair toward a rifle propped on a mahogany rack. One night I told him about it."

Ridicule and spilled wine had drenched her when Nathan grabbed her wrist. Surrounded by "his beauties," Nathan was more intoxicated with power than with spirits.

"I told him I wanted the room locked. He refused. Then I told him he'd come home one day and find I'd sold them all."

For one mesmerized moment, murder had glinted in his eyes. Then ridicule returned. He shoved and her head struck the wall. When she blinked free of tears, he held a pistol.

"He was showing me how innocent his guns were." Christa's hand rose to the level of her temple. "How harmless. Except that it was loaded."

One of the horses snorted and stamped. The dying sun cast a sheen on Imp's black hide.

"How close were you?"

Patrick believed her, even if he didn't comfort her, even if he didn't guess how she'd pressed her hands against her mouth to keep from screaming.

"Too close." Christa looked down at the ink-blue gaberdine bunched over her lap. It was dusty and once she began brushing it, she couldn't stop. She couldn't seem to get it clean. "Too close."

He took her hand again. When had he dropped it? Or had she pulled away?

"I hardly drink." Patrick forced out the words. "And I'd never be so reckless." He tightened his hand until hers was entirely enclosed. "Tell me you know that."

"I do."

A loud rustling preceded Cloud, who emerged from the reeds with mud on his forelock and muzzle, wet grass clinging to his whiskers.

"Been fishin' for dinner, son?" Patrick asked.

The gelding stamped and shook like a wet dog, dousing them.

Christa gasped and jumped to her feet. Relief turned distress to laughter and she blew away a lock of her hair that hung as soaked and dripping as Cloud's forelock. She pushed it back from her eyes and wrung out the hem of her ill-fitting basque. The adobe-gold dusk had turned lilac, and though a breeze chilled her, it felt good.

"Could you bring me back here?"

Not now, with Nathan's ghost hanging between them. Not now, but sometime, this hot spring would be their private oasis. She knew, because the hurried yearning that sawed her nerves like violin strings had slowed. She'd read about this feeling, even imagined it, but nothing had prepared Christa for this low, sweet wanting. They must come back here.

"Sometime, Patrick, please?"

Eleven

Sometime.

Christa looked up at him with eyes dark as violets. But these violets had black centers, spreading to take him in. She had no right to ask him for a future. But *sometime* could be tomorrow, couldn't it? Or next week?

To hell with that. For hundreds of nights, he'd wanted her kiss. He'd tried not to think of her that way. Better to remember her as a weak new mother. Better to hope for her survival and safety. But a man alone didn't always do the right thing.

Right this minute, she wouldn't refuse his touch. Later, she might change her mind. If she had any sense at all, she would. Now, he had to hold her, claim her, and pray God she gave him that right.

"I don't dare."

By the sudden "Oh" on her lips, he knew he'd said it out loud. It was too late to stop. Trick covered her lips with his and his hand crept, at last, to the softness of her nape.

He might have stopped, satisfied with one stolen kiss, one kiss to last a lifetime, but Christa leaned into him, reaching her arms around and up, pressing her palms over his shoulder blades.

He broke away and rested his fingers on her cheekbone. He wanted no question about who was kissing her. There was no room for Nathan here.

"By God, Christa, three years!" Trick lowered his mouth to her once more as she answered.

"Three and a half."

He felt her smile against his lips and he was lost. She'd crushed any chance of stopping short. He kissed her hard, but he didn't dare take down the heavy hair he'd longed to see. Didn't dare—but his fingers quit cradling her neck and worked through the strictly pinned braid. It bounded loose and the end unraveled, making a frayed tassel on her shoulder.

Put-off dreams were a powerful prod to loose morals. When Christa's breasts rose against him, he knew he'd take her right there if she didn't make him stop.

She showed no sign of it, until her cussed, too-big blouse gapped high above her skirt waist. He let his hand take the invitation, never thinking his callused fingers would snag on her camisole, never imagining he'd rip the lacy thing with his clumsiness.

Christa gazed up as if just wakened. Eyes wide, lips parted, face flushed, she looked less like his desert Madonna than ever before. The transformation drove any goodness right out of him. He wanted her.

Poised and staring, Christa didn't move. She knew as well as he that one touch would slide them into madness. One touch and he'd claim her. Forever. After that, he couldn't send her away.

Christa stepped back, holding the tail of her loosened braid in a grip so tight, he fancied she blamed its fall for her own. She didn't seem angry exactly, more confounded. She looked to him to sort it out, and he didn't know how.

"What if I keep the Winchester over the mantel, where you can see to it, for as long as you're in there."

He gave her control of his gun. It wasn't enough, but he couldn't think what else to do. He hoped Christa didn't know how the words raked his throat coming out.

She flinched as if he'd slapped her. But damn it, she'd confirmed his worst fears, leading him astray in plain view of any renegade who rode past. She wasn't bred to this life, and when she tumbled into danger, she'd take him along.

Christa Worth couldn't stay. The quicker he ended that notion, the better.

"Fine." She stiffened, seeming to grow a good foot taller.

Anger was what he'd hoped for. If Christa wept, he wouldn't know what to do.

Trick whistled through his teeth and both horses slogged toward him. Dappled by the last light sifting through the reeds, they looked real pretty, but they'd made a mess of the little hot spring. He wouldn't let them plunge in and stir up the muddy bottom. Next time.

The treeless skyline, black and cookie-cutter sharp, ran in endless, varied shapes against the dawn. Far to one side, Christa saw a single rock with a triangular point. Jagged peaks spiked up, then dipped in a smooth curve before rising to a stone steeple in the pink sky. She noticed this hill each daybreak as she hurried across the ranch yard to the cookhouse. Always, she forgot to ask Patrick its name, but today would be different.

Patrick Garradine had kissed her. More than once. Each time she ran the memory through, her stomach plummeted as if she'd stepped off a cloud.

Patrick had stroked her neck, loosed her hair, and pulled her against him. Five small words had stripped off his mask. "By God, Christa, three years," he'd groaned, and she knew he'd felt it too. Patty's birth had bound them together, but camaraderie had turned to something tender.

And then he'd hurt her.

Christa tapped up the cookhouse stairs and opened the squeaking door. Those hinges really must be oiled.

The yeasty smell of sourdough didn't make her nose twitch, now. She welcomed it as evidence of the starter's survival.

Christa tied on her apron and thought of Patrick's hands, there at her waist. She must feel them again. She jerked the knot tight, then fluffed the bow into a perky butterfly behind her.

Clear-eyed analysis and a knowledge of male thinking drawn from two brothers and Nathan made Patrick's motives clear. With lips warm from her kiss, he'd spoken of her banishment because he was losing control. He wanted her to stay, and it was only a sentence from wanting it to *asking* her to stay. As more than his cook.

Her shaky hand cast too much salt into the biscuit batter. She'd have to triple her recipe to cover that much salt. That's what came of staying up too late.

Hours after Patty begged to "fall asleep in Mama's bed," Christa had mulled over Patrick's ardor and withdrawal. Patty had drifted off with Josh's muzzle on her pillow, and the collie's soulful eyes watched Christa pace. Legs straight, paws properly on the floor, Josh hadn't presumed to jump on the bed. His eyes rolled white in his efforts to track her steps. Occasionally, he whimpered, but he stayed next to Patty.

"No, Josh. Patrick wouldn't like it."

She'd issued the command a dozen times, whispering, then sniffing back tears, finally, through clenched teeth. Christa stopped and stared at the patient dog.

Fighting Patrick wouldn't work. Armored by the arrogance of a man who knew he was right, he'd win.

Her will was strong as his and she might outlast him. But the memory of Patrick's cold eyes and set jaw told her he could absorb more pain. She wouldn't subject Patty to that kind of battle. In the end, she didn't want a man who gave love grudgingly.

Love? She'd returned to help him, to settle a debt no amount of cooking could repay. But last night she'd considered marriage, because the ragtag collection of cowboys felt more like family than Francesca, because the ranch house was warm and her Sacramento mansion frigid, and most of all, because of Patrick. And though Patrick provided the greatest lure to this rugged life, he'd erected the greatest barrier. He feared for her.

By midnight, she'd reconciled herself to proving she was

in no more danger than hundreds of pioneer women who'd come before her. Then she'd given in to a bit of petty revenge.

Reading her posture, Josh's ears had pricked straight. His tail had fanned.

"Go ahead, Josh."

The collie didn't need to be asked twice. Before Christa even patted the bed in approval, Josh leapt, spun around once, and curled on the lower half of the bed.

Satisfaction made a fine sedative. Christa dozed on Patty's pallet, thinking she'd be a fool to believe Patrick's wintry indifference when she still felt the imprint of his fingers cradling her neck.

Now, Christa yawned over the sleepy memory of last night and stamped biscuits from the dough's floury surface. Could a young widow be excused such lascivious reflection so early in the morning? She peeled the trimmings from her biscuit cutter and molded them into a small, heart-shaped bun for Patty's breakfast.

She'd already set the biscuits to bake when the door squalled open behind her.

Patrick had dressed for rough riding. Rawhide chaps, dark brown and scored by brush, were buckled around his waist.

"Good morning," she greeted him.

Why would a woman invest her heart in a man who offered little more than a grunt? She should quit now. What was that expression Nathan's poker chums had used? "Cut her losses?" Or was it "cut and run"?

She bristled at the thought of giving up. Perhaps this was a battle after all. Coolly wiping her hands on her apron, Christa studied his odd attire.

She'd never seen chaps, close up. The oiled leather leggings stopped short of his boot tops, but when he turned to reach for a coffee cup, she saw—well, she saw what a refined young woman would not have noticed.

"What?" Patrick growled, turned to confront her stare.

"The fringe on your, uh, *chaparejos* is quite pretty." There. Let him wrestle with her expertise in Spanish and vaquero gear, while she brought her bounding pulse under control.

"It's not for pretty." He frowned down at the leather strips. "It's for dripping off rain."

"Oh. Let me pour that for you."

He really shouldn't trust her to pour without scalding him. All she could say of chaps was that it was a good thing Patrick wore pants underneath them, so he'd have some denim covering his backside.

Patrick drank coffee and accepted the thin slice of apple pie she'd saved for her breakfast. He couldn't stay for biscuits and gravy.

"I'm going to check the gullies off High Rock Canyon, where the brush is thick and thorny enough to catch a cow if she's not careful." He drained the last of his coffee. "I'm hoping I'll run into that no-account brother of yours, too."

Dan. If she knew her brother, he'd come riding in, swinging a rope, singing his version of a Western song, herding more cattle than Patrick thought he owned.

"He should've been back from California. How long could a man stay cooped up with relations?" Patrick glanced around the cookhouse as if its walls were confinement enough.

As she turned back to the stove, Christa's hand hovered above the coffeepot. *She* was Dan's only California relation, except for Francesca. The two had never met. Mercy, she couldn't imagine two in-laws less well suited.

"He's not the sort to just hightail it off some place, is he?"

"Not since I've known him." She poured Patrick a second cup of coffee, before he could refuse.

"Don't go coddling, now."

"I told you once before, Mr. Garradine, it won't hurt you."

"I might get used to it."

"You might," she agreed.

The tip of his black mustache twitched, hiding a smile, and his eyes glinted blue and happy as never before. Oh, she wanted to twine her arms around his neck and touch the black hair lapping over the neck of his collarless striped shirt. She'd convince him to grow it Indian-long, as it had been before. She'd teach him to laugh.

Then, Patrick remembered to frown.

"I won't be back for dinner, so Bloody Jim is sticking close. When I sleep out with the herd, he'll stay in the bunkhouse."

Patrick swished the last of his coffee around the cup, regarding it as if reading his fortune in the grounds.

"You can have the little one collect eggs. I expect she'll bring you a few that are usable."

Hoofbeats heralded the first riders as Patrick opened the cookhouse door.

"Why won't you call her Patty?"

The door slammed on Christa's question and the smell of burning biscuits.

Every weed in the territory had migrated to the water meant for Christa's baby plants.

She'd dispatched weeds like petals on a daisy. Instead of "Loves me, loves me not," she tried to predict Patrick's ire.

"Appreciate my grit?" she'd asked, working her fingers through roots twice as long as each weed. "Or call me a dim-witted city girl?"

Now, after application of a stiff brush and plenty of lye soap, her hands shone white and clean. She dried them on the towel she'd brought to the pump. Washed free of her after-dinner dirt bath, Christa steepled her index fingers, tapped them against her lips, and stared at her nameless ridge.

Patrick would be piqued if she rode alone to his cow camp, but a flat-iron hot day had tapered into a sweltering evening. She would slip into their camp unobtrusively, without disturbing Patrick's routine. If he complained, she'd use Patty's crankiness as an excuse. That was far from a lie.

"Listen, little girl," Christa called through the open cabin door. The pump dribbled a last spurt of water. Patty didn't answer. "Baby?"

She entered the dim cabin. Patty and Josh lay nose-to-nose on the hearth rug. Both were panting.

"Let's go on a ride and cool off. We could go see Mr. Trick's cows."

Josh rewarded her with a thumping tail.

"No!" Patty snapped.

"Maybe Josh would like to go, too?" Christa offered.

The collie lifted his head and gazed from adoring, almond-shaped eyes.

"No," Patty repeated. "Josh is scared of cows."

The plank floor beneath Patty's chin had the child quite literally gnashing her teeth as she talked. That couldn't be healthy. And for all Christa's high mothering standards, she would resort to bribery sooner or later. Why not sooner?

"I might let you sleep on my bed again." Christa picked up her black riding hat. "With Josh."

"Aw right."

Twenty minutes later, they rode out of the ranch yard.

Patrick's mismatched herd of bovines spread over the horizon like a motley patchwork quilt. Their calls were just as diverse. One bleated like a sheep. Another lowed like a kettle drum, over and over. Still another managed a distinctly enunciated "moo."

"Why do you think their voices are so different?" Christa asked her daughter.

With the evening turned balmy, Patty had become a delightful companion. The same couldn't be said for Cloud. He flattened his ears and cranked his tail in irritation as Betsy plodded beside him. Cloud wanted a run.

"To help the babies find the mamas in all them cows," Patty answered.

"Good idea!" Christa settled her hat against the breeze. "That would help, in all *those* cows."

Her daughter's reasoning pleased her. Christa wondered if it would be too presumptive to address the hands about their grammar. . . .

Cloud side-stepped past a clump of gray-green sagebrush shaking in the wind. *Seein' snakes*, Patrick had called it when Cloud shied at cracks on the playa. The horse tensed beneath her.

"What if I quit leading Betsy? You could ride with just the reins, couldn't you? Like you used to do in the park?"

"All by myself." Patty nodded, vigorously.

Christa tied Betsy's lead rope around Patty's waist for extra security.

"Go, Mama. Let's go see cows."

Christa regarded the arrangement with a twinge of uneasiness. If Patty fell, her weight would anchor the horse to one spot, wouldn't it?

Cloud struck out impatiently with one rear hoof. In any case, Patty was safer some distance from this fretful beast.

They were approaching the cow camp at a sedate and picturesque canter when Christa's hat somersaulted into the breeze and landed between the two horses. Cloud shied and hopped sideways.

"Patty, get back!" Christa shouted. She waved her wide-eyed daughter away, leaving one hand to clutch the reins when Cloud put his head down to buck.

His front legs straightened like broomsticks and the jarring stop sent her hands sliding down his mane, nearly to his ears. He kicked, reared, and only her hand, flat against his rump behind the cantle, kept her from slipping down his tail.

Cloud fell to his front knees as if he'd been shot. In the sudden stillness, she felt his heaving sides and heard her own quick breaths. Christa felt him begin to shake like a horse who'd been unsaddled. Her mind chattered an urgent warning. Unsaddled, a horse shook, then—

She jumped from Cloud's back as he began to roll.

Shouting distracted her as she circled the animal, watching for her chance to grab the bridle reins. Patrick and his men, probably, calling out advice.

There! Christa snagged the left rein at the bit before Cloud completely regained his feet. She swung herself back into the saddle. Turn an uppity horse in circles, Danny had advised her long ago. Horses don't fancy dizziness any more than folks do, he'd said.

It worked. Just when Christa thought she'd vomit from spinning, Cloud hung his head and stood, blowing and snorting. Christa's body remained tight, ready, but she heard admiring shouts and a spiraling Rebel yell from the camp.

"Patty?" Christa remained focused on the horse, but Patty trotted up next to Cloud and the winded gelding only flicked his ears in acknowledgment.

Patty translated her appreciation into an excited garble punctuated frequently with "Mama!" Christa smiled and let her daughter lead the way into the camp. So much for making an unobtrusive entrance.

Patrick's riders, most still mounted, had gathered in camp. Patrick, on foot, stood behind them, by what appeared to be Muley's chuck wagon. Some of the riders applauded.

"Nice goin', ma'am. Nice goin'." Pete's accent soared over the noise.

Christa laughed and pushed her hair, still pinned but sadly sagging to one side, away from her face. She couldn't see Patrick's expression as he walked toward her.

"*Muy valiente, senora.*" Ramon, mounted on a blaze-faced chestnut, appeared at her side and offered her fallen hat.

Valiant? Christa pressed the hat firmly onto her head. The word must have a different meaning in Spanish, because right now her insides quivered.

Patrick's black mustache stood out as if painted on his stark face.

"Looked like he planned on unloading you and heading for the high country."

Patrick's stiff humor said he wouldn't skirmish with her here, in front of his men. He suppressed a disappointed sigh, as if she'd confirmed his worst fears for her safety.

"But I rode him to a standstill."

Cloud pawed the dirt and blew a weary breath between his lips.

"You did." Patrick's eyes focused past her, on an approaching horse.

The smooth-moving red horse carried a man wearing a tattered gray cap. Christa thought she'd found the source of that ear-splitting Rebel yell.

Was it Thad or Arthur? Thad. Arthur's gaunt face belonged to a melancholy poet. Thad looked sunny and boyish.

"See ya got y'all a new rider to smooth out the rough string, huh, Garradine?" Thad drew back, hand on his chest in mock amazement. "Oh! Pardon my mistake! It's the widow Worth, ain't it?" Thad inclined his head in her direction. "I caught the tail end of your rodeo, ma'am, and it was a mighty nice bit of riding."

Thad's eyes feinted toward her waist. Her lips curved in a sly smile. Christa touched the spot and felt a handful of lace. With all her vaulting off and on her horse, her chemise had worked up between her bodice and skirt. Should she stare down Thad Yates and ignore his trespassing eyes?

"What do you want, Yates?"

Christa expected Patrick to snarl. She'd even formed a hasty plan to stuff her chemise back in her skirt under cover of his anger. But Patrick's voice had a lilting cut that the Southerner echoed.

"Why, I was just riding by—but you know that, don't you? You said every time a man steps foot on your land, you know, i'nt that what you said?—and I noticed a heifer wearing your brand, chewed all to hell. She wasn't dead, just bleeding bad."

"From—?" Patrick demanded.

Until now, Thad Yates had gloried in telling the bad news, but the tremor that crossed his face made Christa look around for Patty.

Her daughter contentedly explored the camp and Betsy followed. The gray mare's reins dragged in the dust, but she was towed along by the lead rope tied to Patty's waist.

"I couldn't say what from. Really." Yates paused at Silas's snort of disbelief. "Something had half chewed off her hind legs."

"Cat?" Preach asked, sauntering closer to the discussion. "Or coyotes?"

"There was no tracks. It kind of looked like the heifer had walked a long way, bleeding." Yates scratched his head and replaced his cap. "I can't help but think a cat or coyotes would've eaten her, after going to all that trouble."

"Did you shoot her?" Patrick asked.

When Yates nodded, Patrick cleared his throat and studied his boot toe.

"Take the meat, if you like."

The Yateses were dirt-poor, Patrick had told her. Twin brothers living in a shack, caring for a father who was using up all three lifetimes dying of something that had displaced the gangrene that should've killed him when his legs were blown off, years ago. Considering the groundless enmity between them, she thought Patrick's offer an act of generosity.

Thad Yates's face turned dark red as his horse.

"*You* go eat a two-hours-dead heifer out bloating in the sun, Garradine!" He yanked his red stallion onto its haunches before spurring away. "Go on," he called back over his shoulder. "'Cause I ain't that hard up."

"Some folks is just lookin' to be insulted, is what I think." Preach mounted and called out over the restive cattle. "C'mon, boys, all the commotion has got our darlin's all stirred up. Settle 'em down so we can get some shut-eye."

Within minutes, Christa and Patrick stood alone. The men

yipped and chirped at the cattle. Patty dozed with her back against someone's saddle. Betsy sneezed at the selection of browse.

"I've been surprised at your foolishness before." Patrick stepped close, but no anticipation glowed from his eyes. "But this," Patrick let out his breath, and for a minute seemed unwilling to take it back, "this is like gunplay in Bible class."

Twelve

❧❧❧

"Wait!" Christa felt she might choke on the injustice. "You can't blame Cloud's—"

"This blame's bigger than that, honey."

Christa's stomach contracted until she thought it touched her backbone. The venom in that "honey" made it the worst name she'd been called.

"Cloud's a sly colt and you knew it when you climbed up on him. What I'm talkin' about is that." Patrick stabbed his index finger in Patty's direction.

That? Christa looked at her baby. Bonnetless and slumbering, she was the waif Patrick Garradine had saved with his own breath. He was calling her *that*? Had anger at Thad Yates ravaged Patrick's brain?

"What made you think it'd be a good idea to tie that child to her horse?" Patrick used the same false amiability he'd wielded against Thad Yates.

"I didn't want her to fall, of course." Christa took a deep breath. She tried to feel a sense of relief as she exhaled. This was a trivial accusation. "I didn't want to be holding Betsy's lead rope when Cloud acted up."

She hesitated, covering unsureness with bravado. "So I made sure she'd still have a horse if she did fall off, and I'll thank you not to tell me how to take care of my own child, Patrick Garradine!"

As if she'd blown out a candle, Patrick's rage vanished. Christa remembered the first night she'd come to him, when he'd patiently explained how her disappearance into the pantry had frightened him. That expression—regret? loss?—coated his features like wax.

"Christa, that child is no bigger than a jackrabbit. If a twelve-hundred-pound horse goes down on top of her, what do you think it's going to do? You want her thrown clear, not tied up, with no escape."

"That's not going to happen," she croaked.

Patrick drew a breath so deep she didn't want to hear what he said next.

"Before you believe that, I want you to talk to Preach about why one of his legs is shorter than the other. And he'd already started to jump clear. Or, hell, Christa, ask me."

Her eyes homed to the scar on Patrick's temple, and his fingers followed her gaze.

"After I got sent home from the war, I was laid up with this. I should've been riding toward Montana to help my pa break wild horses. If I'd gone, maybe a rank bronc wouldn't have reared back and snapped both his spine and my father's. The horse got a quick bullet in the brain. My pa"—Patrick's words took moments to form—"was *nine* days dying."

She'd thought Patrick Garradine could absorb pain better than she. He could, but the pain didn't vanish. It roiled about inside him, dulling his blue eyes as he remembered.

"Why are you telling me this? To scare me away?"

"Not to scare you, not to drive you away. I'm telling you—" One hand reached out involuntarily, trying to grasp the words his mind couldn't. "Because, damn it, Christa, someone has to talk sense to you.

"All these men," he said, waving his arm toward the range, "love your cooking. They love your prayers and pretty ways. You showin' off ahorseback makes it all the better."

He wouldn't let her deny it and he wouldn't let her touch him. She ached to be in his arms, to turn back this sinking sun to yesterday.

"But where are those admirin' men going to be if your

little girl gets killed? Are they goin' to hold you while you cry your heart out with guilt? No. And I could not stand it."

She couldn't stop the tears from coursing down her cheeks.

"Jesus!" Patrick turned his back, and his shout sounded like a plea, not blasphemy. Through the blur of her eyelashes, Christa saw him slam his fist against his thigh.

Christa swept aside grief for a death that hadn't happened.

She must think. In the next five minutes she'd either force herself to think like a Westerner, or lose it all.

With the heels of both hands, Christa cleared her tears. She tucked her chemmy back into her skirt, sniffed, and tried to look relaxed.

"What makes you so good at what you do?" she asked.

He wheeled back to face her, hands slung on his hips as if she'd challenged him.

"It's a serious question, Patrick. You weren't born a cowboy. This competence wasn't bred into your bones. Who taught you to ride, to shoot, to know the land and stay safe?"

His eyes narrowed and he glanced around, expecting an ambush. Christa clasped her hands before her, wishing someone had kindled a fire. Except for Patty, she and Patrick stood alone in the darkening camp.

"My pa," he admitted. "He was an Indian fighter, a scout, a mustanger."

And in the end even he wasn't safe. She didn't say it. She wouldn't snap off this thin edge of truce, but the knowledge hung between them.

"How old were you when you learned to ride?"

"That doesn't matter." He nodded to Patty, who rubbed her eyes and wobbled toward them, towing Betsy.

"Patrick, how old?"

"My mother died when I was born. Pa carried me while he worked. He said I went straight from a papoose board to the mule's packsaddle."

"So, perhaps a year old?" she asked. "Or two?"

He shrugged a sort of acceptance as Patty came to lean against Christa's skirts.

"Up, Mama."

Before lifting her, Christa untied the lead rope still knotted around Patty's waist. She let it drop, then hoisted Patty against her chest, crossing both arms over her daughter's narrow back. It was a private thing, closing her eyes and inhaling the scent that belonged only to Patty. It was as primitive as those cows, nosing their young, but for her, it was part of mothering.

Christa opened her eyes to Patrick's bewildered face. No mother had ever held him like this. Poor little boy.

"Patrick, I can teach her how to ride. You saw me with Cloud. I can show her what to do in an emergency."

"No. Mr. Trick." The contrary little minx all but strangled Christa with one arm, reaching the other out for him.

"I could do that. You learn pretty quick, don't you, sugar?"

Like magic, the trident of lines between his brows vanished as he talked to Patty.

"You sure taught those biddies you meant business. They just—whoosh!—move aside when they see you comin', huh?"

Where on earth had his clowning come from? Patrick Garradine was making a fool of himself, just to see a little girl laugh.

"Dark as the inside of a cow, ain't it, sugar?"

Patty rode with Patrick and Betsy followed along behind. Several times during the ride, he'd shared such silly cowboy expressions and Patty giggled obligingly.

True enough, the ranch yard before them lay in darkness. Christa had only made out the looming barn when high-pitched barking began.

"I've never known that dog to bark," Patrick said. "Maybe it's the horse."

With Imp worn out from hunting through brushy canyons, Patrick rode an oddly spotted horse he called a "palousey."

"I smell skunks." Patty giggled into Patrick's neck with a silly joke of her own. "Skunks, Mr. Trick."

"Mmm, you might be right."

Christa dismounted and Josh swirled around her legs, licking her hands, then Patty's, as Patrick handed her down.

"He's saying sorry for barking," Patty explained, patting Josh's head.

"He's supposed to bark," Christa said. "But why are you so wide awake, miss?" She set Patty on her feet, and she only giggled in response. "No joke, now. You're up long past your bedtime."

"Oh, no!" Patty's mock horror said she wasn't the least bit sorry. She skipped in wavering steps toward the cabin.

Overstimulated. Christa heard Francesca's voice as if her sister-in-law stood on the porch. Perish the thought! For their giggling, Francesca would have dosed all three of them with castor oil.

"I'll put these ponies to bed," Patrick said. "You ladies have a nice evening, now."

"Patrick, wait." Christa didn't run after him, didn't stand next to the horse and touch his leather-covered leg as she wanted. "When you're done, come back for a few minutes and just sit. Will you?"

He nodded, then took the horses to the barn.

The cabin looked just like it had the day he'd opened the door to Christa Worth, except that anyone standing in this doorway now would know a woman lived here.

Trick smoothed down each side of his mustache, aware of the dust he wore. He shouldn't go in. He'd left his chaps in the bunkhouse, but still. He stamped off his boots and the lamplight from inside haloed the dirt he'd raised.

"I'd best not come in."

"Don't be ridiculous! This is your house." Christa clucked her tongue before pulling him inside by the forearm.

His table was polished, and a little lace thing no bigger than his fist lay in the middle. Atop that sat his blue speckled coffee mug, filled with white prickly poppies. She'd folded the blanket on his horsehair couch to sort of a point. His chair sat near the hearth at an odd angle and a couple of plants dangled from cups on the mantel. Peering inside, he thought maybe the vines had grown out of sweet potatoes.

"Is it all right?" Christa asked. "I tried not to change anything."

Trick saw her start to wring her hands together, then stop. Next, she commenced biting her bottom lip, and that brought the kind of thoughts he'd pushed back all day. He almost told her hell, yes, he minded. He preferred the smell of gun oil to lavender soap. But he didn't say it, because he'd run his mouth enough for one day, and because, just for a flicker there, he wasn't sure he did mind.

"It's just fine," he said, then blinked. "Why, hello there, Josh."

The collie kept his head to the floor, flat between his white paws. He did not move. He was invisible.

Trick would've kicked the beast out, except that maybe he'd learned to be a watchdog.

Patty came in from his room. With hair slicked back into a braid like her mama's, wearing a long white nightgown, she looked like an angel.

"Hey, sugar," Trick whispered, pointing. "Is that dog hiding from me?"

Patty covered her mouth. Eyes aghast, she looked at Christa.

"He's not good at hiding," she said, shaking her head.

Trick nodded in agreement. In just two weeks, the child had started talking in sentences. He rubbed the back of his neck in confusion. Well, hell, so had he.

"I poured us some sun tea," Christa said.

She handed him pale liquid in a cup. Her last concoction,

that strawberry stuff, had been delicious. This tasted, honestly, like water from a well gone bad.

"I tried to sieve all the leaves out."

They'd left the door standing open for the night breeze and it rushed in, tipping one of the tissue-delicate poppies from the cup. Christa rushed to replace it.

"It's just fine." He sipped a little more and realized he'd said the same thing about the house.

He should leave. He really should. But he didn't want to. He wanted to watch Christa move around his house, fixing things, bringing things, stealing peeks at him. The gal was jumpy as a mouse. No, that wasn't fair—they were both edgy and walking on eggs because of today, and last night.

He watched her gather Patty next to her on the couch, taking the child beneath her arm like a mother bird with a nestling. Then Christa opened a greenish book, and he stared at her without speaking.

Hellfire, he'd sell his soul to go back and get that kiss right. He should've taken her face between his hands and touched her lips with respect. That's how he'd planned to do it, but then he'd never thought he'd have the chance. Anything would have been better than grabbing her by the back of the neck like he was set on bulldogging her.

"Yes, ma'am?"

"I said, this book is *The Deerslayer*, by Mr. James Fenimore Cooper. It's about a frontiersman, like you."

"What's his name?" he asked politely, though he was sure he'd never heard of the man.

"James Fenimore Cooper. But he's the author of the book; he's no frontiersman. I do believe he lives in New York. That is, unless he's dead. The frontiersman is the hero of the book."

She confused him, with her talk of frontiersmen, dead and living in New York, but he gave it another try.

"And what's *his* name?"

"I don't know yet. Uh . . ." Christa paused to flip

through the book. "I think it's Leatherstocking or Natty Bumpy, something like that."

Trick shook his head. They were sure fool names for a man who claimed to live wild.

She'd read a little bit and he'd taken out his knife to whittle a stick of kindling into some geegaw for Patty when the child pushed the book away and tunneled into Christa's arms to be rocked.

Christa held her, moving back and forth about a hundred times until he figured her belly and back muscles must be screaming.

"You need a rocking chair."

"This is just fine," she answered. Then she smiled, because she'd echoed him.

More walking on eggs. That meant they both had something at stake.

He gulped down the rest of her watery tea when she went to put Patty to bed. Then he stood, waiting for her return so he could take his leave. Josh yawned and stretched, too, but he only turned around in a circle and flopped back down before the cold hearth.

Christa had washed her face and tidied her hair. She'd used combs to hold the falling-down hair up from her temples, and she'd unpinned her braid from its knot. The gold tassel end of it swung from one side to the other, peeking out from behind each hip as she walked toward him.

He nodded toward the open door and Christa stepped onto his wooden porch, smiling as if he'd asked her to a ball with kings and fancy cakes. She halted so suddenly, looking up at the stars, that he put out his hands to keep from colliding with her.

A night bird called. Josh's toenails clicked on the plank floor, following Patty to bed. A coyote howled and his hunting pals came back with a ragged chorus of yips.

Christa leaned until the back of her head touched his

chest, then she drew his arms around her waist. Small hands, covering his, held him there.

No, honey. Aw, no. You're making it harder for both of us. His brain said the words, but his jaw didn't get the message. Trick leaned forward. He pressed his cheek against her hair, nuzzling her with closed eyes.

Christa's hair smelled of wind, sage, and her own lavender soap. A good combination. He wished things could be that simple. But he didn't say it, and Christa stayed still, only breathing and wishing.

Then the wind snatched one lock of her hair and teased it out long enough to float back and tickle his cheek. He had no earthly reason to feel so silly and soused, but he did.

"Christa?" he asked at her ear, his arms still locked around her. "At night, have you been sleepin' in my bed? Or has Patty?"

"I have."

He heard the smile in her voice, a smug smile like a little white cat, licking her paws.

"Just thought I'd ask."

He heard horses neigh and that rackety Josh barking his head off. Jehosaphat, once he'd got the hang of it, the fool dog couldn't quit.

Trick rolled over, certain he felt a bunk slat pressing through to his breastbone. Then he heard Patty scream.

Not horses neighing. Patty screaming his name.

He rolled out of bed. He didn't know Bloody Jim was on his heels until he heard the barefoot man curse. An erratic glow swung through the cabin ahead. Fire? Trembling hands trying to light a candle?

"Daddyyy!" Not yelling for him, but he'd thought—

Dear Lord, his mind remained in a nightmare, because he pictured grave-moldy Nathan coming for Patty. Trick kicked in the cabin door instead of opening it.

Josh twisted in midlunge and fell to the porch boards, convincing Trick this was no dream. The dog's hackles stood up like quills as it burst past his legs to go ripping around the cabin.

No one else was there. Trick slipped past Christa, who was holding Patty and trying to light a lantern. He searched the bedroom and found nothing there, either. The pantry?

Bloody Jim was coming out of it, shrugging, when Trick stopped. Both Christa and Patty wore those billowing white nightgowns, and Christa still fumbled with the block of matches, determined to set them on fire.

He took it from her, struck the match and lit the wick.

"What the hell was it?" His dread turned into anger.

The reproach in Christa's face didn't work on him like Patty's outstretched arms and quivering lips. The little scrap wanted him to hold her and he did. How had it come to this? He patted the child's shaky back. Over her head, he saw Bloody Jim rub the side of his nose and grin.

"Sorry," Patrick apologized to Christa. "I can't do this twice in one week without getting a mite testy."

Christa sat on the couch. Centered and alone, she didn't look much bigger than Patty. She leaned her forehead into her fingers, as if trying to focus her thoughts. Then she looked up.

"We all heard something. Josh, too. But at first I thought it was a skunk. Remember the first night, when I asked if you had a cat? Twining and scuffling sounds and something being knocked over. Oh, if he got in my herbs—! Well, we smelled that one tonight, and—dear Lord, I'm rambling like my grandmother." Christa looked down at her hands, trembling in her lap.

"Maybe if I poured Miz Worth some medicine."

"I don't need any medicine," she said.

"In the pantry, bottom shelf, on the right," he told Jim. A drop of whiskey wouldn't hurt her and it might settle her nerves.

Jim returned, holding a bottle by the neck. He poured a couple fingers of whiskey and held it out to Christa.

"It's good for shock," Trick promised.

Christa's lips twisted dubiously, but she sipped.

"Snakebite, too," Jim added.

Christa shook her head as if they were both loco. While she took a second swallow, Patty climbed up him another inch. Her knees clung so tight, he thought she might crack his ribs.

"We heard this sound, and I thought it might be a skunk," Christa said. "Then it moved out from under the porch, and we could hear it come around." Christa pointed, moving her finger from the front door, past the corner, to the bedroom. "There was a little thump and that's when Josh stopped growling and started barking. Then there was a big thud, like a, like a fist. Like someone trying to get in."

The suddenly level tone of Christa's voice gave her away. She'd been scared.

"Show me where."

He followed Christa, but he already knew. Sure enough, she pointed to the two logs whose chink he'd been meaning to refill. With the lantern lit, light would stream outside, showing anyone who had a mind to look—like those sneaky Rebs— that someone was in the room, turning in for the night.

"We'll go out and look around."

"Go too," Patty said, as Trick tried to peel her off.

"No, sugar."

Patty uttered a contentious grunt and held her arms out to Christa.

"You stay awake, though, sugar. I want to ask you some important questions."

Using two lanterns and considerable tracking skill, he and Bloody Jim found nothing but a few scrapes from Josh's claws. This ground didn't take tracks well, but a man might have dropped something or left some mark.

Not a careful man, though. Trick stamped dirt off his boots before reentering the cabin.

"Patty says it was piggity." Christa held Patty on her lap.

"Piggity again, huh?" Trick sank into his chair, though he wanted to sit on the couch, next to them.

"Uh-huh." Patty's nod told Trick she was prepared for his skepticism.

"Sugar, I'm not too clear on what piggity looks like. Could you tell me?"

Patty's hands churned, describing vague dimensions, then she pointed to him. "Like he."

Jim touched the middle of a chest covered by red long underwear. He cocked his gleaming bald head to one side.

Trick sure hadn't expected that. The Nevada territory had its share of freedmen and a fair number of fugitive slaves. Like Jim. But the race had no more than its share of no-goods.

"A black man?" he asked her. "You sure?"

"No!" Patty whined with exasperation, and Christa rocked a little to settle her. "No, his *eyes*."

"Piggity has brown eyes, like Jim's?" Christa asked.

"No!" This time the whine was louder and Trick figured they didn't have much time left for questions. "*Big* eyes."

"Big brown eyes." Jim's deep voice snapped Patty out of her fusses.

"No. Leloeyes."

"Yellow eyes," Christa interpreted.

"Leloeyes, pink nose and ears." As Patty mimed points for the top of her own ears, Christa began nodding as if she knew what this nonsense was all about.

"She's just described the man-eating trolls from her fairy-tale book," she sighed, wearily.

Well, hell. That whole description had been for nothing. Trick motioned Jim to step outside. He did, nodding that he'd picked up Trick's gesture to keep things quiet. Trick didn't want an argument with Christa when he left wearing holsters and carrying the Winchester.

As Jim passed through the doorway, he looked relieved, but Trick felt downright cranky. He was sick of the Yateses and their vicious ways, and he wasn't getting enough sleep. Worst of all, he'd suspected all along he wasn't really missing out by not learning to read, and Patty had just proved it. Man-eating trolls.

Thirteen

At dawn, Arthur Yates half carried his father to the outhouse.

"Just shoot me, son. Send me out of this life, if you care for me," the old man wept.

"Aw, Pa. You just had a bad night. Things'll brighten when the sun comes up."

In the blue-gray dimness, Trick saw Arthur hold the wooden door with one shoulder, circle his father with the other arm and hoist him inside. The hacking cries continued as Arthur leaned his back against the narrow door and tipped a bottle to his lips.

Trick waited for the pair to make their drag-shuffle way to the shack before backing the Appaloosa away from a hedge of wild roses. Such goings-on might make him a drinking man, too.

All night Trick had squatted there, watching the shack, less certain each hour that the Yateses were Christa's intruders.

Time to go home. He set his heels to old Freckles. Cold from standing so long, the gelding slipped on a rock and stumbled. The Yateses' squirrel dog set up a ruckus, and looking back, Trick saw one of the men come outside.

Well, fine. He'd been mighty polite in the face of their orneriness. It didn't do to let them get complacent.

"Eyes like the morning star, cheeks like the rose, Laura was a pretty girl, God Almighty knows—"

Trick shivered. Every time he heard Slim Jim sing that song, the three notes of "pretty girl" made him shiver like rain dripping down his collar.

The rising sun serenade on the cookhouse steps broke off as Trick loped into the yard. If they hadn't seen his dust ten minutes ago, they hadn't looked. So why did they pull on their hats and turn sheepish now?

"Oh, don't stop." Christa gave soft applause and begged Slim Jim to continue warbling. Patty, up early and kicking her heels against the porch, clapped, too.

"You do have a wonderful voice!" Christa continued.

"Humph." Bloody Jim shambled down the steps. "We got heifers harmonizin' better than that."

"You should, you should—"

For a minute, Trick thought shy Bill Williams would actually squeeze out a thought, but he didn't.

"You should hear him with the guitar, ma'am." Pete watched Trick, not Slim Jim or Christa, and he didn't put on his hat or move toward his horse.

"Sinkers are all gone, boss," Silas said, without an ounce of regret.

Trick wanted to kick the sorry gluttons. Christa could have cooked nothing but those fancy Sacramento doughnuts and the hands—him, too—would've walked off wagging their tails.

"I declare, we're so sorry, but we et them all up," Pete added.

Trick surveyed the hands. All moved just a mite slow. All talked just a little too cocky, especially Pete, but not quite cocky enough to punch. Had Christa made them soft? Or were they jealous, thinking he was getting something they weren't? Either way, he'd put a stop to it. They had to work together as a crew, a team, in time for the fall drive.

Trick watered Freckles, washed up, and walked toward the cookhouse, hoping she'd saved him something. Anyone still in camp when he rode out would pull hard duty. The narrow defile leading into Cow Heaven Gorge had been so thick with brambles when he and Imp had come upon it late yesterday afternoon, he hadn't had the heart to force the young horse through. He'd heard cattle, though. Cutting that thorn brush and squeezing the cattle out of one of their favorite hideouts would give these men something to think about besides where their boss was spending his nights.

Without a word of explanation, Patrick Garradine had arrived late for breakfast, then expected her to have saved something for him. She had, of course, but not much. A dollop of eggs—scrambled, since their trip from henhouse to cookhouse had suffered during Patty's romp with Josh—a portion of parched corn with peppers, and two biscuits. She hadn't been able to keep back any more. The men had noticed her rescuing even that much, and followed removal of the plate with as much wolfish interest as they'd shown the velvet ribbon in her hair.

Now Christa had to get two gargantuan pots of beans out to rock-lined pits before her coals lost their gray perfection. Her Dutch oven skills had improved. When Silas taunted her with the information that Western cooks were judged by their beans, she took up the challenge.

She'd made plenty of them, Lord knew. She'd put the beans on to soak last night after dinner, before riding out with Patty. She hadn't known the little pink pellets would swell so. She'd come in this morning to find they'd grown much too fat for their container, overflowing onto the stove and floor.

So she had two pots of beans, entirely too heavy for her to carry alone, and she'd asked Bloody Jim to stay a moment and help her. She started for the door, then spied yet another of the escaped legumes. Mercy! They'd fallen everywhere. She bent from the waist to grab it. When she turned to dispose of it, Patrick's eyes were on her.

A hot blush covered her face. He'd clearly been studying her backside. Now he ate, slow as a cow chewing her cud, and he was smiling.

"Jim?" She ignored Patrick's ill-mannered smirk and called out the door. Pete still stood out by the hitching rail, checking his mount's hooves.

Jim carried out the first pot alone. Then they each took a side of the metal bail curving over the lid of the larger oven.

"Oh, Jim, we can't drop this." They lowered the cast-iron bottom toward the coals. "It's going to be so good. See how I've got the lid turned over? At the end, I'm going to fry bacon on top, and then slide it into the beans."

"You got no business touching a white woman, boy." The venomous voice froze Christa's hand on the pot's bail, where it showed pale and small next to Jim's.

"Pete!"

"Pardon me for saying so, ma'am, but this is none of your affair. Most likely you wasn't raised to know what's right. He was."

She wanted to wash out his mouth with soap. She wanted to push him in the middle of the chest and make him fight her, like he would a man.

Jim rose from his crouch beside her, uncoiling until he reached his full height. Oh, no, truly she *didn't* want a fight, and certainly not on her account. But Jim didn't wear the expression of a man fighting for her honor, and he didn't look the least bit insulted.

"Yeah, I was raised to know what's right, *boy*. And I know there's a lady standing here, and a little girl sitting on the porch, and the man who hands me my pay right inside.

"If you want a fight, you're gonna have to wait for it. Just you keep your eyes open, *boy*. If you feel something itchy between your shoulder blades, better duck."

Bloody Jim swaggered toward his copper mule, Emperor. If he felt Pete's glare between his own shoulder blades, he gave no sign.

A meadowlark fluttered down to land on the pump handle. She inflated her yellow-speckled breast, released a dozen soaring notes, then looked aghast at the site she'd chosen for her song and vanished in a flash of feathers.

"Pete Jessup, what is the matter with you?" Christa began, then she met the blond Texan's surly eyes and stopped. She grabbed his arm before he could leave. "No, that's not right. I apologize, Pete. I'm not your mother. May I start over again?"

"I'm not sure what you're startin', ma'am."

Like dogs circling for a fight, Jim and Pete had blown themselves out of proportion. With Jim gone, Pete looked younger, smaller, as he glanced toward the cookhouse.

"I know if Trick comes out and sees me still jawin' with you, he'll have my hide."

"I'll make it quick." She stooped, then used her garden trowel to shovel dirt over the Dutch ovens. "You're a religious man, aren't you, Pete?"

"Yes, ma'am, I told you I was." He squatted beside her, using a stick to mark idly in the dirt.

"Well, what about the idea that all men are created equal?"

"Ma'am, I went to school," he said, shamefaced for her rather than himself. "That's from the Declaration of Independence, not the Bible."

"Well, I know that," she said. "But who do you think did that creating?"

She scraped the packed ranch yard earth for a mere handful of dirt and sifted it over the pots. Debate had once been her strong suit, but perhaps she'd lost her skills from spending too much time in the kitchen.

"Well, God did, of course, ma'am, but I can't help thinking he created some a lot more equal than others." Pete drew a circle within a circle.

She wouldn't point out the fallacy in that statement. No, she'd attack from a different direction. Christa glanced up to make sure Patty was still on the porch, playing with the spinning top Patrick had carved.

"Pete, is your father a gentleman?"

He puzzled over the intent of her question, then scribbled over his drawing and answered.

"*Was*, ma'am. He died in the war, but, yes, I believe he was a gentleman."

"And did you ever see him in a situation he considered uncomfortable, but unavoidable?"

"Yes, ma'am."

"Think of one." She sprinkled a last bit of dirt over the cook pots. "And tell me."

"Well, there was a time he reprimanded a deacon for making off with a collection plate." Pete's cheeks flushed at the memory, but he watched his stick. "Turns out he hadn't. My daddy himself left the plate on the altar. When he went back in for his sermon notes, he found it."

"And did he apologize?"

"I saw it with my own eyes, but if you're asking me to apologize to Bloody Jim, ma'am, it just ain't going to happen."

"I'm not asking that, although it would be awfully nice. I'm only asking you to conduct yourself in a dignified manner." She watched Pete's face as he turned the request over in his mind. "I know you're capable of that. I wouldn't have a lesser man at my table, certainly not around my daughter."

Pete pursed his lips, nodded, and used his hand to wipe out the scratches he'd made in the dirt.

"I'll work on it, ma'am. I surely will."

As Pete returned to the hitching rail, Christa used the back of her trowel to give the piled dirt a last satisfied thump.

She hummed, "Oh, Laura was a pretty girl," as she tapped back up the cookhouse stairs, so pleased with herself she almost collided with Patrick as he opened the door.

"You've been up to some mischief, Mrs. Worth. Just how many of my hands do you need as cook's helpers?"

He stood so close, and he held her surprised stare with such intensity, Christa couldn't find words to answer. His brigand's mustache rose into an intriguing smile, and she thought he might kiss her. How he loved this. Just when she thought she was so smart, Patrick held her captive and speechless with nothing but his smile.

"See you at dinner, Christa."

It wasn't until he'd mounted Freckles and spurred away that she found her voice.

"You're really going to like these beans!"

"What, Mama?" A string dangled from Patty's fingers and she scowled as she looked up from the top.

"I don't know." Christa struck herself lightly on the forehead. "Baby, I really don't know."

Trick tucked fresh clothes under his arm, slung a horse-hair hackamore over one shoulder, and let a chorus of frogs lead him toward the creek. He felt good.

Christa's beans and bacon had been her best dinner yet, and she'd made plenty of fried cornbread, enough to sop in the beans, then cover with jam and honey.

His Cow Heaven strategy had worked, too. Thirty head, five of them his prized meaty shorthorns, had holed up in there. It had taken all but Pete—who'd ridden watch on the existing herd—to bring them out.

Clearing those flesh-gouging thorns with sweat in your eyes was bad enough. Then the longhorns, wild as deer, proved impossible to herd. And one brindle bull, a shorthorn-longhorn cross of the type he hoped would make his fortune, needed no excuse to rampage.

They'd been forcing cattle down the rock-walled passage to the range when the brindle threw his wagon-sized body sideways. Two cows went down, but the brindle clambered over them, horns lowered for Preach's bay horse.

Trick thanked God and instinct for telling him to keep his eyes on the bull. Only a lucky loop snagged the animal before it struck the bay's belly.

It'd been hell, then, trying to get the rope off, and once Trick thought sure the brindle had broken his neck, struggling, but the bull was too mean to die.

The men were the same. Exhausted, swearing they

wouldn't ride back, even for Christa's beans, they'd emerged from Slick Rock Hole, a hot spring half as pretty but twice the size of Goldwing Seep, restored. All but Preach.

Before leaving, Trick sat back on his boot heels, at the edge of the spring, talking to his *segundo*.

"Comin' in, Trick?" Preach asked. "Feels mighty fine."

"No, I'd rather wash in the creek. This thing's too hot for me."

"Uh-huh. Thanks for saving my ass."

Trick brushed off the older man's gratitude with a wave, but Preach continued.

"I saw that son of a gun coming for us. I felt Red go up on his hind legs and—whoo boy. All I could think of was last time it happened."

The surface of the water rippled as Preach rubbed his leg.

"That is one pony ride I don't ever want to take again."

Ramon burst out of the spring first.

"Ay, I cannot keep company with men who look like you," he scorned the naked cowboys. "With your brown face and hands and white hairy bodies, you look like the pet monkey of my uncle Jorge in Mexico.

"Trick, let these monkeys go in to the ranch. I'll stay with Preach and watch *toro loco*." He indicated the brindle bull with a jerk of his chin. "He'll lead them all to Cow Heaven, if we're not careful."

"Think so?" Preach asked. "Well, that might not be such a bad idea, if we don't get rain soon."

So he'd left Preach and Ramon behind, promising to ask Christa to save them a hat-sized bowl of beans.

That was a promise he'd had to break. As he stood bathing in the creek, Trick pictured the bunch of them— Christa and Patty included—rooting into those beans like hogs at a trough.

Wading toward shore, it seemed the creek was low. Riding in tonight, it had even sounded different.

Except for the fact he still didn't know who'd been sniffing around the cabin, the day had been a dandy. Trick pulled a fresh shirt on, then reached for his boots. It felt good to be clean.

On the pretense of waiting around for piggity—that slippery man or critter, he'd spend tonight sitting on the porch, mending his hackamore and listening to Christa read.

Trick squinted in the dusk, looking for the boulder that held his hat. Then he heard the shot. He climbed the bank, stirring more dust than you could settle with Noah's flood. He ran toward the bunkhouse, telling himself it just figured.

Cowboying must steal one's sense of smell. That was the only explanation for what lay before her. The bunkhouse at Good Thunder Meadows ranch was quite possibly fastidious Francesca Worth's worst nightmare.

Spying on the men had not been Christa's intent, but when Josh's whining escalated into urgent yips aimed in the direction of the bunkhouse, Christa had felt compelled to investigate.

Then she'd remembered Patty's "peek hole." Like most of the outbuildings, the bunkhouse had been part of the fort. With time, one log in the doorless back wall had sagged away from its brothers, leaving an opening that served for ventilation.

Weeks ago, Patty had been examining a nearby anthill when she discovered the peek hole. Since the men were absent, Christa had allowed Patty to peer inside.

Now Christa had quite a good view. Under the best of conditions, it would not be a light and airy place, but this evening the hands had ignited a number of Betty lamps and propped the door open to catch the June breeze.

That was why Christa could not only see but smell Bill Williams skinning a dead coyote. She didn't believe the coyote's passing was recent. A tobacco-spitting contest added to the miasma. Pete and Slim Jim rarely hit their mark outside the front door, but their competition was lively, until halted by Bloody Jim.

"You all are disgustin'." He tilted on the back legs of the

only chair, eyes toward the log beams. For an instant, Christa imagined he saw her. No, he'd said he was recovering from a wound inflicted by a "sassy little dogie." That's why he sat.

"It smells nasty, too," Bloody Jim added.

"Disgusting? And that cow dung poultice y'all have stuck to your leg ain't?" Pete earned a laugh from them all.

The log beneath Christa's fingertips vibrated. She watched Bloody Jim coax Slim Jim and Pete into an alternate means of rivalry.

For all their merriment, only Silas appeared to be drinking spirits.

"Have a li'l rotgut?" she'd heard him offer, but each man declined. Now he slumped in a corner, mumbling morosely. "—even make enough money to have a wife—"

"Shoot, Silas, take mine," laughed Slim Jim. "Can't do nothing but write to the one I have, and I can't do that 'cause my pencil won't spell correct!"

"Never mind, never mind." Silas slurred his words terribly. "She-stuff makes you too particular. Ask the boss, putting us in that ravine full of stick bushes. Too damned particular."

She-stuff. Is that what they thought, these men who looked at her with such respect while she served their food? But the others didn't laugh, or really take notice of Silas's remark. Even Bill Williams had left off skinning that poor coyote to gather over in the corner directly beneath her spying spot. He joined Bloody Jim, Slim Jim, and Pete.

By craning her neck, Christa could just make out two lizards. If it hadn't seemed so ludicrous, she could have believed Pete and Slim Jim had lined them up for a race.

In an instant, she thanked the Lord for the inspiration to figure out their game. If she hadn't, she wouldn't have had her hands pressed to her ears or had time to jump back before Pete shot a bullet through the roof.

Fourteen

Trick stood in the bunkhouse doorway, boots straddling a pool of tobacco juice. He gripped the stone door frame to keep from reaching for his gun.

In his mind, though, Trick Garradine did just that. He slipped the Colt from his holster and shattered the whiskey bottle, *his* whiskey bottle, clutched in Silas's hand. Bill Williams would bite the dust without ever uttering that perfect sentence he'd been building up to, because he gripped a skinning knife and stood over a stinking coyote. Damn it, a man did not flay the hide from any animal indoors. What would Christa think if she should see such a thing?

After that, Trick figured he'd aim for Pete's revolver and send it spinning to the floor. He'd plug Pete and Slim Jim just to teach them some respect, and crease Bloody Jim's scalped pate because he was old enough to know better than to leave a raw herd in the hands of one vaquero and an old man whose nerves were shot and whose bones ached from nearly getting gored. As for the lizards—he'd let the lizards live.

But the bloody, soul-satisfying tumult took place only in his mind. Trick drew a calming breath and hollered, "What the Billy Blue hell are you horses' asses *doing*?"

In a single moment of silence, something scuttled across the floor.

"We were goin' back in just a few minutes, Trick."

"We wasn't planning to leave Ramon and Preach alone all night, boss."

"Just digestin' our beans and playin' a little . . . playin'." Pete hid the horse leg revolver behind his back.

"Well, looky who's got himself as cleaned up as a Chihuahua pup," sneered Silas. "Boys, didn't I tell you she-stuff was real particular?"

Trick's hands dropped from the door frame. He needed this crew kept together—but not Silas. Not after this. But if he shot Silas, no matter how much he deserved it, the crew would fall apart. They waited for him to make his move.

"Silas, you're fired. You can ride one of my horses back into town—"

"Now, Trick, . . ." Silas suddenly sounded sober.

"—leave him at Malloy's and I'll drop your pay at Hacklebord's by the end of the week." Trick stepped inside. Bad as the bunkhouse smelled, he wanted out of the doorway in case he had to throw Silas through it.

"Shoot, Trick." Silas sounded surly even though he couldn't sit up straight. "Don't you think—"

"Silas, you don't want to know what I'm thinking."

The sometime-mortician's muttering didn't stop until he shuffled through the door. Then he hissed something that made Trick follow.

Christa stood just outside, pale above the high neck of her dress, fingers pressed to her lips.

"Did he say something to you?" Trick asked. No matter that she shook her head. He knew Silas had.

"Patty was asleep and I was preparing to do some hand laundry when Josh growled and I heard a shot."

"Christa."

Trick looked at her rounded green eyes and the pale hands she'd clasped together. He watched Silas mount up and ride away, then decided he'd do his best not to sound angry. Christa wasn't guilty of anything but ignorance. He nodded for her to follow him a few steps off.

"Christa. You can trust me on this: When you hear a shot, run away from it, not toward it. Understand?"

She nodded, but her face turned red. She looked like she'd bust from holding something in.

"Now, I want you to get back in the cabin. But first, tell me what Silas said to you." He did his best to sound gentle.

"He didn't say anything, but he did smell unpleasant."

Smell, Lord. All he needed was Bill Williams riding out and leaving that coyote carcass inside.

Trick held up one finger, bent back toward the bunkhouse and called out, "Billy? See that you get that animal out of there."

Then there was whispering and shuffling, socking and laughing. Christa didn't return to the cabin, as he'd told her. She just stood listening, straining forward as if she tried to identify each speaker.

"*Not* with Mrs. Worth standing here!"

"He was already dead, Trick, if you care."

"Billy just found him."

"Like a vulture!"

"Take him out and bury him, Bill. Don't do it here or the boss'll shoot you."

Christa should've shut the door behind her by now, but she'd decided to set down roots.

"Or I will, I swear. I ain't eatin' where some—"

"Whew, Bill, that is a mite whiffy, son. Ol' Paint's gonna take exception to haulin' it."

Not that it mattered that she was listening.

"They're just acting like boys." He felt obliged to explain. "They've had no time off for quite a while."

She didn't say anything, only tried to stare him down. He didn't much like having his directions ignored. Before he insisted, Pete stepped out of the bunkhouse, hat in hand.

"I hope you didn't hear none of that, ma'am."

"Don't worry, Pete." She looked over as Slim Jim lined up as well.

"See you at breakfast, ma'am."

"No, Jim, you're staying out. All of us are staying out."
He had to knit this bunch together—now.

"Mrs. Worth? I'm glad you weren't around earlier."
Bloody Jim shook his head remorsefully. "If you had been,
you might have heard some awful rough talk, though we
was just having fun."

Bloody Jim and Christa exchanged a look Trick didn't
understand. He let the men move off before he spoke again.

"If I'd asked you *please*, would you have gone in the
cabin?" Even to himself, Trick sounded weary. As he waited
for her to answer, he heard a sound from behind him. Bill
must still be in the bunkhouse wrestling with, oh, maybe a
sack of potatoes.

"I would have, and I will, Mr. Garradine." Christa shook
his hand with a formal little yank, and walked away.

Trick wished Silas had left that bottle standing upright,
instead of dropping it on the floor in all that coyote mess,
because he sure didn't know why Christa had her back
up—again.

The mantel clock flew into one of its frenzies, reminding
Christa it was far too late on a Saturday night to do laundry.
But the air was still so blessed hot, water felt good. And the
clean smell of soap banished the bunkhouse stench.

When you hear a shot, run away from it, not toward it.
Patrick's instructions echoed as she sloshed her chemmy up
and down in the washtub, then scrubbed it against the
corrugated board. Better this innocent undergarment than
Patrick's hypocritical hide.

How dare he tell her to run, when that shot had brought
him running to the bunkhouse? With both hands braced
against the bottom of the washtub, Christa stared at the front
window, blank with reflected light. What irritated her was
not that he'd done it, but that she couldn't tell him she *knew*
he'd done it.

Oh, the hour was late and she'd started thinking in circles.
She had only Patty's white pinafore left. Tomorrow was

Sunday, after all, and she considered it suitable to look pleasing on the Lord's day. Not that there was much notice taken on this ranch.

They haven't had any time off in a long while. Isn't that what he'd said of the hands? Excusing their wildness?

Careful, she cautioned herself. She didn't want to scrub off the pinafore's buttons, just because Patrick Garradine hadn't noticed she'd been here for three Sundays and she hadn't had a day off. Wait. Hadn't he told Slim Jim not to ride in for breakfast? That they were all staying out on the range?

Christa rinsed the suds from her hands and hung the garments on the indoor line she'd rigged in the pantry. No one, not even Patty, would see. Not even Patty, since Christa always rose first. Her bloomers, chemises, and Patty's pinafore would dry by morning, since no drop of moisture wet this Nevada air. She yawned, knowing she could take the garments down and fold them before she walked across to the cookhouse.

But what of breakfast? King Patrick hadn't decreed a halt for her. Christa pushed back the damp sleeves of her nightdress and picked up the washtub. She'd drenched the whole front of her gown by the time she'd carried the tub to the porch, poured the water on her struggling herbs, dried the tub and hauled it back into the pantry.

Christa doused the lamps, using moonlight to guide her steps toward Patty, snug and smack in the middle of the bed. This must stop. But not this minute. Her damp gown and baffling restlessness would disturb Patty.

Christa took the blanket from Patty's pallet and returned to the big room. For several nights, she'd risen to pace between the two rooms, checking that the door was barred.

Now, Christa stared from the window. A slip of moon rode high and silver in the sky. She tried to absorb its cool desert beauty, just in case Patrick Garradine got his way and sent her back to Sacramento, where gas lights and rooftops corralled even the Heavens.

* * *

"What's wrong?" Christa leaned against the barred door, disoriented by her stumbling walk from the couch, confused that minutes before she usually rose, someone had knocked at the cabin door.

"Nothing's wrong." Patrick's voice flowed through the door, soothing her as if she were a fractious filly.

Christa stayed there, head pillowed against the barred door.

"Christa!"

"Yes?" She lifted the bar.

Josh bounded past her before the door completely opened, and a chill breeze followed Patrick inside. Christa picked through her muddled thoughts. She was miffed with him. She couldn't recall what he'd done to cause this soggy grudge.

Memory focused and Christa remembered his uppity orders. Somehow she didn't care. She wanted to crawl into his warm hypocritical arms.

Patrick must have felt the same temptation she did, because his arms surrounded her. She kept her eyes closed. *I'm not even awake,* she excused herself, but dim consciousness tantalized her into counting the layers of cloth between them. No chemise, no bloomers, no stays, only her nightdress and his shirt. Two.

"You shouldn't have to wake up saying 'What's wrong?'" His lips moved next to her ear and Christa shivered. His protection was sweet.

Unless. She blinked the table and couch into focus. Unless he meant she *wouldn't* wake asking the question if she returned to Sacramento. Christa pushed off Patrick's chest and stepped back.

"Mornin'." His lazy smile enticed her, but Christa stayed out of reach. "You don't have to cook breakfast. I came for canned goods."

"All right," she said, as he moved toward the pantry.

What would she do with a vacation? She'd dawdle over

mealtimes with Patty. She'd pamper her herbs. She might read on the banks of Mud Meadow Creek and let tiny silver fish nibble her toes. But she'd long for a glimpse of him.

"How long will you be gone?"

"Hard to say."

Christa sat on the couch, frankly appalled at herself. Patrick had seen her in her nightdress, twice. And had she rushed about, squawking over propriety and pulling on clothes? No. She'd only wished the moments at the door had lasted longer.

How shocking. Maybe she had degenerated into what Silas had called her last night. She wasn't sure of its exact meaning. Nathan had been more multisyllabic in his choice of names.

Her laundry. Mercy, her bloomers and chemise hung in the pantry. If Patrick hadn't expired of mortification, he might have been garroted by her clothesline.

He hadn't. He returned carrying a grain sack full of clanking cans and a tin of crackers.

"I want to show you something." His expression hovered between solemn and cautious, mirroring the closed, resisting look he'd worn that first day she'd appeared on his porch.

Hadn't she pulled him past that? Even if he feared for her, couldn't he see the shared days of cooking and eating, digging and riding, had bound them together?

"All right," she said. "Show me."

"Not here."

"Where, then?" Waiting for his answer, she listened as Patty shifted in bed. Routine called for letting Patty doze until the hands finished breakfast. Then Christa led her, tousled but dressed, to the table for a few minutes of society. By those rules, she shouldn't wake for another two hours.

"You need to get dressed." Faced away, Patrick prodded the delicate sweet potato vine creeping along the mantel.

"Is it far or just out in the yard? In the barn? Patrick, stop being mysterious."

"Christa, I want you to come alone. We won't be long."

Outrageous. Impossible that his quiet words cranked her pulse into a pounding torrent. Then a quick shake of his head, perhaps to himself, told her it wasn't lovemaking he had in mind. At Goldwing Seep, with his hands searching out paths to flesh, she'd seen him ardent. Now, he looked wooden.

"You want me to leave Patty? At home, when she woke up and couldn't find me, she was terrified." Even as she spoke, Christa couldn't picture that happening here. *Home* in Sacramento meant a shuttered, hollow house with shadowy corridors and astringent smells. Here, Patty would likely play on the porch with Josh, spinning the top for him to paw to a standstill.

But there could be strangers and snakes. She could get lost. Patrick's worries were real, and deeply imprinted on her.

"I can't leave her alone. What if we take the wagon?"

"It's not far, just upriver. I think there's something you'll like. I'll carry her."

Christa wrapped Patty in a blanket and gave her to Patrick, wondering why he worked so hard at holding himself apart.

Upstream, perhaps a mile, set back from Mud Meadow Creek on a brow of dry yellow weeds, lay the remains of a homestead. Its stone walls had been scattered by weather, animals, and time, but the hands that dug the foundation had built for forever. Though blackened by smoke and fire, the rock underpinnings and half a fireplace remained, delineating the shape of the one-room cabin.

Christa stood in its center. From here, she looked down on Patrick's barn and house, then straight across the creek. The homesteaders had picked a safe place. Intruders could be seen for miles across the river, before they had a chance to ride down the bank, ford the creek, then spur uphill again.

This family would have had plenty of time to ride for the security of the fort.

On the opposite bank, wind stirred a stand of mountain mahogany, then ruffled the trees. She smelled willows, cottonwoods, and sun-dried grass, borne on an updraft.

"Who lived here?"

"Don't know. It was here before the fort."

"Oh?" So, if you saw trouble coming, where did you go? Christa looked behind her, to the sparse grasslands skirting miles of desert alkali.

"Can you tell how the fire started?"

Patrick shrugged and readjusted Patty in his arms.

Had a log rolled out of the fireplace, from under a cooking pot, past a cradle? Had there been an Indian attack? A brushfire?

Christa stepped over the back boundary and studied the ground, looking for evidence of the people who'd lived here, for any sign Patrick was wrong; she would not accept another example of Nature's savagery.

At first, she saw nothing but a hump of grass, greener than the rest, where the outhouse had stood. Then she bent closer to the ground and plucked it from the dirt.

"It's my guess," she said, sashaying over to Patrick as if she were one of Pinkerton's detectives, "that this family departed long before the fire. Want to know why?"

"Sure," Patrick said, but she saw him saving his smile for her fanciful evidence.

Christa held the shard of sun-purpled grass up so it sparkled before his eyes.

"Because this is the bottle from the wine they used to toast their trek to the goldfields of California in 1849!"

Finally, the black tips of his mustache stirred. He looked down at his boots and shook his head, then moved Patty higher on his shoulder. And when he walked closer, to gesture with his elbow, he brushed her skirts in passing. It almost seemed intentional.

"*That's* what I wanted you to see."

Because the ruins were so stark, she'd missed the strawberry plants flanking the entrance to the house. Lush emerald leaves framed tiny white flowers with yellow centers. Vining runners flowed out for yards.

"Oh, Patrick!" She sank so suddenly, air whooshed through her skirts. When she slanted a smile up at him, he returned it. "They're not wild strawberries, either. They're domestic! Someone planted them and they've thrived for . . . When was the fort built?"

He shrugged, but she gestured for him to guess.

"Maybe '62?"

"So these have been here at least eight years, probably longer." She walked around the plants, studying them from every angle. "These delicate little city dwellers survived in the wilderness, alone, for all those years." She crossed her arms in front of her and gave Patrick a smug nod.

"Now, why do you look like that?" he asked.

"Why did you bring me out here?" she countered. He didn't look anything but bewildered.

"Because I thought you might like to move some of them to your little garden. I thought it would be a nice plant and you might make some more of that shrub drink."

He stared at the ruins, frowning, then his blue eyes swung back to her face, realizing what she'd thought.

"Hellfire, woman, don't go looking for trouble. Between us, we got plenty, without making it up."

"I'm sorry." Since he couldn't escape while carrying a sleeping child, Christa stood on tiptoe and kissed his cheek.

Gently, she pinched off starts from the hardy strawberry plants and wrapped them in Patrick's calico handkerchief. With corners tied, it made a nice fat bundle, pregnant with the possibility of pies and jams and cooling drinks. Christa held it with great care as they walked back downhill, toward the creek.

"Look at this." Patrick pointed before they reached the water. "Look how low this is runnin'."

"I noticed the other night. It even sounds different. Maybe it will rain soon."

"And maybe this drought will just keep on, till I've got nothing to sell but jerky on the hoof." He shaded his eyes to scan the banks. "This ain't natural. Want to walk upstream with me? I could go get Freckles, but it's not much further."

It was a lot further. Patty had awakened and walked agreeably beside them for some time before she mentioned her hunger. Christa distracted her, pointing out a silvery trout, a ground squirrel, a pumpkin-shaped cloud.

"I'm starvin'." Patty mimicked Bloody Jim's bass voice to perfection, but Christa knew that if the temptation kept soaring, Patty's good humor would end.

Christa wanted to help Patrick. This side-by-side work was exactly how she'd hoped to prove herself. But not with a hungry child tugging at her skirts.

Three miles from the ranch house, the ground turned marshy beneath their feet. They had reached the source of the problem, but Patty was the first to notice the marker left so they wouldn't miss it.

"My bonnet!"

Patty's yellow bonnet, the one she'd worn for their wild ride to the cow camp, hadn't ended in this tree by mischance. Bobbing from a cottonwood branch, it dangled from its strings, which were tied in a rough bow. Below it, a disorderly stone dam slowed the creek, forcing the waters to overflow and turn the banks into mudflats.

In spite of the eerie placement of Patty's bonnet, Christa searched for a logical explanation.

"Beavers?" Christa hazarded, lifting her eyebrows and shoulders at the same time.

Patrick acknowledged her guess with such sharp disagreement, Christa clapped her palms over Patty's ears and winced.

Fifteen

Since the day started as a calamity, Christa had no reason to think it would improve as the sun rose overhead. It didn't.

Patty sat on the muddy bank, proclaiming her hunger in every word combination she could devise, while Christa and Patrick rolled boulders off the makeshift dam, out of the creek's path. Water rushed forth, causing their smooth-soled shoes to slip and each of them to fall. Christa's knees and backside ached, probably purpling with the same bruises as her palms.

Foot-crushing trial and error taught them they couldn't replace the boulders on the creek banks. The villains probably found it simple to tumble them off the edge, down into the creek, and into a rough dam. Rolling the boulders back up banks slick with mud proved impossible.

If only she'd heeded Patrick's protest that this wasn't women's work, Christa's hands wouldn't sting with blisters, her back muscles wouldn't grab in breathtaking spasms, and her gray calico might be suited for something other than a dust rag.

One hour into the labor, Christa questioned her sanity. Why had she wanted to prove her aptitude for hard Western work? Winning Patrick through seduction, preferably in a cool hotel overlooking foggy San Francisco Bay, held far greater appeal.

Not that Patrick deserved her help. Christa wiped sweat and creek water off her upper lip and glared at him. Patrick had not shown himself to be a paragon under pressure. The

155

riding heels of his boots had felled him as often as Christa's skirts had tripped her, but Patrick took each mishap as a personal affront. Even vigilant Patty had given up reprimanding his curses.

In addition to all that, Patrick vowed to kill the Yates brothers. Since Coyote had no sheriff and the territorial police wouldn't come this far north for anything less than a massacre, enforcement of basic human decency fell to him.

Though Christa objected, Patrick insisted on a grunt-punctuated recital of his case against the Yateses. They'd turned rogue, first killing the heifer, then furiously refusing the offer of the meat.

"You don't suppose you could have provoked him? With your insistence that you'd know if they stepped foot on your ranch?" Christa readjusted her hold on a boulder wide as her shoulders.

Three more to go. She dropped her burden with a splash, glanced up to locate Patty, then heard the echo of her sarcasm when Patrick turned slack-jawed as if she'd betrayed him.

She bent to embrace the next rock. Squatting in icy water didn't improve her subtlety.

"I only meant"—she fought her fingers' numbness as she grappled with the next rock—"that they might have taken it as a dare."

"That's because you're not a man."

"Maleness, I would say, guarantees it."

Only two more boulders. Patty, thank the Lord, had kept to her dry patch of ground, out of the mud.

"Hey." Patrick grabbed Christa's elbow as she slogged toward midstream. "You're not one of them upstart suffragettes, are you? Wanting the vote . . . and all."

His sudden interest in her soaked and clinging dress delayed his last words. The man could provoke temper from a toad.

"I haven't given it much thought, Mr. Garradine, but I think suffragetting might suit me." She slid free of his hand.

"Mama, I want biscuits."

"I know, baby. Soon."

"And there's two more things makes me believe the Yateses are on the warpath." Unhurt by her snub, Patrick returned to his avenger's refrain, toting another rock. He squinted past her, musing, until his arms trembled from the boulder's weight.

"The rocks?" She tried to hurry him along. His forearms' veins bulged as if they'd burst, and still he held the boulder.

"Rocks and the bonnet *and* the sound at the cabin. Never did take that as an animal." Patrick stared at Patty. Frowning and thoughtful, he hefted the boulder and his denims slipped down an inch. "I don't like that a bit." Finally he cast the rock away. "Can't count it as a prank, if it scares a child."

Christa followed Patrick's interested look and recoiled. Belly down, Patty squirmed in the mud like a piglet.

"P—" Christa let the maternal reprimand die.

Absorbed in play, Patty had forgotten her hunger. Cleanliness was probably not truly next to godliness, anyway. Patty sat up and mud flowed down her front like chocolate. Christa tried to avert her eyes, but when Patty took handfuls of mud, slapping them to the front of her like breasts, Christa groaned. It was too late for the nightgown. Patty had just crushed any hope of laundry day salvation.

"Buggy." Patty aimed a coated finger across the plain.

Together, she and Patrick shoved the last huge boulder from the center of the creek. Christa couldn't lift her arms in celebration.

"Yes, sugar," Patrick panted. "If you see piggity, just let me know."

"Not piggity; I think she said—"

Christa shaded her eyes and stared toward the horizon. Water dripped from her cuff to her nose. *Oh, no. Please, no.*

"Bug-gy," Patty enunciated, pointing.

Hannah Hacklebord drove the mercantile delivery wagon. Though the Coyote shopkeeper had been less than civil, Christa dreaded the hike home in these squishing boots and would have welcomed conveyance. Would have, if she hadn't spotted the hat. Purple petals fluttered on a circle wide as a chandelier hoop. The lady seated next to Hannah could only be Polly LaCrosse.

Oh, fiddle. They already thought her a murderess. It shouldn't matter that she stood soaked and gaping like a carp. It shouldn't matter that Patty, at midday on the Sabbath, was dressed in a muddy nightgown. It shouldn't matter that Patrick had deserted them both.

Unperturbed, he shambled ashore. "Morning, ladies."

"More like afternoon, Patrick Garradine," called Polly. As the buggy drew nearer, she added, "Lands, don't be polite when you've obviously suffered a terrible accident!"

The dressmaker's scrutiny made Christa's seemly nature revolt.

Yes! she wanted to scream. *Yes, I forced him to deed the ranch to me! Then I dragged him three miles upstream to drown him!* Maniacal laughter rang so clearly in her head, Christa feared she'd actually cackled.

"Trouble with water flow." Patrick shrugged, as if it pained him to explain. "Mrs. Worth kindly helped me get it goin'."

Heaven knew that Patty was a good child, a sweet, smart, loving child, but her shyness before strangers was hard to tolerate just now. As Christa came ashore, Patty scuttled around behind her. Instead of burying her face in Christa's skirts, she lifted the damp swathes to drape herself like a gray ghost.

"Patty," Christa said, under her breath. "Patty, stop it!" She refused to have her sodden bloomers exposed.

"Hungry!" Patty gulped, then burst into tears.

"Poor little thing." Hannah laid one hand over her heart. "But I have something in my wagon that will cheer her up."

Probably Patrick's new shovel handle, and wouldn't Patty just chortle with glee? Such sarcasm, even unspoken, bordered on unchristian. Christa reminded herself it was the Sabbath, and tried to repent.

"Are we there?" A deeper version of her own clipped Boston vowels rose from the wagon bed, like a voice from a grave.

"Dan?" Christa hurried forward with Patty hampering her every step.

"Sis!"

Dan sat up suddenly, as if he were hinged at the hips. The movement was awkward, unnatural. His white-blond hair hung shaggy over his forehead, reaching to his sun-bleached eyelashes. He looked just as mischievous as he had the day he'd pushed her, "dead," from their tree house. But why did he recline in the back of the mercantile wagon instead of riding a horse?

"Sis, am I glad to see you." He placed both arms behind him, palms down, to support a more upright position. "Got to blame this on somebody!"

"What happened, Danny?" Merciful Heavens, how like him to joke through some tragic maiming or the loss of a limb. "Let me see."

"She always did like to see my wounds. Skinned knee, cut finger, stubbed toe, any kind of mutilation'd do." He winked at Patrick.

Christa's hands trembled as she chinned herself to look over the wagon's sides. A striped blanket covered his legs.

"Aw, Sis, don't look like that. It's just broken!"

He flipped the blanket back. When she saw the splint and binding that verified his words, Christa turned away, blinking.

It was just this whole stupid day! It was just piggity and Patrick, her aching muscles and Dan's sweet familiarity.

"There's something in my eye." She motioned blindly to Patty. "Come see your uncle Dan."

"Uncle Dan is a lucky boy." Polly opened her parasol with a snap, startling the buggy horse into jumping sideways against the shafts. "He'd just arrived from Reno as we were leaving church."

"We took it as a sign we should come visit, Mrs. Worth. Polly and I have meant to, for weeks."

"Where's your horse, Trick?" Dan cut through the mannerly excuses. "Don't see Imp, Cloud, nor none of your string."

Mother might have started up screaming, all the way across the continent from her grave, at Dan's appalling grammar.

Patrick's muttered response snapped Dan's head back on his neck. Apparently he couldn't comprehend a cowboy walking, unless misfortune cast him afoot.

"Then you must ride with us." Polly broadened her invitation with a smirk. "You, too, of course. And your youngster."

"Her name's Patty." Patrick lifted her by both armpits. "Don't kick your uncle, sugar. Though I don't know what a lamed rider's good for."

Patrick settled Patty, then climbed up beside her. Christa marveled anew at Patty's effect on him. Even though he'd wanted to leave her behind this morning, Patty softened Patrick's disposition. Holding her, he'd rattled off more congenial words than he had all morning.

When Patrick reached down to help her into the wagon bed, a smile tilted the tips of his mustache, and Christa saw it dawn on him just what a lamed rider was good for. She handed him the bundled strawberry plants, then Patrick's hand engulfed hers in a gentle tug as he cast his voice back over his shoulder.

"Hey, Dan, since you can't fork a horse and harass my cattle, how'd you like to ride herd on your niece? Just temporary, of course."

Scarlet sunlight fading on jagged mountain peaks . . .
Lavender shadows stretching across the playa . . .

"Mrs. Worth, that will be quite enough tea!" Polly LaCrosse leaned back from the outdoor plank table, fearful Christa's pouring would overflow the cup, into her lap.

"I'm sorry." Chagrined, Christa stopped just in time.

Since Patrick's hand had closed in that knowing squeeze, she'd imagined a dozen intimate evening rides. Those fantasies interfered with the operation of her arms, legs, and mind.

Hard male legs parted the green reeds fringing Goldwing Seep. . . .

"Sis, let me hostess this tea party while you get into dry clothes. You're shivering."

In fact, Dan, with his foot propped on a chair set beside the plank table, had done just that since Patrick departed.

He'd entertained Patty with tales of his jouncing stage-coach ride from Sacramento to Reno and pantomimed the squinty knife grinder who'd conveyed him as far as Coyote. Other than pouring too much tea, serving seed cakes, molasses cookies, and sourdough bread with Hannah Hackle-bord's gift of strawberry preserves, Christa had done nothing but daydream.

Each time she jerked her mind back, she intercepted arched-brow looks flashing between her visitors.

Polly presented Christa with a scarf fashioned in the purple-edged black of half-mourning. It flowed a yard long and floated like thistledown.

"It's the simplest thing I make." Polly stemmed Christa's praise with a dismissive wave. "Just cut and hem, honestly."

But it was the ladies' last offering that convinced Christa to take Dan's advice and withdraw.

Polly snatched a letter from her reticule. "Alvin said to pass it along."

Christa held the letter by one corner, wondering if it had been steamed open and resealed.

"Dan, though I feel a perfect goose accepting, I will let you play host while I see to Patty's nap and changing."

"About time." Neither lady looked shocked by Dan's sibling bossiness.

Stalling, Patty dipped in a curtsy and shook each woman's hand. Polly tolerated the touch, but Hannah was charmed.

"Oh, my Hetty would just eat you up like apple cake." Hannah pressed her cheek against Patty's. "I'm sorry she's away at school."

With round, alarmed eyes, Patty wriggled loose and returned to her mother. Hannah flashed Christa an empathetic look.

"I miss Hetty every day. She's away at normal school, you know, learning to be a proper teacher. She did just fine, being our schoolmarm without any college, but some of the big boys did harass her.

"My Henrietta was the readingest child Coyote ever had and never no trouble." Hannah's boasting ended in a sigh. "Just pray Hetty's back before this angel's ready for sums and reading."

"Will you be here that long, Mrs. Worth?" Polly rolled her shoulders in a slink that caught Dan's attention. "I surmised, from a talk with Miss Pilgrim, that you'd be returning home as soon as the stage runs again." She clucked her tongue. "Silly old cat."

"Our plans are not yet definite." Christa's stiff-necked propriety might not suit her attire, but it matched her mood. "Please, excuse me."

With Patty settled in a fresh nightgown, Christa tried to open the letter. Her fingers refused. No news written in Francesca's ant-tracks hand could be good.

Christa changed to fresh clothes, watching the letter as if it might leap from the table and hurl itself at her. Dressed, she stared at it, turned it over, then lifted the flap. Still, she couldn't remove the letter. Finally she centered it on the mantel, where Danny was bound to inquire about it.

When Christa returned, Dan had Polly and Hannah tittering. No doubt, her Boston-schooled brother stacked up well against Coyote's clever gentlemen.

Yes, she'd let Dan sharpen his wit by performing a humorous interpretation of Francesca's letter. Francesca's misspellings alone would provide amusement, and after lone weeks on the range, Dan must be ready for recreation.

After the women's awkward departure, Christa found herself alone with her brother. She sat in Patrick's hearthside chair, while Dan, propped up on the couch, mourned the passing of Patrick's medicinal whiskey.

"I could have used some, Sis. Because I must ask you a mighty tough question. Explain to me why a man who's been a reasonably good brother for twenty-five years of his life—"

"Dan, excuse me. I'm only twenty-one."

"Don't try to lead me off the scent, Christabel. Just answer me this: Why wasn't I told about Francesca Worth? Why was I allowed to arrive, guileless, suitcase in hand, at her lair?" He shifted and grimaced. "What about brandy?" he added. "If the whiskey's gone. Riding in that grocery wagon has these bone ends reminding me they need peace and quiet to knit."

Christa slipped into the pantry and studied the shelves.

"Would hard cider do?" She pulled out a cork and recoiled at the smell.

"Only if it's not ungodly sweet and full of little black specks."

"Well . . ."

"I'll settle for a tin cup of water."

Once he held the cup cradled to his chest, Christa made her excuses. "I wrote that I was coming to Good Thunder Meadows, but I suppose you were out on the range. And long before that I mentioned how difficult—"

"Excuse me, Sis. A rattler in your bedroll is difficult. A bitch wolf in heat is difficult. Francesca Worth—"

"You needn't curse, Danny." She suppressed a giggle, remembering how Father had stormed at her for encouraging her brother's wit. "I know precisely what Francesca is."

"It's a lack of cursing that got me this bum leg." He patted his thigh. "If I'd been able to tell off the—old girl—I wouldn't have had a yen to scamper drunk through a neighborhood where folks think it's quite the thing to throw decomposed vegetables in the street."

"Ugh." Laughter quaked beneath the arms she wrapped over her ribs. "Not *my* neighborhood."

"Of course not." He narrowed his eyes down a mock snooty nose. "Would you like to know how much extra damage I did, dragging myself a half block to escape the curs guarding that unsavory slum?"

"Poor Danny." This was *not* funny. It was appalling. Sordid.

"Thank God, the constable finally caught up with me."

"Constable?" Christa sputtered with laughter and every rock-taxed muscle punished her.

Satisfied with quashing her dignity, Danny continued in a more sober manner.

"Then the real fun began. For two solid weeks, I could not escape. I begged to be taken to a charity ward, but Francesca would not be deprived of her Christian duty. I remained a victim of her tender care for two weeks."

Pawing sounded at the door and Christa rose to admit Josh.

"Here, boy." Dan offered his hand, palm up. "Hasn't Trick shot you yet?"

Josh skirted Dan and skittered into the bedroom. He paced, then collapsed with a groan. Christa had no doubt that Josh had hidden under the porch, afraid of Polly and Hannah.

"So, tell me the truth, did you finally do in Nathan like I should have three years ago?"

"You know I wouldn't." She stood and arranged her sweet potato vines so they made a symmetrical arrangement. "Dan, there are a few things too serious to joke about."

"Not Nathan Worth's death." A nerve at the corner of Dan's eye beat in an unrelenting tug. "Oh, all right, Christa, hand me that cup of cider. Gad! It's awful! Promise not to give me any more.

"I'm the one who brought him home from school. I'm the one who believed in him enough to ride with you two across the continent, to follow him off to find water while you delivered Patty. God! Was I ever so young and stupid? Thinking Nathan Worth was man enough to teach me what that meant?

"And I left you with him. I'll have to live with that, although I should think that two weeks alone with Francesca counts ten years off my time in hell." Dan waggled his eyebrows, then turned serious.

"I think she has it in for you, Sis. I wouldn't worry much, because I don't think she's as smart as she is mean, but she has a lawyer working with her." Dan frowned at the cider dregs.

Francesca wouldn't have hired the bank's attorney or Nathan's personal consultant. Francesca had hated them both when they'd circled the uncertain estate like vultures. Who, then, and what had changed her mind?

"Who is he?" Christa asked.

"We weren't introduced." Dan wiped his lips. "The curse of this crutch is its stumping racket. I only heard what drifted upstairs. Precious little, but intriguing. So, figuring I had nothing to lose, I asked her about it. In sort of a general way."

"And what did she say?"

"The same drivel as before: You killed him, you hadn't been punished, and for the good of your immortal soul and her bank book, you needed to be punished."

"Francesca did not say that, Dan." Christa interlaced her fingers in her lap. "She knows I'll give her anything she wants. I never want to live in that house again, with those sad-eyed elk and curtains reeking of tobacco. She's welcome to it."

"You're not going back? You're staying here?"

"I—" There would be liberation in saying the words, in

declaring independence from streetcars and lampposts, face powder and stays and damning looks. But it also meant cutting Patty free of education, physicians, and pretty clothes. "I don't know."

"Well, if you plan to marry, don't settle for any old cowboy." He laughed, apparently amused at the mental picture he was about to share. "You ought to put your loop on Trick. He's—" The eyes that teased her sharpened. "He—"

"Never mind, Dan."

"Right. I know you have the horseback skills to remain, and that sourdough bread was first-rate. How long have you been alone with him, Christabel?"

"I said never mind. Finish telling me about Francesca and the lawyer."

"She never gave me a logical answer, but she'd been quoting scripture—not very accurately, I might add—so I asked if she shouldn't let Jehovah do 'Vengeance is mine' accounting for Himself."

"I doubt she liked that." Christa resettled in Patrick's chair. The scent of wood smoke wafted up from its cushion and she found it strangely comforting. She grinned at the image of Francesca's wrathful face.

"Actually, I think she set me up." Dan swigged down the dregs of the cider. "She told me 'God helps those who help themselves,' and flounced out of the room with her nose in the air."

In the end, Christa took the unopened letter to bed with her. With Patty asleep on her pallet and Dan ensconced on the couch, Christa tried to imagine the letter's contents. Invocation of God, of course, because Francesca believed comfortable circumstances proved He was on her side. Faulty spelling, since Francesca's schooling ended at grade six. Perhaps threats?

In her final determination to get it over with, Christa ripped open the envelope, wrinkling the sheet inside. She shook the paper straight and began reading.

Dear Christabel,

Trust this letter find you and Patricia healthy in the Godless desert of Coyote. Such sudden leaving pushes some to an admishant of guilt. Nathan's daughter deserves more than banishmnt. Come back and face the questions and your rightfull punishment or you may expect a sipena from Mr. Frost, Atty at Law.

Remember what happened befor. When you were so headstrong.

Yours in Christian sisterhood,

Francesca Worth

Remember what happened before, when you were so headstrong? Oh, poisonous Francesca.

Sixteen

Trick sat his horse on the ridge overlooking the Yates place. He'd been there long enough that all five dogs but the wall-eyed one had quit barking, long enough to shrug off the pity he'd feel seeing all three Yateses together. By that time, damn it, he'd dulled the edge of his anger, too.

He loosed his reins and let Freckles pick his way downhill. The horse shifted left, right, left, balancing the rub and weight of the saddle scabbard as he negotiated the steep path. The Yateses had plenty of time to heed Trick's approach.

When Arthur stepped out carrying a rifle and Thad followed, wearing his holster tied down gunslinger style, Trick knew he'd been noticed. The old man leaned against the front wall of the house, crutches spread to take his meager weight. Every week, the brothers took Daddy Yates into the Pilgrims' to tempt his appetite. For all their coaxing, the old man lived on corn bread and stubborn pride.

"What in hell you want, Yank?" the old man yelled, his voice high as a girl's.

Arthur shifted. His rifle barrel reared up a notch. Trick knew they expected him to show his hands clear of the reins. But the backbreaking morning and Patty's bonnet bobbing from a branch had soured his disposition. And Arthur wasn't likely to shoot him. It wasn't the Southerner's style.

Luckily, Freckles didn't share Imp's jackrabbit nature. When Arthur's bullet kicked dirt at Freckles' front feet, the Appaloosa only shifted his rump in disapproval, then rolled his eyes at the five ugly hounds snapping around him. Thad whistled, the dogs subsided, and Arthur spoke.

"My daddy asked you a question, Garradine."

Trick had figured on dismounting and having a civilized conversation with them. Civilized. He knew just where that fool idea had come from. Christa.

Just because Christa had tenderized *him* didn't mean the Yateses would act civilized. Arthur's shot had proven it. Trick stayed mounted.

"I want your sons to stay off my land if they don't know how to behave."

"Seems like we've heard that before," Thad taunted.

"Yank's talking to me, boy," the old man said. "Go on."

"There's been several things, but I spent all morning today clearing boulders out of the creek."

"Couldn't do it alone, could you?" Thad gibed.

"You sat around and watched a female do a man's job?" Trick started to mention Southern chivalry, but his mind snagged on the image of Christa wearing wet, clinging calico.

"The little blond widow?" The old man dismissed the idea. "Yateses wouldn't let her do that. Why did you?"

Trick couldn't answer the second part of the question, so he tackled the first.

"I won't argue. Someone blocked the flow and hung the little girl's bonnet so I'd be sure to see. That bothered the child and her mama. This ain't no neighborly joke."

To wipe that grin off Thad's face, he'd probably need a gun. Too bad. Any other man in the territory would heed a fist's warning to stop relishing the way Christa had looked, wet down and working.

The wall-eyed cur growled. Trick let his hands and legs tell Freckles he was doing just fine. Trick waited.

The old man wouldn't grill his sons in front of an enemy. When old Yates's pallor turned more sickly, Trick confronted them with the rest of it.

"Another thing. Someone's been sniffing around my

ranch house." Trick let his eyes stop on each face. "I don't hold with scaring children. Mrs. Worth's brother Dan is staying with her. Dan keeps an old Sharps that'd blow a man from here to breakfast. You know what I keep." Trick let his hand fall to his saddle scabbard.

"We'll pass it along, Garradine," said Arthur.

"To the bogeyman." Thad nodded.

Trick felt an itch in his knuckles. Nothing but Thad's chin could cure it.

Arthur caught his father's nod and motioned with the rifle barrel. "You're making my dogs nervous. Ride on."

Before Trick turned his horse, old Yates slumped, then sagged. Thad spun to support him and eased him down to the porch. Arthur reached for a flask. From one of them came a sound like a mewling babe.

Maybe that's why the war never ended. Folks, and not only those who'd fought, were still dying from it.

This was Heaven. This was how a man was meant to live.

As Trick rode out, blue sky vaulted up and over him. Madrone and sage shook in the breeze, releasing incense and sound like a Paiute's prayer for good medicine. The horse under him—a mustang he'd caught two days ago—tested him at every turn and he'd caught every feint. Behind him a couple hundred head of cattle lowed, almost ready for that long walk to the railhead.

All the good medicine he needed was here, but five days without Christa had Trick feeling like this bronc's flinty hooves had stove in his chest.

It wasn't the grub. Hot canned goods beat lizards and berries, and he'd lived on both before. It wasn't muscles tight from sleeping on the ground. He wouldn't weep if he never saw the inside of that bunkhouse, again. And it wasn't Christa's pretty face, or even her child's, though their sweetness worked magic on a man who lived among men.

It wasn't worry, either. Trick knew Christa was doing fine. Before riding out, he'd checked everything from the buckles on the harness they'd rigged for Betsy to the hinges on the henhouse door. He'd even cast a quick eye over the roof, since Heaven knew the U.S. Cavalry wouldn't build roofs to last. Crippled as he was, Dan would act as her fearless protector. Instead of him.

A cold wind kicked up and the crazy claybank colt humped his back and bucked. He spun. He sunfished. He showed his heels to the larks. Though the unplanned rodeo cheered Trick, the colt's contortions were tame compared to the twisted confusion in his heart.

"I didn't have anyone to take care of—" Christa began.

"Except for me, Patty, Josh—" Dan sat in the buckboard beside her, pretending he could rattle off names all day.

"—so I decided," Christa talked right over her brother, "I'd bake enough cinnamon cookies that everyone could have as many as they wanted." She crossed the ends of a shawl over her breasts. With barely any help, she jumped down from the wagon and lifted a hamper from the back.

Trick had captured two steers that had been castrated and branded, then escaped last year's roundup. Satisfied and ready to brag, he'd run the beasts back and spent an hour easing them into the herd before he loped into camp to discover why he was the only one riding herd.

Once there, he heard Christa's voice and saw the men's enthusiastic surge toward the wagon. Trick led the mustang to the edge of camp. From there, he watched her.

Christa pushed her sleeves halfway to her elbows, then let down the tailgate of Muley's chuck wagon and propped it. She folded a white cloth back from the basket.

"Preach, is your leg acting up?" Even with her back turned to the men, she coddled them.

"No, ma'am, just sidestepped a contrary bull. It's fine."

"Billy, don't be so shy. I haven't seen you in days. Have you decided what to do with that coyote hide?"

At his silence, she didn't turn, knowing that would have scared even the gestures out of him. Instead, Christa glanced over her shoulder to catch Bill Williams spreading his hands wide enough to span a horse. He poised his fingers near his collar bone and made rolling motions. Christa nodded, still fiddling with the cloth. Then Bill frowned profound enough to start up a poem.

"Like a collar for your coat?" Christa suggested.

Trick went slack-jawed as every other man in camp. Did she really understand Bill? She couldn't be funnin' with him. That wasn't Christa's way.

Bill's slow smile hid behind his coffee cup, but not a soul missed it.

Trick peered over the claybank. Christa wouldn't recognize the horse, so he stood behind it, watching over his saddle as Christa doled out cookies and affection. Her quick fingers tucked wisps back into her braid as she scanned the camp. She watched Patty ride Bloody Jim Black like a pony. Her green eyes brightened as Dan jawed with his buddies. She rubbed her neck as if it were stiff and wheeled around to study the terrain behind her.

Me, Christa? Is it me you're looking for?

He felt a catch in his chest as she took a cup of coffee from Pete, gracious as if he'd offered a diamond necklace. The young Texan was head over heels for her, even after the talking-to she'd given him.

Dan leaned from the wagon bed to confide something and Trick decided it was a good thing Dan had returned when he did. Otherwise, he'd have left Pete, with his horse leg revolver, as Christa's guardian. That would have been pure disaster.

"I thought you hated wild animals dead and stuffed," Dan muttered. "Why are you taking notice of a butchered coyote? Not that Bill isn't beside himself with joy."

"That's—" Christa began, but Ramon's low laughter covered the rest.

Enough. Ramon, a true vaquero, his best hand, had deserted the herd for Christa.

"Would've been back sooner if I'd known the circus

come to town." Trick strode out with the skittish mustang hanging at the end of the reins.

Christa's eyelids lowered and blood sprang up in her cheeks. She looked rosy and excited with promise, making Trick wonder where he'd got the nerve to hold her in her nightgown, to feel no stays, no underpinnings, nothing but woman flesh under the smooth linen. That look disappeared when she caught his sarcasm, when the others—with handfuls of cookies—remounted.

"I'm sorry if our arrival took your men from their work, Mr. Garradine."

She was all stiff disappointment, calling him "mister" and staring down at the half-emptied hamper so he wouldn't see how she'd counted on him. And what if *he'd* been the one, running to her with a bunch of flowers or some such? What if she'd acted too busy to notice?

Trick swallowed and gritted his molars until he felt it at the top of his skull. He deserved her disdain. He'd asked for it, because he wanted her to desert him. Then he'd be out from under this heartache.

A loud clatter and tumble signaled Dan had found a way down from the wagon. He caught himself and stumped a couple steps away, probably sick of simmering in the heat waves running between his sister and Trick.

"I'm going to check on Patty and Crow, see how you've been treating my old pony." Dan sounded congenial enough, but Christa would be in for a grilling later.

"Betsy was glad to get out." She folded the cloth and closed the basket.

As if he were the tinker come to sell pots and pans, she smiled pleasantly, remotely. It took no mind reader to tell him she wasn't in the market.

"She looks good."

"I curried her." She moved over to the gray and when Betsy rubbed her face against the bodice of Christa's gown, knocking her back a step, she didn't mind.

"I planted the strawberries, too. They're almost ready to

bear. Even though it was a bad time to transplant them, they've perked up. I put some on each side of the porch."

Her voice was like sweet water, running on by, reminding him he'd thrown away five days with her.

"You had plenty to keep you busy," he said. "Why'd you come out here?"

Her eyes flashed from middle distance to his. They were spittin'-cat mad, but she didn't say a word, just rubbed Betsy's neck hard enough to remove the hide.

"I heard you say you didn't have anyone to take care of." If that didn't sound lame, he didn't know what did.

"Eavesdropper."

Hell, he deserved anything she wanted to dish out. It was what kept him from getting out of range.

"But I said it." She turned and plaited a piece of Betsy's mane. "It's not a chore— No, it *is* a chore, but I like taking care of your men and animals, Patrick."

That "Patrick" forgave him. He heard it, and he wanted to spin her around to face him. He wanted to pin her between him and that horse. He wanted to kiss that solemn talk right out of her. Instead, he pretended to straighten Betsy's harness. It brought him right next to her.

"One of the Gretchens is missing."

"Coyote." Come to avenge that travesty's of Bill's, maybe, but he didn't say it. He stood close enough to take her hand off Betsy and kiss it. Would that make things better or worse? *And how come he didn't know?*

"The creek's running fine, now."

"That's one thing you didn't like takin' care of, I'll wager."

"I hated it, at the time," she admitted. "Being all clumsy and wet. But last night, the three of us and Josh walked down there and the frogs were loud again, and the swallows dove down to say thanks. It was worth having wet feet for a few hours."

It was just how he felt: The work and discomfort paid off. How could Christa understand?

"The worst part was having Polly and Hannah show up." She laughed a little and started a fourth plait. Betsy'd look like a kinky-maned cart horse when she got done.

"What did they want, anyhow?" He barely cared, but Christa warmed to the gossip and proved, again, that she was no angel.

"They wanted to see how far I'd fallen. Seeing me drenched was a bonus, but I think they were a little disappointed by my seed cakes."

"What? Must not have any tasters on their tongues, then."

"No, I think they were disappointed because they couldn't keep from eating half a dozen each."

"Is that all?"

Her hands stilled. She seemed on the brink of confiding something, but she stopped, then veered the conversation back the way they'd come.

"You know, maybe that's what's wrong with Polly. She doesn't have anyone to take care of."

Why would Christa concern herself over such a witch?

"She had a cat," Trick said. "Till Alvin told her they spread disease. She drowned it."

"So she has no one. If she married, or if she adopted an orphan—"

"What's wrong with you, girl? Why would she want to take on extra work? It's not natural! Folks want to please themselves."

"What about all those chores you did, just before you left?"

"They would've had to be done sometime." What was she getting at?

"Didn't I see you checking the *roof?*"

"It could rain." She knew how to make him squirm, all right. "Besides, I don't mind doin' for you and— Hey, sugar, where you been?"

With a long lead on her uncle, Christa's daughter came running up to hug his knees.

"Careful, this new horse isn't quite broke. I don't trust

him. Get back, sugar, over by your uncle Dan. At least one member of the family knows how to stay out of harm's way."

Dan approached the wagon bed like he would a feisty horse. "Trick, can you give me a leg up here?"

He did and Christa stood at Betsy's head, though there was little chance the horse would go anywhere without being prodded.

"This tricky ol' cayuse has slipped his bit." As Trick reached across Christa to fix Coaly's bridle, his hand grazed her shoulder.

"No, I loosened his headstall when we stopped."

His fingers moved on their own, slipping the bit back to Betsy's mouth, working the strap and buckle on the headstall. He waited for her to say whatever was poised on her lips. Seemed she didn't want Dan to hear, by the way she kept glancing back.

"I like doing for you, too, Patrick Garradine," she whispered. "The only thing better," she raised her voice, then, and Dan's ears pricked right up, "would be learning to take care of your cows, and I'm working on that."

She vaulted into the driver's seat, touching him in passing, and her skirts rustled by his cheek. She unwrapped the driving lines and took them in each hand.

Christa left him standing speechless. He tried to get up the energy to remount. He watched the windswept tail of dust corkscrewing up from the wagon wheels and saw her pass Preach, who lifted his hat and kept coming.

"What the hell's wrong now" Trick asked, but he was smiling, feeling spunky as the claybank.

"Nothing. Not a thing that couldn't be fixed by you marrying that girl."

"Not another word, Preach, or you're going to be picking up your pay at Hacklebord's, along with Silas the mortician."

"Go ahead and fire me if you like, Trick, but sometimes I don't think you got nothing under that hat but your hair."

Seventeen

❧

At creekside, a hen flapped with a broken wing. Her pitiful squawks attracted Josh and they'd heard his distressed barks for ten minutes before they reached the ranch house. Dan limped down to check on the commotion while Christa hustled Patty indoors.

"Chicken and dumplings," Dan diagnosed, sticking his head inside, then withdrawing it.

Christa followed after him. Patty lay drowsing fitfully on the couch. For the first time in weeks, she'd asked to hold her charm, Trick's medicine bag, as she fell asleep. Christa closed the door behind her. "What did you do?"

"The only merciful thing, Sis. Wrung her neck."

Dan looked sheepish and Christa wondered who had taught her polished Boston brother to do such a thing. Muley? Then she remembered the other chicken.

"That's two. Two dead hens in two days."

"Maybe you miscounted. Sums were never your strong suit."

"No, there were twelve hens when Patrick left. He told Patty to count them every night when we locked up."

"Perhaps Gretchen grew tired of the barnyard and eloped with a cock from Coyote."

"You said she went for a ride *inside* a coyote," Christa reminded him.

"How clever of me." He rubbed his leg and shook his head. "No coyote would leave one out there, wounded."

"Maybe Josh scared it away."

179

Dan stared pointedly at Josh, who'd stood cowering since Dan dispatched the suffering hen.

"All right, maybe the sound of the wagon scared it."

"No. Coyotes are bold. It would have run with that Rhodie still squawking in its mouth. Rhode Island Red," he clarified with a superior nod. "That's the kind of hens you're tending. And White Leghorns."

He leaned heavily on his crutch, tilting his head to that side as if listening.

"Now, that's interesting. I wish Josh and I hadn't made such a mess down at the creek. There might have been some fascinating tracks."

"Like what?" These mysterious comings and goings chafed her nerves.

"Like . . . Not the Yates brothers, I don't expect."

"No, of course not. Two adult men wouldn't maim a chicken! I think you need a rest, Danny."

"You're right." He maneuvered back toward the house. "But I can guaran-damn-tee that's what Trick will say."

"Don't cuss."

"Why not? My niece has usurped the only place I can stretch out," he moaned.

"Trick thinks the Yateses are responsible for everything that's gone wrong, lately." Christa carried Patty to her pallet.

"Oh, that's better." Dan collapsed on the couch. "You want to let the dog in, too, Sis? His scratching is real annoying to a man trying to relax."

Christa resisted the urge to thump the white-blond head pillowed on crossed arms.

"I'll be more than happy to, Danny." She opened the door and Josh padded in to guard Patty. "Because when you're rested up, you're going to pluck that hen."

"I'd like to, Sis, but that sounds like the cook's job to me."

"Tragically," she said, standing beside him, "the cook doesn't want to. And she's far too dainty to disjoint it." Christa turned her palms up.

"We could have jerky and day-old cornbread. Patty wouldn't mind. Chicken and dumplings with black pepper gravy and green snap beans are nothing compared to those leftover cinnamon cookies."

"Who's taught you to bargain, Christa? I find it extremely unbecoming."

"That *grimace* is unbecoming. Remember what Mama used to say? Your face may get stuck like that. Now, I'm going out to tend my herbs. Have a nice nap, Danny."

They were sitting inside the cookhouse, feasting on savory if oddly shaped chicken, when Josh announced a rider. Patrick had tied his horse and already stood at the pump when Christa defied Dan's caution and left the table to see who'd arrived.

"They were eatin' rattler." Patrick explained his return and pumped a last sluice of water over his hands. "I can't abide snake when I know a real dinner's cooking."

"Hey, Trick," Dan greeted as they came in together.

"'Course I didn't tell them that." Patrick pulled a chair to the table, gave Dan a nod, and waited for Patty to look up from her dumpling. She did, then went back to eating.

What had perturbed the contrary little soul? Christa reviewed the day and came up without one slight. Even when Patrick asked Patty to step back from the young mustang, he'd complimented her.

Patrick frowned, started to speak, then covered his flash of hurt with a long drink of water.

"I told them I had to work the kinks out of this colt."

"Think they were fooled?" Dan ladled another dumpling from the kettle.

"I wasn't trying to fool them. I was trying to spare their feelings." He aimed the remark at Patty.

When he caught Christa's eye, Patrick only smoothed the damp edges of his mustache and forked chicken onto his plate. He tried to arrange it at a recognizable angle and looked like he might have joked about it with Patty, except she still wouldn't look up. Her disdain made Patrick snappish and defensive.

"If I want to sleep in a real bed and eat real cookin', that's my prerogative as boss."

"So I hear," Dan said.

"What's that supposed to mean?" Patrick lowered his fork.

"Patty, how's that gravy?" Dan asked.

"Hot!" Patty fanned her mouth in pantomime and Christa discouraged her with a stern look.

She would have made more of the rudeness if she thought she could draw Patrick's attention away from Dan. Clearly the other men had confided something Dan didn't dare tell Patrick.

"I asked what you meant, White."

Dan looked dismayed, not scared. "Nothing."

Patty kicked her feet against the chair rungs. Christa might have scolded for that, too, except it was the only sound besides chewing. The silence continued until Christa stood to clear their dishes to the wreck pan.

"No, ma'am." Patrick waved her away. "Guess I can see to yours, too, Dan. Save your leg." He juggled plates like a waiter in a Sacramento chophouse. "What about you, sugar?"

Patty hung her finger like a fishhook in the corner of her mouth. Patrick reached for her plate and she pulled the finger lower. When Patrick turned to her for advice, Christa shrugged. What had gotten into the child?

Patrick took the edge of Patty's plate, but as he eased it away, Patty slapped her palm in the middle of it, amid a smear of mashed potato, and glared at him.

"Patricia Rose Worth, you stop that!"

Patrick met Christa's anger with a mystified smile.

"Apologize to—" Patrick shook his head curtly and Christa stopped. Though she knew more of child-rearing, Patrick ruled in the arena of stubborn beasts.

She bowed to his expertise as Patty slumped over the

tabletop, burying her face in crossed arms which were, mercifully, to one side of her plate.

Patrick had scrubbed the dishes and set them to drain when he said, "I been thinking about giving them all a night off."

"That would be a nice gesture, Trick. I know they'd appreciate it." Dan leaned back in his chair as if awaiting an after-dinner brandy.

"Not till dawn, mind you, just sundown until midnight." Patrick turned, drying his hands, and Christa thought domesticity sat well on him. "Give them time to ride into Starr's and whoop a little, but not enough to get booze-blind."

"Looked like a pretty rough herd to handle alone."

"That's a fact, Dan. One heifer even broke her own neck. I'll need some help nighthawking."

"I'd like to do it." Dan studied the leg he'd propped on a bench. Christa saw his good judgment crumble. "Do you think—?"

"I think you on any horse would be suicide just now. But Mrs. Worth said she wanted to learn to handle cattle."

Dan slapped a palm on the table. Very like his niece, Christa thought. Then she met Patrick's gaze and her levity faded, leaving her mind filled with a single word.

Yes. Patrick's open-sky eyes clouded and he looked down. Was he afraid she'd spurn him? Like her sassy daughter had? She couldn't tell what he was thinking. She was thinking *yes.*

"What?" Dan demanded. "I heard her say it, but I don't think she meant it."

Still seated beside him, Christa considered kicking Dan in the ankle.

"I think she did." Patrick leaned back in his chair, arms crossed behind his head as he regarded the rafters.

Christa smiled, entirely too pleased. The front legs of the chair slammed down and this time, when Patrick met her eyes, he held them.

"Now, why would a Sacramento housewife need to know such a thing?" Dan asked.

She wouldn't.

I'm never going back. Never.

"Beats me, Dan. Ask your sister."

"Christa?" Dan tipped his head, trying to snag her attention from Patrick.

"Would you stay with Patty for me, if I went?"

Dan threw his hands up. "If you're even thinking of doing it, *you're* the one needs watching."

"Dan, I could use the help," Patrick said. "I've seen her ride and she ain't bad. Said you taught her everything she knows."

"She did?" Dan's incredulous laugh gave her hope. "We'll talk about it. Maybe me and my niece could spend an evening reading about trolls and piggitys."

Patty's head snapped up from her arms. She clapped and pointed at her uncle.

"*Maybe*, I said."

Patty ignored his cautioning tone and her cheer expanded to include Patrick.

"Mr. Trick," she wheedled. "Do *my* plate."

"You are a night owl, aren't you?" Trick asked.

His voice made her jump. Even though he'd walked to the river and back, even though Josh, lying beside her, had lifted his head and yawned in greeting. She'd probably thought herself invisible, working next to the front porch, taking a moonbath as she weeded her herbs.

"I am." Christa dusted her palms together and looked up at him. The full moon lit her face and he thought he'd choke over the feeling it struck in him. "I like to be out in the night."

"It doesn't scare you?" Trick asked.

"Not here. In Sacramento, sometimes it did, because people were out, mainly drunkards."

Patrick sat on the porch, looking away, treating her like he would a skittish animal.

"Nathan warned me about robbers, but once you learn night sounds, you find most noises are only wind and cats."

"Where's piggity fit in?"

Christa rocked back on her heels and Trick realized she'd squatted there like an old cowpoke. He saw the points of her knees spread for balance, making a triangle of her skirt. He'd best get out his knife and a whittling stick, for distraction.

"I think—" She broke off, looking toward the room where her daughter slept. "Patty's just tired and cranky." Christa set to digging again. "Don't take her behavior to heart. I don't want you to—"

"Hush, honey. I know."

Christa swiveled toward him, trowel held shoulder-high, surprised as he was by what'd jumped off his tongue.

"I think," she hurried her words so neither of them could ponder what he'd said, "I think piggity is real."

So did he. The hell of it was he couldn't blame all of piggity's deviltry on the Yateses. They *might* have hung back on the edge of his herd when Christa rode in with her cinnamon cookies and smiles and taken the chance to break that heifer's neck with an ill-placed loop and a quick horse. They *could* have ridden over and busted a hen's wing, but the blocked creek was more their style. Irritating, but harmless. When Christa didn't ask for his opinion, he was thankful.

"Don't you have any worms?" She tapped the dirt in mild frustration.

"Worms." He mulled it over. "I can't say."

When Christa shook her head, her braid snaked back and forth over her spine. Tomorrow night they'd be alone under this silver-dollar moon.

"Maybe if you did this by day, you'd see what kind of vermin are in the dirt and wouldn't have to worry about touching one."

"They're not vermin. You *want* worms in your dirt."

Trick heard it again. Her voice held the solid conviction it had before, when she'd talked of coyote's cries, of how moving rocks had paid off in the creek's free-flowing song. Christa could come to love his ranch.

She brushed her hands together again. This time, Josh stood and stretched, thinking she meant to go in.

"Who taught you farmin'?" Trick tried to stall her. "I thought only potatoes got planted by moonlight."

"My mother."

"Shoot, you mean she's not a Boston lady like you?"

"She is—was, I mean." Christa's head bowed before she looked up, smiling. "Shall I tell you something no one else knows, even Danny?"

"I'd be honored," he joked, but her offer pulled tight within his chest.

"One night after the house was quiet I snuck out to check Merlin—our horse. I told you how our games involved death-defying horseback stunts? This time, Merlin fell. But he was fine."

Even after all this time, she sounded relieved. Trick remembered how she'd felt Cloud's legs after his bucking spree. It wasn't that she treated horses like pets; she cared about them, so she cared *for* them. If she had a pen full of pigs and shoats, fields full of milking cows and calves, and a cat with kits, she'd coddle them all.

"Coming back from the stable, I noticed a glow and plopped down on my belly in the deep grass to watch it. I was about nine, and I thought I'd seen a ghost."

Christa's face softened, and Trick wanted to pull her onto the step next to him.

"I parted the grass in front of my face and saw my mother. *My mother,* in the garden at midnight. As I watched, a vee of geese came drifting down to our neighbor's pond. With the moon all silver on their wings, they crowned her, and she looked like some kind of goose goddess." Christa laughed, but her voice still held a catch of childish awe.

"My mother was buxom and well-bred. She gossiped and did good works and played the cello. Except"—Christa shook her finger at an imaginary family—"she fooled all of us. We thought she slept all morning because she was lazy, but she did it because she worked all night, wearing a servant's work smock, in dirt up to her elbows."

Trick turned the stick in his hands, wondering if he could make a whistle of it, thinking again of Christa moving rocks out of the creek bed.

"Mother spotted me, called me to her, and took this *worm* out of the garden. It was no helpful earthworm, either. It was what she called a cutworm. Among vegetables, they're disastrous, but she—my *mother*—Patrick, I don't know how to tell you how shocking this was. She was forever scolding me for skinned knees and ripped jumpers, and my *mother* held out her hand and showed me this pale, disgusting creature, and said, 'Doesn't it gleam like pearls?'

"I thought she was crazy. Not because it didn't have the same glow as a pearl—it did—but because I couldn't reconcile her with my corseted, perfumed mother.

"So, I started sneaking out with her. I think she liked having a cohort. Oh, how she scrubbed her knuckles, knowing what Father would think, knowing the danger of playing the cello, which focused attention on her hands.

"She taught me gardening and constellations and showed me how caterpillars have two sets of feet to hold on with."

Christa stared off as if hearing her mother's voice, and the look on her face cut him deep. How wondrous to have a mother with secrets to share and things to read, just because you were her own.

"Caterpillars can crawl anywhere, you know. She said that second set of feet was the reason. 'Let that be a lesson to you,' she told me. 'When you marry, make sure you have a second set of feet—something besides your children, because they'll grow up and go. Something besides your husband . . .' And then she said words that still shock me. 'Your father hasn't had his nose out of his books in so long,

he couldn't describe me to the constable if I disappeared.' "
Christa covered her lips.

Trick wondered why Christa hadn't taken her mother's
advice. He had this ranch, the cattle and horses on it, the
improvements his labor had made, and the future. In spite of
the drought, he owned a damn fine ranch. Except for Patty,
what did Christa have?

Then he kicked himself for forgetting her Sacramento
house full of lamps, rugs, pictures, and the whatnots of
civilization. He thought of Christa and Patty in frilly
dresses, posed under one of those chandeliers with tinkly
crystals shooting rainbows.

Somehow, the picture didn't set right. He switched to a
question he could understand.

"How do you suppose she was creeping out of his bed for
all those years and your father never noticed?"

Christa uttered a wobbly laugh, and though it was a
private matter, his question brought her up from the dirt to
sit beside him on the step. His pulse flared hot at his wrists
and forearms as she settled.

"I suppose he never knew, probably still doesn't. I don't
think they ever shared a bed—not regularly."

He guessed by the way she ducked her head that Christa
blushed, but he teased her just a little, keeping himself on a
tight rein.

"What's the use, then," he said, "of gettin' married?"

"You're shameless, Mr. Garradine."

Christa pillowed her head against his shoulder and he
caught her in the bend of his arm and touched his cheek to
the thick smoothness of her hair. He heard the creek rushing
past the croaking frogs, past far, lowing cattle, then dwin-
dling, going underground, out in the Black Rock Desert.
Mud Meadow Creek tied them together like they'd been all
those years ago, when only the river had known it would
happen all over again.

Her head grew heavy, then bumped up suddenly. "I'd
better go in or I'll sleep through breakfast."

Her husky voice reminded him of the hours he'd held her between the pains of birthing Patty. Memories of that straining woman dimmed before this Christa, this pretty and daring female who craved his nearness as much as he did hers.

"Don't worry about cookin' for me," he told her as she stood. His side felt cold with her gone. "I'll be drinkin' Bloody Jim's forsaken coffee with the boys before you get the stove started."

"Still." She stepped nearer the door, retreating as he followed. "We'll have a late night tomorrow."

Anticipation glinted in her voice. More than her words, *that* aroused him. How long had he sat there, holding her, wordless and *kissless*, damn it? Would she have let him? Welcomed him? Why had her story held him spellbound, making him a flimsy Boston dandy instead of a man? Hell's bells.

"Yep." He answered too loudly, but the word was wasted as Christa snatched the last flicker of skirts inside his cabin door.

First off, Christa burned the double batch of biscuits she'd planned to feed them all day. Her roast turned out fine, and she rolled and cut her egg noodles to perfection. In fact, they were so perfect, Patty ate too many, too fast, and was sick.

I am not staying home. Christa stood in the bedroom, fighting guilt, while Dan and Patty pouted in the main room. Christa had watched Patty twist and complain on her pallet, then rise and totter in to her uncle. Christa lectured herself. Of course she would have stayed if Patty were truly sick, but overindulgence in what amounted to flour and water? No. Dan could handle this crisis.

"I don't know." Dan's dubious voice invaded the bedroom.

Christa laced her boots, folded her cloak, and raised her voice to reassure him. "It was just from overeating. You saw how she stuffed those noodles in with both hands. I should have stopped her sooner."

"Why didn't you?"

He hadn't mentioned the intimacy of tonight's meeting with Patrick, but she knew he'd take Patty's illness as a reprieve.

"She was having fun." Christa studied the mirror, dissatisfied with the way the basque gapped above the skirt. The ink-blue habit had been designed and stitched years ago, before she had Patty. Frankly, her figure had changed.

She wished she dared wear the white blouse, the last garment she'd purchased before Nathan died. And there was the problem. Nathan had been dead three months, not nearly long enough to break formal mourning.

"So for supper, Patty and I can have cold beef on burned biscuits. Is that it?"

"With apple pandowdy for dessert. Grumble about that and try to sound convincing."

Mercy, this collar grated on her throat each time she turned her head from side to side.

Christa stared at her image. Her cheeks glowed pink as if she'd labored in the fields, and her eyes looked tearful. How absurd. No one stood at the door, ready to condemn her white blouse. Francesca was hundreds of miles away. No one would notice the rough leather charm tucked beneath the fine white lace blouse. No one except Patty, who hadn't asked for its magic today.

"I guess it will be all right. . . ." Dan moaned.

Amen. Merciful Heavens, Dan could not still be complaining about the best dinner he'd had in weeks!

"—if I don't have to have that damn dog inside."

"Do what you like with Josh." Christa fastened the dozen pearl buttons leading from throat to waist. Patty would grind down Dan's resistance and have Josh inside before the dust from Cloud's hooves settled in the dooryard.

Christa picked up her dove-gray cloak and folded it over her arm. She snugged the new chin strap on her hat and surveyed the room. The top blanket on Patty's pallet was turned back, and they'd rehearsed the act of a "big girl" tucking herself in, since Dan couldn't stoop to do it.

Christa's bed was turned back, too. Between now and the time she slipped into it, would Patrick have kissed her again?

Christa strode out of the bedroom to find Dan teaching Patty to identify suits of cards.

"Diamond."

"Good."

"Clover."

"Close, Patty cakes. That's a club, though, remember?"

"What are you teaching my daughter?" Christa pulled her gloves up over her wrists.

"A Western skill equally useful as that which her mama's about to learn." While Patty tugged the next card from his hand, Dan looked askance at Christa's white blouse.

He couldn't see through to the pouch around her neck. She was sure of it. Still, she whirled the cloak around her shoulders and buttoned it to her chin.

"Heart?"

"Exactly. It's July, Sis. Don't bundle up on my account."

Christa watched as Patty arranged all the face cards into a family.

"What about Grimms?" Christa asked them both, bending to kiss her daughter's cheek.

"Later," said Dan.

Patty returned the kiss, then pushed Christa's hand away from the cards. Christa sighed. Her baby was occupied. Completely, if not suitably.

"I'll wait up," Dan said.

"I wish you wouldn't."

"Somebody's got to show some sense around here. I'll be sitting on the porch with my old Sharps."

"We'll be prepared if we get charged by a herd of buffalo." Christa slipped outside before Dan could tell her not to do something she'd regret.

Eighteen

He had the itch.

It brought back the memory of Loco, the only paint horse he'd ever owned. Loco hungered for lupine and it twisted him into knots no cowboy could ride out of him. Some horses ate the wildflower and just got belly flutters. Not Loco. Soon as he caught the scent, Loco started shaking. Chewing a mouthful, he'd snort and stare. After a swallow, he neighed, flung his head, and bucked like the juice prickled him inside and out. His craving never stopped until it finally killed him.

One morning Bloody Jim roped him out of the remuda and rode out. Two hours later Jim came back, afoot, elbows bleeding through the rags of his shirt.

"Lead poisoning," he'd grumbled, when Trick asked what had become of Loco. Then Jim had patted his holster.

Trick half wished someone would do him that favor. If he didn't get his hands on Christa—past her cotton, linen, or whatever kind of cloth she wore, onto her skin—he would surely die. If he did get his hands on her, it figured to kill them both. Once he started, he wouldn't stop. Dan putting a bullet through him would kill Christa, too, since Trick knew he wouldn't release her, even with the Sharps's muzzle pressed against the back of his neck.

As Christa trotted into camp, sitting like a princess on Cloud, Trick tried to stifle his lust. They didn't suit each other. He didn't have bloodlines like hers. He couldn't read or talk about the people in books or the folks who wrote them. He couldn't offer her a satin-lined carriage or a downy bed.

While he waited for guilt to take him, Trick noticed Christa's skirt move as her knee tightened against Cloud's moon-colored hide. What wouldn't he give to have her knees naked to his touch?

He'd throw away bloodines and books and settle for not having a herd to watch. He'd tackle her from her horse, roll her into the tall grass, and love her next to the creek. It wouldn't be civilized, but he didn't have much time.

"One beer and I'll be back, Trick," Preach had promised when he learned Christa had ridden in to play second nighthawk.

Well, hell, he hadn't really hoped for a whole night alone with her, had he? And they had a skittish herd to watch. Christa swayed in the saddle, body following each slide of Cloud's muscles as she rode toward Trick.

"Ride slow and far back."

She nodded, cheeks blushed from working outside without a bonnet, green eyes intent as if he held the secret of buried gold.

"Keep away from that brindle bull," Trick added. "He's a troublemaker."

He'd almost blurted that the brindle thought with his *cojónes* instead of his bovine brain. But who was he to criticize? And, in spite of what he'd been thinking, he couldn't talk to Christa that way. Trick gritted his teeth until he felt the bones in his skull grate. Christabel Worth was a lady.

"Half of the herd is wild as deer and the other half's been branded and cut. That gives 'em a healthy respect for men ahorseback."

"Or women?"

A sharp wind with an edge of fall blew right in her face, flinging back her gray cape to taunt him with the white blouse underneath.

"Or women." What in hell had happened to him when just

the word *women* twisted his gut, when he thought that blouse was a white flag of surrender?

Trick squinted past her, wishing she'd ride a few steps off. Cloud nuzzled Imp's neck, and Christa's nearness made it tough to rattle off more directions.

"If one breaks for open range, a raised hand or yip will send him back to the herd. If Cloud notices first, his ears will twitch and you'll feel him tighten up. Then grab that saddle horn." Trick reached for her wrist. He felt a flicker of resistance before she let him place her gloved hand atop the leather-wrapped horn. "Like that." He formed his fingers over hers. "Tight, or he'll move to cut off a calf and shift right out from under you."

She understood perfectly, so he removed his hand. Trick took what pleasure he could from the fact that being city-bred didn't slow her down a bit. She took to riding herd like she'd watched it from a cradle board.

They circled the herd in opposite directions, coming face to face every twenty minutes or so. None of the cattle wanted to break. This bunch didn't clatter horns or slam chests in territorial disputes.

Except for the brindle bull. His black-orange head rose above the herd as he went after a cow. With uncooperative grunts, the female pulled away. Her refusal caused only ripples in the calm gathering of bovines. They'd bedded down for the night, chewing and dozing.

Each time Cloud loped past, Christa's white blouse glimmered. This time he pulled Imp to a stop and sat waiting. By the time she reached him, he'd made up something to tell her.

"My cows wear slit ears and a crazy T brand." He pointed out marks on a bald-faced steer. "I know we're losing the light, but if you see any different brands, let me know."

He cleared his throat, planning to go on, but his mind fixed on brands. What if he burned an interlocked T and C on some hapless cow? What if he carved them into a tree trunk, deep, so they'd haunt him when he was an old man, riding these hills alone? What he really wanted was to mark Christa as his own. And it wasn't possible. Nathan, damn his eyes, had marked her first.

"Patrick, am I doing all right?"

She fidgeted in the saddle, still waiting for him to go on.

"Am I riding far enough from the herd? Tell me. If something's bothering you, I'd like to fix it."

Oh, and I'd love to have it fixed.

"Naw, we just ate jackrabbit for supper," he joked, slapping his reins on his palm. "Made me kind of jumpy." Trick jammed his heels in against Imp with undeserved energy and the black leapt into a rollicking lope.

The next time they passed, Christa slowed to a jog, then pulled Cloud around to shout after Trick.

"Patrick, when's your birthday?"

"What?" He couldn't have heard her right.

"When's your birthday?" She tilted her hat brim up to see better. He'd have to send that hat sailing before he kissed her.

"I have no idea." He hoped she'd only used a little overhand knot to tie her hat strings. "Only thing Dad mentioned was my mother dying. Didn't make me real eager to ask more."

"I daresay not, but when do you celebrate?"

"I don't."

"Never?" She reached a hand toward him, but Cloud jostled her away. "You've never had a birthday party? Or even a cake?"

"Now take that little-lost-lamb look off your face, Mrs. Worth." His teasing tickled her, because she burst into laughter. "I'm not a child whose life you're going to set right."

"Patrick," she grinned down at her saddle horn, "I never mistook you for one."

The words sizzled along his nerves and he couldn't let her go. He took her wrist again—perhaps too tightly, since she pulled away.

"What do you mean by that?" He couldn't say it straight out. He had to clear his throat.

"I mean, I've never seen you as anything but a man."

"Jesus, Christa," he said, but by then she'd wheeled Cloud away, and he didn't know if she'd heard.

His words flew after her, mixing with the summer wind. Both filled her with contrary feelings. Hot wind, laced with a trace of autumn, felt like brewing passion, chilled with the fear of good-bye.

Patrick's first kiss had been tender. There by Goldwing Seep, a warm pool guarded by high reeds, she'd felt cherished. But the Patrick who'd just grabbed her arm and demanded her thoughts was different. Here, on this open plain, he moved abruptly, a male reminding her that they were alone.

Christa eased Cloud down to a walk, afraid to pass Patrick. She must admit she'd tried to tempt him. Not in a wicked way, but he'd misunderstood. The way he looked tonight, simmering with heat, made her a little afraid. Not that she didn't want his kisses. Not that she feared a carnal alliance . . . Yes, she did.

Christa stopped Cloud. She touched the amulet beneath her blouse and wished it contained true magic.

If she'd never lain with Nathan, she'd sigh over the prospect of Patrick's strong hands and wide shoulders. She'd fantasize how he'd gaze into her eyes as he rose above her.

Long ago, she'd come to her marriage bed eager and bristling with energy, full of dreams. If only it stopped with kissing. A month of the marriage act had left her sad and disgusted.

She knew how it felt to offer everything and get nothing in return. Patrick's lovemaking wouldn't mean he wanted her to stay. It would only mean he wanted her. Christa knew this much of men: They weren't ruled during the day by what happened at night.

She loped Cloud past Patrick and he did nothing to stop her. Cloud's ears flicked to catch Christa's mutter. Had she imagined Patrick's lust? Had he only grabbed her arm to stop her chattering?

Mercy, what a confusing tangle. When Pete and Preach hailed her, riding in at a gallop, she couldn't decide whether she'd been delivered or robbed. Fate had given her one night alone with Patrick and she'd wasted it.

The full moon's globe silvered the desert at Goldwing Seep. Instead of riding straight for the cabin, Patrick had detoured, bringing her back, just as she'd so boldly asked. They stood at the hot spring's edge, and Christa again wished for its warm water lapping between her toes.

Vaulting excitement wavered as she wondered if even a good man could plunder her body, then send her away. Men lived by different rules. Patrick Garradine had saved her baby's life, but he was as male as that troublemaking bull.

With a proprietary move, he took Cloud's reins and ground-tied him alongside Imp.

"Christa, what's got you afraid of me? You are, aren't you?"

"A little." Inside, she pleaded with him not to ask why. She could discuss anything except men's physical appetites.

"I guess I'm kind of clumsy. I've never been with a decent woman."

"And you're not going to 'be with' me!" She sounded like a shrew, but Patrick's words confirmed her worst fear. He thought she was his for the taking.

Christa stepped away so quickly, her ankle wobbled and her hat fell back on its chin strap. Patrick steadied her against falling, then embraced her.

"I only meant to kiss you."

It *wasn't* all he meant. Patrick lied before he even started. She felt it in a kiss so hard her lips parted at his urgency. His hands held her shoulders as if preventing escape, and she didn't try. She leaned into him. Traitorous, unthinking body to cover her mind's warnings like thunder over the faint crackle of lightning.

He lied. She forced herself to shrink, to pull in on herself so that his hands hung empty.

"I'd never hurt you, Christa." He took back his hands, folding his arms, hiding his fists beneath his elbows. "It's the last thing I want. And I'd think—"

Patrick paused on a sigh that made guilt surge up in her like bile.

"—I'd think that you'd know that."

Every word was steeped in disappointment, and Christa wanted to hold him. What had she done? For weeks, he hadn't offered a crumb of affection and she'd been starved for it. Now he'd reached for her, and she'd cringed away, as if he were unclean. Wielding her own fear, she'd cut off his feelings, leaving him hurt and embarrassed.

"I'd best get you back to your little one."

As always, Patty provided a safe space between them. Maybe this time, Patty could bridge their tumultuous feelings.

"Why won't you call her by her name? It's always 'the little one' or 'sugar.'"

"If you don't want me to call her that, I won't. It's just because when you brought her in that first day, you had her perched up there on Betsy, along with those sugar sacks." He scrubbed the heel of his hand between his eyebrows. "Hell, I thought she liked it."

"She does. *I* do! But why won't you call her Patricia or Patty?"

"I can't!" He snapped his jaw closed.

With narrowed eyes, he stared across the safe, cold plain. She'd lost him. Oh, foolish girl to throw away painstaking closeness, that link fused by hard work and respect.

"Patrick." She put on a schoolmarm's voice and it surprised him. "Take off your boots. Yes, just do it." She removed her hat and set it on a rock, then whisked her skirt aside and unlaced her boots. "I'm going to take mine off, too."

She threw the first boot aside and hopped on one foot to tackle the other.

"Then, dangle your feet in the warm water." She eased herself down to the edge of the spring and plunged her bare feet into the lapping darkness.

She glanced over her shoulder to see him still standing, staring out at the desert. "You might as well give in, because I'm sitting here until my toes go numb. We've got all night. Danny's not about to come after us."

She stared at the other side of the pond, forcing her eyes to separate individual reeds from the dark wall that wavered, protecting the pond from the wind. She heard Patrick's boots scuff.

"If that's what you want."

She took his words as a small victory and thanked God. She didn't deserve even that.

He settled on the pond's edge, three feet away from her. Christa scooted closer.

"Is it because I named her for you?"

Patrick sagged against palms he'd braced on his thighs.

"You did, didn't you? I tried to tell myself it was a family name. But you named her for me."

"Of course I did. You saved her life."

"But she's *his* daughter." He expelled the words as if he'd pried them loose with his knife.

"Never, never as much as she is yours. He abandoned her and you breathed life into her. He tolerated her, you love her."

His eyes closed so tight, denying, that wrinkles fanned across his eyelids.

"I know you love her." She closed her own eyes, then, against the shame of what she had to tell him.

"Our marriage was a sham. It's my fault. I saw him as a means to escape Boston and come West. He thought I'd act as the perfect hostess for the rich businessman he planned to become.

"I tried. I polished crystal goblets and brass sconces. I directed servants to beat the rugs and dust the moldings over the doors. I arranged flowers he made me buy, because gardening was beneath me. And I served brandy and cigars to his friends."

She shuddered. Had any Sunday morning in her house smelled of something other than Saturday night "meetings"?

"Couldn't you get outside?" Patrick's shoulders shifted with the imagined confinement.

"He allowed me to ride twice each week, while Patty napped."

"That must have been a comfort. I'd've gone crazy, inside all that time."

"I did. So did Dan. That's why he came back here."

"He never once told me he was your brother. I would've liked knowing."

"He watched you strike Nathan. He didn't want you to—" Christa broke off when Patrick nodded, then circled back to her confession.

A tendril of underwater grass, or perhaps a fish, brushed her ankle. She ignored it, drawn back by the dark undertow of life with Nathan.

"At least you got to ride."

"For a while." She slid her fingers inside her high lace collar, swallowed, and decided to tell the rest. "Francesca, Nathan's unmarried sister, came to stay. She put it into Nathan's mind that the reason I couldn't conceive was my riding."

"Oh, that's not right."

"Logic had no impact on her arguments, and Nathan believed her. Just to torment me, I think. Then I did."

"Did—?"

"Conceive."

"Christa, you had another baby?"

She watched memories of her first labor build and crest over his features. Then Christa saw his alarm.

"For a few minutes," she told him.

Cloud wandered toward the water. Patrick raised his hand and the gelding backed away, hooves sucking air from the mud.

"Nathan and I had a loud discussion by a hitching ring on the public street—about riding and its effects on my unborn babe." Christa pulled her feet from the water, suddenly too hot. "Our marital discord was no secret."

"Don't tell me he went off and left you like he did before."

"Oh, no, Nathan was right there, with a doctor known for handling difficult women." Her chuckle sounded peculiar, even to her own ears. "But the baby came early. And, just like Patty, she didn't breathe."

Patrick trembled beside her and she clasped his hand.

"I told them to breathe for her, like you did. They thought I was out of my mind. I screamed for them to let me do it. Nathan sent a maid to look. Yes, she said, people on the street were staring up at our windows. So he and the doctor gagged me. And tied me, so I couldn't 'injure myself.' She died."

"Jesus, Christa, the man was a monster. Why did you stay?"

"Because he was my husband, Patrick, and I was reared to think that meant something."

"He didn't deserve to be. God, he shouldn't have been allowed to touch you."

She saw guilt take him, as if he could have done anything about it. Then, she realized he had. All memories of numb copulation with Nathan sickened her, but deep in that humiliation was something she could offer Patrick.

"When Nathan came to me, I hated it. Most nights I tried to think myself out of that room into this clean, white desert. When that didn't work . . . I closed my eyes and saw you, in your buckskins, in the lantern light. . . . That must be some kind of sin. But I thought of you."

Christa leaned her cheek against his chest, nestled her head beneath his chin, and wrapped his arm around her. His breath came harshly, and his hand moved in three awkward pats.

"I'm here now."

Christa kissed the cloth of his shirt, then came to her knees beside him. Patrick's legs still dangled in the hot spring when she lifted his Stetson and placed it on the rock next to hers. She draped her arms on his shoulders and tilted her head to kiss his bottom lip. Then she brushed the Indian-black hair back from his face and kissed his temple.

"Christa, this is killing me," he said hoarsely. "If you want me to leave you alone, you're going to have to stop."

She burrowed her face against the side of his neck. He shivered when her lips moved. "I don't want you to leave me alone."

With a splash and a shower of warm droplets, his legs broke the spring's surface. Patrick searched for a way to hold her. He dragged her across his lap, cradling her neck in the crook of one elbow while he kissed her lips. His bent knees supported her back as he kissed from the flesh beneath her ear to her high lace collar. When she reached, with drugged slowness, to undo her highest buttons, he snatched her hand away. He released them all at once, to the curving top of her chemise.

Christa gasped for breath and for good sense, but Patrick's lips, dusting against her collarbone, kept both out of reach.

"What's this, now?" His fingers lifted the buckskin thong that held the leather medicine pouch. "You kept this?"

Her nod was a spur and he surged against her, as if the pouch conferred ownership. Christa arched her neck backward, encouraging his lips, but he only gripped the pouch.

"Patrick." Her beseeching tone might have been anyone's but hers, and Patrick kissed her savagely. There was no softness in him, and she didn't care.

"I'm glad he's dead." Patrick took her face between his hands. "He never deserved you for one night."

Christa's kisses raged back at him. Where did this rising heat come from? This yearning for him to touch her breasts instead of gripping the pouch so tightly its thong bit against her nape? It took several heartbeats to meet his sad eyes and hear what he'd said.

"What am I going to do without you, Christa? Tell me?"

They both felt it break. A fragile thread of moonlight had spun out and bound them together, but now the dark had come again.

The horses might have led a funeral train, except they walked under a full moon.

He'd insisted on seeing her home.

Except that it was not and never would be her home, only Patrick's. His plea had confirmed it. He craved her kiss, but he could live without it. She wanted to howl. Heels beating a wild tattoo on Cloud's ribs, she'd burrow her face in his mane and let his huge strides take her away. Except Patrick wouldn't allow it.

A distressed bray announced that Emperor and Jim were near, but even the full moon didn't show where.

"Man," a drunken drawl stretched the word out for seconds. "It's a sin to Moses, drownin' yourself over a mule!"

"Jump, hombre, while you still can."

"Ramon?" Christa called out, but Patrick had already ridden forward at a cautious trot.

Pete, Bloody Jim, and Ramon were drunk and the mule couldn't have been angrier. It brayed again. Then Christa heard sodden splashing and she knew what had happened.

The playa's crust looked hard as marble, but it could collapse, dropping horse and rider into a wet reminder that this desert had cradled an ancient sea. Muley had warned her of a slurry of sand, salt, and water that gave no footing and drowned its victims. He'd called it quicksand.

"Don't worry, pard. I'll rope you off and drag you free."
The voice sounded like Pete's.

Christa urged Cloud toward the drawl as she heard
Patrick beside her. "Hell, he can't rope sober."

Patrick sent Imp ahead faster, following Christa a bit east
of where he'd aimed before.

"Not leaving my mule." Bloody Jim's baritone blotted out
every other sound. "He brought me all t'way from Mississippi. Not gonna jump ship at the slightest—"

There was the sound of whipping rope and a subdued
bray.

"Don't duck yer head, hugging around that stinkin'
mule's neck! Now, what're you thinkin' to do me like that?
Huh, partner?"

Bloody Jim. Ramon. Pete. And Bloody Jim and Emperor
were sinking fast, by the sound of it. She should feel amazed
that such experienced riders had stumbled into trouble, but
what truly shocked her was Pete Jessup calling the black
man "partner."

Patrick galloped past her, and by the time she reached the
mess, he'd dismounted.

"Well, if it's not the blamed cavalry!"

"Hush up, Jim. Let's see what you've got yourself into."

Patrick's level voice warned Christa. The situation called
for more solemn consideration than the hands gave it.

"The mule's lost, Jim. All his thrashing's just making
things worse," Patrick said.

Dark humps and shapes, jingling bits, creaking leather,
and the sour stench of beer painted a vague scene, and
Christa wondered how Patrick could make his diagnosis.

"Let Ramon rope you," Patrick said, over Pete's protest.
"Then hit the muck spread-eagled and swim out."

"Swimmin' in a desert!" Jim chuckled. "No, sir, ain't
swimmin' away from my Emperor."

"Then drown with him, amigo, but I'm doing as Trick
says."

Again Jim ducked, but Ramon's rope settled over the

mule's neck. Emperor's groan and crunch of horse hooves setting and backing told Christa that Ramon was trying to pull them out.

Christa edged close enough to make out the mule's striving head and neck. Bloody Jim had sunk to midthigh. He leaned forward, urging the mule with body and voice. A platter-sized patch of Emperor's hindquarters gleamed above the muck, and Pete flogged it with his rope.

"Here, now! Don't go whipping Emperor. He's such a good mule." Jim sounded as if he'd weep.

"Steady up, Jim. This one's going around you," Patrick called. "Son of a bitch, you dodged!"

"*He* moved. I swear, Trick, for a minute he got his feet underneath of him."

That decided her. Christa could see what needed doing. She dismounted and surprised Pete by jerking the rope from his hands.

"Miz Worth!"

She ignored him and started giving orders before it was too late. "Take this end. Not that way—around his rump."

"Yes, ma'am."

"Then we'll both run it under—"

"Christa! Watch out! Get away from the edge."

Christa blocked out Patrick's voice, ducked Jim's flailing arms, and squinted to make sure Pete was following instructions.

"That crust'll crumble and we'll have all three of you in the soup."

Patrick's predictions made it hard to concentrate.

"Four," Bloody Jim said.

Patrick continued to yell from Emperor's front, and when Christa matched Pete's rope with hers and ran both through the chin strap of the mule's bridle, Patrick grabbed for her.

"For the last time, woman, get away!"

Judging by his nodding head and extended hand, Ramon understood what she was doing.

"Christa! I'm warning you!"

She slapped the rope ends into the vaquero's hand and wheeled on Patrick, shouting through the darkness. "Hold my horse or hold your tongue, Patrick Garradine, but after tonight, you're sadly mistaken if you think I'm ever taking orders from you again!"

Jim's disrespectful hoot lasted only a second before he shouted, "He's moving!"

Christa ran around behind the mule. She leaned against the gritty bit of haunch that had emerged.

"Do you hate that, Emperor? Do you hate that rope under your tender tail? Get away from it, baby. Come on." She petted and urged and strained along with the mule, then stumbled back as it lurched free and fell sideways. The mounted men whistled and whipped their mounts, dragging the mule onto the solid playa.

Bloody Jim kicked weakly, trying to free himself from his muddy stirrups. Christa hurried to help.

"If you haven't broken their backs, you've saved them." Patrick joined her beside the panting man and mule. "That was the foolhardiest thing I ever did see."

Jim wriggled loose and lay flat on his back, like a man shipwrecked.

"Nice thinkin', ma'am," Pete congratulated. "But don't count on Emperor feeling quite the same about you."

"I know. I hated to do it."

"He's not suckin' mud up his nose. He can be grateful for that." Patrick jerked his rope out of the mud, gathered it into a neat coil, and tied it on his saddle.

Pete gave Jim a hand up. Emperor scrambled to his feet and shook. Her blouse would never again be white, but there was no sense standing in range. She snagged Cloud's reins and remounted. The gelding minced sideways, snorting a comment on mules.

"I don't mind walkin' if you want to take my pony," Pete told Jim.

"It takes more than a mud bath to get this mule down. He can tote me."

"You three go on, now. I'll see Miz Worth back to the ranch."

The hands didn't pretend they'd missed his uppity shouting or his use of her first name. Even though they sounded half-sobered by Jim's accident, they chuckled at their boss.

Ramon spurred ahead of the rest. A laughing stream of Spanish flowed back to them.

"You know I don't understand your jabber," Patrick grumbled. "What'd he say, Pete?"

Bloody Jim urged his dripping mule into an amble as Pete tried to interpret. "I'm sorry to say I had a few sips of joy juice, Trick." Pete scratched his head.

"Give it your best shot, if you want to keep your job, amigo."

"Went something like this: 'Holy Mother of God, *jefe*' — that's like boss — 'hold onto that priceless woman!'"

"I'm ridin' on back to camp, now, Trick." Pete cleared his throat and set his heels to his horse. "Adios!"

Nineteen

When Christa stepped outside, a cloudy dawn had mottled the peaks orange and gold as a calico cat. Dan and Patty still slept, deaf to the rumbling thunder. Only once, just before Patty was born, had Christa witnessed a desert rainstorm.

Christa pulled her gray cloak closer and faced her punishment. She stared at the cougar skin nailed to Patrick's stable. Nailed wide apart, the cougar's taupe legs spread in a last appeal.

Christa imagined how the cat's nostrils had tickled with man scent. But she'd had cubs, so she'd answered her drive to eat. Movement had flickered at the edge of her vision and her tail had lashed as she bolted one last bite. A quick lift of curiosity had come as she faced the intruder. Then she'd folded her ears and flashed a snarl of queenly disdain to send him running.

Thunder rolled overhead, leaving Christa hollow and weary. Like the dead animals stuffed and propped in her Sacramento house, this cougar's beauty lay in memory.

Damn Patrick Garradine! Rain splattered her cheek. Christa left her hood down and let herself cry. She'd come back to help Patrick build this ranch. He had a good start: healthy cattle, earth from which herbs and strawberries could be coaxed, a crew of cowboys who finally pulled together, and this.

Christa regarded the cookhouse and cabin with pride. Patrick had moved into the army's structures, but she'd turned this scatter of buildings into the heart of his ranch. The hands felt it as they relaxed around her dinner table. Dan saw it in the contented scratching hens, sleek horses, and fresh-swept floors. Even Patty loved the ranch. She chattered and drew pictures to show to Rosebud the next time she visited. She ran, leggy and laughing, along the creek. Only Patrick refused to see the harmony.

Because he was afraid.

Trick had nailed the cougar skin to the barn to discourage others of her kind. His vigilance over her was just as senseless. If predators came, this limp totem would do no more good than a "Keep Out" sign. If danger stalked her, Christa knew she'd be as vulnerable walking down a city street as riding a desert playa.

She wanted to despise him. Staring at these slain beasts, she should. Instead, she saw what Patrick tried to do. He wanted to protect them all—his herd, his woman, his child—wielding death if he must.

Was it because he'd had no mother to protect *him* that he insisted on guarding others? Was it because—oh, curse such sympathy! She didn't want to understand! He believed he could shield her and Patty by sending them away.

She'd cooked, planted, ridden, shoved rocks, moved a mule, and barely scuffed her palms along the way. Patrick had told her his was no life for a lady, but she'd snatched up his dare and proven she could lead this life and love it.

Christa crossed her arms and stared up into the misty rain. She couldn't force Patrick's eyes open. She would not beg to be his wife. She'd only come here to help him. Perhaps her debt had been paid, and she should leave.

Just as she'd felt a stitch in her side from laughing as a child, she now felt a stitch in her heart. Oh, Patrick.

Christa lifted her skirts above the damp earth and walked toward the woodpile. She'd run out of stove lengths, and that ax wouldn't lift itself. Chopping wood and drinking a cup of strong coffee would banish her melancholy before the sun rose over the Calico Mountains.

*   *   *

For three days it rained. Laundry piled up until Christa zigzagged clothesline across the cabin's main room. She told Patty stories, played cat's cradle, and made finger shadows on the wall. She sewed matching jumpers of old pink wrapping flannel found stashed in a strongbox inside the stable. When Patty whined over standing still and pinpricks, Christa asked her to play with Uncle Dan, who protested he could do nothing but teach her poker. Christa ignored them both to pop corn and alphabetize the canned goods in Patrick's pantry.

And she baked cakes. With a streak of perversity she hadn't expected from barnyard fowl, the hens produced a record number of eggs. Finally, Dan suggested she make pickled eggs like those served free in John Starr's saloon.

Rain and clouds made day four of the storm dark as December. Christa lit rush lamps to lend light to Patty's games. Wouldn't Francesca expire if she saw her niece sprawled on the cookhouse floor, matching and stacking playing cards?

In three tiresome days—now four—Christa hadn't decided what to do about Francesca's letter. Oddly, she wanted Patrick's opinion, though he'd probably see Francesca's threats as another reason to return to Sacramento.

Christa set a full dozen eggs out on the plank table. Thank the Lord she and Dan had rigged a pulley to get it back inside before the rain settled in. That was far more important to her than Francesca's Mr. Frost and his subpoena.

Taking care not to slop water on her new jumper, Christa set a cauldron to boil, then answered Patty's tug.

"Mama, Josh wants in."

The collie sniffed loudly at the cookhouse door, then barked.

"Sorry, baby. Not near the food. Mr. Trick doesn't even like Josh in the house."

"Mr. Trick's gone bye-bye." Patty showed Christa a face card, then laid it down.

"Yes, he has, hasn't he?" *The coward.* She poured a measure of vinegar. Had her response to his kisses convinced him she was a hussy? Probably not. What man would abandon her for *that?*

"Jim gone bye-bye."

"Mmm-hmm." Patrick had simply caught her in a weak mood.

"*Other* Jim gone bye-bye." Patty raised her voice over Josh's insistent barking, and added a third card to her stack.

"Right." Christa asked herself why she hadn't taken off that medicine bag yet.

"Josh, hush!" Christa shouted.

"Preach gone bye-bye. Pete gone bye-bye."

"All of them, Patty. You're right."

Such recital expanded Patty's memory. It would help her learn to read. And to count. Christa gritted her teeth.

"And Imp is gone bye-bye and Freckles."

Rain hammered the cookhouse walls, making it risky to open a window, but if the stove made the room any hotter, Christa would do it. And if her daughter planned on naming off the livestock, Christa refused to listen to Josh bark his meager brains out. She jerked open the cookhouse door.

Patrick stood so close, his hat brim dripped rain on her nose. His duster blew in on a gust of wind, surrounding her, and she wanted his kiss more than air to breathe.

"Morning, Mrs. Worth. Mornin', sugar." In the shelter of his duster, he touched her waist and she swayed against him. "I've got a hurt boy out here. He said he'd probably die if he didn't get tended by you."

"What? Who?" She leaned to peer around the wet canvas covering his shoulders.

"It's me, ma'am." Pete's Texas drawl identified him. With his hat pulled down and collar turned up, he hunched on a wet, miserable horse. "Don't come out in this frog-strangler, ma'am."

"Nonsense." Christa rushed down the steps.

The rain's needle darts ricocheted up from the ground.

Once she stood beside the horse, Christa held her arms up to Pete as she would to Patty. Patrick's sound of dismay only made her smile, as the young cowboy tumbled down with one arm slung around her neck.

"What happened to you?" Christa murmured. She braced her knees, trying not to stagger under Pete's weight.

"Hey, now, if this is a rain dance, I wish someone would've invited me." Without a crutch, her brother Dan hobbled across the yard from the house.

Patty clapped from the porch and Patrick said Dan looked ready to mount up, while Pete insisted he wouldn't feel right bleeding in Trick's cabin. Besides, he hankered for some of Christa's coffee. Patrick took Pete's weight from Christa and eased the boy up the steps to the cookhouse.

"It's just as well." Christa held the door ajar. "There's water boiling on the stove. Whatever's wrong, I'll need to clean you up." Christa shivered when Patrick's rain-wet mustache wet the wisps of hair next to her ear.

"It's nothing much," he said. "Might as well use that water for coffee."

It turned out there was water enough for cleanup and two pots of coffee. Pete refused to be hoisted onto the dinner table for examination, so Christa sat the young cowboy down and propped his leg on a second chair. She sent Patty scurrying to the house for the remaining pink flannel, then squatted to examine the wound.

"That brindle bull finally got a good excuse to hook someone." Patrick hunkered beside her as Christa laid back the edges of Pete's denims.

"It looks like more of a puncture than a hook," she said. "All I can do is clean it and put on a tight bandage."

"Trick already poured whiskey on it." Pete gazed up with trusting eyes and Christa flinched with imagined pain.

Dan sucked in a sympathetic breath. "I hope you poured some in the boy, first."

"Tried to." Patrick rested one boot on a bench and leaned forward to study the exposed wound.

Before Christa gathered words to protest, he lay crossed arms on the long denimed expanse of his thigh. If she spoke now, she'd end up stuttering. She noticed Patrick's duster dripping on her fresh-swept floor and the muddy boot he'd planted on her bench; she just didn't care. The lean rider's muscle in that thigh entranced her.

"I wanted to wait." Pete's boyish faith made Christa whirl away to dip steaming water into a bowl. "Didn't want to drink spirits without Mrs. Worth telling me it was the right thing to do." Pete's eyes followed her as Patrick shook his head.

Patty returned and Christa used the flannel to swab the wound.

"No need to be so gentle," Patrick said.

Christa looked up from the wound, hoping her hands wouldn't shake as she frowned at Patrick. "There's no need to be rough."

"He was only homesick for you."

"You're cringing more than Pete is, Sis." Dan ignored Patrick's assessment. Instead, he limped to the coffeepot and poured three cups.

Her brother was probably right. Christa took a long sip of coffee before finishing up.

"I'm so sorry, ma'am."

"Hush, Pete. What else would I be doing on a rainy morning, with no one to cook for but Patty and Dan?"

Pete relaxed in her hands. His leg rolled slightly outward, his shoulders sagged, and his head fell back against the chair.

"He'll be asleep before I get back with the 'required' dose of whiskey." Christa pushed yellow bangs back from Pete's face. He couldn't be more than fifteen years old.

"That's if we didn't pour it all into you that night," Patrick said.

Dan cleared his throat as if he'd eavesdropped on something illicit.

"*That night* piggity pounded on the wall," Christa explained, but Dan's smirk hadn't changed since he was eight years old, and nothing she could say would wipe it from his face.

"I'll find another bottle if that one's gone," Patrick said, standing as she did. "I'll go with you."

Wind flapped Christa's skirts as if they hung from a flagpole, but the rain had thickened into fog. They moved across the yard in silence and found Dan had left the cabin cold, still, and gray.

"I'll just light the lantern." Christa hurried across to the hearth, then turned when she heard the door bar fall into place.

Behind his stallion's-tail mustache, Patrick looked boyish.

"Have you locked us in, Mr. Garradine?"

His blue eyes crinkled at the edges as he sauntered toward her. "No, ma'am. I've locked them out."

Christa clasped Patrick's hands and stood tiptoe to reach his lips. A brazen move, but his kisses came sweet and slow. *There's no need to be so gentle,* he'd said over Pete's wounds, but his tenderness melted her. Patrick's hands pulled away from hers to flow up the back of her flannel jumper.

"Pink?" He tilted his head one way, then the other, to kiss each corner of her mouth.

Following his lead, Christa stroked Patrick's blue denim shirt. Worn and washed, its softness barely concealed his muscled back.

She wanted to see it. Her heartbeat stampeded, making her delicate touch a disguise for desire. Why did he bathe at the creek, instead of at the pump, where she could peek? Patrick's muscles slid beneath her fingers as his hand flattened at the small of her back. She swayed forward, felt his hardness, and pulled apart. She tried to cover the moment with teasing.

"You see what a little gentleness can get you?"

Patrick didn't look like a man ready to laugh. Every line

of his body strained. When she took his hand again, forking her fingers through his, his control snapped.

"Hellfire, Christa."

In one swoop, he lifted her legs from under her and carried her to the bedroom. He took her down to the bed and pulled her to face him, lips to lips, chest to chest. He kissed her ruthlessly, and when she opened her lips to his tongue, a wave of relief swept her.

Oh, yes. She pressed her hips against his as if translating the kiss. One of his hands came up to her breast and she pushed it into his palm. Shameless, she flushed from hair to toes and didn't pull away.

Closer. She raised one leg nearer his and he swept the web of her skirt away, forming his hand over her calf, her knee, then her thigh.

He mumbled words that sounded like "no stays," and Christa might have laughed, except the cacophony of feeling ringing in her mind left her breathless. And when his hand dove under the hem of her chemise and his fingers fumbled for the tie to her bloomers, she let him. His fingers stayed there, weaving back and forth, touching her waist and her waistband, waiting, waiting.

Yes! She arched her back impatiently.

"Patrick, please."

Christa's whisper stayed on his lips and one of his hands pushed her hair back, over and over. Her whimper would have drowned in their mixed breaths, except that Patrick suddenly turned from rousing to soothing her.

"Shh, honey."

"I'll hush, but don't stop." It was the most complex thought she could muster. "Patrick."

"You don't want this. I'd be a sorry son of a bitch to take you, with the way—"

"I do want you. I don't care—"

He weakened and kissed her again, then set her shoulders away from his so firmly it hurt. His voice shook as he tried a feeble joke.

"See what a little roughness can get you?"

They lay on their sides, face to face, and she glared as if her eyes could set him afire.

"Don't think you can come back to me, after this." Embarrassment choked her. Why had he stopped? Why had he given her time to see herself like this, a panting beast? "This is no joke, Patrick. I've never— Damn you!" She clutched his shoulders as if her fingers could meet through his flesh.

"Is that the way you want it between us?" He jammed his body atop hers, grinding his denims against her softness. "Is it? Me doing it because you're mad?" He held her chin in one hand, forcing her to meet his eyes. "Because I can. Lord, yes. I'll be inside you so fast you won't have breath to change your mind."

Her head reeled. Heat consumed her from the core outward and his ragged breaths were frightening balm.

"It's not anger. I'm not mad at you. I just—" She hugged him with all her strength, but she could not say she loved him. Not after coming back to him. Not after proving herself. Not *first*.

Christa surged closer. If her body surrounded his, if his ached and he knew her for the cure, then he'd tell her. He kissed her throat, and behind closed eyelids her world swirled fire-orange.

"Just tell me, Patrick. Can't you at least—"

His mouth covered hers, milking her lips for forgiveness, pressing so hard her teeth cut her lips. Then he rolled away. The chaos in her mind, the pounding in her veins, stopped as if a lid covered her in darkness. She lay still with arms and legs straight. As if she were dead.

The bed creaked as Patrick sat up. He smoothed a hand down her bodice, closing a button. He patted her skirts over her legs, and Christa opened her eyes to his frown of profound sadness.

"Christa. *Christa*."

He snatched his hands back, laying them on his legs,

fingers stiff and extended, as if he'd pull something from her by sheer will, without touching.

"What, Patrick? Tell me." Could her chest cave in from such pain?

"Don't cry, honey. Oh, don't."

She didn't. Not when Patrick shook his head and touched one finger to her lower lip. Not when he stood and she watched him find the bottle of whiskey and walk to the door, moving as if his legs were jointless planks. Not even when he lifted his hat from the hook and hefted the bar from the door.

Only when she was alone, staring out the window at the hard, barren land, did Christa cry.

What if you had a little boy and his mama died. What if you carried him on your back while you killed Indians and wild animals. What if he never went to school, never played with other children, never had a birthday cake. Would you, in your tattered buckskins and harsh beard, ever tell that little boy he was loved?

And if you never did, how could he ever grow up and know what it meant?

Twenty

Christa refused to explain her reasons for breaking Patrick's most adamant, unquestioned rule.

"Christa, you can't ride into town alone." Dan stood beside Cloud, watching Christa saddle up. "Knowing the gracious town of Coyote, you've excited enough talk by killing your husband and alienating your sister-in-law."

"Not to mention burning an entire batch of stew." She refused to rise to his bait.

"How are you going to answer Francesca's threat, anyway? Christa?"

It had been a mistake showing her brother Francesca's letter. Now he expected her to do something about it. Christa shrugged, then tightened Cloud's girth. The gelding swung his heavy white head back to look at her, then blew a disappointed breath through his lips as if he'd decided it was a poor day to test her.

"That's all? A shrug? Christa, Francesca would delight in taking every penny of what Nathan left and spending it on—laxatives!"

Christa patted Cloud for his good judgment and wished Dan learned as quickly.

"I refuse to worry what people, including Francesca, say. The best thing about being ruined, Dan, is freedom."

"You're not ruined. Sakes, Christa, it's just that with you and Trick sort of, well, being out here alone, with all these men and no chaperon . . ."

She checked the buckles on her saddlebags, made sure

Patty was out of heel range, and mounted Cloud. "Dan, if I weren't ruined before, I am now. Coyote's no different from Sacramento. It doesn't matter what I've done. They'll think what they want."

Between her legs, Cloud tightened, reconsidering his urge to buck. Christa smacked him with the ends of her reins.

"Since you're set on going, why don't you ride Betsy?"

"Cloud's just being a scamp, because of the rain. I'll use his energy fast enough." She kept the horse dancing in place. "Patty babe, your job is to find a piece of rope about twice as long as you are. Can you do that?"

"In the barn, Mama?" Patty's earnest face made Christa flinch. Her child deserved a better mother than this hussy preparing to gallop into town. "Should I look there?"

"Good idea. When you find it, get Uncle Dan to teach you how to skip rope. If he won't"—Christa raised her voice over Dan's protest—"we'll do it when I get home. When I get *back*," she corrected. "We'll play all afternoon. It's our last day of vacation, since Mr. Trick is going to let all the cowboys take turns coming in for supper."

"Oh, goody."

"Oh, goody, indeed." Turning to her brother, Christa tugged the brim of her hat in true cowboy fashion. "Adios."

"That means 'go with God.' Did you know that?"

Christa lifted one hand in a despairing gesture, but she couldn't speak.

"Hurry back, Sis."

"Bring me candy, Mama."

Each time her mind replayed yesterday, Christa's heart dropped through a trapdoor. Each time she remembered his indecent warning, her stomach fell away with desire. And that, she supposed, was how a woman could tell whether she loved a man. If obscene words turned you to jelly, you knew. It was not, however, a hint she'd pass on to Patty.

Christa and Cloud were winded and calm by the time Starr's Saloon blotted the horizon. She was determined to accomplish the errands on her list quickly. By the time she returned *The Deerslayer*, retrieved Patrick's mended branding iron from blacksmith David Malloy, purchased a slate for Patty, a nutmeg for a spice cake, candles and fresh saleratus from the mercantile, and begged Rosebud's company as an overnight guest, she should be drained of all passions and a fit mother once more.

Passing Starr's Saloon, Christa kept Cloud at a smart trot. She considered it a good omen when the odd prospector, Monk, failed to greet her with wild pronouncements.

The proprietor of Malloy's Livery and Smithy watched her ride toward his establishment. David Malloy's red-gold hair, open smile, and hasty buttoning of his white shirt, might set some women—especially the sort looking for a home in Nevada—aflutter with heart palpitations.

"Mrs. Worth!" Pigtails flying, long legs churning below a cranberry-colored skirt, Rosebud cut across the street from the mercantile, straight into Christa's path.

Rosebud coughed and leaned both hands against her knees, trying to get her breath, and Christa was struck again by the knife-sharp part in the child's black hair.

"Rosebud Kathleen Malloy, you're to get yourself straight back into bed. What am I to do with her?" David Malloy transformed himself from admirer to worried father with just his outflung hands.

Rosebud looked up, pained and pale.

"Don't talk. Save your breath. It's my fault for allowing you to go over to Hacklebord's." He gently unfolded Rosebud from her bent position. "Give yourself room to breathe.

"All night, I've sat up plying her with squaw tea. Garlic paste on the chest is what my mother swore by, but will this little miss tolerate it?"

"S-smells funny."

"Well, were they in? Push your breath out all the way before you draw a new one. That's the way." He rubbed the child's back in hard circular motions.

"Not yet," she wheezed, then added to Christa, "We ordered my spectacles."

Rosebud managed a glorious smile before her lashes closed on ash-colored smears beneath her eyes. Christa could well believe the child had been up all night, struggling for breath.

"Mr. Malloy, you must let me help. Do you need anything from the mercantile? I've heard some plasters and aromatics help with breathing troubles. Please."

"No, no." He glanced inside his dark shop, where Christa made out a stableful of tethered horses. David followed her glance. "The faith healer," he explained. "He's bringin' in folks from all over."

"As a fellow parent, if not as a friend, you must let me help." Christa met his eyes more boldly than usual and he sighed.

"Well, you wouldn't be seein' Lucy Moore, now, would you?"

"I don't know Mrs. Moore yet." She hazarded a guess, to keep him from turning away help. "Does she work with Miss LaCrosse?"

"Never in a hundred years. Lucy Moore is a Mexican girl, sister to Trick's vaquero, if I'm not mistaken."

"Ramon?"

"That's it. She's a chandler, after a fashion. Makes candles and honey candies, keeps hives of bees that're forever swarming and making folks miserable." He flashed a hint of his usual smile. "Not really. It's happened only once, but ask Polly LaCrosse and they're buzzing down her chimney near every day. Lucy makes some medicinal candles that ease my Rosebud's breathing."

Christa didn't let him finish his explanation. "Fine. And is there anything else?"

"Nothing." He gave Rosebud a push toward their cottage behind the smithy. "Back to bed with you, now. Draw Patty some more pictures and Mrs. Worth can take them when she comes for this fine boyo." David Malloy took Cloud's reins.

"Wait." Rosebud opened her fingers as if they'd stuck to the crushed paper within. She extracted it, frowning over its condition, and gave it to Christa. "For you."

"Thank you." Instead of stashing the paper in her saddlebags, Christa loosened the drawstring on her reticule and slipped it inside, charmed by the little girl's gesture. "You rest, Rosebud. I'll be back with those candles and maybe a surprise. But I'll only leave it with your father *if* you're fast asleep."

She found the chandler's shop with little difficulty, but she couldn't get through the door. A bell tinkled the exit of a tall male customer. Christa tried to avoid him as he backed from the shop, talking with arms loaded.

"Lovely work, as usual, Luz. And thanks for the sweet. It's a pleasure doing business with you."

His unfamiliar accent and splendid black suit made it clear the man didn't belong in Coyote. For an instant, as he protected his burden, Christa thought he carried an infant. Then she saw the tips of ornate ivory candles. He tried shifting his parcel from both arms to one and finally gave up.

"Excuse me, ma'am." He wore sparkling white linen, pricked with diamond shirt studs, and she'd never seen brandy-brown eyes glitter with such utter self-possession. "Both for backing into your path and for not tipping my hat."

"That's quite all right," she said, but he showed no inclination to move out of her path.

"Mrs. Worth? I'm John Starr."

That explained the too-forward speculation in his eyes. The saloon owner supposed they were two of a kind. She nodded politely and stepped around him.

"Your grit has set this town on its ear, ma'am. Congratulations."

Had the tinkling bell confused her? Half inside the shop, Christa stared back over her shoulder. John Starr winked.

In the moment it took the shopkeeper to hurry from her

back room, Christa read a small hand-carved sign: MRS. LUZ SEYMOUR, CANDIES AND CANDLES. Had she misunderstood the name, as spoken by Coyote's denizens?

It hardly seemed polite to ask the soft-spoken woman for clarification, so she merely made her purchases, including two herbal tapers for Rosebud. Shy as she was, Luz Seymour evidently listened to Coyote gossip. She insisted on giving her two paper-wrapped slabs of honeycomb— one for Patty and one for Rosebud.

Glancing up the street, Christa saw Monk lounge against a hitching post. Before she looked away, he made a throat-clearing sound and drew his index finger across his Adam's apple. She turned the other direction. A curtain twitched, but did not open, as she passed the dressmaker's shop.

What had Dan called it? "The gracious town of Coyote"? His sarcasm was small comfort, but when she stepped into Hacklebord's Mercantile, Hannah's nervous smile helped. At least Hannah tried to be friendly. Then Christa did a mental tally. David Malloy, John Starr, and Luz Seymour had been cordial. Only Polly LaCrosse and a crazy prospector had not. If Hannah Hacklebord fell somewhere between, that wasn't so bad.

"Hope I sweetened those strawberry preserves enough for you." Hannah glanced from the basket of peaches she was arranging to survey the store, as if she didn't want to be caught in her friendliness toward the "black widow."

"Delicious. I must admit we were selfish enough to be glad Mr. Garradine had the hands out on the range. Patty was just silly over them!"

"I'm so glad." She placed the last peach. "Can I offer you a cup of coffee before you begin shopping?"

"No, I won't drink your coffee when I only need a box of saleratus and a nutmeg." Christa surveyed the four nutmegs. Would it be rude to produce her hat pin and prick them? Muley had told her that was the only sure way to check for freshness.

"You haven't heard anything from home, have you?" Hannah's jittery laugh made Christa look up, but the woman had turned away.

"Nothing since the letter you brought, but wouldn't any letter come here?" Puzzled, Christa approached the counter. "I thought, because of the stage not running, there wouldn't be anything."

Hannah swept a pile of spilled white powder together. "Oh, we get the occasional rider through, mostly headed toward Starr's, or like today, in for the faith healer. The healer isn't expected until tomorrow, you know, and Pilgrims' is already full. But you're right. Mainly we get all the mail."

"What do you hear from your daughter? Hetty, wasn't it?"

"Nothing since I was out to your place—"

Christa almost sagged under the weight of those words. Good Thunder Meadows would never be "her place."

"—wishes she'd find some nice young man and settle down, but the other half wants her home. Sweet Jesus knows no young city boy would settle in Coyote."

Spare, thin-haired Alvin Hacklebord appeared from the back room. "Sounds like a bunch of gabbling geese, from out back. Man can't do his bookkeeping with all the racket."

"Sorry, Alvin." Hannah's hands shook as she folded the top on the box of saleratus and placed it on the counter, next to the nutmeg.

Alvin Hacklebord's froggish eyes shifted behind his wire-rimmed spectacles, probably searching for Patrick. Christa remembered how he'd retreated before Patrick's no-nonsense defense of her.

"Blame me for chatting, Mr. Hacklebord. I'm lonesome for another female voice." Christa had barely placed her coins on the counter when the mercantile door opened on Jeremiah Smit.

"My dear Mrs. Worth!" Orange muttonchops and a green windowpane-checked waistcoat made the attorney impossible to miss. "Just when I'd despaired of never seeing you again, here you are. When David Malloy asked if I'd seen you this morning, I told him no! Told him I feared that you'd found the climate so harsh you just blew away like these god-awful tumbleweeds!"

In spite of his frenzied wringing of her hand, Christa greeted Jeremiah Smit with a smile. He had just evened her mental tally of friends and foes.

"You must allow me to escort you to Pilgrims' for dinner. I will not accept a refusal. Tell Mrs. Worth about the sisters' delectable turkey dinners." He wheeled on Hannah and Alvin so quickly his gold watch chain made a slap.

"Lands, I haven't eaten there in years. It always smells good, though." Hannah's wistful voice sounded like a reproach.

"Humph, such sauces and gravies. A man likes his meat plain." Alvin pushed his spectacles up his nose.

"Not this man." Jeremiah gathered Christa's purchases, offered his arm, and nodded to the door. "The aroma of sausage stuffing and sweet potato pie has wafted into my office all morning. Mrs. Worth, I insist. Besides, I have a bit of news for you."

"News? Good-bye, Hannah! News?" Christa asked again as soon as they reached the boardwalk outside. If the news had originated outside Coyote, she couldn't imagine it was good.

"During our meal, I'll tell you. Otherwise, I'm afraid you'll gallop off on that wild white stallion."

"He's not a—" Christa stopped. Explaining the difference between a stallion and a gelding would be indelicate. "I promise not to gallop off, Mr. Smit."

"Jeremiah." He patted the hand she'd allowed him to wrap through his elbow.

"Jeremiah." Christa remembered how Preach had glared at the round attorney. Heaven knew what Patrick would say, if he came upon them. But Patrick had forfeited his right to an opinion by his callous rejection of her. If Jeremiah Smit

patted her hand and called her by name and she allowed it,
Patrick Garradine could go whistle!

"How goes your estate?"

"Your news, Jeremiah?"

"You promise I don't need to bribe you? All right, then."
He adjusted his bowler to a jaunty angle. "According to a
rider at Starr's last evening, we're just days from going
home, m'lady!"

"Home?" The word sounded a knell in her chest, evoking
the marble-eyed trophies trapped forever in her Sacramento
house.

"It seems the uprising that so frightened our intrepid stage
driver was something of a tempest in a teapot."

Christa matched his steps, fighting the need to bury her
face in her hands.

This journey had been a gamble from the first. She'd had
nothing to lose. Ironically, over these past weeks, she'd
gained something she'd never expected. Now she saw no
way to keep from losing it.

"Just let me step inside my office for a moment." He held
up one finger for her patience.

"Jeremiah?"

He turned with such delight, she felt guilty. "Yes, my
dear."

"If there were to be trouble with my husband's estate,
could you help me?"

"Of course. Of *course*. There's nothing I'd like better! If
this village had a telegraph office, I'd handle it for you like
that!" He snapped his fingers, inclined his head a bit too
near, and brushed at his impeccable muttonchops. "What
would the problem be? Greedy relatives?" He chortled at
her gasp. "It's the usual, my dear Mrs. Worth. I'll be right
back."

Christa stared at the horizon, but she couldn't see her
Calico Mountains from here. It shouldn't take a fortune to
buy acreage in Nevada. With Daniel's help, she could
manage a ranch. How much could it cost to buy cows? As

if she'd find it therein, Christa fumbled in her reticule and encountered Rosebud's drawing.

Except it wasn't a drawing.

The folded and refolded scrap was part of a letter in Francesca's ant-tracks hand. Someone had given it to Rosebud to deliver. Who? The salutation had been ripped off, and the letter's tone made it clear it was not written to her.

Christa tried to puzzle out Francesca's charge. Her sister-in-law believed her a murderess and would make her pay. Nothing else was terribly clear.

But that wasn't the oddest thing. Across the letter, printed in blue ink, were additional words: "Be wary. Friend."

At the jingling of keys, she stuffed the letter back into hiding. Probably she should share this with Jeremiah. He was the expert. And yet, she couldn't. First she'd ask Patrick who he thought had warned her. He couldn't read handwriting, but he read people as easily as he did the land and animals. Effortlessly, he'd made Alvin Hacklebord leave her alone and kept Polly LaCrosse at arm's length.

Too worried to feel hungry, Christa apologized to Jeremiah and urged him to go on to Pilgrims' and eat a serving of sweet potato pie for her. Then Christa delivered Rosebud's candles and rode out of town.

It wasn't until Christa had urged Cloud into a forested shortcut that she realized Patrick had read her just as easily as he had the others.

On the very day she'd returned to Nevada, Patrick had called her foolhardy. He thought she took risks. He said he couldn't protect her from her own recklessness. She'd denied it with cooking and cleaning and planting and protests, and yet here she was, alone, compromising her safety exactly as he feared.

Cloud shied at a tree's bobbing shadow. To an animal born to open terrain, accustomed to seeing miles around him, this spare copse seemed cramped and dangerous. Patrick probably wouldn't have brought him this way.

Christa was cursing her rash decision to take the shortcut, when it struck. As if someone had swung a full grain sack against her head and shoulders, she plunged off Cloud, to the earth.

Damn it to Hell. He might as well marry an orphan asylum as Christa.

Startled by the turn of his thoughts, Trick might have spurred home alone if he hadn't caught a flash of white up ahead. If it was Cloud, he'd pull Christa right off the gelding, turn her over his knee, and give her the paddling a wayward child deserved.

He hadn't been due back to the ranch until tomorrow. It had been sheer luck that he'd ridden in to check on Pete. Truth to tell, he'd been checking on Christa. She'd held off, brave as could be, but he knew she'd broken down after he closed the door. He'd left her on his bed, crying in the rain.

She didn't deserve that. Not when she'd come into his arms so willing. Not when she'd touched his face like he was the most important thing in her world. Damn.

Imp shied into a stutter step, then continued loping. Trees. Desert horses didn't care for the confinement, but he'd take it slow and hope Christa had done the same.

Everyone in town said he should have passed her—him riding out, her riding back. Everyone. Right. *Every man, more like.* Christa had by God talked to near every man in town: David Malloy, John Starr, Monk, Alvin Hacklebord, Jeremiah Smit.

Now there was a sorry-ass excuse for a man. That soft, ginger-whiskered lawyer reminded him of a lady's pet.

He was a lot like Nathan. When Christa admitted the coldness of her marriage, she'd set fire to Trick like nothing else could. Each time he pictured Nathan's hands on her, he raged to replace them with his own. When he imagined that fool mindlessly rutting atop her, he wanted to show Christa her body could be worshiped.

He should have killed Nathan three years ago, just put

him down like a destructive animal. But he couldn't kill a dead man. The best he could do was protect Christa this time.

At least this Smit character worried over Christa. The fool had rushed Imp and started tugging on Trick's stirrup leather like he'd pull him down, all the while accusing him of ruining her. He'd settled down enough to do business later, but—

Suddenly, Cloud came toward him at a shambling trot, cautious, sideways, limping. A smear of blood marked his neck.

Oh, dear God, no. I don't want to be right about this one. He didn't stop to check if the blood was Cloud's or hers. Trick spurred Imp into a gallop, trusting his eyes to stare off the black's left side, following the trail. Cloud ran along behind, fishtailing from one side to the other.

Cloud shied, ramming Imp from behind, just as Trick saw her.

For the first time, he knotted Imp's reins to a branch. He didn't trust the gelding to stay ground-tied, and he couldn't chance the horse running off, not with Christa lying before him, facedown and still.

Twenty-one
❧❧❧

She was breathing. Thank God for that. Trick knelt beside Christa, one hand just touching the back that rose two notches, then fell. *I love . . . her. I love . . . her.* Trick's confession kept pace with her breathing at the same time he cursed her for coming back. It had been so easy loving a faraway angel. This headstrong woman, who defied—no, denied—his authority, then surrendered in his arms, would wring the hearts out of both of them.

He was doing no good sitting here. Lifting her hat, he started at her neck. With careful fingers, he felt down the length of her spine, then checked her arms and legs. No broken bones. Closing his eyes, he let his fingers touch her hair. Blood. His heart lurched at the stickiness, yet nothing showed on this side of her.

"Christa? I'm going to have to turn you over. Let me move you just a little bit, honey. Then I'll take you home."

She stirred, stifled a cry, and her hands moved in the dust, like Patty's did when she was napping. She'd heard him. He supposed that was good, but he still had to turn her. *Sweet Jesus, please don't let me hurt her.*

She'd hit face first. Blood smeared her brow and she'd have a black eye, but the rest were only scratches, red and dirty on her pale skin.

Her lips moved and he cleared a thread of hair from the corner of her mouth.

"I'm here, Christa. I've got you, honey." *Tell me you're all right. Tell me I wasn't too late.*

Her little skull was no bigger than his outspread fingers. How much shaking around could she tolerate?

"I'm awake." She said it on a disgruntled sigh, as if she didn't want to rise and cook breakfast. Then her body jerked, realizing where it lay. "Did Cloud fall?" Her eyes fluttered open. "Did he fall?" she demanded, then her hand came up to her head.

"Cloud's fine. He's eating leaves or some such, over there."

"My head. Oh, I told Patty we'd— What time is it? Not night yet?"

Did she think it was dark? Gooseflesh puckered Trick's arms. It was bright noon, even in this grove.

"It's early yet. Patty won't be worried. How bad does your head hurt? How'd you fall off?"

"I didn't fall. Ow!" Indignation made her sit up, but the injury forced her back down. "Oh, I feel sick." She grimaced and covered her lips with the back of her hand. Small rocks had shredded her palm. "I didn't fall. Something hit me in the neck, in the top of my shoulders, and threw me off. Patrick, I feel awful."

"Are you sure?"

"Mercy, Patrick, I think this is *one* thing I do know—" Her voice flared from outrage to giddy amusement and he couldn't tell if it was the head injury or her normal tangled emotions.

"No, honey. Are you sure someone knocked you off? Maybe you rode under a branch."

"No one could ride up behind and me not . . . Patrick, credit me with having ears."

No one could ride up unnoticed, but what if they'd already been there? Trick squinted up at the sparse leafy canopy. Not many hiding places, but a rider kept his eyes forward, especially with a demanding horse. She might not have heard anything until the bastard jumped.

"Patrick, I feel sick."

"I'm taking you home."

Her eyes opened, questioning the sudden change in his voice.

Christa hadn't been jumped by an animal. Unconscious, she would've been dinner. Any beast crazy-brave enough to ambush a human had to be starving. No, her attacker was human, and all Coyote's misfits were in town, accounted for. This time the Yateses had gone too far.

Patty was crying. Her daughter's fingers clutched hers. Christa wanted to comfort her, but only managed a squeeze.

"Mamaaa," Patty said in a quiet sob. She gave Christa's cheek a delicate open-palmed pat, then laid her face against her mother's, matching breaths.

"Mama's all right," Christa whispered. Poor little girl, to lose her father and worry over a reckless mother.

At least Patrick had brought her home. The ride had been both a nightmare and a dream. Pain had lanced through her head and shoulders, but Patrick cradled her against his chest, soothing her, loving her—even if he didn't know it.

Dan's voice jarred her back into this cabin. "I ought to kick your ass, Garradine. Bringing her out here—" Dan spoke from the other room, but Christa felt Patty startle at the bite in her uncle's voice. "—and what did you do to her, in here yesterday, to make her ride off like that? I swear to God, if you—"

"Me? Hell, I wasn't exactly the one standing here, watching her saddle up, was I?" Trick's voice was low, conversational, and Christa hoped Dan knew how to duck. "You're the one who stayed home, knittin', until you got scared, and when I—"

"Scared? Smart, maybe. I got to thinking about the way you've been sniffing around her. Every time she turns her back, you're like a he-dog—"

"Shut up!" Christa wanted to shout, but the tearful croak was equally effective. "Just shut up."

They hovered over her. Like the deathbed scene in *Uncle Tom's Cabin,* but who'd been dying? Little Nell? Uncle Tom? Weariness weighed her down, fogging her memory.

"My mama's sick!" Patty scolded. "Shut you up!"

Christa knew she shouldn't have let Patty hear her speak that way, but the men's altercation had been even worse.

"I know, sugar. I'm sorry we talked so loud. Careful, now, don't jostle her. You want to come up to me?"

Through her lashes, Christa saw Patrick hold out his arm.

"No. She's got a bandage." Patty bounced on the bed, staying put.

"Sis, can I get you something?" Dan's paternal tone made it clear he'd elbow Patrick from her sickroom.

"I need to get off my back. I can't seem to turn over alone." She heard them move to help her, muttering. She didn't have the energy to referee. When she faced the sheets, her nightgown bunched up around her legs and her spine complained of the forced curve, but her neck hurt worst of all. "Is my neck bleeding or something?"

Dan started to lift her hair, then stopped. Did he gesture at Patrick or just glare?

"Hell, what do you think I'm going to—?" Patrick's sigh came up from his boot toes. "I've seen lots of riding injuries. I'm a fair hand at tending 'em. I'd as soon cut off my arm as hurt her."

"All right. Patty, go play over by the hearth," Dan ordered.

"Let her stay," Christa mumbled against the pillow. "Let her see it's just like a skinned knee."

"If you could unbutton it in front," Patrick said, "I could slip it down far enough to see."

Burning with embarrassment, Christa did as he said. Callused fingers pulled the neck of her gown back, and the jolt through her senses did not come from pain.

"It's purple and black," Patty observed.

Patrick's fingers drifted from her neck, across her bare shoulders, to the space between her shoulder blades.

"Just bruises, sore muscles." The hand withdrew. "Give it a few days and you'll be fine."

"You're bringing the men in tomorrow. I can't coddle myself while they go hungry." Even if she could sit up and put her feet on the floor, could she lace her shoes?

"That'll wait. Trick has other business."

"What?"

"Sis, that kind of twisting around is what's going to keep you in bed. I swear!"

"What other business?" Gathering the herd, tending the ranch, that was his business. What could take him away?

"I need to hire a trail cook. The drive's going to commence in a week."

Did he do that intentionally? Hint that their time had shrunk to a few days, so she'd ignore the vengeance she heard brewing in his voice? Dan sounded no different than he had as a child, planning feuds with the neighborhood bad boys. Other business, indeed!

"Don't go after the Yates brothers." She struggled into a half-sitting position, though her stomach lurched.

"Lay back down, Christa." Patrick exchanged a glance with Dan.

She closed her eyes, but the room still spun in a sickening parabola. "There's a treat for Patty in my saddlebags." She had to say some harsh things to Patrick, and she didn't want an audience.

"That honeycomb?"

"I could eat it, Uncle Dan."

"It's a gooey mess, Sis."

"I would like to eat it now." Patty beguiled her uncle with a smile.

"Just tie a dish towel around her neck and let her eat it, Dan." She yawned, and Patrick made settling motions as Patty led Dan into the other room.

"Don't go after them. Not for me."

Patrick squinted at the wall, as if a window had opened over her head.

"Don't you dare kill someone in *my* name. What if they did find Patty's bonnet and then block the creek? Is that a crime?"

"You're set on talking about this, so go ahead. I'll sit here and make sure you don't hurt yourself, but I ain't listening, because you don't make sense."

Silence simmered between them, until Christa continued. "Think. The bonnet and the rocks. It's a childish thing to do. Kind—finding the bonnet and wanting to return it—then spiteful, because the kindness embarrassed them." She watched him as her words sank in. "I bet it was Thad. Patrick, think how those boys live. With their father like he is."

Patrick pulled her sheet up higher and folded it neatly at her waist. Then he rebuttoned the neck of her gown.

"Show a bit of mercy, for your own sake, if not theirs."

"Christa, I follow lots of your philosophizin', but what in hell is that supposed to mean?"

"You're awfully good at feeling guilt, Patrick. Over me and Patty, over your hands not getting along, over your cows and chickens dying!

"How would you feel if you shot someone over a mistake? Maybe I *did* fall off! Didn't you say Cloud was tricky as a back road after dark?" She lowered her voice when Josh walked stiff-legged into the room, regarding them both with suspicion before he scooted his nose under Christa's hand.

"You talked me into not killing that dog, but this is different." He brought her a glass of water and cupped the back of her head to help her drink.

"I didn't talk you into anything." She looked up at him then, and for a minute he watched her so intently, he failed to see the empty glass.

"Patty, then." He turned away.

"Neither of us, Patrick. You saw for yourself. You were wrong. Josh just took a while to grow up."

The collie growled a squeaky sound and plopped on the floor.

"Christa, we're not talking about a dog that's afraid of cattle. We're talking about men terrorizing you at night. I watched you shiver and slug down that whiskey, remember? We're talking about an 'accident' that might have snapped your neck!"

"Not about you being able to protect me if the hand of God strikes me down?"

"Now why would you say something like that?" Patrick rubbed his hands over his face before flinging them down in frustration. She grabbed the nearest one, but he wouldn't sit.

"Because you can't be everywhere at once, Patrick." Her eyelids sagged and she wanted nothing more than his warm, heavy weight beside her in this bed. Asleep. "Because you are the most wonderful man in the world, but you aren't perfect. You could make a mistake."

"I won't." He disengaged his hand and touched a kiss to her hair.

Behind closed eyelids, she heard him move through the pantry, jumbling food into a gunnysack. She heard his boots stop before the hearth. Looking toward her room? It didn't matter. The last thing she heard was the Winchester's polished wood stock, sliding from its rack over the mantel.

By the end of her first full day in bed, Christa convinced herself that she'd taken worse falls as a child. She ached, of course, and her black eye was quite the ugliest thing ever to blemish her face, but when she regained the ability to swivel her head from side to side, and saw the cluttered cabin, she wanted up.

"Dan, I've asked you three times to wipe the honey off that table. I can see it from here. It's going to drip on the rug and stain!"

As Dan's deliberate footsteps approached, she realized he was not only mad, he was walking without a limp.

His shaggy white-blond hair had always been great camouflage. When he swept it out of his eyes, Christa saw she'd pushed her big brother as far as he'd allow.

"That's it. If you're well enough to sound like Francesca, you're well enough to get your fanny out of bed and back into the cookhouse." He untied a dish towel from around his waist and threw it on the foot of the bed.

"Patty is driving me mad with this piggity, biggity,

whatever it is. I can't pretend I see it, Christa. Call me a rotten uncle, but I'm sick of that game."

"Dan, I appreciate—"

"What's more, I can't cook. And I won't clean. If Trick Garradine has a stain on his rug, I don't give a fig.

"He got on his horse and rode out of here yesterday, just like he always does. And I don't know if he's waiting in ambush for the Yateses, needing me to cover his back, or laying dead on their doorstep, or in jail."

Christa swung her bare feet onto the floor. It wouldn't help Dan, Patty, or the hands for her to sit here mulling over those same thoughts. She stood, straightened her knees, and took an exploratory step. Her head felt as if she balanced it on a platter.

"I'm sure he's not dead, Christa. Sorry." Dan steadied her arm and adjusted the misbuttoned neckline of her gown, staying beside her as she hazarded a step.

Once she got her bearings, she'd be able to walk just fine. Perhaps she could make a simple dinner, like chipped beef and gravy over biscuits.

"Are you two in love or something?"

She grimaced at the thought of wielding a rolling pin with her sore shoulders. Perhaps no biscuits. She couldn't answer Dan, nor could she let him think her frown applied to his question.

"Or something," she said.

"That's enlightening." Dan stepped back to watch her, then blushed. "If he'd taken advantage of you, would you tell me?"

"Yes." She pulled a shawl around her shoulders. "If I'm ever stupid enough to let a man take advantage of me, after the lessons I learned from Nathan, lock me in an asylum."

"That wasn't quite what I meant, Sis." He folded his arms. "Has he made improper advances?"

Not nearly often enough.

"I'm a seasoned widow woman, Danny, don't worry."

"Mama!" Patty, flushed with sun, Josh dancing at her heels, burst into the cabin. "Can we skip rope?"

Patty's fine blond hair had only gone unbraided for twenty-four hours, but it frizzed around her head in a halo of snarls.

"Not yet, baby. My head still hurts."

"I'm sorry, Mama." Just then, a far honking sound made Patty turn. "Mama, come see!"

Her tug telegraphed pain from Christa's hand down her spine, but Christa went, following a sound from her own childish memories of her mother.

On the porch, she held Patty before her, warm against the front of her gown, as Canada geese floated in a drifting vee. Black satin, with white-throated necks extended, the geese swept so low, Christa heard the silken whisper of wind whisk through the gray feathers of their wings.

The wondrous, upturned face of her daughter made her weep.

"Does your head hurt, Mama?"

"No, baby. Sometimes adults are silly. They cry because something is beautiful." *And because it's autumn and my life here is over. I had nothing to lose, so I built something. And now I've lost it.*

"Do you like those birds?"

"I do. I like them a lot."

"Why don't they live in Sacramento?"

"I don't know. They might. Just not where we do. Maybe they need open space to land. Do you suppose?"

"I don't want to go back to Sacramento." Patty's hands came to her hips, and she twisted away to face Christa.

"What would you think if we bought our own ranch?"

"I like Mr. Trick's ranch." Her jaw took on a stubborn jut.

"So do I, Patty babe—"

"What about the Gretchens? And piggity and all those cowboys, Mama!"

"Mr. Trick is going to go on a long trip soon, with his cows."

"Why doesn't he take us, instead of his cows?"

Christa laughed and wiped the last tears away.

"Why don't you ask him that, when he gets home?"

When Patrick didn't return after two days, Christa had Dan saddle up Freckles and ride out to the cow camp for news. She hoped he'd stay several days. With one of her cranky housemates gone, she turned her attention to Patty. For the first time in her life, Patty acted like a brat. First, she used Christa's fountain pen to splatter "rain" on Patrick's oak table. Next, cradling her book of Grimms' fairy tales, Patty ripped off the corner of each page bearing an illustration.

Christa sent her to bed with a stern lecture on destroying beautiful things, then sat on the bed next to Patty until long after she'd fallen, sobbing, to sleep. As their life unraveled, Christa blamed herself for loving a man so unlike her that he couldn't see where she'd fit in his life.

She slept late. With Dan and the hands away, she had no one to please but Patty. At dawn, Josh scratched to leave the cabin. Stiffly, she walked across the bare floor and stood in the doorway, admiring the marmalade and cream of her Calico Mountains.

Sleep hadn't erased her troubles, but she'd reconciled herself to them, and instinct told her Patrick would return today.

"Patty?" Christa crawled back into bed, bringing her sleep-limp child along. "Do you want to help me make a birthday cake?"

Eyes closed, Patty inserted her thumb between her lips and nodded. She sucked idly three or four times. Christa removed the thumb and braced for another battle.

"Is it my birthday?" Patty opened eyes of such surpassingly beautiful blue, Christa wanted to say yes.

"I think it's Mr. Trick's birthday."

"Is he home?" Patty scuttled upright, kicking blankets and quilts and Christa.

"Not yet, but I have a feeling he will be."

"Will he make us go out of his house?" Patty frowned.

"No, Patty. Mr. Trick likes us."

Patty didn't look convinced. Was her naughtiness really anger at Patrick? For fighting with Dan and Christa?

"Is he still taking his cows on a trip?"

"I'm afraid he is, but not today." Christa tried to change the subject. "Shall we wear our pink flannel jumpers?"

Patty slipped from bed and went to press her palm against the window.

"It's not cold," she said dubiously, then stripped off her nightgown and waited, arms extended, for Christa's approach.

Dressed in matching jumpers, they picked sixteen fat red strawberries—half of Christa's crop—and ate them with cream and sugar. Then Patty sifted flour while Christa grated the nutmeg she'd had in mind for Patrick's birthday spice cake, three days ago.

"Piggity won't go to Sacramento."

"Oh, I think piggity would like Sacramento." Christa reached for a big mixing bowl and almost dropped it at Patty's vehemence.

"*Biggity,* not p-piggity!"

"I'm sorry, babe, I misunderstood. How are you doing with that flour?" The stove's heat had nearly convinced Christa that Patty was right. The day was too warm for their festive jumpers. When Christa turned to tell her so, Patty had vanished and Josh was barking.

Patty hadn't gone far, but she had tied Christa's silk shawl from Polly LaCrosse on Josh. Then she'd taken him wading at the creek. Alone.

"Young lady, I don't know what to do with you." *Oh, that was a fine thing to tell a child who already had the upper hand!* "Get yourself into the cabin and stay there until I've baked this cake, and then we're going to have a little talk."

"No talks!"

"Yes, talks. Josh, you stay outside."

"Mama!"

* * *

In peace, Christa finished sifting and stirring, separating eggs and measuring cinnamon and cloves. She drank a cup of coffee as the cake baked, almost dozing with placid thoughts of Patrick.

She pictured his night-black hair and mustache, his body over hers as it had been for just a moment, and she wondered what their own child might have looked like. She'd never know, but even if she couldn't stay with him, she'd make sure he remembered her. Every August, he'd remember the only woman who'd baked him a birthday cake.

The spice cake sat cooling on the sill when she roused herself to go back to the cabin. It had been over an hour, a sufficiently long punishment. Even Josh had tired of waiting and trotted off on some errand of his own.

All was quiet inside. Christa untied her apron as she crossed to the bedroom. Patty had cried herself to sleep.

No. Christa turned fully around, surveying every corner of the tiny bedroom. She bent to look under the bed, noticing that her back didn't hurt. That was a mercy, but Patty wasn't there.

"Patty?" Christa strode to the pantry. Patty was never still. Christa knew she'd hear her, even if Patty was hiding.

Empty.

Christa walked back onto the porch and stood silently, repinning her chignon and listening. Chickens, a cawing jay, the creek's murmur, Cloud stamping.

"Patty?" Her voice hovered for a minute, then fell, leaving her quite alone. Christa crossed to the center of the yard and turned again, looking in every direction. "Josh!" she shouted.

"—osh!" Her echo came back from the stone stable. By the time she'd searched the stable, the bunkhouse, and the creek bank, she knew Patty was gone.

How far could a little girl go in an hour?

Twenty-two

His bones had turned to mush and his eyes burned from watching. Trick rubbed a hand over his jaw and the sharp black stubble bit back. He stood and rolled his shoulders and wondered how Christa's were, just as he had every hour since he'd set up camp above the Yateses' homestead.

He hadn't felt like this since Shiloh, and he probably looked like one of those hollow-eyed, stiff-legged skeletons he'd seen wandering Southern roads.

But he wouldn't give up. Both red Tennessee Walkers, the wagon horse and wagon, were gone. With every minute Trick hunkered in the sagebrush, his conviction grew. The Yateses' had ambushed Christa and afterward hightailed it for town. They were lying low, probably at Pilgrims', hoping he'd lose interest or wouldn't want to make a ruckus in town. It didn't matter how long they hid. Sooner or later, the Yateses were dead men.

For three days he'd remembered how Christa had looked, facedown in the dirt. She looked *dead*, damn it! Trick worked his jaw and swallowed against emotion that refused to be diluted, no matter how often he poured it out. He saw her gold braid caked in dirt and her black hat back on its string. His medicine bag had twisted backward around her throat, and he'd thought of keeping it for Patty. Scuffs in the dust at her feet showed how she'd struggled to rise.

The dead couldn't hear. Those words had echoed in his mind as he walked toward her. If the dead couldn't hear, Christa would never again answer Patty's cry and wrap her in gentle arms. If the dead couldn't hear, Christa would never shiver at the wild sweet calls of coyotes. Christa, dead, would never hear a cowardly man finally confess he loved her.

And when she awoke and he carried her home, when he'd touched her bruised back in the cabin, he still wasn't brave enough to tell her. It had been a hundred times easier to pick up the Winchester and walk out.

She'd urged him to feel mercy, but he couldn't. Not to the Yateses, not to her. Mercy had no more place here than Christa did.

Soon as the Yateses showed their heads, he'd plink down all three. No discussion, no excuses. They'd had three chances too many. By the time the U.S. marshal made his way to Coyote, Trick would have raised a week's worth of trail dust, bound for Reno with his herd.

Trick stood, tightened Imp's cinch and slipped the bit back into his mouth. The black shook his forelock back from brown eyes and stamped, eager to go home. Trick shook his own head, trying to clear it.

Thinking like a criminal didn't come natural. A dunk in Mud Meadow Creek would drown this dizziness, and a few hours of sleep would harden him. Then he'd be back. The Yates family would be dead before they could hurt her again.

As soon as Trick saw Dan riding toward him, he thought of offering an apology, but Dan beat him to it.

"Sorry about that squabble."

In silence, Trick wrestled with an answer, but none came. He'd gone inside himself, like he had in the war. Christa's brother got only a nod, though Trick felt happy to see Dan riding, and glad to have company for the last mile into the ranch.

The light was odd, outlining weeds with gold, showing shadows in forked prints where quail had scurried from one sagebrush to another. Tumbleweeds, like metal balls too heavy to roll, sat beside rocks. Neither hot nor cold, it was ungodly still, as if the desert held its breath.

She'd ridden right up to him, the horse's shadow mingling with his, before he realized Christa was no mirage. Trick took his old cavalry canteen from his saddle and dashed what water he had in his face. He scrubbed both hands hard against his face, then shook the moisture from his hair.

"Haven't been sleeping." Water dripped from his eyebrows and he sniffed. "Damn it, Christa, are you trying to cripple yourself?"

"Patty's gone. I've looked everywhere."

"Josh—"

"Is gone, too. I saw her half, no, an hour and a half ago."

"Did she just wander off while you were taking a walk?" Dan asked. "Maybe she's hiding from you."

"I was punishing her. She didn't want to go back to Sacramento, and—"

"You punished her for that?" Dan slapped his hat against his thigh.

"Doesn't matter." Trick's mind hadn't gone so numb that he didn't think of Patty falling, crying, facedown in the dirt like Christa. "Dan, ride to the cow camp and tell them to come in way close. How far could Patty walk in an hour?" Her name was out before he could catch it. Patty. Patricia. Named for him. "Ride with me?" he asked Christa, and she nodded.

They checked the shade of every boulder big enough to cast a shadow, and rode into each gully deep enough to grow a sticker.

"She knows better." Christa closed her eyes, blaming herself, and he couldn't find words to comfort her. They wouldn't work anyway. Not for either of them, until Patty was found.

They skirted Goldwing Seep, flushing a band of three bachelor mustangs who would have spooked long since if Patty and Josh had passed.

"Do you think she fell in the creek?" Christa choked out words so horrible, it had taken her this long to say them.

"Josh would've barked his head off on the bank. He wouldn't have gone with her. Come on, honey. You know that dog hates water."

When Preach caught up with them, his dun's sides heaved and Preach was almost as winded. "Where's 'the little house that isn't there anymore'?"

"What are you talking about, man?"

"When you rode out with those cinnamon cookies, ma'am." He turned to see Christa nodding. "The little girl was telling me and Ramon about 'the little house that wasn't there anymore.' I don't know if it's another one of them things like piggity." Preach frowned in concentration. "She said you could pick strawberries there."

"Shit!" Trick pulled Imp on his haunches so hard the horse squealed. He wheeled in the opposite direction, upstream from the creek, and put his spurs to him.

If he knew the Yateses, they had a hideout right where they'd rigged the avalanche. No wonder he'd sat at the homestead, waiting for men who never came. Would they be satisfied, this time, with just flaunting Patty's bonnet?

Cold reason came back and he slowed Imp, letting him pick his way along the rocky creekside. No wonder they could come pound on the cabin and kill hens, then get clean away. The burned-out cabin was a half-hour walk, tops.

He'd ridden out into full sun when Imp pricked his ears and snorted. A big red horse came toward them at a fluid, loafing walk. Trick pulled the Winchester from his saddle holster and chambered a bullet.

Thaddeus Yates looked damned proud of himself, toting Patty on the saddle before him. Trick hoped Thad enjoyed his smug satisfaction, because he'd never feel it again, ever.

Trick centered his sight between the Tennessee Walker's ears. Just a little closer. The horse turned his head sideways, maybe scenting Imp. Trick wiped his right palm along his pant seam and sighted all over again.

Thad waved. Something not quite right in that, but he'd always been a cocky bastard. He'd show Thad Yates what mercy was about, invading a man's land, scaring his woman, taking his— You could make a mis— Now!

Trick pulled the trigger. Patty bounced up, trying to see over the horse's head, hailing Trick with a wide wave and a shout.

The warning shot kicked up an explosion of dust at the horse's forelegs.

Thank the Lord. If he'd kept that sighting, she'd be dead. Now Josh was barking his narrow collie head off and the red horse threatened to bolt. He would have killed her. Instead, she chattered about piggity, both arms flailing fit to knock Thad Yates onto the ground.

Alive and jabbering, Patty Worth was the prettiest thing he'd ever seen in his life.

"Shucks, Garradine, if I'd a-known you felt that way about it, I'd of left her where I found her." Thad nodded toward the fist-sized rock Trick's bullet had split.

"Mr. Trick, Mr. Trick, biggity eating—"

"Bet your ass he was a big kitty—pardon me, ma'am." Thad nodded to Christa as she galloped up with Preach. Patty struggled to go to her mother and Thad released her inches at a time until her kicking feet reached the ground.

"We were coming back from town, havin' taken Pa in to the faith healer, though just between you and me, the only thing I think that fella has faith in is the power of the collection plate. Anyhow, we were coming back and found her down by the burnt house—you know it? She was squatting there by the river, watching a half-grown cougar eat a deer." Yates pretended to shiver at the memory.

"We were worried he might turn on the child if we scared him, so none of us took a shot."

"Thank God you didn't." Christa tried to lift Patty, but the child was too excited to be hugged. "Patty, was that biggity? Big kitty? The one you saw by the river and out the window that night?"

"Yes. He was eatin' a poor deer. I was trying to make him stop, but he wouldn't listen to me." Patty pumped both fists down at her side and shook her head.

"A lot of people think you shouldn't bother animals when they're eating." Christa sounded a little faint.

He could never tell her it had been her mercy lecture, three days ago, that saved Patty. His hands began to shake, and then his legs. Trick was afraid to dismount, even though he longed to hold Patty in his arms.

"You know what I think, Trick?" Preach pulled at his lower lip. "I think that's the cub you been lookin' for all these months. Teachin' himself to hunt, rather than havin' his mama do it, might cause him to make a few mistakes."

Trick rubbed the back of his neck and wished he had more water. He needed to think. First there'd been the piggity by the creek, eating fried chicken from the two little girls. Sure, that could have been a cougar, skulking around on the other side of the creek. The butting at the windows? If the cat smelled food or saw movement, it was possible. The attacks on the cattle, then hens, and Christa.

"You still blocked my creek." He pointed a less than steady finger at Thad Yates.

"Shoot, you go daring a man to step foot on your property, Garradine, what do you expect? But I was right insulted, and so was Arthur, when you suggested we'd been messin' around your cabin. No, sir, that's not a gentlemanly thing to do, and ma'am, you'll always find us— Ma'am, you're lookin' a mite peaked."

Christa sank down onto a rock, holding her struggling daughter. "Don't you ever run away from me again!" The tears in her voice didn't obscure her words' intensity. "Do you understand, young lady? Never."

"I'm sorry, Mama." Patty sniffed and rubbed her knuckles against her nose. "I don't want to go to another house. I like Mr. Trick's house. And Josh."

"Hey, sugar. Why don't you ride up here with me and we'll talk about it."

"I want my mama."

"I know that, but remember she hurt her back. Don't you think it might be easier for her not to hold you on Cloud?"

"My mama took a fall. Her back looks like a skinned knee," Patty reported to Thad Yates. Before Christa could hand her to Trick, Preach dismounted and boosted her up.

"Does it, now?" Thad asked. "Are you all right, ma'am?"

"I am, but Mr. Yates, I haven't even thanked you!"

"That's quite all right, ma'am. Nothing you wouldn't do for me if I had a child. Isn't that right? That's what neighbors are for." Thad smirked.

"Yes," Christa said, settling herself carefully in the saddle. "Mr. Yates, I have no idea what we're having for supper, but I've baked a birthday cake for dessert. Would you be able to join us?"

"I knew there was a reason I volunteered to bring the little gal back. Mrs. Worth, I'd be delighted."

With all Yates's preening, Trick decided to stick with his original assessment: Yates was a cocky little bastard.

When the triangle rang for dinner, Trick lay flat on his back in the bunkhouse. From his aching dry throat, he knew he'd probably been snoring. Clean from a dunk at the creek, he rolled out of bed and into fresh denims. He'd told Christa she was silly to dream up this fiesta, but she'd ignored him. She'd assigned Dan to nighthawk and told all the other hands to come on in.

The men had latched onto the holiday, with Slim Jim and Ramon bringing guitars and Preach volunteering to cook. The results smelled pretty inviting.

Trick pulled on his boots and jogged out of the bunkhouse. No way in hell was he going to be late for his first birthday party, even if it was his twenty-eighth. Or thereabouts.

Fried steaks and fried potatoes cast a cooking mist inside the cookhouse and out. In spite of the air's autumn chill, someone had hauled the long plank table outdoors again.

It'd be a wonder if the thing didn't fall apart just from all the moving.

Trick stifled a yawn. He should douse his head to wake all the way up. But before he reached the pump, he heard heels clatter down the steps from the cabin and turned. Patty ran to hug him around the knees. Sweet baby girl. How could she make him feel like a fist was crushing his heart? He stood with one hand on her head, watching Christa.

Maybe sore muscles made her move with such slow grace and maybe she looked so elegant because she'd looped her hair up in a smooth city style. She wore a green skirt that clung to her hips, then flared to ruffle around her feet. If she spun herself around, like Patty had commenced doing, the skirt would make a perfect circle. Her blouse, ivory-colored and sheer enough to make him stare, convinced him. She looked good out of mourning. In fact, Christa looked better than any woman he'd ever seen. He couldn't wait to kiss the warm curve of her neck, where she smelled like sweet female and lavender.

"Mrs. Worth, may I escort you to dinner?"

She touched her lips as if thinking, and he wanted to kiss that finger, then push past it to kiss her lips.

"I believe you may."

"You look lovely." A dandy's word, but damn it, the right one. "I never knew until now that I'd fancy a woman with a shiner."

She gasped in embarrassment, but he held her hand tight in the crook of his elbow. What if he could have her to tease every night? Every day and every night, he'd think of more outrageous things to wrench that shocked little gasp from her.

"Don't blush, honey. You're just beautiful."

Christa's cheeks turned redder still by the time they reached the table. Slim Jim and Ramon sang one of his favorite songs as Christa and he approached, but they'd changed the lyrics a bit.

"Eyes like the morning star, cheeks like the rose, our Christa is a pretty girl, God Almighty knows—"

"I think you two have been drinking before dinner." Her prim words failed to shame them into silence.

Every verse made her blush deeper and hold his arm tighter. Trick liked the men's singing just fine.

Preach wasn't a bad hand at cooking, as it turned out, but Trick knew boot leather would've gone down as well as beefsteak, with Christa sitting beside him. The plank table was crowded with all of the hands, plus Thad Yates, and none of the men even tried to keep their eyes off Christa.

Not that he was jealous. That little Texan probably didn't mean a thing by his mealymouthed compliment on the way Christa said grace.

"Ma'am," Pete said, "I never heard any preacher, on this side of the Brazos or t'other, who included horses in prayer. Thank you."

Of course, Ramon, good rider or not, wasn't to be trusted. When the vaquero's eyes turned molasses-gooey and he fired off a romantic-sounding sentence to Christa, then translated it as "I like your shirt," Trick had his doubts.

Bill Williams didn't make any great pronouncements, but the kid drew Christa's brightest smile by putting his chin on the table and peering across to say, "Hello, Patty."

But he almost thanked Thad Yates for flirting with her. When Yates remarked on the candlelight color of her hair, Christa's ankle crossed over Trick's boot, in a sort of ankle hug. It could have been an accident, but when he glanced sideways and saw Christa's intense preoccupation with her food, he didn't think so. He wanted to pull her over against him, feel her thighs brush his as he lifted her onto his lap.

In all, Trick found himself in a poor state to follow Christa's directions about rising from the table to eat birthday cake at the cabin.

As they scuffed across the yard, Bloody Jim Black offered half a dozen suggestions for after-dinner songs that didn't involve horses, cattle, or lost love, but Ramon and Slim Jim scoffed at every one.

Inside, Bloody Jim pursed his lips and nodded, then announced that Christa had worked a miracle by getting that pitiful strawberry vine to bear. When the others saw the white-frosted cake topped by candles and strawberries, they agreed with applause.

Pete built a fire against the evening chill and Patty insisted on bringing in every blanket and quilt from the other room. Everyone got so settled and cozy, Trick wondered if they'd ever leave.

". . . I looked in the window and spied a young cowboy, all wrapped in white linen and cold as the clay . . ."

Ramon and Slim Jim had gotten to the sad songs. Trick would've told anyone who asked that those songs had turned him melancholy, but that would have been a lie.

He studied Christa, a city girl with country eyes, leaning against the back of his horsehair couch with her daughter curled under her arm. This week alone, she'd been scorned by townsfolk, attacked by a cougar, and nearly lost her babe to a misdirected bullet. Because of him.

She sat amid rude wood and rock walls, an educated woman with a covey of untaught cowboys. She hummed with a look of contentment sweet as any man ever hoped his wife would wear. Wife. He couldn't deny that's what he wanted from her. With every day in this cabin, she'd been that. She'd studied him, accepted him, embraced him, in all ways but one.

He wanted the rest of her.

"Will you forsake your house and home, will you forsake your baby? Will you forsake your husband, too, to go with the gypsy Davy?"

Ramon sang directly to Christa. Trick watched her. Blushing and laughing, she shook her head and cuddled dozing Patty all the closer, but she wouldn't look at him. Slim Jim sang a high-pitched response.

"Yes, I'll forsake my house and home and I'll forsake my

baby, and I'll forsake my husband, too, to go with the gypsy Davy."

The cowboys whooped and clapped, fancying themselves gypsies of a sort. Under cover of their noise, Christa glanced at him. She turned away, staring toward the hearth, as Ramon and Slim Jim leaned their heads together and howled a final verse.

"Last night I slept in a feather bed, sheets turned down so bravely. Tonight I'll sleep in the mud and rain . . ."

Look at me Christa. It's what you've given up, feather beds for a shuck mattress, hot tea in warm parlors for dawn with the wind in your hair. You love it all, but it's me too, isn't it? Isn't it?

". . . by the side of the gypsy Davy, by my darling gypsy Davy!"

The guitars' ending strums were loud, but when Josh stood, shook, and scratched at the bedroom door frame, they all noticed. Christa moved with a start and refused to look at him. As if she'd come to some cold conclusion.

"I figure that means it's time for Patty to go to bed." Preach jerked his head toward the door.

Christa wrapped Patty in a blanket. She stood beside Trick, far enough away that he couldn't bump her elbow with his, couldn't feel her skirts touch the seam of his denims.

Each cowboy shuffling toward the door thanked Christa for the party. She gave each man who'd helped in the search for Patty a heartfelt peck on the cheek. He wanted her to stop. He wanted the men to finish congratulating him on being such an old codger. He wanted her alone.

Finally, the line dwindled to Thad Yates. His kiss was for Patty, placed on her slumbering head. "Gotta have me one of these, sometime soon."

"I can never thank you enough, Mr. Yates. I wouldn't know how to begin."

To his credit, Thad Yates shrugged off all flirtation.

"She is a sweet little thing, Mrs. Worth." With an index

finger thick as a sausage, he touched Patty's downy cheek. "She surely is." He tipped his hat and left.

The door hadn't closed when Christa spun away from him. Her slippers tapped across the floor, into the bedroom, and he heard the mattress take Patty's weight. Enough light shone in to show him Christa curving over Patty. She was a silhouette of prayerful thanks and he didn't deserve her. Patty deserved her, and though once he'd given that baby life, today he'd almost killed her. He couldn't tell Christa, ever.

Trick gathered the dishes, ate a last crumb of cake, and moved around the room, doing evening chores he'd always done. Tonight they felt purposeful, a right end to a day. And he wasn't yearning for the night to pass, so he could ride out on a good horse and join his men. He left the quilts strewn around the room. Tonight he wanted to be right here.

He stared at the mantel clock, ticking off its eleven o'clock frenzy of minutes. Three days ago, Jeremiah Smit had said the stage would arrive any day. By this time tomorrow, Christa and Patty could be gone. If he let them go.

Until the songs ended, he would have said it was his choice. *He* could say whether this would be a last bitter-sweet night, with a kiss at the door, or if it would be the first glorious night of a lifetime spent in Christa's arms. But when she returned in a silken rustling of skirts and stopped at the edge of the braided rag rug, there was an odd formality to the way she watched him. He felt at a loss.

That last rainy moment on the bed, she'd told him not to come back to her after *this*. He'd assumed she'd meant the trespass of her body, the way he'd just helped himself. But maybe he'd cut off the feelings she had for him. Maybe Patty's distress over leaving Nevada meant Christa had set her mind on going.

She straightened a chair at the table, then swept a blanket up from the floor and folded it with practiced precision.

When a coyote's call intruded, she went still, holding the blanket against her, as if memorizing the sound.

He'd lay all his cards on the table and give her a chance to change her mind.

"Will you sit with me for a minute, Christa?" He nodded to the hearth, but he was surprised when she sank down before it with the blanket still in her arms.

She gathered her knees under her wide green skirt and locked her arms around them, all tight in a tidy package, with him locked out. He sat beside her, but he didn't know what to say. She wasn't going to make it easy. But when he met her green oasis eyes, he knew Christa wasn't holding him off, or being stubborn.

She'd called her marriage a sham. She'd hated her husband coming to her bed, and covered her revulsion with thoughts of him. Christa had confessed all that and he'd cast it back in her face. He'd kissed her and touched her, then abandoned her by talking of sending her away.

Christa wasn't being stubborn; she was waiting to see how he'd hurt her. This time he wouldn't stop.

Trick felt desire gathering low in him, but he wanted more than entry to her body. One flesh. That's what they had to be, different as they were.

"Christa." He touched one fingertip to the faint bruise beneath her eye, then let it touch the smooth curve at her temple. She made a faint withdrawal, as if holding her breath, and her eyes were wary. "I know things have been uneasy between us."

She cinched her arms tighter around her knees and talked into the fire. "If you wanted to say good-bye, to say let's remain friends, you could have said it at the door like the others. You didn't have to close the curtains and bar the door."

"No. That's not it." His throat kept threatening to close up on him. "You've taught me an awful lot of things, bein' on this ranch. Most all of them involve thinkin' and talkin' — things I didn't do much of. But I can teach you one thing —"

Before I go? He saw the question in her eyes as she pulled the blanket up in front of her like a shield, but she said something altogether different.

"I don't want to walk away from here any more ruined than I am, Patrick."

He let out a long breath, and kissed her. A quick touch of lips, then away. "There. Are you ruined?"

"Don't make fun of me." Her arms dropped and she tried to untangle her feet from her skirt.

He trapped her in his arms, kissing the temple he'd touched, kissing her cheekbone. He held the back of her neck with a gentle curve of fingers.

"Christa, you never asked. You're the one who's good at talking, and you've always told me what I thought of you. Let me teach you what I think."

Confusion wavered over her face as she searched for a trap.

"You're in control, Christa. You tell me when to stop."

"I will," she said, but he was going to make sure she didn't.

Twenty-three

❧

Curved like the outline of a windswept wing, the branch burned brightly. It had smoldered in the back of the fireplace, untouched, all the time Christa watched. Smug, silly piece of wood, to think it could escape once the match had been struck.

Patrick loosened one of her hands from the blanket. He splayed her fingers and kissed the end pad of each one. Then he turned her hand, kissing the scuffed, healing palm. It seemed a sweet, almost fatherly thing to do, until his teeth grazed the swelling of flesh at the base of her thumb and he raised his eyes to her startled ones. He wasn't quite smiling.

Well, he'd taught her one thing, then. A hand could feel more than soap and bread dough and baby's hair. When he closed his teeth in a second nip and she shivered, he moved his lips to her wrist.

Tease, she thought, because the glitter in his eyes was playful, and when he kissed her lips, it was almost nothing—the flutter of butterfly wings. Quicker than she might have liked, in fact, disappointing.

She should have expected it. At first, their kisses had been flavored with three years of separation and yearning. Maybe this was all that was left after turbulent emotions had been leeched away.

"Your back and your neck—?" His sentence began in such a normal tone, she wanted to gnash her teeth.

Would he *teach* her, as he'd promised, or ask after her health? Disgraceful as it sounded, she'd expected instruction in the proper art of loving. Not that she would have allowed his teaching to progress *too* far.

"My back and neck are fine. Nothing on me hurts. Except my knees, which ache from sitting in this awkward position."

"Good." He bowled her over onto a quilt, and then he was above her on all fours, grinning like a wolf as he dusted another brisk kiss on her lips.

Her irritation built only an instant before he lowered his body to fit the length of hers. He kissed her fully, tongue darting inside her mouth. Then he rolled away, tipping her to face him, but keeping her nearly an arm's length away.

A wash of cold air separated their bodies. Frustration cranked tight in her belly. This childish come-hither, go-thither game made her nerves scream. It would serve him right if she said "stop" now. She'd do just that, as soon as he ended this kiss.

Instead, he lengthened it. The aggravation of touching only at the lips, of being kept at arm's length, made Christa tag his tongue with hers. Perhaps she could lure him closer. He responded, holding the back of her head. His fingers sifted through her hair, plucking pins, loosening coils, making it impossible to escape. Her body moved on its own, sliding against his, closing the gap of cold air.

The answering pressure of his hips told her it was time to tell him to stop. What had Patrick said that day? With hard hands and clenched teeth? "I'll be inside you so fast, you won't have breath to change your mind." She hardly had breath now.

A swathe of loose hair had fallen over her blouse, and it attracted all his attention. Now she should be able to align her thoughts and tell him to halt. It was only her hair, after all, that he kissed. He couldn't know the warmth that passed through her blouse and chemise, until her nipples hardened with a tug like pain, straining for his lips.

He must have guessed, because he brushed the hair aside and formed his mouth over the material of her blouse.

No! She must have gasped the word. She must have, but Patrick believed her arms instead, as they tightened around him. His hands cupped the undersides of her breasts and he slanted his mouth over hers, silencing her "no." And that must have been what she'd been trying to say, mustn't it? Because her mouth opened even wider as his hands worked at her buttons.

"Patrick." But she didn't say no as he stripped off her blouse, then rose to his knees, towering over her as he shed his own shirt.

He wasn't going to stop. He'd told her she was in control, but if that was so, why was he taking off his clothes?

His brown muscled chest collided with her ribs and her skirts twisted. His weight should have crushed her. She should have complained, but his lips pulled again at her nipple, with only her chemise between them now. And then he slipped the strap down.

She arched her breast against his mouth, and the keen pleasure had her falling. Behind her eyelids, flame flashed black and gold. And when his hand moved beneath her skirt, "stop" became a mere fragment of the alphabet, odd letters without meaning.

He kissed her, gently, thoroughly, and while she waited for his fingers to pull the tie of her bloomers . . . he didn't. A rush of hot humiliation and passion made her struggle against his kiss as his fingers spread the modesty slit in her bloomers and touched her.

His mouth kept her trapped. Stop. Say it now . . . say it. She couldn't. Her throat uttered animal whimpers and she was too ashamed to open her eyes. She could only respond to his low sounds of encouragement as she rose shamelessly against his hand, and he plied her with a touch she'd never felt.

He turned to unfasten her skirts, to raise her chemise.

"Leave them," she moaned. "Don't stop."

His breath caught loudly and he left everything tangled around her to lower his denims.

"I won't come to you with my boots on."

She felt the smile on his lips as he managed to kiss her and undress them both.

His arms were braced on each side of her when she opened her eyes. Every dream she'd had of him had ended here, with Patrick rising dark above her.

But now he lowered his skin to hers and she wanted him even closer. Each time he pressed against her, she followed his retreat.

"Now, Christa." He held her face between his hands, kissing her as he came fully inside her.

She cried out against his mouth, shrinking away from the burning shock. Then she found herself struggling forward, closer, closer. He took his mouth from hers, stilling for a minute, and when she shook her head, he stopped her.

"Christa, look at me."

She opened her eyes to his firelit face. It loomed so close, she couldn't look away.

"Please don't stop."

"Never. Never." He moved deeper into her, but when she would have let her mind fade away, once more, he called her back. "Christa, I love you."

"I love *you*."

At her aching echo, he came into her as he hadn't before and his power lifted her from the floor. She gasped, sinking her fingers into his flesh. His hands below her tried to meld them into a single being. With every thrust, he strove to make them one.

I love you, I love you, she mouthed the words against each patch of skin she could reach, until he arched, pouring his life into her, and she said it again, aloud.

"You won't be sorry."

Christa lay on her side, facing the fire. His hard knees nested in the curve of hers. His hand wandered the length of her thigh and his lips nuzzled her nape.

"I'm not."

His fingers caught her chin and turned her for his kiss. Then his lips nuzzled back into her neck and he seemed to inhale her before he spoke.

"When the stage comes, don't go."

He loved her. That was enough. More than enough, because Heaven knew, his passion alone could have kept her from going.

"What are you thinking?" He rolled her back to face him. When he stirred against her, she smiled.

"That it really does make a difference, loving someone, when—"

"Hellfire, lady." He lowered his head to her breast and kissed it. "Am I going to have to teach you to *say* it, too?"

"They're not nice words," she said primly.

He laughed, and his hands flowed down her back and back up.

"Some are."

Open-eyed and deliberate, he kissed her.

How could it be that she already felt hollow, without him inside her? How could she be so eager, trembling for him all over again? Because he didn't invade. He possessed, and it was possession dearly urged. She slid her hands over him.

"Teach me the nice words," she whispered.

"Lovemaking." He rolled the syllables off his tongue.

"I knew that one."

"Are you going to stay here and wait for me, Christa?" Patrick's lips brushed back and forth against hers as he watched her eyes. "Will you stay and take care of my ranch while I'm gone? And be here for Thanksgiving and Christmas, too? Stock prices are high. I need to leave soon. This week, or I won't be able to bring you baubles when I come back."

"I don't want baubles."

Traitorous body, to keep telling her love was enough. She didn't need promises.

"Say you will, and I'll teach you another word."

Through his teasing, he looked anxious. Christa rolled onto her back, guiding him astride her.

"Yes," she answered, gasping as he joined their bodies. "I'll take care of your ranch, Patrick Garradine."

He moved full inside, until he lay along the length of her, lips at her ear.

"Coupling," he sighed, making her shiver as he stroked into her. "That's always been one of my favorites."

Then he set about banishing the question mark from her heart.

The hands stayed away that morning, but Christa knew Patty would wake soon. When Josh scratched to go outside, Christa escaped Patrick's arms. She wrapped a blanket around herself, hushing Josh's whining as the dog sniffed the top of Patrick's head.

"Go ahead, you useless mutt." Patrick looked up through half-open eyelids. "In case I failed as teacher . . . last night, what I was trying to tell you . . . you're beautiful, Christa." He lifted the bottom edge of the blanket and kissed her ankle bone.

"Thank you." She felt her cheeks heat and ignored Josh's whines a moment longer. "I never used to blush, you know."

"Mmm." He stretched, smiling. "I think I like the sound of that."

She felt cozy, loose-hipped, ready to spark back into passion if he wanted her again. Christa sauntered toward the door and opened it. A fist appeared at her eye level.

She'd never before seen the man trying to knock on her door. Gray-haired and stocky, he wore a travel-stained shirt and a marshal's star.

"Pardon me, ma'am, for calling so early, but I figured you'd want time to prepare." He re-collected himself, looking away from the blanket and down at a sheet of paper. "Are you Christabel White Worth?"

"I am." She pulled the blanket closer.

"Then this summons is for you, ma'am."

Summons. Although the lawman stared the other way, she was afraid to take the offered piece of paper for fear of dropping her covering.

Tall and firm as a tree trunk, Patrick came to stand behind her. He reached for the paper and let his eyes skim down it with practiced artifice.

"You want to explain this?"

The man's badge said U.S. Marshal, and he considered whether Patrick had issued a challenge or a request.

Bare-chested, with hastily donned denims hanging low on his hips, Patrick ran forked fingers through his hair. The marshal relaxed.

"Pretty much as it appears, Mr. Garradine. Francesca Worth is charging this lady with hoodwinking her brother. Sorry if that's offensive, ma'am, but I'm plainspoken. Your sister-in-law's claiming your child," he lowered his voice, cautious in case Patty was about, "isn't her brother's. She'd get his entire estate, in that case. That's what I'm thinking's got her all stirred up."

He'd addressed most of this to Patrick, but now he took in Christa's tousled hair and the bare shoulder that peeped from the yellow blanket.

"Marshal, may I offer you coffee?"

"No, ma'am. My guts ain't what they used to be."

"Cake, then. I have this nice spice cake sitting here, drying out. I insist." She whirled inside to get it, and he continued talking to Patrick.

"I rode in last night at about the same time as Circuit Court Judge Leland Pinkwater got off the stage in Coyote. He'll hear the case.

"Between us, Garradine, he's a nasty little bulldog of a man, and being cooped up in that stage with Francesca Worth didn't do his temperament no good. He's a particular sort. Takes mostly to Western women. The type who's good for something besides—"

"Francesca's here?" Christa pulled the door wider as she handed him the cake.

"In Coyote. Thank you, ma'am. Mmm, smells like cinnamon. Seems the boardinghouse gave Judge Pinkwater its last room, so some lady modiste took Francesca Worth in."

"Cozy as a bed of rattlers," Trick snorted.

"If you say so. I can tell you Miz Worth's been on my boss's tail to get this accomplished.

"Thanks again for the cake, ma'am." The marshal brushed crumbs from his mustache and started to go. On the first step, he turned back. "Word to the wise: Don't keep Pinkwater waitin'. Hear tell he's getting married over in Silvervale, and he's nervous as a whore in church. Pardon me again, ma'am.

"Pinkwater already put the blacksmith to finding a fast horse to get him there, soon's he's finished with you."

Christa cast off humility and focused her mind on the facts: She was educated and articulate. She'd worked well with bankers and cowboys. She could certainly talk things out with Judge Pinkwater.

"Thank you, Marshal. We'll ride in first thing tomorrow, and the judge can meet with us at his pleasure."

"Tomorrow? No, ma'am! That won't do atall! Judge Pinkwater wants you in the courtroom—that is to say, John Starr's saloon—at two o'clock this afternoon. His nuptials are at sunset and Silvervale's a good hour's ride.

"Adios, folks! Good luck!"

"Did you understand any of that?" Christa slid gratefully into Patrick's arms. "I think I'm having a nightmare."

"I understood enough to know you'd better get Patty up and dressed for town."

"Wait, I have to think. I have to read this."

"I don't see the point in it."

"Wait." She sat frowning over the legal document as Patty entered the room.

"Mama, I'm hungry." She took in the room's disarray. "Those cowboys forgot to put the blankets away."

"Yes, they did. It's quite a mess, isn't it?"

"Hey, sugar, do you know how to measure coffee?"

"I can measure all kinds of things."

"Well, I'm going to poke up this fire while you get out the things for coffee. We'll make your mama a cup while she's reading. How's that sound?"

"That's fine." Patty yawned and stretched on tiptoe as if reaching for the rafters. "Mr. Trick, did you know your shirt is buttoned funny?"

It took only ten minutes for the idea to seize Christa.

"Jeremiah!" Her coffee almost spilled when she bumped the table with the force of her revelation.

"Pardon me?"

"What, Mama?"

"Jeremiah Smit is an attorney. His specialty is estates. This is not a problem." She jumped up from the table, eager to throw her arms around Patrick's neck. Instead, she lifted Patty clear off the floor and spun around with her.

"Patrick." In one whirling flash, Christa caught his glare. "Go ahead back out to the herd. Get ready for your drive. Patty and I will ride in to see Jeremiah Smit and everything will be fine."

Patrick looked at her as if she had the brains of a gopher, then addressed his words to Patty.

"Sugar, why don't you take this basket out to gather eggs. And pay real close attention."

Patrick rubbed his jaw as if deep in thought. The faint rasp of his fingers on last night's growth of beard was unbearably intimate. "It seems to me it's about the time *one* of those Gretchens starts laying blue eggs. Yes," he nodded, "it's gettin' on toward fall, and that's when she does it. Hides them real good, though. I'm not sure a little girl like you could find them. Never mind. Hand me that basket on back."

"No!" Patty snatched the basket and scampered out the door with Josh on her heels.

"Now, Christa."

She slung her arms around his neck. Even as the blanket unwrapped, she walked backward toward the bedroom, leading him like a balky horse.

"Christa, this isn't going to be as simple as you think."

"Why not?" She let the blanket drop, but when his eyes followed, modesty got the best of her and Christa reached for fresh garments. "I'll help you make this ranch into something fine. Let her keep the money."

"Think, woman. They're not just accusing you, they're accusing me."

Like a hammer falling on a nail head, he drove the word in. She listened and understood.

"Patty's name." On his fingers, Patrick ticked off the evidence against them. "You coming here, just weeks after Nathan's death, and the way he died." He scrubbed his hand through his hair. "Didn't you say there'd been talk before you left, and not just from Francesca?"

"Yes. It's part of the reason I had to get Patty away. I knew that when she grew older, it would hurt her."

"Honey, it's still going to. Scandal follows folks. Hell, it got here before you did! You've got one more chance to protect your little girl from folks talking about her for the rest of her life."

"Wait! I thought of something else." Christa turned away from him to tie her laces in an energetic knot. When she looked back, Patrick's eyes were hungry, not logical. "Patrick, Jeremiah Smit saw me pregnant. He traveled with us. He knows when Patty was born. He knows—!"

Before she could don her chemise, Patrick pulled her into his arms, twisting her hair into a long rope, then tickling between her brows, where she felt certain a frown line had appeared.

"We're doin' pretty good on second chances, us two. But it won't do to get cocky. We better go." He pushed her away

with a swat that turned into a caress. "I hope Judge Pinkwater has a good breakfast. Even then, he may lose his
reputation as a hard case. 'Cause lady, I think you could talk
the hide off a cow."

Salvation came in the shape of Rosebud Malloy. As
David paraded a lovely long-legged thoroughbred mare—
the horse he'd secured for Judge Pinkwater's sunset dash,
the mare Pinkwater would give his betrothed as a wedding
gift—Rosebud begged Patty to stay and play while Christa
and Patrick conducted business. Selfishly, she hoped Patrick
would suggest a midday meal at Pilgrims', where she might
show off her fine serge riding suit and revel in the
possessiveness that still lit Patrick's eyes. But she didn't
dare be so forward.

"We might be some time, Mr. Malloy. I seem to have
blundered into some legal trouble." Christa twisted her
fingers together at the blacksmith's knowing nod.

"Here, now, Electra, me beauty, back in your stall."
David turned the horse into an open box, then placed his
hands on his hips.

"Mrs. Worth, I'd like to say 'There, there, that's private,'
and put an end on it. But your sister-in-law and Polly
LaCrosse have made no secret of what's going on. I'm not
believing a word of it, nor are many folks. But some others
are feeling like the circus has come to town. And I do wish
you hadn't brought that Winchester, Patrick. Feelings're
running high, and you might be tempted to use it."

"Oh, no." Christa met Patrick's eyes. Even if they
married, even if she and Patty lived forever at Good
Thunder Meadows, the story of Patty's illegitimacy would
live on.

Small towns had long memories. Now it was even more
important to convince the judge of Francesca's lies.

"Let's go see Smit." Looking as if he'd invited her to a
funeral, Patrick took her arm.

"That'd be Jeremiah Smit, the lawyer, now? Wouldn't it?"

Christa thought of how hard she'd tried to muster the word "no" just last night. Watching David's face, she didn't think it would be nearly as hard in today's bright light. She did not want to hear what the blacksmith had to say.

"Afraid he left on the same stagecoach that delivered the judge and the sister-in-law."

"Not last night?" Patrick dared the blacksmith to say it.

"No. You know how Potter likes his tarantula juice down at Starr's. They left near daybreak—say, two or three hours ago."

Patrick stared past Christa, scanning the stable. His eyes fastened on the thoroughbred, Electra.

"Oh, no, me boy." David saw the direction of Patrick's stare, but moved too slow to block him.

Patrick slid back the bolt on the stall door and led the mare out.

"Patrick. Patrick Garradine," David shouted. "I try to be a good friend to you, man. I've always done my best—"

"Malloy, I count myself your friend, too." Patrick swept his hand over the mare's deep chest and muscled shoulders. He nodded. "I'd follow you right up to hell's back door." He looked up from beneath the mare's neck. "But if you try to get between me and this mare, I'll show you what this Winchester's good for."

"Of course, Trick. Always a pleasure doin' business with a man who knows what he wants."

Twenty-four

Christa accepted David Malloy's offer to sit inside his tidy parlor. Even as she resolved to fold her hands in her lap and watch the girls play with Rosebud's porcelain dolls, Christa's mind wandered.

The stagecoach carrying Jeremiah Smit had a two-hour head start, but the thoroughbred, Electra, could run. Patrick had refused to burden her with the extra weight of a saddle. Rushed but deliberate, Patrick had tied back his hair with a leather thong. Then he'd insisted on taking precious minutes to limber up the mare, warming her muscles for the exertion ahead. Finally mounted, he'd ridden like an Indian, low to her neck, and they'd galloped down Coyote's main street, vanishing before shopkeepers came to their doors to investigate.

Christa took off her gloves. She twisted them, then smoothed out the wrinkles and put them on again. She wouldn't allow herself to check her brooch watch until she'd watched the girls finish their tea table and floor bed for Rosebud's dolls. Before that, Patty's voice intruded.

"Mama, are you whispering real quiet?"

Her daughter cradled a flaxen-curled doll, but her puzzled blue eyes studied Christa. Too polite to stare, Rosebud blinked and adjusted her spectacles. Christa covered her lips with one hand, afraid she'd mused aloud. At the very least, her lips must have twitched as she planned a defense against Francesca's lies.

Before she answered, the girls had returned to their game.

"I'm going for a walk." Christa stood and crossed the room to the flat brown rug where the girls sat, playing.

She stood behind Patty, looking down at her child's wispy blond curls. Christa swept a few loose tendrils back toward her own chignon. So much depended on her respectability.

Without glancing up, Patty reached behind her and patted Christa's skirt. "Go walk," Patty said.

With that dismissal, Christa made excuses to David Malloy and turned right on Coyote's main street, certain where she was headed and equally certain she shouldn't go. *Don't do this, Christa.* She lifted the full riding skirt high, so she wouldn't trip. *Go on down to Pilgrims' and have a cup of tea.* The determined stamp of her boots attracted the attention of two boys rolling a hoop between two tumbleweeds. *Cross the street and chat with Hannah at the mercantile.* She stopped in front of Polly LaCrosse's modiste shop.

Why, when she so detested confrontations, did she seek them out? In front of Polly's spotless glass window, Christa pretended to peer in at covers from *Peterson's Magazine* and *Godey's Lady's Book.*

She might have kept walking toward Luz's candle shop, except that the marshal had been right. Through Polly's window, Christa saw the dressmaker and Francesca seated side by side at a cutting table. Cozy as a bed of rattlers, Patrick had suggested. Indeed. Both neatly coiffed heads, one light and one dark, bent over a stack of papers, so intent they hadn't noticed her.

She took a few more steps. When she reached the other side of the shop, she stopped and clutched the strings to her reticule to keep her hands from covering her stampeding heart.

Within the shop, a clock bonged the hour. Noon. Polly and Francesca sat conniving a legal strategy that would strip Patty of her inheritance and Christa of her reputation. For all their malevolence, the women were smart. Two solid hours might be enough.

Christa opened the shop door with such energy, the door hit the wall and rebounded. Christa barely stopped it from hitting her nose.

Her invasion brought both women to their feet. Christa admired Polly's gown, designed in rich spills of pale yellow, and took it as her inspiration. She'd remain just that smooth and unruffled.

"Good afternoon, Francesca." Christa inclined her head with an attempt at regal elegance. "Polly, your shop is wonderful. I've never been inside."

A quick glance showed her that Francesca had put on a good deal of flesh in the last two months. In her rich brown cisele velvet gown, Francesca looked like a fat Persian cat next to Polly's canary daintiness.

"Do let me show you around." As Polly took her arm, Christa felt the dressmaker's fingers test her wool serge sleeve for quality.

"I'd like that." Christa ignored Francesca's labored huffs.

A shaft of autumn sunlight eased through the front window, turning a shelf of trims into a pirate's cache. Bottles of round jet buttons and iridescent bugle beads glittered next to coils of lace and ruching. Spindles of rainbow ribbons—peacock and primrose, heliotrope and hunter green—glowed beside two dressmaker's dummies. One, in a flounced frock, wore a garland of silk flowers around its blank-faced brow. The other was headless, and covered by a ghostly drape.

"As you see, I select only the finest trims for my creations." As she spoke, Polly's eyes totaled the cost of Christa's riding dress.

The cutting table rocked on its stout legs as Francesca lunged upright and stood, turning a thick document over and over in her hands. Christa looked away, concentrating on a shelf stacked with fabric.

"These are beautiful." Christa's fingers hovered above two lengths of cotton sateen, one printed with feathers, the other with leaves.

"Aren't they?" Polly straightened the cloth before Christa could disturb it. "You can see why I don't do my dressmaking house-to-house, or trade my gowns for a dollar's worth of butter and eggs."

Francesca's stare frayed Christa's nerves. She wanted to grab the woman, shake her for ruining the most glorious morning of her life, for threatening Patty, and for insinuating herself into Coyote. Given time and no "black widow" letters, Christa knew the little town would have welcomed her.

"I brought these, from Sacramento."

Christa recoiled from the bolts of bilious egg-yolk and lavender corded silk Francesca thrust into her face.

Before Christa could respond, Francesca tripped. Her bulk slammed Christa into a dressmaker's form. Polly gasped as a head rolled across the floor, strewing silk pansies and roses.

"I'm sorry, Polly, I—"

The dressmaker's condescending frown and Francesca's self-righteous sniff made calm impossible.

"All right, Francesca, it's time to talk." Christa sighted down her index finger.

"I have nothing to say to the likes of you." Francesca's fingers snaked up her sleeve. She pulled out a hemmed linen square and blotted her lips.

"Oh, yes, you do." Christa pulled a chair screeching toward her and plopped into it. "You've accused me of adultery. Now sit down."

Francesca sat and so did Polly. Christa folded her hands on the tabletop, then buried them in her lap to hide their trembling. As she stared at Francesca, her sister-in-law's nostrils flared open and closed.

"Well, Francesca? Where did you get such an idea?"

"You are a scarlet woman. I told the judge that in my letters. You never cared for my brother. You only used him to come out here." Francesca's jowls wobbled mightily as she added, "To this wasteland."

Tears sprang into the woman's eyes and Christa felt a sickening stab of guilt.

"But Nathan *was* Patty's father." Patty's image wavered in Christa's mind. "Francesca, think. For every bit of me, Patty has twice as much of Nathan. Her quick mind—why, the child can practically read!—her blond good looks and blue eyes. *Blue.* My eyes are green, Francesca."

Polly flounced against the back of her chair and pursed her lips. Christa pleaded for an angel to curb the dressmaker's tongue. If anyone in town had gazed into Patrick's open-sky eyes, it was Polly.

"Then why did you leave?" Francesca demanded. "Why did you call her Patricia—?"

"Francesca, you know very well why I left. People were agog over Nathan's death. Although I could have borne it—"

Beyond her own voice, Christa heard Francesca gobble like a turkey. Christa hardened her conscience against twenty years of manners and tried to outshout the other woman.

"If I hadn't had a child, I might have waited for the sick excitement to dissipate, but I was afraid for Patty."

Francesca rushed on, her voice rising still louder.

"—then why did you come back out here to that wild red Indian of a man—?"

"Patrick is not a wild—" Christa pressed her lips closed. In the sudden silence, Francesca and Polly faced each other and smirked.

"Polly, might I beg you for a cup of water?"

The dressmaker flushed when Christa called her hospitality into question.

"Of course." Polly bustled into the back room. No hand pump creaked before she reappeared with a crystal pitcher and cup.

Christa sipped water while her mind crabbed sideways, eyeing her situation. Why on earth should she be less than candid?

"How did the two of you meet?" Christa set the cup on the table. She didn't look up until the water quieted to a smooth surface.

Polly's face had flushed again, but Francesca responded. "After my letter, Polly wrote to me." Francesca's lips pressed into a flat seam and her chin jiggled in defiance.

"That would be the letter calling me a black widow." Suddenly weary, Christa ran a fingertip around the rim of her empty cup. "What made you do that, Polly?"

Jealousy charged Polly's features with such anger, Christa read the answer easily. *Patrick*. Polly wanted Patrick to suspect Christa. The interloper. The scarlet woman.

"Did you write Francesca before or after you brought me a gift?" Christa touched the cool cup against her temple.

Polly shrugged peevishly. "Why don't you take your child back to Sacramento?"

Francesca gasped as if she'd been betrayed, but Polly continued.

"Split the inheritance and live in two different houses. I'm sure Sacramento is big enough that you never have to lay eyes on each other."

The screech of Francesca's fingernails scoring the smooth tabletop kept Christa from speaking. Together, she and Polly stared. Lips slick with saliva, Francesca muttered a word Christa had never heard spoken. What hellish thoughts writhed in her sister-in-law's mind?

Soundlessly, Christa rose from her chair. Clouds had blotted the sun from Polly's only window, and Christa longed to go outside. She preferred the company of the impatient drunks waiting outside Starr's Saloon to this.

Oblivious to Christa's movement, Francesca continued to scratch. Only twice had Christa seen Francesca's odd behavior: after the baby's death, and after Nathan's.

Christa stepped over a shower of silk rose petals and slipped out of the shop.

On the boardwalk outside, Christa gathered her wits. The boys with the hoop had gone, but another tumbleweed jostled its fellows, riding a forlorn autumn breeze down the dirt street. A lone Canada goose honked, wings whisking across a leaden sky. Christa drew a breath of cold wind scented with piñon pine. She wished for a shawl, for the midmorning warmth of the cookhouse, for a clean floor littered with crumbs. She wished for Patrick and the home they'd patched together.

If only Patrick caught up with the stage and sent Jeremiah riding back, she'd never pray for another thing.

No.

Christa stopped and rubbed her gloved hands together. She craved Jeremiah Smit's assistance less than she needed Patrick's safety. She vowed to save her prayers for that single blessing. Still, if God had a spare moment, Christa hoped he'd set His celestial finger against the lips of anyone telling Judge Pinkwater that the scarlet woman's lover had stolen his sweetheart's horse.

Christa walked as far as Pilgrims' boardinghouse and paused to scrutinize the crowd outside Starr's Saloon. The men saw her watching. They meant no harm, returning her stare, but Christa found the mob of denim and suspenders, whiskers and perspiration, quite overwhelming.

With Patrick beside her, she wouldn't have balked. Of course, Patrick would have tied her to a hitching rail before allowing her to approach these men alone.

"It's a rough crowd and no mistake, Mrs. Worth." Sharlot Pilgrim stepped from her front door, hastily pulling a shawl over her blue dress and work-smeared apron.

Sharlot rubbed her hands together. They smelled of rosemary. Sharlot had so obviously left her cooking to stand there in the street beside her, tears gathered in Christa's eyes, leaving her mute.

"Those tumbleweeds seem to have followed me in off the range," Christa managed.

Sharlot nodded, eyeing the brown thistle balls, rounded from rolling with the wind. "I often wonder where they came from."

The gang in front of the saloon guffawed at some coarse joke and turned to ogle the women. Did they know what she'd been accused of? Is that why they gawked? Christa edged a step closer to Sharlot.

"They're not dried sagebrush?" she asked, hoping the older woman would stay.

"Lands, no. They're prickly as porcupines, and just as brassy. Simply showed up on the main street of town one day, scaring horses wherever they went."

"And where do they go?" Caught on an errant draft, one of the tumbleweeds bounded away from the others. Christa imagined it bouncing right into the crowd of men.

"Pile up out in the ravines, I imagine. Drop their seeds and come back for another run at us the next year."

"More meddlesome intruders who outstayed their welcome." Christa hugged both arms around herself and shivered.

Sharlot shaded her eyes and looked up the street toward Polly's shop. "Here comes that hideous woman. Francesca, your sister-in-law, isn't she? Lord give us bliss, Mrs. Worth, for putting up with such a harridan!

"Excuse me for saying so, but how she wailed when she found we'd no room for her. You'd best get on to the saloon before she does. The judge went over a good half hour past."

Christa tugged down her blue serge cuffs and cleared her throat, girding herself to wade through that throng of men.

Sharlot laid her hand on Christa's arm, though she didn't look at her directly. "You'll do fine. Tell the judge what he needs to know and then bring little Patty over for a treat. Seems to me, I've got the makings for rice pudding with raisins."

Only when Sharlot left did Christa focus on the dust plume far out on the desert, past the men, beyond the edge of town. Could it be the coach?

John Starr's bartender couldn't mix a more intoxicating brew than the dread and excitement rushing through her. In her hurry to see more clearly, Christa reached the edge of the gathered men. She started when one spoke.

"I heard tell this judge don't get no salary, nothing but what he fines folks." Monk, the mad prospector, rolled his eyes toward Christa.

She'd heard, of course, but Christa felt so certain the approaching flurry was the coach that she gave the grizzled reprobate a grin. He responded, not with a pantomimed throat-slashing, but a grudging yellow smile of his own.

In spite of the fact that she stood, the lone woman in the midst of a half-dozen drunkards, Christa's spirits catapulted even higher.

"*I* heard Leland Pinkwater told folks on the Comstock that he'd found a heap better enforcement from a Colt than a law book."

Christa ignored the speaker, staring until her eyes burned. Wiping them, she thought she'd made out a lone rider, instead of a coach. The horse was dark. Was it a bay, like Electra?

"What I want to know is why's she here if she ain't guilty?"

Christa had never been inside a saloon. Most decent women hadn't. Surrounded by these unsavory men, she knew why. She should probably just push past the batwing doors, but she continued to wait for the horseman to draw near.

The horse, this much closer, look soul-deadeningly black.

"That son of a gun's ridin' fit to kill that horse." Once more Christa recognized Monk's voice. He spat off the boardwalk to punctuate his disgust. When commotion erupted behind her, Christa turned.

"I demand to see Judge Pinkwater." Francesca brandished a paisley parasol. "Clear the way."

The men opened a path to the boardwalk. As if summoned by Francesca's command, John Starr stepped from his saloon.

"Hey, John, you don't need to keep us waitin'! Just have

old Pinkie pound the gavel and . . ." A gabble of agreement covered the rest and Christa sighed her relief.

In the cloud-strained sunlight, Starr's shirt glared white
against his black vest and trousers. Diamond studs glittered
on his shirtfront and a crimson rose pinned to his lapel made
him look like a bridegroom.

Christa glanced back down the street. The horse was
definitely black, and some sort of odd trappings flapped
around its galloping legs.

"Mrs. Worth?" John Starr's voice cut through the men's
banter. "May I escort you inside?"

Christa took his arm. The black gabardine felt civilized
and fine beneath her fingers.

"Ma'am?" John Starr raised his voice and beckoned
Francesca to join them.

"No lady would step foot in there!" Francesca shook her
parasol in his direction.

"C'mon over here, sister. When a woman's with me, she
ain't no lady!" Monk's offer set the other men whooping.

"How dare you!" Francesca's parasol cleared so wide a
space around her that Starr tucked Christa behind him. "You
see what kind of man you are, encouraging such riffraff!"

"Madam, you remind me of my wife." Starr raised his
hand as if tipping his hat, though he wore none.

"Do you mean to say that a woman lives with a wastrel,
a bottle imp, a *devil* like you?" Francesca withdrew the
handkerchief from her sleeve and wiped her lips.

"No, ma'am, she lives in New York City."

Starr had taken Christa one long stride away from the
outraged Francesca when the black horse, flecked with clots
of foam and trailing stagecoach traces, skidded to a stop.

"Jehoshaphat!" A man slid from the horse's back and
leaned both palms against the hitching rail. "Mrs. Worth."

Without the clue of his voice, Christa could not have
identified Jeremiah Smit. His clothes and face were coated
with dust and he appeared so exhausted, she wondered
whether to rejoice or send for a doctor.

"'Cut 'im loose, or I shoot all four.' Glory be, Christa, that's what your Mr. Garradine said, then cocked that big revolver, just in case the driver didn't take his meaning!"

Jeremiah Smit's eyeballs rolled white while the men raised a cheer.

"Ha!" Francesca tucked her parasol under her arm as if the trial were over.

Christa hoped Judge Pinkwater was nowhere nearby. Besides calling her so familiarly, by her first name, Jeremiah had portrayed Patrick as a gun-toting renegade.

The saloon doors slammed open so suddenly, only John Starr's shoulder protected Christa.

Topped by a bowler hat, cigar jutting from the corner of his mouth, a man who stood exactly at Christa's eye level emerged from the saloon. He removed the cigar and pointed it toward Christa.

"You the accused?"

Christa nodded. Before she found her voice, he pivoted toward Francesca.

"You the litigant?"

"Why, I never—"

"Be that as it may, I don't have time to gossip on the front steps." The judge stopped his high-pitched yap by replacing the cigar. Then Jeremiah shambled up and the judge spoke around the sodden tobacco. "What's this, now?"

"An attorney, sir." Jeremiah used a knuckle to clear white smears beneath each eye. "Counsel representing Mrs. Worth."

"Not in my courtroom you're not. Take a bath and maybe we'll talk. Ladies, in or out?"

Twenty-five

❧❧❧

Honey-wax candles scented the huge room, making it smell more like a church than a saloon. Only when she drew a deep breath did Christa catch the lingering odors of tobacco and liquor beneath the fresh pine sawdust. Starr's Saloon boasted a walnut bar polished to a glassy sheen, faceted bottles with many-colored labels, and a crystal chandelier and wall sconces alive with Luz's delicate candles.

So bedecked, the saloon felt no more like a den of iniquity than the mercantile or Polly's dressmaking shop. And it was lighter than either of them.

As Christa followed, Judge Pinkwater tossed his cigar into a knee-high brass spittoon. Christa gulped back nausea at the sputtering sizzle and set her feet after the man, determined to be on his heels when he reached the document-laden table far left of the door.

She glanced back over her shoulder. Her head cleared considerably when she saw that no painting of naked women defaced the saloon. She'd heard lurid tales of such things, but over John Starr's bar, Christa saw only a huge silver mirror and swathes of red, white, and blue-starred bunting.

Christa seated herself in the chair the judge indicated, wishing Patrick sat beside her. The stolen Electra might be a racer to her bones, but her legs had looked spindly. If the mare fell and took Patrick down beneath her, Christa vowed to shoot the horse herself.

With that thought came panic. This whole escapade was ending as it had begun. That first summer day, she'd faced Patrick and realized she had no one to count on but herself. Today was no different. Patty's future and Patrick's depended on her. Christa felt responsibility lower, like a lead shroud.

She watched Judge Pinkwater toy with his gavel. Rumor said territorial judges needed no more credentials than that: a gavel and a yen to hand down pronouncements. With Francesca finally seated, he commenced.

"Although court convenes, strictly speaking, at two o'clock, since both litigant and accused are present, I declare court in session." He struck the table with his gavel and plunked into an upholstered chair at the head of the table.

He glanced between the two of them, apparently waiting for someone to speak.

"Miss Worth."

"Yes," Christa began, and heard Francesca's echo.

"No, you're *Mrs.* Worth, if I'm not mistaken." Judge Pinkwater aimed his gavel toward Christa. His sarcasm probably reverberated in the street. Christa ducked her head in a nod.

"Miss Worth, tell me why you believe your sister-in-law's child is not your brother's flesh and blood."

As if her corset suddenly tightened, strings yanked taut by giants, Christa's breath stopped. Her chest swelled with silent gasps. She needed air and her lungs could draw none.

"Steady, there, Mrs. Worth." Judge Pinkwater patted her hand hard, as if she were a horse. Though it hurt and though she felt profoundly embarrassed, Christa found his gestures reassuring.

"First of all, there's the child's name." Francesca stared pointedly at the stack of papers beneath the judge's elbow. "As you might know, if you'd troubled to read the papers I filed."

"I've read every one, Miss Worth, and I could've ruled

through the U.S. mail, if I didn't want both parties to look me in the eye."

Further comforted by signs that the judge couldn't bear Francesca's audacity with any more grace than she, Christa leaned back in her chair.

"What of that, *Mrs.* Worth? Why'd you name the child Patricia? Tell the truth, now." He glanced toward the black Bible next to the stacked documents. "Consider yourself sworn to tell the truth."

Christa regarded the Bible. "Nathan and I had not discussed names for a girl child. He was so sure she'd be a boy." Christa had forgotten that fact until just now. "He— Nathan—wasn't there when she was born, so I couldn't ask his opinion. The man who *was* there saved my baby's life."

"And who was he? Tell the judge *that*, Christabel."

Christa squared her shoulders and faced the judge head-on. "His name is Patrick Garradine. He was a mustanger for the cavalry, riding in the desert where Nathan—" Christa stopped. Defaming her dead husband would probably soil her assertions. "Since Patrick Garradine saved my baby's life, I named her Patricia, in tribute."

"And your husband knew this?" Judge Pinkwater turned his gavel end for end, watching her.

Christa blinked. "He never asked." She blinked again. "We never discussed it."

"Humph." Judge Pinkwater's lips twisted and he turned to face Francesca. "What else?"

Francesca's fingers wiggled up her sleeve. Her fingernails caught one corner of her handkerchief.

"Nathan's death. My brother was shot to death."

"But you haven't been charged? Correct?" The judge swung back Christa's way.

"No!" The word was a gasp. Oh, mercy, did she sound guilty? Hooves clopped in the street and Christa prayed it was Patrick. Please, God, let it be him. Please let him come sit beside me.

"Steady, young lady. It's just a question."

"Next?" he asked Francesca.

"He was shot in the head!" Francesca slapped both palms on the table.

Christa forced herself not to cower. *How close were you? Too close.* But the judge didn't ask.

"And no sheriff or constable filed charges. You, Miss Worth, even you, filed no charges, correct?" Pinkwater thumbed the stack of documents with a sound like riffling cards.

"Correct, but she left town right after the funeral."

"Right after." His head tilted right, then left, like a scale. "How soon is *right* after?"

"One month," Francesca said.

"How long have you been a widow, now, Mrs. Worth?"

Had he noticed her riding dress was colored dark blue, not black? Had he seen a flicker of ivory lace on the blouse underneath?

"Three months."

"So, you're a new widow." It didn't sound like a question. His tone sounded peculiarly male.

"Yes, sir."

"And why did you leave so soon? Why did you come to Coyote, of all the godforsaken places on earth?" He glanced back over his shoulder. For the first time, Christa noticed John Starr, polishing glasses behind his bar.

"*Mrs.* Worth?"

"I left because of what Francesca's saying. E-everyone said Nathan's death was strange. I never contested that. It was a terrible accident.

"I came to Coyote because my brother Dan works here. On Good Thunder Meadows ranch."

"Why didn't I know that?" The judge turned to Francesca, but he seemed to address the world at large. "She has a brother in town."

"Two hours' ride away," Christa amended. "Besides, I like ranch life."

"Just like Junie," Pinkwater muttered, but Christa only

noticed Francesca had extracted the entire handkerchief from her sleeve. She blotted her lips.

The judge placed his gavel on the table, matched his fingertips together, and asked Francesca, "What else?"

"She whored when he was alive," Francesca whispered. "And she's whoring now."

Christa closed her eyes and flashes of light swirled behind her lids. This time, her corset might suffocate her. This time, she truly could not get a breath. She heard a glass touch down on the table and felt a ring of moisture gather around her fingertips. She also heard Francesca's nails, scratching.

"Water," a voice told her.

"You're too kind." Christa mouthed the words without opening her eyes.

"See? See how she is?" Francesca's cackle brought Christa's eyes open again.

"I see a gently reared young woman," Judge Pinkwater answered Francesca. "Now, Mrs. Worth, is your sister-in-law telling the truth?"

"No." How could he ask such a thing? "Patty is Nathan's daughter."

"Yes?" His rising inflection led her toward something else.

What? What else was he asking?

"And now?" he urged.

Christa shook her head, at a loss. What else did he want from her? Was it possible she'd misunderstood the word? Certainly no one had ever defined it for her. Christa pushed the sides of her hair back toward the messy chignon, as if the stimulation could wring some sense from her brain.

"Your sister-in-law is implying," Judge Pinkwater's voice dropped, "that you are now, even if you weren't before . . . That Mr. Garradine is enjoying carnal knowledge of you."

The judge looked longingly at a beer barrel, and Christa stared in the same direction. Little white towels hung on hooks beneath the bar. She didn't care to know why. As she watched, John Starr turned his back to the room.

"See her searching for a lie? What do you think now?" Francesca scratched with renewed frenzy.

"Madam, I think you're crazy as a bedbug. Unfortunately I don't know of a law against it. Now quit that infernal scratching on the underside of the table. It may frighten this young lady, but it's making me downright testy.

"Which brings up another thing." The judge unbuttoned his suit coat, opened it, and checked the inside pocket for cigars. "Mrs. Worth, did Patrick Garradine give you that black eye?"

Christa's hand flew up to her face. "No, of course not. I fell from my horse."

Pinkwater's face brightened with amusement and he took up the gavel once more. "My Junie wouldn't fall from her horse."

"Has she ever had a cougar pounce on her?" Christa straightened in her chair, good and sick of men leaping to the wrong conclusion about her horsemanship!

"No, ma'am, I'm quite certain she never has."

"It tends to make you fall off."

"I daresay it does." The judge turned to the commotion at the bar behind him. A stranger whispered to John Starr, then scurried from the saloon.

"Judge Pinkwater, would this be a bad time to interrupt?"

"You already have, Mr. Starr."

"It seems someone has stolen your mare." John Starr glanced quickly at Christa, then back at the judge. "The thoroughbred mare."

"Son of a bitch!" Pinkwater's gavel ricocheted off the saloon wall. He shot up from his chair and stormed over to pick it up, then proceeded back with stately demeanor. "Mrs. Worth, answer my question."

That question. She might lie. Leland Pinkwater wasn't God. He knew nothing. She owed him nothing. She hadn't laid her hand on the Bible. Still, she could not lie.

"Mrs. Worth, I'm asking because it establishes a preexisting relationship."

"But it doesn't. Patty is Nathan's daughter."

"So, you're telling me you have never been intimate with Patrick Garradine." The judge nodded his encouragement.

Christa took a long drink of water. "No."

"You're not telling me— Wait. You *have* been with the man? Intimately?" The judge gripped his temples as if squelching a headache.

"Once."

Francesca's wail rose like a dog's howl, and the judge nearly rapped her with his gavel. "Oh, hush that keening. Do you think she is the first young woman or the last who's let her feelings run away with her?"

Knuckles struck one of the batwing doors, and Christa's heart soared. As it swung in, she saw Jeremiah Smit. Not Patrick.

"Your Honor, I have something else to add to these proceedings." Jeremiah wore a tight flannel shirt and denims, but his carroty whiskers were fresh-washed and his watch chain gleamed.

"Humph," the judge greeted him. "I was about to send them outside so I could deliberate."

"It's beginning to rain."

"No help for that. This is Nevada. We could just as easy be having a dust storm. You don't like the weather, just wait around for a few minutes." Judge Pinkwater's levity flagged as he appeared to remember Electra. He jerked his head toward the swinging doors. "Ladies."

Christa let Francesca go ahead and the doors rocked closed. Christa's feet refused to follow, though she should feel safe now. Jeremiah could point up any detail she'd forgotten.

"Mr. Starr, how about one of those 'biggest five-cent beers in the territory' that you brag about?"

"Coming right up, Judge."

Christa might have laughed, except that she was afraid to

go out there, afraid to leave a saloon—where such sins as hers were commonplace—for the world of decent folk.

When she saw Patrick's black Stetson above the doors, she swallowed down a sob and eased outside to meet him.

Right there on the boardwalk, with light rain blowing, Christa burrowed against his chest. Smelling of horse and leather and wind, Patrick's arms surrounded her.

"Are you hurt, honey?"

"No." Christa's lips moved against his shirtfront, engraving each moment on her mind. "Are you?"

"Me?" Patrick stepped back.

"You. All this time you've talked about *me* being foolhardy and taking risks—" How long had this sense of injustice built up in her? Was it only worry that made it erupt? "—and you go riding off on that nervy Elec—"

"Mama." Patty hung to one side of Patrick, small fingers clinging to his thigh as she would to a post. Patrick had brought her daughter to a saloon.

"She wanted to come," Patrick explained.

"Mama, you hugged Mr. Trick."

Patrick laughed out loud, delighted Patty had taken him off the hook of Christa's irritation.

"I know that," Christa admitted. She looked past Patrick's broad shoulders, hoping the crowd of waiting drinkers had dissipated. But if anything, their numbers had grown. Patty wasn't the only one who'd seen them embrace. By tomorrow, everyone in town would know.

"So?" Patrick nodded toward the saloon.

"I'm not sure."

Patrick's dust-smeared face and the raindrops plopping on his hat brim resurrected a memory so tender, she'd tried to keep it buried—in Sacramento and especially here. But she needed to tell him, now.

"You kept your promise, Patrick Garradine."

His blue eyes darkened, but he looked confused.

"Out there, you promised that if I stayed—alive, I think you meant—that you'd give me something to live for." She wrung his hand and lowered her voice to a whisper. "And you did." She saw his eyes lower to Patty. "Not just her, though she's the greatest gift—" Christa shook her head and leaned over her daughter to grab Patrick's shirtfront. She pulled him near enough that she could kiss him. "I mean *you*. I love you, Patrick."

The onlookers had only a minute to gawk before Jeremiah Smit reappeared.

"Well?" Patrick demanded.

Jeremiah looked nonchalant, in spite of his tight, obviously borrowed, garments. "I think he'll rule in our favor. I convinced him that you were in a delicate condition when you started your journey." He turned half away from Christa, but she saw him grimace and heard him mutter, "I had to tell him."

"Tell him what?" she and Patrick asked together.

"About our business arrangement?" Jeremiah hinted, rolling his hand in midair as he stared at Patrick.

He wasn't talking about cattle. That much was clear. But Patrick seemed to have no more idea than she did what Jeremiah meant.

"About deeding the ranch to Christa." The angry words ejected from his orange-mustached mouth. "It showed your honorable intentions, even though you—got the cart before the horse, otherwise."

"What in hell are you talking about?" Patrick shouted.

Christa stepped between the two men. Had Jeremiah said—

Patrick turned on her as Jeremiah's words sank in. "Just what did you tell them in there?"

Christa hauled his head down to her level and whispered, "He asked if we'd—been—I don't know." Tears of embarrassment pricked her eyes. "He asked if we'd carnally enjoyed each other?"

Patrick bit off a surprised laugh. "And you told him?"

"Should I have lied?"

"Honey, you lied about knowing how to make beef stew."

"Did you deed me your ranch?"

All laughter deserted him. A solemn mask fell over his features, and Patrick nodded. "In case I died on the trail or something."

"When did you do it?"

"Before the cougar jumped you."

Christa tried to think. Before he lay with her, before confessing he loved her, Patrick had given her his ranch.

"You didn't just leave it to me, in your will?"

"Mrs. Worth, when he deeded you Good Thunder Meadows, it was a transfer of ownership," Jeremiah explained.

"You were going to let me return to Sacramento—" Christa wrestled with the vision, irritated by Patrick's renewed smile. "—*owning* Good Thunder Meadows."

"I figured if this drought lasted much longer, I might need a rich woman to cover my debts." Patrick removed his hat and turned his face up to the gentle rain. He closed his eyes, still chuckling.

"Instead of giggling, Mr. Garradine, you might better serve yourself if you considered where you'll go when I evict you!"

Hard, uncompromising Patrick Garradine looked like a boy, opening his lips to catch raindrops on his tongue. If Monk's raucous voice hadn't intruded, she would have thrown herself back into Patrick's arms.

"Now there's something I never expected to see, sober." Monk shuffled away with a comrade, apparently set on remedying that sorry state. "Trick Garradine swillin' thundercloud droppin's like they was fancy champagne!"

Trick shook his head as if he'd slept. Truth was, he had no idea what'd gotten into him, making a spectacle of himself on the main street of town. Relief, maybe, or mooncalf longing for Christa. Maybe just a tad of Christa's foolhardiness had rubbed off on him. Whatever it was felt pretty damn good.

"Ladies!"

Trust that feisty little judge to bawl like a gut-shot steer and haul them back inside the saloon. He hoped the man had a sense of humor. Electra wasn't ruined, but no way was she running to Silvervale. Not tonight. Still, Trick had a plan that should tickle everybody.

Christa had worn as many petticoats as she could ride in, and their teasing rustle almost covered Pinkwater's verdict.

"I've ruled in your favor, young woman." Pinkwater glared at Christa with fatherly temper. "Immoral behavior not withstanding."

Trick felt his hackles rise, but then Patty hung on his left arm, nearly pulling him over, and Christa made a brushing move with her hands, saying "Don't." Trick let a blast of pent-up air rush past his lips. He'd do for Pinkwater later. After they talked about the mare. And about marriage.

Francesca didn't stay to listen. She straight-armed the doors back on their hinges, leaving all the rest of them to wish her good riddance.

"Case dismissed," Pinkwater called after her, then the cocky son of a gun stabbed his pointer finger just above Trick's belt buckle. "Did you steal my mare?"

"Do you perform marriages?" Trick fired back.

"What?" Judge Pinkwater stopped cold and Trick couldn't tell if Pinkwater's eyes or Christa's bulged the biggest. Pinkwater, though, pulled himself together first.

"Only if they happen in the next ten minutes." The man's head leaned back on his neck and his eyes narrowed like he was bargaining at an auction. "And only if you have a middling fast horse that'll get me to Silvervale by sunset."

Trick cleared his throat and shuffled his alkali-bleached boots. "Well, now," he said, but he couldn't have put it better himself. Then he shook his head, like he'd given in but was saving face. "No problem."

Christabel White Worth, for the first time since he'd known her, stood speechless. Telling her about the ranch had made her dizzy. Now this. Now marriage. Her shoulders made a twitchy movement like she was snarled up in her own loop.

He needed to get her loose. Pointing at the judge, as if telling a dog to stay, Trick handed Patty into Jeremiah Smit's arms and pulled Christa outside. Rain like hail peppered the overhanging roof in front of the saloon, and damned if the dusty street wasn't turning a wet, soft gray.

"Two rains in two weeks. Maybe the drought's broke." He turned back and looked down into Christa's eyes, and knew for sure it had.

Love cranked tight inside his chest as he moved a strand of hair back from her temple, hoping his rope-ragged hands didn't hurt her. He'd always figured a man about to get married would feel cornered, but it was just the opposite. As if Christa had chipped a hard crust off of him, he felt set loose.

"Patrick?"

He should have known better. Christa wouldn't stand silent for long.

"Christa, will you marry me?" The first words weren't tough, but they dragged out a rock slide of others that he'd sworn not to say. "Just promise you won't be so crazy brave, so reckless—" He stopped, though she looked stunned enough not to balk at his conditions. "Let me start over.

"I trust you, Christa." His eyes winced shut with the ache of saying it. "I trust you to take care of yourself for me and for Patty. Will you marry me?"

"Now or never, cowboy!" Pinkwater hollered from inside the saloon. Trick thought maybe he'd shoot him, after the wedding.

"I'll marry you." The green of Christa's eyes sparkled like dewy grass, and the little black centers opened like they wanted to take in the whole of him.

He let his arms swallow her up, instead. His heart thudded louder than the rain and he wondered if she could hear it. She sighed, going limp against him, and he thought she could. Lord, how he wanted to take her home.

"Patrick, I promise to be careful, but Patrick—" She wriggled like a pup, leaning back in his arms to see his face, and Trick knew he was in for it. "—nothing's riskier than love, and we—"

"I swear, Christabel, you are the talkingest woman."

Once he'd used peppermint candy to quiet her down, but now he tried something still sweeter. Even if his lips had got all dry from galloping into the wind, even if his beard rasped the soft skin underneath her ear, Christa liked his kisses.

The townsfolk of Coyote were downright fortunate they'd scuttled in out of the pounding rain. They wouldn't strangle on their gasps as Christa's fingers burrowed up under the back of his hair. Their jaws wouldn't drop as he tugged that buckskin shaman's bag out of the neck of her dress, fingering its emptiness, while he kissed the side of Christa's throat.

"Francesca poured all the magic out of it." With her head thrown back, Christa's whispered regret quivered the skin beneath his mouth.

"Oh, no, honey. It's gotta be magic that's got me thinking that foolhardy might be good, just this once."

Our Town

...where love is always right around the corner!

_**Take Heart** by Lisa Higdon

0-515-11898-2/$5.99

In Wilder, Wyoming...a penniless socialite learns a lesson in frontier life—and love.

_**Harbor Lights** by Linda Kreisel

0-515-11899-0/$5.99

On Maryland's Silchester Island...the perfect summer holiday sparks a perfect summer fling.

_**Humble Pie** by Deborah Lawrence

0-515-11900-8/$5.99

In Moose Gulch, Montana...a waitress with a secret meets a stranger with a heart.

_**Candy Kiss** by Ginny Aiken

0-515-11941-5/$5.99

In Everleigh, Pennsylvania...a sweet country girl finds the love of a city lawyer with kisses sweeter than candy.

If you enjoyed this book, take advantage of this special offer. Subscribe now and get a

FREE
Historical
Romance

No Obligation (a $4.50 value)

Each month the editors of True Value select the four *very best* novels from America's leading publishers of romantic fiction. Preview them in your home *Free* for 10 days. With the first four books you receive, we'll send you a FREE book as our introductory gift. No Obligation!

If for any reason you decide not to keep them, just return them and owe nothing. If you like them as much as we think you will, you'll pay just $4.00 each and save at *least* $.50 each off the cover price. (Your savings are *guaranteed* to be at least $2.00 each month.) There is NO postage and handling – or other hidden charges. There are no minimum number of books to buy and you may cancel at any time.

Send in the Coupon Below

To get your FREE historical romance fill out the coupon below and mail it today. As soon as we receive it we'll send you your FREE Book along with your first month's selections.
